# The Wind
# Leaves No Shadow

*Books by* RUTH LAUGHLIN

CABALLEROS

THE WIND LEAVES NO SHADOW

# The Wind
# Leaves No Shadow

by

## RUTH LAUGHLIN

*Enlarged Edition*

*2001*
*Caxton Press*
*Caldwell, Idaho*

First printing October, 1951
Second printing December, 1952
Third printing December, 1959
Fourth printing June, 1962
Fifth printing August, 1968
Sixth printing January, 1973
Seventh printing August, 1978
Eighth printing February, 1986
Ninth printing May, 1992
Tenth printing March, 2001

Printed and bound in the United States of America
167197

*For* SANDY

and in Honor of my dear dear friends

Pat and Betty Clancy

from

Rene and Laughlin

# Cast of Characters

(In their order of appearance. Fictional characters are printed in italics. Translations of Spanish songs, and a glossary of phrases are given in the back of the book).

Tules Barceló (Maria Gertrudis), daughter of Luz and Joaquin Barceló.
Luz Barceló, mother of Tules, later called "Nana Luz"—grandmother.
*Don Miguel Salazar*, owner of a Taos ranch.
*Doña Carmen*, his young wife.
*Caterina*, old nurse for Salazar baby.
*Bernardo*, foreman of Salazar ranch.
*Marcos*, foreman of Salazar caravan to Mexico.
*Alfredo, Juan, Cruz, Ramona, Mercedes, Lupe*, servants in Salazar household.
*Don Florentino Salazar*, uncle of Don Miguel.
Governor Facundo Melgares, Spain's last governor of New Mexico.
Colonel Antonio Viscarra, successor to Melgares.
Juan José, Apache chief and bandit.
*Señora Ortega*, mother of
*María, Ramón* and *Augustin Ortega*.
*Don José Sanchez*, father of Doña Carmen and owner of ranch and salt trade at Manzano.
*Doña Prudencia*, maiden sister of Don José Sanchez.
*Pedro Bustamente*, cowboy foreman on Sanchez ranch at Manzano.
*Celso*, in charge of horses at Sanchez ranch.
*Cuca, Rosita*, servants of Doña Prudencia.
*Antonio*, cowboy on Salazar ranch.
Rafael Sanchez, husband of Luz.
Rafaela, Trinidad, Lucita, children of Luz and Rafael.
*Dionisio Sanchez*, partner of Ramón.
Don Francisco Ortiz, owner of Ortiz land grant at Dolores.
Don Damasio Lopez, father-in-law of Don Francisco.
Don Manuel Alvarez, U.S. Consul at Santa Fe.
*La Casimira*, the witch woman.
*Tia Apolonia*, midwife.
*Carlota* and *Lourdes*, neighbors of Maria and Tules in Santa Fe.

vii

Pepe Cisneros, buffalo hunter from Alcalde.
Don Manuel Armijo, governor of New Mexico.
Doña Trinidad Armijo, his wife.
*Jim Mathews,* a New England boy.
Santiago Flores, manager of gambling rooms.
*Vicente Mares,* lookout at Tules' monte table.
Nicolás Pino, son of Don Pedro Pino.
Don Albino Perez, governor of New Mexico, 1835–37.
*Victorio,* hunchbacked orphan adopted by Maria and Tules.
*Flavio Martinez, Evaristo Tafoya, Felipe Durán,* Santa Fe citizens.
Don Juan Rafael Ortiz, Don Juan Esteban Pino, prominent leaders and
  friends of Don Manuel Armijo.
General Santa Anna, president of Mexico.
Santiago Ulibarri, sub-lieutenant under Armijo.
José Gonzales, Taos chief and ten-day governor of New Mexico.
Colonel Justiniani, commander of Mexican troops at Chihuahua.
*Jackson,* Santa Fe Trail trader.
Don Pedro Perea, rich rancher from Rio Abajo.
*Rómulo,* footman for Tules.
*James Collins,* merchant of Santa Fe.
Augustus de Marle, lookout for Tules' monte tables.
Dr. Josiah Gregg, trader and author of *Commerce of the Prairies.*
Antonio Chavez, son of Chavez family in Albuquerque.
Alcalde Rubidoux, sheriff of Santa Fe.
Padre Antonio José Martínez, parish priest at Taos.
Padre Leyba, parish priest at San Miguel.
Padre Juan Felipe Ortiz, vicar of Santa Fe parish.
*Conchita Mondragon,* coquette from Mexico.
Diego Archuleta, second in command under Armijo.
Don Mariano Martínez, governor of New Mexico, 1844–45.
Don Carlos Beaubien, prominent French-Canadian leader at Taos.
Charles Bent, Taos trader and first U.S. governor of New Mexico.
Kit Carson, famous scout whose home was at Taos.
Doña Josefa Jaramillo, wife of Kit Carson.
Doña Ignacia Jaramillo, sister of Doña Josefa.
Cerán St. Vrain, St. Louis trader over the Santa Fe Trail.
Juan Escolle (John Scolly), early Santa Fe merchant.
Don Santiago (James) Magoffin, leading trader and U.S. emissary.
Adolf Speyer, partner of Armijo in Santa Fe Trail trade.
Captain Phillip St. George Cooke, of First Dragoons, U.S. Army.
General Stephen Watts Kearny, commanding officer of American Army
  of the West.

# Contents

# Part One: Taos 1821-1822

## 1

"Viva Santa Fe! Viva Santa Fe! Salud! Salud, amigos!" the stowaway child heard the men shout from all the oxcarts ahead of hers.

As the long caravan wound down the red hillside and into the town people answered, "La caravana! Welcome, welcome! Stop and visit! Come in, come in! You will be hungry before you eat the good bread of Chihuahua!"

The child, hidden under heavy rolls of buffalo and sheep pelts inside the carreta, forgot her caution in the excitement of entering Santa Fe and the mention of food. Tules was starved, for she had eaten nothing but a few cold tortillas during the four-day journey from Taos. She climbed quickly over the stiff bundles of pelts to peer out the side of the cart. She knew that any noise she might make would be lost in the tumult of creaking wheels, clattering pots and pans tied at the back of each cart, snorting horses, barking dogs, and whips cracking as the drivers guided their oxen. She looked quickly at Bernardo's fat buttocks bulging over the seat and saw that he leaned out to shout to people standing beside the road. She sighed with relief that he had not discovered her so far and would leave the caravan at Santa Fe. After he left, she would ride on to Mexico, free and happy.

The homemade carreta was swung over a single pole between the two solid wheels and jolted with every plodding step of the oxen. A sudden jerk threw the child's slight body against the tough cedar sticks that formed a high crate around the bed of the cart. She clung with wiry, ten-year-old strength to the shifting pelts, rubbed the scratch on her thin arm, and drew the worn saddle blanket closer over

1

her small shoulders. She forced the cedar sticks apart, pulled up the white sailcloth that covered the cargo and came down over the sides. She pushed back her mat of red hair and peered out with one bright hazel eye.

She saw low adobe houses lining the narrow road and was disappointed that they were no larger than houses in Taos. She had expected to see great mansions in the famous capital. And the houses were not white like those at Taos but a warm golden color. The late afternoon light gilded the dark faces of men, women, and children who smiled and called as the caravan passed. She watched a black-haired boy, a little older than herself, jump up and down with excitement and wave his arms. He was with an older girl and a little boy. Tules wished that she dared wave back to them. Suddenly the boy pointed to her cart and called, "Are you taking a cat to trade in Chihuahua?"

Tules realized that he had pointed to her eye and hastily dropped the canvas. She held her breath as she heard Bernardo answer, "No, chamaco, no one buys cats, dogs, or pert little boys in Chihuahua. The journey is only for brave men like our Marcos here."

"But I saw a cat's eye . . ." the boy shouted.

Tules trembled as she pulled one of the bundles of pelts over her head. Now Bernardo would discover her, whip her, and send her back to Taos. Curse that boy! But the carreta lurched on, and the boy's taunt faded. Above the rumbling wheels she listened intently to find out if Bernardo suspected the extra cargo, but he was grumbling to Marcos on the seat beside him.

"Válgame Dios, it burns me to think that I have to return to Taos to look after a spoiled young mistress, and you will take charge of the caravans to Chihuahua! After all the years that I have been mayordomo of the Salazar carretas! You haven't had my experience, Marcos. You'll let the beasts die of thirst on the Jornada del Muerto, and the Apaches will scalp you."

"You forget that I have been in charge of the caballada on other trips," Marcos said. "I know all the three hundred dusty leagues of the Chihuahua Trail. Besides, we will have one hundred and fifty

2

carretas in the caravan this year. Added to these from the Upper River there will be the Santa Fe carretas and those from Albuquerque. With so many carretas and the military escort the Apaches won't dare attack us."

"Por Dios, man, there will never be enough water for all those beasts and men. It's been a dry year, and the water holes won't even be muddy. You'll go crazy with thirst! Then Juan José and his warriors will stampede the loose stock, and you'll pray for an easy death with an arrow through your throat. I know. . . ."

Tules crossed herself at the mention of the dreaded Apache chief who was the terror of the harried caravans. She shivered at this danger ahead but heard Marcos laugh and say, "Then why do you want to go again?"

"Pendejo, I want to make money! Men are so rich in Chihuahua that their horses are shod with silver. I can trade one bundle of sheepskins for the twenty-five pesos Don Miguel pays me in wages in a year. Beside sheepskins we've got buffalo and beaver pelts, tanned white deerskin, copper, turquoise, homespun blankets, and the wool sheared last spring. Don Miguel owns most of it, but he let the peóns put in everything they could find. They expect a good profit, but they don't know the difference when I make a better bargain for myself. Válgame Dios, I haven't thought of anything else for the last six months but this annual departure of the caravan for the great fairs in the south. . . ."

"We will have a hard trip for eight weeks, but it will be warm when we get there," Marcos said.

"Yes, you'll be warm while I freeze in the snow, curse you. You'll dance with beautiful girls and sing and drink in the great cities of Chihuahua and Durango. The traders will swarm over your carts, and you'll come home rich. You'll bring back chocolate, sugar, wine, silks, and velvets. . . ."

"I'll do well if I buy my wife enough calico for a skirt."

"That's because you are not a good trader, Marcos. Por Dios, a mayordomo has more power than a general. When I went with Don Miguel to the fair south of Chihuahua at Valle de Allende two years ago, to get the trousseau for his bride, you should have seen the silks and velvets, laces and jewels he bought. The merchants give the mayordomo a good commission for bringing them a rich master. And now, this year, Don Miguel leaves me at home. . . ."

The carreta pitched clumsily as the wheels ground over stone. Tules heard the drivers ahead shout to stop their oxen, wondered what had happened, but dared not look out again.

"You know the danger if the Navajos raid Taos," Marcos said. "They'll steal the horses, women, and children, kill the men, and set fire to the houses. I don't like to leave my family alone. . . . You should be proud that Don Miguel trusts you to take care of his hacienda and Doña Carmen. The baby was only born last week."

"But I am the mayordomo, not a wet nurse," Bernardo growled. "Don Miguel pampers his wife until she is as spoiled as a queen. But she can't boss me. If I have to go back, I'll see that Doña Carmen stays in the house with the baby where she belongs, and I'll run the ranch for the six months Don Miguel is away. Pues, here we are at last. Get your carretas in line and make camp. Oiga, Carlos, feed the horses first and see that they are hobbled. And tell the 'madre' to hurry supper. I want to go to the plaza."

Tules heard the men bustle to make camp, feed the neighing mules and horses, and dig into the frozen earth to make holes for the cooking fires. The carreta tipped forward when the oxen were unhitched, and she slipped down with the rest of the cargo toward the front seat. When the men left she cautiously lifted the side canvas and looked out.

They were camped in a wide, sandy valley near the Río Santa Fe. She looked toward the east where the flat roofs and towers of the town were framed by the arch of a bare gray cottonwood branch. Beyond the town high mountains piled up to a round white dome. They were covered with deep snow, but it glowed like rose quartz in the afterglow of the early December sunset.

Beyond her carreta Tules saw the white covers of dozens of other oxcarts forming a half circle around the campfires. They tipped forward in a tired droop, and the wheels looked too heavy to turn. The

4

wheels were cut out of solid chunks of wood that bulged toward the center for extra strength around the axles and were crudely rounded to fit the wide iron rims.

She heard the loud squeaking of more wheels as the carretas from Chimayo and Santa Cruz straggled into camp. They were followed by a large band of sheep, who bleated when they smelled river water and stirred up shimmering dust. These were driven into a rock corral beyond the enclosure for the loose stock in the caballada. Near the wall Tules saw a man sitting beside a solitary campfire. He was the guard for the two dozen young Navajo captives who were chained in pairs and would be driven to Mexico to be sold in the slave markets.

She watched hungrily as men gathered around the cook fires and dipped their tortillas into pots of steaming beans. Each held out his gourd cup to be filled with tasty, hot atole. Her mouth watered as she saw them drink the corn-meal gruel. She was so hungry that she pressed her arms tight against her gurgling stomach and wriggled her bare toes. It seemed years since she had been warm or tasted good food.

But it was only four days ago that she had run away from Taos. That day of December 1, 1821, everyone in the Salazar household had been at work long before dawn to finish the last preparations for the journey. She shut her eyes and saw the big, dark kitchen and the glow of the fire where her mother baked tortillas on a low griddle. There was a steady throb in the warm, steamy air as other servants patted dough into thin, round cakes and handed them to Luz. She ran to her mother to beg permission to send a saddle blanket to be traded at the fairs for enough red cloth for a new skirt. It was a good saddle blanket of narrow black-and-white stripes with a red band at either end and only a little worn in the fold. She held it up as high as her eager arms could reach to show her mother, but Luz shook her head.

"Tooo-les!" Her high, plaintive voice drew out the first syllable of the child's name in long-suffering reproach. "Put that blanket back where you found it. You know it belongs to Don Miguel. Every day you've brought something to send that doesn't belong to us. Don't molest me again. The saints know that I haven't a moment to spare with that Bernardo barking at us to finish the tortillas."

If her mother had given her permission to send the old blanket, she would still be at home. It must be God's wish that she should take the blanket herself and find riches in Mexico. As she thought of this she pulled the saddle blanket around her defiantly and tilted her small chin.

That morning, as she handed the muslin-wrapped tortillas up to Bernardo to pack, she noticed a small space between the stiff bundles of pelts. As soon as Bernardo left the carreta she climbed over the high wheel, squeezed under the canvas and through the cedar sticks, and jumped down between the pelts. Almost before she had settled herself, the carretas rumbled off to Taos to join the caravan. She crouched in fear and listened for her mother or Bernardo to call her, but in the commotion no one missed her. No one suspected that a child would hazard a journey that tried the strength and courage of the hardiest men.

She had nearly frozen in her hiding place, but she pulled the saddle blanket over her head like a tent and sat on her bare feet. There was no warmth in her patched skirt, short-sleeved blouse, or cheap black cotton reboso. She munched the cold, thin tortillas she had pilfered and moistened her tongue with small icicles that formed on the edge of the canvas. She was sick with terror when Bernardo unfastened the canvas at the back, but he reached for a hunk of meat without looking inside. Another time Alfredo, the ox driver, heard the pelts squeak when she moved and suspected pack rats. After that she hardly dared to stretch her cramped legs or relieve her excited bladder through the cracks in the floor of the cart.

She listened to the oxen groan as they pulled up steep mountains and Bernardo shout as the brakeless wheels plunged downhill. The first night two Navajo captives escaped, but they were brought back and flogged by Bernardo at Don Miguel's command. The men were restless that night and talked of a Navajo or Comanche attack on the small Taos party. The second night, when they were reenforced by carretas from Abiquii and the upper Chama River, Bernardo

6

drank too much with the new men. Tules remembered that her mother and the other servants dreaded Bernardo's brutal treatment when he was drunk.

She looked at Bernardo now, talking with other men at the campfire. His face was heavy and pock-marked, and there were gray streaks in his coarse black hair. His stiff knee was a good excuse to make others do his work. She shuddered as she watched him and longed for the safety of her mother's arms. Her eyes filled with tears because her mother had not kissed and blessed her before she left. She could hear her mother's harsh voice say that she was thankful for shelter, scraps of food in the kitchen, and fifty centavos a month in wages. She could never understand why Luz would not give her a copper instead of giving it to some strange thing called "debt." Luz said "debt" made her a bound peón and she could never leave Don Miguel.

Tules brushed away her tears in the fierce pride that she had gotten away. Now she would visit her mother's country, Sonora, come back rich, and rescue Luz. She did not know that the caravan would not go near Sonora. To her Mexico was Sonora, a warm, beautiful place where children picked luscious fruit and flowers. She had asked her mother why she had left such a heavenly homeland, and Luz had said, "Your father was a soldier named Joaquín Barceló, and he was ordered north to fight Indians. What could I do but carry you in my reboso and go along to cook for him? The Indians killed him and all the soldiers, and we hid in the rocks. The Blessed Virgin sent a party of traders who took us with them to the salt fields near Manzano. I found work with good Don José Sánchez, and when his daughter, Doña Carmen, married Don Miguel Salazar, she took us as her own servants for her new home in Taos."

Then Luz had added proudly, "Your father's family came from Andalusia to Mexico. He had red hair like yours and the blood of the Right People. You must mind your manners to be worthy of a fine family."

Tules pictured herself now, returning to her grandparents' rich home. She would curtsy and say, "I am María Gertrudis Barceló, at

7

your orders, grandsire. I am called 'Tu-les' for short." Then the grandfather would bless her, dress her in fine clothes, and send her in a coach to bring her mother from Taos.

At last she saw Bernardo swing his stiff leg and start for the plaza. The other men followed him, and the few guards huddled around the fires with their backs to the carretas. Tules stealthily wriggled through the side and jumped down from the high wheel. She landed in the snow, and her bare knees shook with fright and cramped muscles. She darted through the shadows to the bank of the small river, dropped flat on her stomach, and took long gulps of the ice-crusted water. She washed her face, scrubbed her greasy hands with sand, and combed her tangled hair with her fingers. She brushed at her skirt, pulled the saddle blanket over her head, and shrugged her small shoulders. Tonight she had no fiesta finery, but she would come back from Mexico in silks and jewels.

A sentry stood at the gate of the wall around the western edge of the town. Tules eyed him cautiously, but he paid no attention to the ragged children running in and out like starved mice. She darted through the gate and ran toward the distant bonfires lighting the towers of a church at the end of the dark, narrow street.

She came abruptly into a large plaza and blinked at the many bonfires and pine-knot torches flaring from long poles. Men crowded around the fires to warm the backs of their tight leather pants and short jackets. The teamsters' red flannel sleeves glowed in the firelight.

Many torches illuminated a long, one-story building facing the northern side of the plaza. Before its double middle doors, sentries paced under a long portal supported by round wooden posts and carved corbels. Tules knew this must be the Palace and squirmed through the crowd for a closer view. She wished that she could press her nose against the mica panes in the deep windows and watch the Governor and Don Miguel dance with elegant ladies.

Beyond the high tower at the western end of the Palace she sniffed the odors of hot, spicy food and ran to the market. Women sat on their heels before wares spread on mats on the ground and called in shrill voices the price of three white eggs, a handful of shaved dry buffalo meat, or a round pat of goat's-milk cheese. Others squatted beside small braziers where savory chile stew or tamales simmered over glowing charcoal. Tules sidled over hungrily to a sharp-nosed crone who was bargaining fiercely with a good-natured ox driver.

"Two tamales for a cuartillo, señor. That's my best price," she croaked and pulled her black reboso with an uncompromising jerk.

"But, señorita, for the love of God, I am a poor man far from his own kitchen," the driver laughed. "Por favor, give me three tamales for a cuartillo. Ah, your generous heart shines through your beautiful face, comadre. . . ."

Tules's fingers pulled at her skirt with famished hunger as she looked at the fat corn-meal tamales in their golden husks steaming in the old woman's kettle. Her mouth watered as she stared at circles of red oil floating around the tamales. She leaned over the old woman quickly, tapped her bony shoulder, and whispered in a frightened voice, "Take care, tía. The Alcalde comes to arrest you."

When the old woman looked backward in terror, Tules grabbed a handful of tamales and ran.

"Thief! Thief! Stop her! Catch her! She stole my tamales," the old woman shrieked.

But Tules hid the tamales in the fold of her blanket, wriggled through the crowd, and crouched breathlessly in the shadow of a deep doorway. She unwrapped the steaming corn husks and crammed the hot mush into her mouth. Nothing had ever tasted so good as the meat and chile in the center of the tamales.

She ran back to the plaza where the gay, noisy crowd celebrated this greatest fiesta of the year in honor of the caravan that would leave in the second dawn. Country people from near-by ranches stared at the red velvet collars and cuffs on the uniforms of officials who hurried into the Palace. Wine-warmed drivers sang in high falsettos and called to girls with flashing black eyes. Tules hugged herself with joy and excitement and wished that her mother could see the laughing faces.

She heard the staccato music of a fiddle, guitar, and drum and

9

squirmed through the men at the open door of a dance hall. Couples whirled in the quick steps of a polka, and Tules looked enviously at the women's flaring silk skirts.

The hot air made her sleepy, and she crept into another lighted room where everyone gambled. She looked cautiously at ragged boys, peóns, and drivers, afraid that someone from Taos would recognize her. They were all strangers, and she edged closer to the officers and girls with black braids hanging over their half-bare shoulders and crept between them to the monte table.

She drew in her breath, and her hazel eyes widened as she saw the stacks of silver near the quick hand of the man who dealt the cards. And gold—there were also stacks of shining gold doubloons! She did not know there was so much money in the world and wished she was the dealer. She could live forever with one of those stacks of silver.

The silver pesos clinked as men placed their bets on a green cloth. The blue haze of tobacco smoke hung in the air below the candle-lighted chandelier. Suddenly she recognized a familiar, dreaded voice, jerked her blanket over her head, and peered out with one eye. It was Bernardo, his heavy face purple with wine. He shouted, "Cabrón! I won that. That's my money on the knave."

"No, it's mine, you damned cheat!" a short man yelled.

Bernardo and the man began to fight, and soon other men were fighting, shouting, drawing their pistols or knives. An iron-nailed boot ground into Tules' bare instep as she ducked through the fighting men and out the door.

The plaza was quiet and deserted, and she wandered forlornly up a dark side street. A dog yapped at her, but she called to him softly and followed him through a corral to a horse shed. She found hay inside, burrowed into it, and sneezed with the sweet dust. She rubbed the torn skin on her instep, snuggled into the hay, and was soon dreaming of warm golden Mexico.

# 2

THE COCKS woke her the next morning, and she scrambled out of the corral before anyone discovered her. She was cramped and cold and limped on her bruised foot. Smoke from a hundred breakfast fires curled into the sharp, clear air, and she smelled the sweet fragrance of newly baked bread. She stealthily opened the door of a hive-shaped adobe oven outside a kitchen door and hugged two warm brown loaves against her famished stomach. She hid behind a wall, broke the warm crust, and ate ravenously. When the six o'clock matin bells rang she stopped chewing for the required minute of silence and gave thanks for the stolen bread.

Later the bells clanged for high mass in the parroquia and a special blessing for the caravan, leaving at the next dawn. Tules passed through the wide doors and knelt on the dirt floor beside black-shawled women. She was dazzled by dozens of twinkling candles on the high altar that gleamed on wide gilt frames of dark paintings and priests' gold brocade vestments. Above the altar incense from silver censers drifted to high windows that were covered with red curtains. Sunshine filtered through them to flood the white walls and gleaming altar with crimson radiance. Tules looked at the wonderful light and felt folded in divine blessing. She closed her eyes tight to hold within herself this beauty and warmth and remembered it all of her life.

When mass was over she jumped as a cannon roared outside the church, followed by a volley of muskets. She pushed close to the woman next to her and whispered with terror, "Have the Navajos come to kill us?"

"Don't be afraid, child," the woman smiled. "They are only warding off the evil spirits in the air. They filled the anvil with gunpowder, covered it with a playing card, and set it off with a hot poker. The

11

cannon and the muskets will frighten evil spirits that might harm the caravan."

"Thanks be to God, señora," Tules murmured and crossed herself with the blessed assurance that her journey would be saved from peril.

In the plaza she joined a large crowd who watched Governor Facundo Melgares review the military escort for the caravan. She pushed her way under the wide portal of the Palace to stand close and look with awe at the Governor's short, corpulent figure with the gold fringe swaying at the shoulders of his dark uniform and the tinted plumes in his cocked hat.

Under the bright midday sun thirty-five soldiers came around the plaza at a clattering gallop and pulled up before the Governor. They presented old-fashioned muskets, lances with iron prongs, and bows and arrows. A few were in ragged uniforms, but most wore flannel-sleeved jackets and fox-skin caps lined with scarlet cloth.

"I hoped to send our soldiers to Mexico in smart uniforms, but the treasury is empty," the Governor said to Colonel Antonio Viscarra, standing beside him. "I have led them in battles against the Indians for fifteen years. Their bravery should be rewarded with something better than this motley. At least we can give them extra rations today."

Tules scanned the crowd for Taos men and loosened the blanket over her chin when she saw only strange faces. In the crowd of urchins at the front she recognized the three children she had noticed yesterday as the caravan rolled into town. She edged toward the older girl with the black reboso over her thin face, the little boy, and the other boy who had called attention to her "cat's eye." They were barefooted and ragged like herself, but the boy looked lively and full of fun. She drew close to them through loneliness and curiosity, but their eyes were on the gaudy officials.

The Governor returned the last salute and was turning to go into the palace when he noticed the ragamuffin children staring at him. He smiled, dug his pudgy hand into his pocket, and threw them a handful of coins.

The children scrambled wildly for the rolling coins. Tules clawed into the dirt and grabbed a copper tlaco in one hand and a thin silver real in the other. Her bare foot clamped over a round silver peso.

A big boy yelled, "That's mine," and kicked her leg to snatch the peso. She pushed him away with all her strength, reached under her calloused sole, and clutched the peso in her tight fist. The big boy pulled her hair with one hand and shook her with the other.

"Let go! Thief! Bully! Son of a pig!" she screamed.

The boy knocked her down and twisted her arm, but she bit at his hand until the blood came. He kicked and cuffed her but could not make her open her hands.

"Leave her alone! You've got your share. I'll make you cough out the peso you've got in your mouth," another boy cried.

The other children kicked and pulled at the big boy, and Tules jerked free of him. She spat at him as he ran away, her green eyes flashing. The older girl picked up Tules's blanket, shook it, and handed it to her. Tules thanked her and tucked her coins into the safety of her tight red sash.

"Where do you live?" the girl asked.

"In Taos," Tules said, still panting. "But I am going with the caravan tomorrow."

"Who accompanies you?" the girl questioned.

"My father is in charge of the caballada—".Tules tossed her red head proudly—"and my mother returns to her beautiful home in the south."

"Caramba! Your father must be a man of influence! And rich!" the 'cat's-eye' boy who had rescued her exclaimed. "Would he take me? I could help with the caballada. I am Ramón Ortega, and this is my sister, María, and my little brother, Augustín."

"I am María Gertrudis Barceló, at your orders," Tules said formally to impress the children with her fine manners. "But I am called 'Tu-les' for short."

"Tooo-les!" Ramón laughed and mimicked the way she had drawn out the first syllable. "Come with us to the market to buy sweets, and

13

then we'll find your father and ask if I can go with the caballada."

Tules had never before had a centavo of her own to spend. Now she squandered her copper tlaco for sticky quince candy and shared it with Ramón. She spent the silver real to see a wonderful puppet show, but she hoarded the round, hard peso for Mexico. She ran with the Ortega children as they tagged after wandering musicians in the plaza and laughed and sang with the joy of being part of this great fiesta.

Toward evening she saw Don Miguel ride by on his black stallion. Silver shone on the rich trappings of his saddle, bridle, spurs, and the cord around his flat hat. His long blue broadcloth cape was thrown over his shoulder, half hiding his small moustache and arrogant young face. Tules shielded her face with her blanket until he passed and then boasted, "That's my patrón from Taos. Isn't he handsome? He invited us to go to Mexico."

"I could give him good service." Ramón looked at Tules admiringly. "Let's find your father now and see about the caballada."

"I've lost my father and mother." Tules shook her head quickly, and her red lips drooped. "I don't know where to find them. I will have to sleep in the plaza."

"Stop talking of the caballada, Ramón. You are always full of wild plans," María scolded and then turned to Tules. "Come and have supper with us, and we'll find your mother later."

Their home was a two-room adobe with clean white walls and a cheerful blaze in the corner fireplace. Tules hung back at the door and looked shyly at the broad, kind face of Señora Ortega.

"Our poor house is at your disposition, child," she smiled. "Come in and eat your supper. Afterwards you can wash and find your mother."

Tules was ashamed of her dirty face and patched skirt, but she forgot them as she gorged on hot posole. She scooped into the kettle with many tortillas and ate until she could hold no more.

After supper the boys were sent to chop wood, and the mother broke brown amole roots in a copper bowl of warm water and washed

Tules's matted hair and thin body. She handed Tules a blanket, washed her clothes, and hung them beside the fire to dry. María used a wooden comb on her tangled hair, and Tules touched her first tight braids. She felt shorn and alone and afraid of going into the dark night. Tears glistened in her eyes as she looked at the friendly room and faces.

"Stay here tonight, and we'll find your people tomorrow," the mother said.

Tules clutched the peso in her hand as she lay beside María that night and watched the firelight caress the white walls. She reminded herself sleepily that she must hide in the carreta before dawn.

A man's voice roused her, and she stared at the strange room. María and her mother patted tortillas, while the father built up the fire. It was already daylight. Tules jumped up, jerked on her skirt and blouse, tucked the peso into her sash, and grabbed her blanket. "A thousand thanks for your kindness, señora. Pray that I am not too late. . . . Adiós!" she cried, as she ran out the door.

She was out of breath when she reached the camp. It was bright daylight now, and she would have to wait for a chance to climb into the carreta. She cursed herself for oversleeping.

The camp was in an uproar. Mules brayed, drivers cursed the wheels frozen in the mud, vaqueros cut the air with their lassos as they rounded up the loose stock. Sheep bleated and surged against each other in confused panic. Only the chained Navajo captives were grimly silent.

"Hurry, you lazy swine. They've started from the plaza," Bernardo shouted, as he inspected the six oxen hitched to each of the Taos carretas. "Get ready, Marcos, and hold your place."

Tules watched him desperately over the fold of her blanket. She prayed that he would leave, but he stood close to her carreta. She heard the drumbeats as the military escort rode down the road from the town, and she saw the horses dance under the soldiers' spurs and the newly sharpened lances glitter in the sunlight. Then the ricos pranced by on their nervous stallions, silver glinting on their saddles

15

and their full capes thrown over their shoulders with haughty grace. They were followed by the white-topped Santa Fe carretas with women running beside them to call last farewells.

The excited Taos mules reared, and the drivers clung to their halters. Everyone was set to fall in line. Bernardo stood beside his oxen, ready to bawl his last command. In another minute they would start.

Tules took a desperate chance, ran to the wheel, set her foot on the axle, and grabbed the iron rim, when a boy's voice called, "Adiós, Tules! Good luck for your journey!"

Bernardo turned to see who had called and then stomped toward the carreta. Tules poised on the high rim and pulled frantically at the canvas and cedar sticks. Bernardo caught her bare ankle and jerked her to the ground. "Keep away from there, you bastard brat. What have you stolen?" he shouted.

"Let me go. I'm going with the caravan. Let me go," Tules screamed, writhing to get away from his hand.

"You are not going with the caravan, you thief," Bernardo shook her, and the blanket fell away from her terrified face. "Válgame Dios, you are Tules Barceló from Taos! How did you get here? I'll fix your mother for not watching a runaway brat. Beggars like you don't ride. Keep clear now. They're starting."

Marcos shouted his command to start, and Bernardo bellowed a sulky "Adiós!" The oxen strained at their load, and Tules sprang for the slowly turning wheel. Bernardo's heavy boot kicked her light body through the air, and she sprawled in the snow.

"Keep away from there, you bastard," he cursed as he caught Tules and bound her to a cottonwood tree with a rawhide thong. "That will hold you until I am ready to leave for Taos. Here's a taste of what you're going to get." He cracked his whip over her bare legs and turned to shout to the departing caballada.

Tules sobbed with fury and despair and pulled against the thongs until they cut her wrists. Through her tears she saw the last of the caravan wind down the snow-covered valley and listened to the high, incessant bleating of the sheep. Soon the caravan was only a dark line moving toward the west where the distant blue Sandías humped against the cloudless sky. Beyond the far shimmering rim was Mexico.

The camp was deserted. Only the litter of animal droppings, sodden hay, mud, and dead fires showed that men had camped under the bare trees. Nothing was left but a pony, some shaggy burros, and the child bound to the cottonwood. They waited in the cold wind, while Bernardo drowned his disappointment in the cantina on the plaza.

Tules's head drooped, and she shivered with the cold and the pain where the thongs cut her wrists. She could not wipe her nose nor the tears streaming down her face. She lifted her head in new fright when she heard a rattle in the bushes near her. She saw María and Ramón crawl over the bank of the arroyo and look at her anxiously.

"Tules, I didn't know. . . . I'm sorry," Ramón called.

"Get away from me, you skunk. Go away," Tules cried and shook her head wildly. Shame burned through her that the children knew she had lied and witnessed her disgrace. "If it hadn't been for your long tongue, I'd be safe in the carreta now. Go away. Curses on you."

"But I didn't know. . . . You said . . ." the boy protested.

"Get out. Go away. As soon as I'm free I'll put the evil eye on you," Tules screamed, furious with shame and disappointment.

"I brought you tortillas," María offered timidly. "I'll put them behind this rock. Mamá said to bring you home. . . ."

"Go away!" Tules spat at her. "I wish I'd never seen your home. Ay de mí!"

"If we could help . . ." Ramón urged.

"You have ruined everything. You will make things worse. Leave me alone," Tules sobbed.

"Listen! Someone comes!" Ramón said.

Tules choked back her sobs to listen to Bernardo's nasal voice boom as he lurched down the road. He sang,

> Triste es la vida del hombre
> Que viene decirte adiós. . . .

"Go. Go quickly. If he forgets that I am here, come back with a knife to cut these thongs," Tules hissed in a loud whisper. "Mother of

17

God, help me. . . ." She flattened her body, praying to make it invisible against the tree trunk and held her breath. The children disappeared behind the arroyo.

"Get a move on you, Alfredo," Bernardo shouted to the clumsy boy who plodded behind with two heavy sacks on his back. "The sun is high, and we have to make ten leagues today."

Alfredo hung his jacket over a burro's head to blind it, while he tightened the cinch and balanced the sacks over the wooden pack saddle. A baby burro with long ears nickered and ran to suckle its mother. The other burros lifted their long heads, bared their yellow teeth as they brayed, and started to run away. Alfredo chased them, and his mouth gaped when he saw Tules. She shook her head wildly, and he nodded and turned to saddle Bernardo's pinto pony.

"Look around and see what you have left," Bernardo called. "Did you pack the flour, sugar, coffee, and the onions and potatoes from Durango? Caramba! To think that I should descend to hauling this stuff for Doña Carmen! Don Miguel is a fool to pamper her like a princess. Beat a wife, and she'll appreciate a good master, I say. But I'll get even. If it wasn't for her, I would be on my way to Mexico now."

Tules hardly breathed as she watched Bernardo stick his foot in the covered stirrup and pull himself into the saddle. If only he would ride away now! The pony jumped under his spur, reared, and stopped stiff legged facing the trees. Tules saw Bernardo stare at her in tipsy amazement. Then a coarse laugh puffed out his heavy cheeks, and he flicked her bare legs with his whip. She ducked her head and winced but did not cry out.

"Válgame Dios! That's no way to dance after you've come all the way to Santa Fe for the fandangos," he shouted. "Loosen her, Alfredo, and see if she can't do the jota with more spirit. Tie one end around her waist and the other to the tree. Give her enough room for pretty steps."

Bernardo sat on his pony and whirled his whip as Tules ran madly from side to side at the end of the rawhide. Bernardo rocked with drunken laughter and shouted, "That's it! Dance! Point the toe—

18

one, two, three! That's it! Higher! Faster for the great fiesta! Quick steps! High steps! That's the way!"

She ran frantically to avoid the whip and ducked each time it whirled. It was like hot iron on her bare legs, and blood trickled down them, but she clenched her teeth and kept from screaming out at the pain and terror. She looked for Alfredo, but he turned a helpless back and loaded the burros.

"Do you expect to ride back to Taos on a white mare with a red velvet cushion?" Bernardo jeered, when he tired of his play. "How did you get here? I should leave you with the other starving dogs, but your mother might hear of it and bawl to Doña Carmen. But I'll make all of you pay for the trip. Alfredo, give the brat two varas length of the rawhide and tie her to that one-eared Mocho. She'll have to run to keep up."

Tules rubbed the welts on her legs and sobbed. The rawhide pinched her waist like a cinch, and the other end was tied to the pack saddle. The burros shoved against each other and started to trot. She ran among them, afraid that their small, sharp hoofs would trample her bare feet.

They scrambled up the red hill north of Santa Fe, but Bernardo did not turn to look back. The snow-covered foothills were covered with piñón and cedar shrubs like the whiskers on a sick man's jaw. Bernardo set the pace as he hunched sullen shoulders and rode on toward the glittering white peaks that barricaded their way toward the north.

# 3

THE LONG leagues to Taos stretched out in torture and exhaustion for the child. She panted as she ran to keep up with the shaggy burros and watched their heels anxiously. If one burro nipped a crowding neighbor, the heels would fly in her face. She tried to keep close to Mocho's mournful brown eye and the flapping split ear that branded him for stealing corn. A dark stripe ran through his coarse gray coat from his ears to his short tail, and another stripe from his forelegs crossed it on the shoulder. Tules crossed herself as she remembered that Nuestro Señor had blessed burros with His cross since that Palm Sunday when He had ridden the ass. She prayed for forgiveness and help.

Alfredo's long legs dangled behind the packsaddle of his brown burro. He kept his eye on Tules and the pack train behind him, while he tried to keep up with Bernardo's sturdy pony. Bernardo drained the last drop from his bottle and raised his voice to carry his threat back to Tules's ears.

"I'll give that runaway brat to the Indians in Taos pueblo, and they can feed her to the Bibirón."

"Not to the B-b-b-bibirón!" Alfredo stammered with fright. Tules gasped with horror.

"The Indians feed girl babies to that great serpent they keep up the cañón," Bernardo said thickly. "I have seen with my own eyes the fetish they keep in the underground kiva. It's a stone as big as a skinned pig and white as tallow, with turquoise eyes and a red coral mouth. When the Bibirón gets hungry, this fetish grows slimy white fur and the Snake Clan have to find food. They leave girl babies at the mouth of the cave, and the huge, bleached serpent crunches them. . . ."

"María S-s-santísima!" Alfredo gasped.

Tules retched with terror, tripped on a rock, and fell headlong into the snow. Mocho jerked her up, and she screamed, "No, no, I can't walk. My ankle's broken."

"Stop! You're pulling off the packsaddle," Alfredo called and ran to her. "Tie it with this," he whispered and dropped a dirty blue bandana beside her. She bound it tightly around her ankle and hobbled on. By afternoon her aching head rolled from side to side, and she mumbled, "Bibirón! Bibirón!" to the burros' hoofbeats.

They stopped overnight at a little ranch, and the next dawn Tules was tied to Mocho again and limped on her swollen ankle. When they turned off for the short-cut trail over the mountains, Bernardo let her ride on Mocho to make better time. He hunched morosely in his poncho as his pony broke the trail through the deep snow. They climbed toward white peaks outlined with pulsing radiance against the winter sky, but Bernardo growled about storm clouds gathering behind them. Black buzzards flew up and circled heavily. "Wolves have killed something," Bernardo called.

Tules held her blanket around her with one hand and clung to the packsaddle with the other. Mocho's coarse hair chafed her legs, bare except for her patched skirt, but she was grateful for the burro's warm body in this freezing wilderness. Deep cañóns twisted between mountains, and mountains crowded against each other to the sharp, glittering peaks. They were alone in an ominous white world, as silent and uninhabited as the mountains of the moon. The only sounds in the muffled stillness were their petty efforts to crawl through the snow like half-frozen ants.

Before nightfall they stopped in the shelter of high rocks where the river ran between ice in a deep cañón. Alfredo piled stones in front to pen the animals, and the dry oak leaves rattled as the burros browsed. Bernardo stretched beside the little fire, rubbed at the pains in his stiff leg, and ordered Alfredo to boil coffee, a luxury reserved for the ricos.

Bernardo looked with contempt at Tules, curled up near the fire on a saddle pad and at simple Alfredo doing the chores. "See that both of you keep your tongues quiet at home," he threatened as he drank the fragrant coffee. "Someday the pobres will have coffee and tobacco like the ricos. Coffee costs three pesos the pound, but Don Miguel can afford to give it to me for the profit I will give him. Last year the Godoys paid four hundred pesos for a healthy girl of twelve. I will offer Tules to them for three hundred pesos. . . ."

"No, no, you can't sell me. My mother won't let you," Tules cried and pushed the tangled red hair away from her pinched face. This was worse than the threat of the Bibirón. Tonight Bernardo was sober, and he stopped at nothing to put money in his pocket.

"Your mother is a miserable peón." Bernardo twisted to warm his other leg and light a corn-shuck cigarrito. "She owes Don Miguel twenty pesos at the store, and she'll never live long enough to work that out. Put out the fire, Alfredo, and keep watch the first part of the night."

The acid odor of wet coals penetrated the terrifying, sudden darkness, and the wind moaned through the high pines. Tules pulled her blanket over her head and sobbed in hopeless despair. Nothing was as bad as being sold as a slave. She would never be free, never have a chance, for no one could hope to pay off three hundred pesos. If she had only stayed at home, safe with her mother and Doña Carmen! She listened to Bernardo's deep snores and wished he would choke. She thought of running away, but where could she go in these dark mountains where savages, wolves, and bears prowled?

The next morning she said timidly to Bernardo, "I'll do anything you say if you won't sell me."

"You make too much trouble," he growled. "I'll let another master teach you to work."

Tules sobbed and clung to Mocho, her legs aching with sore muscles and cold. The burros pulled up a steep trail, grunted, and stopped to rest at the top. On all sides the world spread below them in the white glare of midmorning and sparkling sun. Bernardo pointed to the blue melon-shaped mountains far to the south and grumbled, "The caravan is beyond the Sandías now. They will be warm, while we freeze."

To the north the high Taos Valley was cut by a deep, narrow gorge whose purple shadow twisted through the white mesa like the trail of an enormous, writhing serpent. It reminded Tules of the Bibirón, and her frightened eyes leaped beyond it to the tiny white houses at the foot of the high blue mountains. Tears ran down her cheeks as she recognized the settlement of Don Fernández de Taos. The Salazar house was only a league from there, and before night she would be safe in her mother's arms.

It was almost dark when Alfredo swung open the home corral gate and Bernardo shouted to the servants to help unload. Eager voices asked a hundred questions about the journey. When Tules saw her mother's lean figure at the kitchen door she slipped off Mocho and ran across the corral calling, "Mamá! Mamacita!"

"Tooo-les! Thanks be to God!" Luz caught the child in her arms. "Where have you been? We thought the Indians had stolen you. I prayed to San Antonio, and he brought you back."

Tules sobbed out her story and clung to her mother's scrawny neck as Luz carried her into the kitchen. The servants chattered over the child's miraculous return until Caterina, the old nurse, announced that Doña Carmen wanted to see Tules.

The child hung back at the bedroom door and saw that Doña Carmen rested against the white pillows in the wide bed. There were still shadows of hard childbirth under her dark eyes, and her beautiful, delicate face turned toward the baby fretting in his spindle crib in the corner of the room. She was only eighteen and seemed too young to carry the responsibilities of a large, isolated hacienda, but her finely molded features gave the impression of latent strength and decision. She smiled eagerly when she saw the dirty, ragged child and beckoned to her.

"Come in, Tules. You were a naughty girl to run away. You caused us great worry." She shook her head gently and motioned to Tules to come closer. "Tell me about Don Miguel. And Santa Fe. Was it a fine fiesta? When did the caravan start? Was Don Miguel dancing with beautiful girls?"

"Oh no, patrona, he could not dance when his heart longed for you. You are more beautiful than the Santa Fe girls," Tules said

23

quickly and watched Doña Carmen smile. "Don Miguel was busy with the Governor. I saw him ride around the plaza with his cape thrown over his shoulder and the silver tassel on his hat jingling like the silver fringe on his saddle. He had more style than any of the ricos. . . ."

"It will be so long before he comes back," Doña Carmen sighed. "If he had only waited a month I could have taken the baby and gone to my parents at Manzano. He has left us in the cold with all these Indians around. . . ."

"This is your house," Caterina said firmly. "You must be as brave as your husband's mother who lived here for forty years. Don Miguel had to take charge when his father and mother died of the fever three years ago. With this dry year and the grasshoppers it was necessary for him to go to Chihuahua to trade. . . ."

"And, patrona, he rides at the head of the caravan, and he will come back rich," Tules said. "If you would only let me stay until he comes. . . ."

"Stay? Are you going to run away again?" Doña Carmen asked.

"No, no, patrona, never, never again. I know I did wrong, and I beg you to forgive me. I will do anything you say if you will let me stay. Bernardo says he will sell me to the Godoys. . . ." Tules fell on her knees beside the bed and sobbed.

"Be quiet, child. Bernardo can't sell you. He is not the master," Doña Carmen said and turned to Caterina. "Por favor, send Bernardo here."

Tules prayed fervently when she saw Bernardo limp through the door. He twisted his old hat in his hands and spoke with false humility as he told of the trip, Don Miguel's departure, and the supplies he had sent back.

"We were delayed because we had to bring this runaway child home. Don Miguel would sell her and be well rid of her." Bernardo's tone suggested that women knew nothing of discipline or business.

"I am in charge here, Bernardo." Doña Carmen's voice carried authority. "While my husband is away you will take orders from me.

24

Tules and her mother are my servants. I brought them from my home. I will punish the child, but there will be no talk of selling her."

Tules sat back on her heels with a deep sigh of relief and looked from Bernardo's small, mean eyes to Doña Carmen's young, stubborn chin. When Bernardo left Tules kissed the patrona's soft hand and hardly heard her scolding in the joy of being safe.

Luz exclaimed over the round silver peso Tules brought her from Santa Fe and hid it with their few coppers in the dirt under the sheep-skin pallet. She bound a flannel cloth filled with wet ashes around the child's sore throat. For a week Tules tossed with fever and frightened everyone with her nightmare screams about the Bibirón. At last Doña Carmen herself brought the curandera, who boiled malva leaves with goat's milk for a gargle and cut the child's arm to let out the hot bad blood. When Tules was better she stayed close to Doña Carmen to run errands or walk behind her holding the baby.

On Christmas Eve she watched the patrona with awe and adoration and thought she looked like the Madonna. Doña Carmen sat beside the corner fireplace with the baby held to her round, young breast, and candles burned on either side. She wore the reboso de Santa María that Don Miguel had sent from Santa Fe. It was a wide scarf of sky-blue silk with pure gold threads woven above the long fringed ends, and it hung from her shoulders to the floor like the azure robes of the Blessed Virgin.

Four days after Christmas Tules heard someone pound at the zaguán gate and ran to see who had come for an unexpected visit. The zaguán was the covered passageway which served as the one entrance into the inner patio and the twenty rooms of the house. It was wide enough for a coach to drive through, but the two heavy wooden gates were seldom opened. A small door, cut in three scallops at the top, had been fitted into one gate. This was only high and wide enough to admit one person at a time. The peón, who was always on guard within the zaguán, now opened the small door a crack and argued with the boy from the village who demanded to see Doña Carmen.

25

Tules ran for her, and Doña Carmen cried, "Did the Apaches attack the caravan? Mother of God, is Don Miguel—hurt?"

"No, señora," the boy said. "Don Florentino said to assure you that his nephew is well. Don Florentino and the Alcalde will bring you the letter from Don Miguel this afternoon. It is something about the Viceroy in Mexico."

"The Alcalde will come? It must be bad news. Por Dios, why didn't Tío Florentino send the letter with you? Now I will have to wait for hours to hear from my husband. Tell them to come early," Doña Carmen urged.

Tules followed her swift heels to the kitchen where she set the servants a dozen chores. "Get the house in order quickly. This is the first time I have received a formal visit without my husband. At least I have too much to do to worry. Bernardo, start the fire to warm the sala and pour more dirt on that leak in the roof. Lupe, make fresh sopaipillas, and, Ramona, get the mincemeat ready for the empanaditas. Come, Tules, and carry the things from the storeroom."

The wind caught at their skirts as they ran across the big back corral. The storeroom was between the servants' quarters, the stables, and the pens for the milk goats and chickens. Tules sniffed at the mixed odors of the ample provisions. There were chicharrones, brown cracklings packed in rendered lard, sacks of freckled beans, dried peas, peaches, apricots, and grapes. Eggs were put down in coarse salt, and precious table salt was stored in another sack. One corner was heaped with corn, the purple cobs in a separate pile for sweet blue meal. Three red-breasted finches flew up from deep bins filled with yellow wheat.

"Shoo! Shoo! Drive them out, Tules," Doña Carmen called. "Bernardo has neglected to fix that hole over the window."

The finches rattled strings of dry red chile and rosettes of garlic hanging from the rafters as they flew around. They bumped against long whorls of dried pumpkin, squash, and melons and sent down a shower of mint leaves from the bunches of dried herbs.

"Fill your skirt with apples and take a pail of lard," the patrona said, as Tules stopped to lick a trickle from the cask of syrup. "I'll

26

carry the beef and come back later for the wine. Look, someone has been in here!" She pointed to tracks in the dust around the casks of wine.

In the kitchen Doña Carmen questioned the cooks. Each boasted of her specialty and allowed no one else to touch her copper pots hung on the wall. "Let me taste the mistela, Luz." She nodded over the fragrant brew of brandy, spices, sugar, and chimajá leaves. "Now seal the jar with dough and let it simmer. Serve it so hot that Tío Florentino will smell the vapors and forget his rheumatism."

Tules ran with her across the patio to the zaguán where a door to the left opened on Don Miguel's store. She opened the one to the right and hurried into the cold, formal reception sala. Beyond it there was a small, private chapel, richly furnished by Don Miguel's mother as a thank offering for safe deliverance from a Comanche raid.

The sala was seldom used, but now servants hastily brushed the homespun woolen carpet of black-and-white plaid that covered the hard clay floor. The narrow shutters were opened, and dust motes danced down from the dark, round vigas in the ceiling to settle on the sofa and two tables. Spanish dignity reserved the uncomfortable high-backed chairs for men, while women sat on the hassocks or dyed goatskin rugs. The bright sunlight brought out the opalescent tints in the white walls and the soft rose, green, yellow, and indigo in the striped blankets that covered the low adobe bench running around the room. The colors were repeated in a painting of the Virgin of Guadalupe in a wide, silver frame, the embroidery on the white woolen draperies, and the pink feather flowers on the mantel under the gleaming gold crucifix.

"Brrr, it's as cold as a tomb in here. Tell Bernardo to put on more logs, or it will never get warm." Doña Carmen shivered and pointed to the wide fireplace with the conical opening where three logs were already burning. "Dust the long mirror, and put a drawn-work cover over that burned place on the table. Dios mío, there's so much to do, and now I must feed the baby!"

Caterina ruled over the bedroom, which was also Doña Carmen's sitting room and the heart of the house. She was the only calm person in the excited household and was more concerned over the baby's hungry cries than the Alcalde's visit. Her authority was unquestioned, for she had been Don Miguel's wet nurse and had given lifetime devotion to three generations of Salazars. Her brown cheeks caved in below her high cheekbones, and her smooth white hair was drawn back in a knot. She looked like the Mother of Sorrows until her dark eyes smiled and her pale lips revealed one snag tooth.

She handed the baby to the young mother to nurse and jerked at the tight door of the high wooden wardrobe. She laid out Doña Carmen's black silk dress with the jet buttons and blond lace ruffles at the throat and wrists. On top of it she placed three petticoats—a short woolen one for warmth, a starched cambric with lace, and a third of red ruffled taffeta. Tules washed the patrona's feet with scented soap from Mexico and slipped on the fine white stockings and black slippers.

"Tules, you shall fix my hair like the ladies in Santa Fe. Heavenly Hat, how many pretty girls must have smiled at my husband in these five weeks!" Doña Carmen pouted.

Tules dabbed her thick dark hair with sugared water, made ringlets above the arched eyebrows, and pinned the shining coils high on the patrona's head. She adjusted the tortoise-shell comb, draped the black lace mantilla over it, and held out the blue silk reboso. Caterina heard hoofbeats and voices outside and said, "They have come. Tules, wash your face, and brush that red mop of hair before you follow the patrona."

The sala was warm now, and Doña Carmen greeted the two elderly men with the formal embrace. She motioned to her husband's uncle to take the seat of honor on the sofa near the fire and offered the Alcalde a high-backed chair. She spread her rustling skirt over the hassock, and Tules curled up on the floor beside her, ready to run any errand.

While the proper salutations about the health of all the families were exchanged, Tules looked at Tío Florentino's ruffled lace stock, fine white shirt, and the silver buttons on his short jacket and tight

28

black pants. These were open to the knee where white cambric drawers flared to his polished boots. Long gray hair curved up from his high forehead, and his great beaked nose curved down below it. His dark eyes were solemn, and his full lips looked naked in his gray goatee.

Tules turned from his severe, aristocratic features to the round red face of the local politician. The Alcalde's bald head looked like a round river boulder with three charcoal dashes for his straight eyebrows and moustache. He pulled at his tight collar and velveteen jacket and spread his farmer feet far apart. He was proud of his temporary importance, but habit held him silent until Tío Florentino nodded. Tules wached Doña Carmen's fingers twist the fringe of her reboso, impatient to get through the formalities and hear from her husband. Etiquette required that she wait until Tío Florentino mentioned his nephew. At Tío Florentino's nod the Alcalde cleared his throat and began his studied announcement.

"With your permission, Doña Carmen, we have brought the great news that reached us this morning. It came from Chihuahua in only thirteen days. Our country has won her glorious freedom, and we are no longer under the heels of Spain. The illustrious General, Don Augustín Iturbide, rode into Mexico City last September 16 and was proclaimed Liberator!"

"But what of the King? The Viceroy?" Doña Carmen exclaimed.

"Ferdinand VIII is practically a prisoner and is called 'The Faithless' from breaking his promises so often," Tío Florentino explained. "How well I remember his court when my father took me there as a boy! The soldiers revolted in Cadiz and refused to fight against the overseas possessions. All the American colonies that Columbus brought to Isabella have now freed themselves from Spain."

"But we are helpless without Spain!" Doña Carmen's voice was shocked and frightened.

"The old days are over, my child," Tío Florentino said. "The colonies were tired of paying tribute to a Spanish court, rotten with intrigue. For fifteen years Napoleon tried to conquer the world and brought French overlords to Spain. But Napoleon died last year, a prisoner on an island in the sea. By God's mercy the world may have peace now."

"We refuse to be used as pawns for Kings any longer," the Alcalde declared. "Mexicans have worked for liberty for eleven years, ever since the Grito de Dolores. Now we have it, and we can run our own country. The officials in New Mexico will not be changed. They have set January 22 for the elections, and our province will be represented in the Mexican Congress."

"You mean that we will not have a Mexican King?" Doña Carmen asked.

"Mexico now calls herself a Republic like those foolish United States who freed themselves from the British. These seeds of heresy and sedition come from the French Revolution." Tío Florentino's eyebrows lifted with fatalism as he added, "The child is born, and the cord is cut."

He sighed with relief as servants brought in heavy silver trays of food. Doña Carmen poured foaming chocolate into thin china cups that rattled with her nervous impatience. Tules helped to pass the sugar-sprinkled sopaipillas and triangular mince pies. Tío Florentino smiled for the first time when he smelled the heady aroma of the hot spiced brandy. He raised his goblet to his niece with old-fashioned courtesy and said, "Salud! To your good health and happiness, my child, and that of your husband and son!"

"Tell me of Miguel," she cried, now that his name had been mentioned.

"But of course. We have delayed too long in giving you the letter he sent." He motioned to the Alcalde. "We brought it to see if Miguel sent further news of this revolt. . . ."

Doña Carmen's hands trembled as she broke the red wax seal. Tules saw that half the highly taxed paper was left as a margin of respect and the other half was covered with fine, shaded script that ended with a rubric. She watched the patrona's cheeks blush as she read.

"Does Miguel mention the new Government?" Tío Florentino demanded.

30

Doña Carmen nodded and read, "He says, 'You will know by this time that Mexico is free and General Iturbide may be proclaimed Emperor any day. There were great celebrations in the capital last September 16, el día glorioso. The victory was three months old when we reached El Paso del Norte, but our caravan had a belated celebration of its own. My men are drunk with new wine and the new watchword, "Dios y Libertad!" We leave for Chihuahua tomorrow. . . .' "

"Then it is true," Tío Florentino sighed. "This is an important date in history, niña. Since Coronado came here in 1540 Spain has protected this country with her might and power. Now we are a newborn Republic, weak and poor. An empty sack never stands straight. Who knows what will be our destiny? The Indian legend says white men from the East will conquer all of us."

"But we have the Three Guarantees of the new order—Independence, Union, and Religion," the Alcalde said stoutly. "We are free, and our country will become strong and glorious. Governor Melgares has proclaimed great celebrations throughout the Province for this week. The people will shout, 'God and Liberty!' with glad hearts, instead of the weakling cry of 'Long Live the King.' "

"The puny cries of men in this land are like the wind," Tío Florentino shrugged. "The wind travels swiftly before the sun but leaves no shadow."

Tules stood on the long portál at the front of the house and watched the two men ride away. Her small face was puzzled. She had not understood what they said, but she knew it was something important. She looked across the wide, silent land from the fading glory of the Spanish sun to the rosy eastern reflection that was like the promise of dawn. Over the mesa the wind died to a whisper in the sagebrush. This noon that country had been Spain. Tonight it was Mexico. Yet the country looked the same. She shook her head and slipped through the little door to question her mother in the familiar kitchen.

# 4

THE SUN, wind and snow of eighty years had molded the Salazar manor house to the rounded contours of a mound of earth. It was built of earth, plastered and roofed with the same red-brown earth as the ground around it. The outside walls were as thick as those of a fortress and bare of trees or shrubs where Indians might hide. Between the long portál at the front and the sparkling mountain stream a grove of venerable gray cottonwoods made a pleasant shade. The house had been enlarged for each generation, and now Doña Carmen supervised twenty rooms besides the sheds and stables.

Behind the walled corral at back, the red mesa sloped up to leagues of land that had been granted the first Salazar by King Philip V of Spain in 1742. Its boundaries were vaguely described as a certain rock and a lightning-blasted tree and extended "two days' ride" from the manor house. It was high, arid land, covered with sagebrush and cut by a few small creeks. Its drought-resistant grasses were sparse feed for Don Miguel's cattle and sheep.

The house stood in lonely isolation at the eastern edge of the grant. It was half a league from the nearest neighbor and a league from the settlement of Don Fernández de Taos. Once a week Doña Carmen dressed in her long, full skirt and rode to the settlement to pay the required visit of respect to Tío Florentino, the head of her husband's house. Tules clung to the sidesaddle behind her, and a groom accompanied them.

She loved to go to the village and explore another house. While Doña Carmen sat through the long family dinner, Tules snatched delicacies in the kitchen and listened to the servants gossip of jealous quarrels, scandal, and intrigue. At home she put on airs and traded the gossip for special favors.

Once a week Tío Florentino left his ailing, childless wife to return the visit. His long, solemn face always looked more cheerful after a game of casino with Doña Carmen and a cup of hot, spiced brandy. Tules hovered close to Doña Carmen and watched the cards with avid curiosity. She learned quickly and pinched herself to keep from speaking out when Doña Carmen muffed a chance to build on her stack of cards. She suspected that the patrona let the old man win to sweeten his temper. Then he would lay out the cards for monte, show his niece how to place her bets, and tell long stories of how he had won and lost fortunes at the monte tables in Mexico City.

Tules pushed back her red hair and memorized the layout, the deal, and how the bets were paid. She remembered the monte table stacked with silver and gold in Santa Fe. If she could learn to deal, she would have all that money. She found a discarded pack of the narrow Spanish cards and amused herself with shuffling, placing the layout, and dealing.

One day she discovered Alfredo and two boys playing monte in the stable. She squatted beside them and watched them bet with kernels of corn. Alfredo's round, simple face beamed when she admired his skill at card tricks. He showed her how his fingers moved faster than her eyes. She practiced with him until her agile fingers learned the tricks.

They were intent on the game when Alfredo put his finger to his lips and all four of them burrowed into the loose hay like mice. They listened to limping footsteps outside the door. When they passed Alfredo looked out through a crack and whispered, "Bernardo! He's stealing wine again. He lost twenty pesos at monte in Don Fernández last week, and now he'll sell enough wine to play again."

"But that's Don Miguel's wine! He's a thief!" Tules whispered indignantly, her voice sharp with her hatred of Bernardo. "You should tell Doña Carmen. . . ."

"And have Bernardo string me up by my thumbs?" Alfredo shook his head. "Doña Carmen can do nothing against that son of a pig. Don't you tell her, either. It's safer for her if she doesn't know. When Don Miguel comes home Bernardo will get an ax in his back."

After that Tules looked at Bernardo with greater fear and kept out

33

of his way. All the servants avoided him and hated the extra work he piled on them in the winter tasks. The men repaired tools and mended harness to be ready for spring planting, and the women worked under the tailor and shoemaker stitching homespun cloth into skirts and rawhide into moccasins for the peóns.

In the long room next to the kitchen women gossiped as busily as they sewed, but there was one silent corner where three dark Indian slaves wove blankets on narrow looms. Their shuttles beat steadily below the whir of distaffs where two more sullen Indian women spun wool into fine, twisted strands. Hanks of yarn hung on the white wall in the soft shades of vegetable dyes and indigo.

Tules spent one hour each day learning to sew and another at lessons with the patrona. Doña Carmen had an exceptional education, for few girls in the province could read and write even among the gente fina. When Doña Carmen began the lessons two years ago, Luz lectured her daughter, "You must study hard to repay the patrona's kindness. I can only put a cross beside my name, but your father could read and write. With his blood you must never be an ignorant peón. You must learn fine manners and the ways of the gente fina from the patrona."

Now Tules could write a simple letter, sign her name, and read the large print in Doña Carmen's prayer book. She still held the quill clumsily, but sums were an easy matter to be counted on ten brown fingers. She never failed to answer that eight tlacos made one real and eight reales made one peso. She gloated over the secret that she had one peso and a few coppers hidden in the dirt floor under her pallet.

As a reward for good lessons, Doña Carmen often told stories and played cards with Tules. The patrona was lonely, and the child was an adoring audience for tales about her parents, Don Miguel's courtship, and her fine wedding. In turn, Tules entertained her with the new card tricks.

"The child is a magician," Doña Carmen laughingly told Tío Florentino one afternoon. "Her fingers move too fast for me to see how she does the tricks."

The late February wind had made the old man's joints ache, and he frowned at his niece and ignored the child curled up at her feet. "You lessen your dignity when you play cards with your peóns. Our safety depends upon the authority of the master. This loose talk of the equality of men in a Republic will ruin the old families. It comes from these wild Americans who have invaded the Spanish settlements under the new laws. Spain knew that foreigners always made trouble and refused their entry for two hundred years. If foreigners trespassed, they were thrown in dungeons in Chihuahua."

Tío Florentino paced the room and took a pinch of snuff. Tules jumped when he relieved his bursting head with a tremendous sneeze.

"I tell you, Carmen, these foreigners should be stopped at once." He shook his long finger at her. "Last week a gringo named Jacob Fowler came to Don Fernández with his black servant and a French trapper. They bought supplies and returned to their traps in the San Luis valley but the women could talk of nothing but the fine build of the black man. And an American, Colonel James, has had the boldness to open a store in Santa Fe to trade with the Utes. If the gringos trade guns to the Indians, we might as well take the last sacrament now. The Indians could wipe out the handful of whites in this province. . . ."

"Don't the new laws prohibit the sale of guns to Indians?" Doña Carmen asked anxiously.

"The new laws are a farce," Tío Florentino stormed. "They will give foreigners equal rights if they pay the same taxes as our people. New money will fatten a few petty officials and ruin the rest of us."

Doña Carmen's feet moved restlessly in the footstool of Tules's lap. She knew that Tío Florentino only dared to explode against the new Government in the privacy of her room, but his talk frightened her.

He took more snuff, sneezed again, and continued, "Last fall a gringo named Becknell brought pack loads of merchandise from the United States. He knew the Spanish exclusion law had ceased with Mexican independence. His party almost died of thirst crossing the dry plains, but they reached Don Fernández and Santa Fe and made so much money that they will return next year with a larger amount of goods. Men already talk of the big trade that will come over this Santa Fe Trail. Miguel will make nothing from a long, hard trip, at his own expense, if these gringos bring in cheap goods."

"It is so long since he left, and another two months before he returns!" Doña Carmen cried with tears in her eyes.

Tío Florentino patted her bent head and said in a softer voice, "There, child, forgive an old man for adding to your worries. Miguel is safe for this year, and when he makes a good profit you will be glad he went. But I must give you one warning. There is seditious talk among the peóns. They say they should not be bound by debt. They expect the patrón to supply them with everything and pay them money besides. The leader of this talk is your Bernardo."

"Bernardo! But Miguel trusted him, left him in charge here. . . ."

"Miguel thought Bernardo had the most experience, but he is as greedy and cruel as a sow. He says he would have more if he worked for himself; but he would never work. I hear he is selling your wine and aguardiente to the Indians, though that is against even the new laws. Some night the Indians will come here drunk. . . ."

"God forbid!" Doña Carmen cried. "I dream of the Indians coming to attack us. Miguel should never have left us here alone. . . ."

"There is no danger if your peóns are loyal. But you must watch Bernardo," Tío Florentino warned.

When he left Doña Carmen picked up the baby, held his soft, warm body close in her arms, and murmured a prayer over his silky head. Tules watched her and wanted to tell what she knew of Bernardo's visits to the storeroom, but she was afraid that Bernardo would find out and arrange some scheme to sell her.

She was nervous when she followed the patrona for an inspection of the storeroom the next morning. Bernardo smiled slyly when Doña Carmen ordered him to fill a pitcher and good red wine spurted out of the cask. She tipped other casks and satisfied herself that they were full. Tules suspected that they were full of water. Doña Carmen hurriedly counted the casks at the back, and Bernardo complained about the heavy expense of running the hacienda and about how much food the cooks wasted. Tules ran to her mother and told the whole story.

"Hush," Luz warned. "Bernardo will drive us out, and we have no place to go. Doña Carmen is a helpless girl. It is better that she does not know. Don Miguel will see for himself when he comes home. We must pray to Our Lady for protection and the patrón's early return."

The next day a messenger brought a letter from Doña Carmen's father saying that he and her mother would come for a visit. They would arrive the day before the feast day of San José, the patron saint of the grandfather and his namesake grandson. Doña Carmen laughed with happy anticipation, though she worried over the long coach journey for her frail mother. Their home at Manzano was many leagues south of Santa Fe.

She hurried the spring housecleaning to finish it before her parents arrived. One group of women spread a fresh layer of mud on the outer walls and smoothed it with wet palms. Others baked lumps of yeso, ground them fine, and spread the whitewash over the inside walls with sheep pelt. A final trim of tierra amarilla, the yellow clay shining with flakes of mica, made a band of golden luster around the conical opening of the wide fireplace and the floor edges of the walls.

"Get the men to hang the picture and the long mirror, Luz," Doña Carmen called, as she stopped to nurse the baby. "We must finish everything tomorrow to show my mother that I am a good house-keeper. And how she will love this little grandson! Caterina, are you sure he won't walk until next winter? His little back is so strong. See how he straightens out when I hold him. Ay, qué hombrecito!" She kissed the warm creases in his neck as he cooed.

She sent Tules to the patio to wipe up the last spatter of tierra azul under the inner portal. It was a clay that turned the rain and dried to a pale blue, a shade lighter than the spring sky. Tules noticed that the large rosebushes growing beside the covered well in the patio still held their red berries and russet winter foliage. Long ago they had been planted by Don Miguel's mother, who taught the servants to throw a little water on them every time they drew up a bucket from the well.

Tules could hardly wait for June, when the bushes would be fragrant with the small, yellow roses of Castile, and she would put one over her ear.

She played with the rope dangling from the big copper bell near the ladder that led to the roof. The bell was the voice of the house. It rang solemnly each evening for vesper devotions, called merrily for fiestas, and clanged in frantic alarm in times of danger. She looked around quickly to be sure that no one saw her and climbed up the forbidden ladder. She ducked through the small opening in the house wall and ran out on the flat dirt roof. No one was permitted to step on the roof except to repair leaks or defend the house. She skipped to the outer fire wall, crouched behind it, and pretended to shoot through the loopholes made by the roof drains.

She looked at the red willows and smoke-gray cottonwoods that traced the course of the little river through the high, lonely valley and beyond them to the faint blue outlines of mountains on the way to Mexico. In another six weeks the returning caravan would pass them. She pouted because she had missed the great fairs and wonderful bargains and turned away impatiently to run across the roof to look over the back corral. She hid behind a chimney when she saw Bernardo moving stealthily toward the corral gate. His poncho stuck out over something round that he held with both arms.

"Cabrón!" she spat toward him. "This is the last day you will steal from Doña Carmen. Her father comes tomorrow, and you won't dare cheat him."

She backed down the ladder to be caught at the bottom by Caterina, who boxed her ears and threatened to tell the patrona.

# 5

AT NIGHT, after the cooking was finished, the women rested on the kitchen floor before the warmth of the coals in the fireplace. Luz and Tules sprawled beside them, tired and drowsy. Everyone had worked since dawn on last preparations for Doña Carmen's parents who would arrive late tomorrow. The next day Padre Ignatius would say the saint's day mass in their own chapel, and then family and friends would have a bountiful fiesta dinner.

Mercedes had baked dozens of loaves of sweet, crusty bread in the mud ovens in the corral. Ramona had blistered the dry chile and squeezed the hot red pulp until her hands stung. Lupe had prepared posole, soaking the corn kernels in lye until the outer husks were loose. Roasts of mutton, beef, pork, and venison were ready and the chickens drawn. The pantry shelves were loaded with cakes, biscochitos, and triangular fried pies.

Suddenly Lupe raised her hand to silence the women's drowsy talk and exclaimed, "Válgame Dios, he is here again. Listen! This is the third night he has come."

All of them sat up and listened to the long, whirring hoot of an owl. "Who-who-whoooo," the plaintive call rolled down the chimney from the outer darkness.

Tules lifted her head from her mother's arm and stared at Lupe's burning eyes as she croaked, "When a witch takes the shape of an owl and comes for three nights, it's a warning of death."

"Go speak to him," Caterina ordered, but no one moved. "Then I'll tell him myself," she said. Her joints cracked as she got up stiffly and marched to the door, her black skirt as prim as a nun's. Cold air rushed through the door as she opened it and called firmly into the dark, "Come tomorrow for salt."

When she sat down again the women avoided her scornful eyes.

They whispered that the first person to cross the threshold after that invitation for salt would be in league with the witch. They asked who it could be and crossed themselves as the owl hooted again. Tules burrowed closer to her mother.

"There's that old witch Concha who lives by herself beyond the plaza at Don Fernández," Ramona whispered. "Maybe she could break the spell. . . ."

"I wouldn't go near her house," Lupe protested. "I went there once long ago. Her black hole of a room was cluttered with herbs hanging from the vigas and bags of leaves and hoofs and horns of animals. It stank worse than a slaughter pen. And there were a dozen blind cats mewing and rubbing against her legs. . . ."

"But she has powerful charms . . ." Ramona said.

"They didn't work for you," Mercedes laughed. "Bernardo got you with child, and then he went for a younger girl to father another bastard. Charms won't hold him. Nothing but money holds him."

"That witch Concha can put the evil spell on you," Lupe insisted. "Before I was married I bought some soap from her. It smelled nice, but when I washed my hair with it my face and neck broke out like the pox. I warn you, if you ask Concha for charms, you'll get nothing but beatings from your husband. Even the Indians are afraid she'll put the brujería on them."

"But if she has taken the s-shape of an owl and comes three times as a w-warning . . ." Ramona stammered.

The words stopped, but her mouth stayed open as they heard someone fumble at the heavy door leading from the corral. This would be the first person to cross the threshold, the witch's accomplice. They drew in long, hissing breaths as Bernardo pushed through the door. His feet were heavy with mud, his eyes bloodshot, and he reeked of sour aguardiente.

"Caramba! You lazy sluts sit here dry and warm while I work in the cold," he growled. "With all there is to do, you think of nothing but resting your backsides. I'll tell Don Miguel you should have beatings instead of beans. If Doña Carmen would listen to me—she'd better heed me now. . . ."

40

"Where are you going?" Caterina demanded as he lurched across the kitchen to the patio and left mud droppings on the clean floor.

"To warn your fine patrona of murderers," he sneered.

"Murderers!"

"Yes, murderers. Navajos are raiding again. Can you understand that? They have left a trail of blood and smoke all the way up the Río Grande. They're headed north. They'll cross the trail of her father and mother tomorrow. . . ."

"Stop. You can't tell her that tonight," Caterina said. She was the only one who dared cross Bernardo. "What could she do, a helpless girl? This may be another false scare. Anyway, Don José will hear the report in Santa Fe; maybe he will come with an armed guard. Doña Carmen is tired out with worries this winter. You let her sleep tonight."

Bernardo caught at the edge of the table to steady himself and belched. "All right. This is a fine house of soft women. If trouble comes, it's on your head. I warned you."

The women shivered as the door banged on his curses.

"Not a word of this to Doña Carmen," Caterina ordered sternly. "We will not frighten her tonight with drunken talk. Now get to sleep. We must be up early tomorrow. And each of you pray to Our Lady for protection."

The women whispered to each other as they went to their room. Tules huddled close to her mother and saw witches even after she pulled the blanket over her head. She fell asleep listening to Luz say her beads an extra time.

The copper bell was ringing, "Clang—clang—clang!"

Tules rubbed her eyes sleepily, sorry that it was morning already. Darkness had thinned into the light before dawn. The bell rang again —sharp, urgent. Luz sprang up from their pallet fully dressed. "Indians!" she muttered, as she grabbed Tules's hand and ran toward the bell and Doña Carmen's room.

"Jesucristo, hurry! Call everyone," Alfredo yelled as he jerked the bell. "The Navajos have come. . . ."

Tules heard the high savage war whoops outside the house and clutched at her mother's skirt. The Indians were pounding at the zaguán gate leading into the patio. She shut her eyes and prayed that the heavy wood, locks, and bars would hold.

The bell rang furiously again. Alfredo pulled at the rope with frantic strength, hoping that the distant neighbors would hear the alarm. Terrified women crowded around him and called aloud for the help of their favorite saint. Men hurried by with set, stern faces.

"Patrona!" Tules cried out, as Doña Carmen came toward them.

Dark, frightened eyes stared out of her pale face, and her hand pressed her pounding heart, but her voice was firm as she gave orders. "Where is Bernardo? Tell him to come at once. Until Bernardo comes, you, Juan Lucero, take charge of the men. Get the guns and go to the roof."

Juan distributed muskets and powder to ten men.

"Cruz, take three men to guard the corral gate," he said. "Jacobo, take your men to the roof. Don't shoot until each man is behind the wall and ready. Aim for the ones at the gate. Don't let them get in." The men ran up the ladder and through the small opening in the wall to the roof.

When the first shots were fired the savage cries increased outside. Blows on the zaguán gate redoubled. The wood splintered, and the iron locks creaked.

"Quick, Lupe, take charge of the women," Doña Carmen ordered. "Caterina must guard the baby. Ah, Mother of God, help us! Luz and Ramona, stay by the ladder to help the men. Chona, Mercedes, Tules, all of you, bring the mattresses to pile against the windows."

Tules pulled frantically to drag the mattresses to the deep bedroom windows and heap them against the wooden shutters for greater protection against sharp arrows. In the sala they stuffed hassocks, blankets, sheepskins against the front windows and dragged a heavy cupboard against one opening.

"Tules! The fireplace!" Luz cried between clenched jaws. She grabbed the child's arm and shook her to make her understand. She

42

pointed to the fireplace and cried, "If they break in, you crawl up the chimney and hide. Don't forget. You will be safe in the chimney. Madre de Dios, help us!"

Tules locked her hands in her mother's skirt when she heard a piercing scream from the patio. A woman started the death wail and shrieked, "Alfredo! My son! They've killed him. Ah, Dios. . . ."

Doña Carmen ran to the mother, shook her shoulder, and smothered the death wail. "For the love of God, be quiet! The Indians will hear you and know they have killed one of our men. Get up there, and take Alfredo's place. You can load the muskets. . . . Where is Bernardo? Why hasn't he come?"

"María Santísima! The ugly brutes!" Ramona screamed as Jacobo's body dropped from the ladder, an arrow through his neck. Ramona tried to stop the foaming blood that ran from his mouth.

Muskets barked from the roof, and the frantic yells from beyond the gate increased in frenzy. Blows redoubled on the gate, but the strong bars still held. Cruz and Pedro ran to guard the zaguán, where arrows whirred over the opening above the gate and plowed into the ground. They reached the narrow shelter of the gateposts in the passageway and sprang up on the adobe bench to shoot over the gate. Luz ran after them, carrying extra guns and powder. Tules followed her.

"No, no, Tules," Luz called. "Don't come here. Go back. . . ."

The child began to cry, alone and terrified. She crouched close to the corner wall and watched in terror as her mother darted after the men. Luz tried to keep within the protection of the narrow side walls.

The men fired wildly above the gate, and arrows whizzed like hail into the passageway. Cruz steadied his arm against the right post and shot into the mob. An arrow pierced his eye and sank into his head as he fell over backwards. Another arrow hit Luz. She screamed, pulled at her breast with both hands, and fell against the wall. Pedro leaped from the bench on the left side and ran toward the patio.

"My mother! She is there! Save her!" Tules screamed and started to run to her mother.

43

"Don't go back there. You can't help her," Pedro shouted. "Run, child! The Indians have brought a log. Now they will break down the gate. Run. . . ."

But Tules would not leave. "Mamá! Mamacita!" she cried.

Her mother did not move, and no voice could have been heard as the heavy log rammed the gate. Two muskets cracked from the roof. The savages answered with high, fiendish cries as the log smashed at the gate and the bars splintered. The great lock broke, and the gate began to give.

Tules screamed as she saw the gate move and ran backward in terror. She could not go to her mother and didn't know what to do. Her mother had said the chimney. She ran to the sala and climbed over the logs on the hearth, placed in readiness for the fiesta. She thrust her hands into the black chimney and pulled herself up. Her bare toes gripped around solid boulders, and her small body twisted into the goose-necked opening. She was out of sight now and braced herself with her palms against the opposite wall.

The zaguán gate had burst open, and Tules heard the Indians yell like demons in the patio. Tomahawks smashed at wood as the war whoops increased. She held her breath when she heard Doña Carmen's voice near the sala door.

"Stop!" Doña Carmen ordered. Her voice was cool and commanding. "What do you want? Get out of here. I will give you money. . . ."

"Yes, we take money, sheep, horses, women," a man defied her in guttural, broken Spanish. "You take our sons away in chains. You keep our women here as slaves. You kill our people. Now we kill you. . . ."

"Your sons are not here," Doña Carmen said clearly. "You have no right to come into my house. Send your men out. I will give you food and money if you will go now. Come tomorrow, and my father will give you more money. . . ."

"Money? Spaniards think only of money," the man grunted. "I will have a white squaw to weave my blankets, cook. You will come with me. . . ."

44

"Don't you dare touch me." Doña Carmen's voice broke into a high, terrified scream. "Miguel! Mother of God, help me. . . ."

Tules shook with a violent tremor when she heard the scream. Her fingers dug into the chimney, and a pebble rattled to the hearth. She loosened her frantic clutch, afraid of dislodging more dirt. The Indians would see it on the raised hearth and find her hiding place. She forced her body to stop shaking and held herself rigid in spite of her pounding heart. She bit her lips to keep from sobbing aloud.

Wood crashed as locked doors were battered down. The savage yells never ceased. She heard women shriek and plead. Sometimes they prayed, sometimes the cries stopped in their throats. She recognized one voice in the tumult. It was Caterina crying, "For the love of God, not the baby! Jesucristo, help us!"

Tules dared not breathe when she heard the Navajos come into the sala. Their quick feet raced over the floor, searching for hiding places. The covers ripped as their lances plunged into the mattresses at the windows. A man groaned when they found him.

"Where is the wine, the aguardiente?" an Indian demanded. "Where is the lame bear who limps? He sold us wine. Now we will take it. . . ."

"Take that, you devil!" a woman screamed in crazed panic.

Tules recognized Ramona's voice. It was followed by a shot. The smell of gunpowder filled the room. Ramona screamed again as the Indian fell on her.

Tules's throat closed with terror. They would find her next, kill her. Her head was dizzy, and she clung to the cold stones and took a deep breath to steady herself. She was terrified that her hold would loosen and she would fall. She bit her tongue to stop the dizziness.

The chimney funnel intensified the sounds from outside the house. She heard the horses neigh with fright when they were brought from the corral. Then women screamed, pleaded, cursed, prayed. Their terrified voices stopped when they were gagged and tied on the horses. She heard Doña Carmen's clear voice plead, "I cannot leave my baby. Let me take him. I will give you anything. . . . Ah, Mother of God, help!"

45

Tears ran down Tules's face when she heard the loved voice. She thought of Doña Carmen holding the baby in her arms like the Madonna last Christmas. Now, if she lived, she would be an Indian slave. Even if they got word to Tío Florentino this morning, he would never catch the Navajos. She remembered tales of captive women, ugly scars on their faces, their backs bent double from carrying burdens for tyrannical squaws. After a few years Spanish women were ashamed to come back to their own people and preferred to live out their miserable lives with the savages. She shook her head with anguish as she thought of Doña Carmen's happy face yesterday, her kind heart, and gentle hands. "Ah, Mother of God, help her!" she prayed.

Then she held her breath as she heard the Indians come back. Some crossed the patio to the kitchen looking for food and wine. Others pillaged the house for guns and blankets. Her back pushed tensely against the chimney when they came into the sala again. Glass from the mirror splintered and crashed. They prowled around the room and struck a flint. The woolen draperies at the window began to smolder.

Flames hissed from dry wood, and smoke followed the draft up the chimney. Tules held her nose and mouth to keep from coughing, while tears ran from her smarting eyes. Her body ached and trembled from the strain, and she was sick at her stomach, but she dared not move. She heard horses moving outside. The Navajos left as swiftly as they had come.

She listened intently to the strange silence of the house. She could not hear a sound. At last she felt her way down, her bare toes sliding cautiously. She dropped to the logs and peered out.

She hardly recognized the once stately room. The sofa, chairs, tables were knocked over. One table was charred, and the draperies smoldered. The picture of Our Lady of Guadalupe had been gouged by lances; the long mirror was shattered, and one corner had fallen to the floor. She froze with fright when she saw a black face moving in the mirror. Then she recognized herself. Her face was black, her hair, hands, and clothes streaked with soot.

Bodies lay on the floor in strange, still heaps. There was fat Ramona with her arm twisted under her; beyond her, Pedro; then the stable boy, Joaquín; and José Lucero. Their heads were raw, bleeding masses where they had been scalped. She crept over to Ramona and stared at the stricken terror in the full, sagging face. She had killed the Navajo. Tules peered intently at the Indian's still body, his bronze face, and coarse black hair. The scalping knife was still in his hand. She pushed his shoulder with her foot and watched, ready to spring away, but he did not move.

In the patio she looked in surprise at the clear, bright sunshine. It was not more than an hour after sunup. The sky was a calm, innocent blue.

She ran to Doña Carmen's room and almost stumbled over Caterina's body. Her black skirt was caught above her bony knee, and Tules pulled it down. The long white hair fell over her shoulder, and a wide bleeding band ran back from her forehead where an expert knife had cut out the scalp lock. Her eyes stared, but her wrinkled face was exalted. Beyond Caterina Tules saw the baby's long white dress. She knelt beside him and saw that the soft skull was crushed. "María Santísima!" she sobbed. "They killed the baby and took Doña Carmen. What shall I do?"

She looked fearfully at death and destruction around her but heard no sound in the quiet, sunny morning. She ran to the kitchen, hoping that someone would be alive in that familiar place. The unaccustomed silence terrified her. Food was scattered over the floor, and milk from a half-upset pail spread in a white pool. She lifted the pail, gulped the remaining milk, and stuffed a broken cake in her mouth.

Near the corral gate she saw a man's arm claw at the dirt where he lay on the ground. As she ran toward him she recognized Bernardo, wisps of hay caught in the back fringe of his leather jacket and an arrow sticking through it. A last groan rattled through the bloody foam on his lips as she stood over him. His heavy body writhed and was still.

"You hid in the hay, you son of a pig!" Tules cried, tears of hatred and terror running down her cheeks. "You brought this on us with

47

your greed. You killed the baby and Caterina, and now Doña Carmen is lost. And you killed my mother! There is no one left. Madre de Dios, what shall I do?"

She ran to find her mother in the zaguán. The gates stood open, broken and sagging. The passageway, filled with yelling demons at dawn, was now silent with death. She stepped around men's huddled bodies and peered at their faces. She did not find her mother and cried in despair, "Mamá! Mamacita. . . ."

She noticed the end of a reboso back of a corner of the gate. She ran to it and saw her mother's body caught between the gate and the wall. One corner of the gate had dug into the ground, and she pulled at it frantically. She jumped as the gate fell forward and her mother's body rolled over with it.

"Thanks be to God," she cried, as she pulled her mother's reboso away and found the arrow sticking out of the right breast. "Mamá, I am here. Mother of God, help me!" she called in a frenzy, as she clutched her mother's arm.

A tiny sound came from the ashen lips, and Tules saw a faint pulse beat in the thin neck. Her mother was still alive! She ran for water and splashed Luz's face. The eyelids trembled. Tules straightened her gently on the ground and drew the reboso around her. Then she raced down the road to get Tío Florentino.

# Part Two: Manzano 1822-1828

# 6

Doña Carmen had been lost for six years. Her fate was as mysterious as the inscrutable desert that had taken her. That morning after the massacre, when Tules ran to Tío Florentino, breathless and soot-streaked, he could hardly believe her. By the time he had ridden out to verify her story and had collected men for the pursuit, the Navajos had gotten away on their swift horses. The next day Don José Sánchez sent trackers to trace his daughter, but the raiding party had disappeared beyond the mountains. Six weeks later Don Miguel returned from Mexico and left at once to seek his wife in the desert. He came back with haunted eyes and a bitter, haggard face to offer rewards and employ spies and trackers. When they gave him no hope he left for Chihuahua.

"I pray that God in His mercy let Carmen die," Don José groaned when Luz finally packed his daughter's belongings. He paid off Luz's debt in memory of Doña Carmen and urged the curandera to cure Luz's cough, a constant reminder of the arrowwound in her breast. Luz and Tules returned with Don José and his wife to Manzano, but the bad luck of Taos followed their jolting coach, and frail old Doña Octavo died soon after they reached home. In his grief over the loss of his daughter and the death of his wife, Don José let his domineering maiden sister, Doña Prudencia, take charge of his home.

Luz had gone to live with a Sonoran cattle herder named Rafael, and their two rooms on the loma were soon filled with the hungry cries of three children—Rafaela, Chico, and the ailing baby, Lucita. She left Tules in the Sánchez household to be trained by Doña Prudencia.

Every evening the peón girls brought drinking water from the clear, bubbling Giant's Spring, El Ojo del Gigante. It was up a little cañón beyond the rubble walls of the hacienda. The girls shouldered the wooden yokes and heavy casks of water eagerly, glad to get away from Doña Prudencia's despotic eyes and reach the trysting place where the vaqueros came to water their horses.

One April evening Tules climbed the trail with two other girls, paying little attention to their chatter. She was seventeen and restless with the fear that she was too old to get a good husband. Her body was slender with long legs and high, pointed breasts. She held her handsome red head proudly, and her clear green eyes scorned every local youth except Pedro Bustamante. She thought that her good looks might have challenged him if she had had a dowry and a father to arrange a marriage letter.

"Hurry up, Tules, you dawdle like a funeral procession. Antonio promised to come early this evening." Rosita's soft red lips pouted, and she shook the waving black hair that grew thickly from her low forehead. Her big brown eyes under the curling lashes knew how to plead.

"You count too much on Antonio," Cuca mocked, patronizing the two younger girls. Her bold black eyes laughed at them as she thrust out the curves of her full hips and breasts. Doña Prudencia bewailed Cuca's loose morals, but the lectures had no effect on Cuca. "Don't set your heart on one man. I sample all of them and take my pick. But Tules is worse than you are. She won't even look at a good offer. That Ignacio sighed for her, and she turned up her nose. . . ."

"He's a sheepherder and as dumb as his sheep." Tules's green eyes flashed. "He smells of sheep, and I'm sick of their stink. For a month I've washed the wool in the patrona's mattresses and dried it in the sun, and it still smells of sheep. I'll turn into mutton tallow with the fat I've made into soap and candles. Everything here reeks of sheep —the skins we sleep on, the tallow soap, and the stringy mutton floating in white grease. In Taos we had beef and pork. . . ."

"For six years you've talked of nothing but Taos," Cuca said. "You should have stayed there."

50

"Ojalá that I could have stayed there!" Tules cried. "I could have been one of the gente fina if I had stayed with Doña Carmen, God rest her soul."

"Pues, you needn't put on airs. You're no better than the rest of us now," Cuca reminded her. "You can read and write, but you have no chance to marry a caballero. You aim for Pedro Bustamente, but you'll have to offer more favors than a sharp tongue to trap that captain of the salt carts."

"My tongue may be sharp, but it's cleaner than yours," Tules cried and slammed down her casks and wooden yoke. She leaned over the spring to hide her burning face and watched the minnows dart through the swaying green plants. She was furious that Cuca's shrewd eyes had discovered that Pedro was the only man who stirred her ambitious heart. She watched the bubbles rise from the clear depths of the spring, but she thought bitterly that Pedro ignored her with the other barefoot peladas.

She looked up at the tall, straight pine tree guarding the spring like a sentinel and thought of Pedro's short, stocky figure. She knew that he wore high-heeled boots and a high peaked sombrero to increase his height and wished that she was a small, pretty girl like Rosita. Pedro could have any girl, and he would not choose one he had to look up to. He was Don José's best foreman, and his future was assured.

Tules filled her casks with the clear, cold water and wandered impatiently onto the new grass that covered the bank of the stream gushing out of the spring. After a short distance it disappeared into the sand and ran out again lower down to fill the blue storage pond. It finally seeped through underground channels into the brine of the distant lagoons.

She looked toward the lagoons where the shimmering desert stretched east as far as her eyes could penetrate. This had once been the floor of an ancient ocean. Now, like a shell that holds the echo of surging seas, the desert rippled in waves of tawny sand until it stopped behind her in the solidified green billow of the high Manzano range. In the central depressions of this Salinas basin, dead-sea lakes evaporated into glistening rims, and men risked their lives to pry out the cakes of salt. It was the most important deposit north of Chihuahua and a large factor in the success of Don José's trading post.

Tules's gaze returned to the near-by settlement where the red houses of the peóns were terraced on the first sandstone ledges above the basin. She looked down with critical eyes at the manor house built around two patios and encircled with high rubble walls. Near the zaguán gate there was a two-story rock tower where a guard signaled the alarm if the fierce, roving Apaches approached. All the walls were as rusty red as the earth around them and strengthened with narrow sandstone masonry, but she preferred the smooth brown adobe and white plaster of Taos. After the cold blue and silver of the high northern sierras the violent reds, purples, and gold of this southern country filled her with strange, unsatisfied desire.

Her heart was bursting with the urgency of spring like the red-tipped buds in the apple orchard beyond the house. Don José had planted the orchard twenty-five years ago, and, because of the rare delight of fruit trees in the far desert, the Sánchez holdings had become known as "El Manzano," "The Apple." Don José took pride in the only orchard and small lake in the province and said they made his home as beautiful as a city in Spain. Tules acknowledged the promise of beauty in the budding orchard, but her eyes followed the twisted branches that were bent with the sweep of the west wind. She sighed with despair that she also was rooted forever in that red clay soil and would grow as bent and gnarled as the dark branches.

She walked back toward the two girls at the spring, adjusted the wooden yoke over her shoulders, and said impatiently, "Come on. It's getting late. We must start down."

"I want to wait for Antonio," Rosita protested.

"They are bringing the wild horses today, and Antonio won't come until after dark," Tules said. "If you will carry my casks home, I'll stop and leave a message for him at the pasture with Celso."

"She's a sly one!" Cuca laughed. "She thinks Pedro will come to the pasture instead of the spring."

52

Tules ran down the trail to get away from Cuca's tongue, left the casks halfway, and hurried toward the wide gate. If Pedro came she would try not to look so tall, and she would smile into his eyes when he teased her about her curly red hair and called her "la china."

No one was there but old Celso with his greasy hat pulled down to his ears to hide the scar on his head where he had been scalped. Another scar twisted his brown face from his mouth to his right ear, but his dark eyes always smiled when he saw Tules. Both of them loved the patrón's fine race horses.

For years Tules had listened to Celso's stories of a mythical white mare with flowing mane and tail who led her band of wild horses over mountains and plains and always escaped the hunter's lasso. He also often repeated the Indian legend of the turquoise horse who rode across the arc of the sky each day and carried the sun as a dazzling shield.

He touched the scar on his face that was the result of an Apache raid and told how the demons had killed all the Christians after the padres had started to build the three great missions at Abó, Quivira, and Quarai in 1629. He said the roofless red walls of those deserted churches had been the only reminder of Spanish life in the Manzano mountains for almost two hundred years. In spite of the ever-present scourge of Apaches the Sánchez family had settled on their land twenty-five years ago, and other small settlements had followed them. Celso taught Tules to shoot with his old musket to protect herself, and the vivid memory of the massacre at Taos made her an eager pupil.

"Hola, Celso, see what I brought you," she called and gave the old man the cookies she had stolen from the kitchen. "Have they brought the wild horses yet?"

"They are driving them toward the upper corral now," Celso mumbled as his toothless gums crunched the cookies. "They found a band of wild horses and drove them into a trap at Cañón del Infierno. They were without food or water for eight days and should have been weak enough to drive, but the vaqueros have had trouble bringing them in."

53

"Pobrecitos!" Tules said. "They will hate the plow and the hard bits in their mouths."

"You are like the wild horses," Celso smiled. "You don't want to be tamed."

"At least I would like to be a race horse like Bonita and get ahead of everyone else. She will win the June race." Tules called to the palomino mare who came to nuzzle an apple from her hand. She stroked the mare's golden neck, admired her high haunches and straight forelegs, and begged, "Por favor, let me ride her down the road and back, Celso."

He looked around to see that no one watched from the pasture. In the distance they could see the dust rise into the slanting evening light above the milling wild horses. Celso slipped the bridle over Bonita's head and said, "Take care. You know how much Don José thinks of this mare. Only go to the bend of the road and back."

Tules sat sideways on the mare's warm back and trotted down the road. She raised her face to the rush of spring air and exulted in the flying rhythm. She felt free and light and wished that she could ride this way forever.

She heard shouts and looked over her shoulder to see that the wild horses had broken away and were running toward the plains and freedom. Bonita snorted when she heard the pounding hoofs, turned, and leaped after them. Tules threw her right leg over the mare's side, rode like a man, and laced one hand in the creamy mane. The vaqueros raced after the mustangs, and a man on a roan horse dashed ahead of them. Through the dust Tules recognized Pedro Bustamente. She smiled at her good luck, thinking this was the chance to make Pedro notice her.

The mustangs raced with outstretched necks toward the level ground that led to the plains. If they could be driven into the arroyo at the side, the vaqueros could get ahead of them and turn them back.

She urged Bonita on. The mare flew over the ground, overtook the rear horses, and raced beside them. Tules held a firm rein, afraid that Bonita might stumble in the blinding dust. She thought more of the danger to the mare than to herself, though both of them might be

54

trampled under the pawing hoofs. The mustangs' eyes were wild, and their nostrils distended.

She kicked Bonita before they reached the arroyo. The mare drew ahead and headed the mustangs off. They swerved into the arroyo, slowed up in the heavy sand, and crowded each other as they ran through the narrowing banks.

Pedro passed her, yelled, and whirled his lasso as his horse tore along the bank above the arroyo. Other vaqueros closed in on the wild horses and turned them back toward the corral.

The sand stung Tules's face as she galloped back behind them. She realized that she had disgraced herself by riding astride like a man. She drew up her right leg quickly, crooked her knee on the mare's shoulder, and pulled down her skirt. She hoped that Pedro had not noticed how she rode. Her braids had come loose, and she tried to smooth her flying red hair. She noticed the sweat on the mare's neck and slowed down to cool her off. Even Don José's gentle heart would not forgive an injury to his favorite racing mare.

She slid off at the gate, patted the mare, and led her into the pasture. Celso and Pedro came toward her in the dusk. Pedro's face was swarthy, with a hint of Indian blood, and his bowlegs looked shorter in the heavy leather chaps, but he walked with a swagger. The brim of his peaked sombrero was rolled at each side and set at an angle over his thick black brows.

"Stop worrying, Celso. Here's your mare," he said and looked at Tules. "So you were the she-devil riding that mare! I didn't believe a girl could ride like that. . . ."

Tules looked at him but kept still. He might threaten to tell Don José.

"The mare needed exercise," Celso excused himself. "The girl has a light hand, and I told her only to go to the bend in the road. . . ."

"Lucky for us that she was down the road, or all those wild brutes would have gotten away," Pedro said. "Rub your mare down, and she'll be none the worse. Caramba, you should have seen that mare fly! I'm going to put my money on her in the race. But you'd better let the girl ride her. She makes a better cowboy than water carrier."

55

Tules gave him a wide, flashing smile. She lowered her lashes modestly, but her heart pounded with triumph.

"She straddles a horse like a man," Pedro laughed, and his bold eyes appraised her figure from her high, pointed breasts to her long legs. "I'll bet Doña Prudencia doesn't keep this handsome wench under lock and key."

Tules's face burned with shame. She wanted to impress Pedro, but, because she had ridden astride, she had lowered herself in his eyes. She turned to go, but Pedro caught her arm and said, "Do you dance as well as you ride?"

She turned to smile at him and tossed her head. She hesitated a moment and then said, "I've waited a year for you to find out."

"Bien, I will remember that at the next dance," Pedro promised. "Válgame Dios, you're a beauty, now that you've grown up! I've been blind not to see you before. . . ."

"Keep your eye open, hombre," Celso chuckled. "In the land of the blind the one-eyed man is king."

Tules blushed with happiness this time and ran home on flying toes. Maybe her luck had changed.

During the next month she met Pedro often at the pasture. She drooped her straight shoulders and leaned on the gate so that she could look up at him. He teased her about her race with the mustangs and laughed at her ready wit. Her tongue was sweet with flattery, and her eyes gave him adulation.

"By the sword of Saint Michael, I can't wait to dance with you," he said and caught her bare arm with his strong hand. "You're a witch. I dream of your eyes, your hair. I go to the salt lagoons tomorrow, but when I come back I have something to ask. . . ."

When she and Celso were alone the next evening the old man clucked his tongue and winked at her. "Pues, our proud capitán eats out of your hand like Bonita. All the girls have tried to lasso him, but he escaped until he saw you. Now he sighs like any other lovesick fool when you leave. Invite me to dance at your wedding, niña, and I'll buy myself a new hat."

56

"Pedro only teases me. He says nothing of a wedding," Tules pouted to draw Celso out.

"I'll give him a hint. He is smart, but he takes his time because he will be a man of property some day. Hold a light rein, child. He is as ugly and vicious as a wild stallion if you prick his pride."

# 7

IN THE CLOSE life of the Sánchez hacienda nothing escaped Cuca's bold eyes. She teased Tules about Pedro but treated her with the respect due Pedro's position. Rosita looked at her with wistful eyes, called Pedro her novio, and asked when he would send the marriage letter to her mother.

Tules guarded her tongue. So far Pedro had only flirted with her and caressed her bare arm. She drew back from his hungry hands to let him know that her morals were better than Cuca's. She wanted a home and the security of marriage, and she did not intend to barter her virtue for anything less. But she used flattery, charm, and provocation to lead him on. She hoped that she could bring him to speak of the marriage letter when she danced with him tonight. She might even goad him by dancing with handsome strangers.

The baile tonight was in honor of the carreteros from Sante Fe who came to the lagoons to get salt. Each spring and fall their overnight stop at Manzano was celebrated with a dance. Every woman from the ragged peóns to dowager Doña Prudencia counted on dancing with the men in the military escort and carretas.

For the past week Doña Prudencia's nose had been at Tules's shoulder as she stirred the soap kettles and made dirty gray jelly from tallow and wood ashes. She had to strain a special batch for fine white cakes of soap for the patrona, but she slipped out a couple of cakes for her own bath in the willow thicket by the pond. She washed and ironed her round-necked white blouse and full red skirt, but the red skirt faded. She forgot it in the pride of new red slippers strapped over her trim ankles. Before the dance she looked at herself in the broken corner of a mirror, patted the copper waves in her hair, and whitened her long nose with a ball of powder to hide the freckles. She thought her mouth was too wide, but Pedro might forget that if her white teeth flashed in a smile.

58

In the crowded dance hall the air was heavy with the odor of sweating bodies and leather jackets. Tallow candles burned on crossed sticks hung from the rafters. Three musicians sat on a platform and scraped tunes on a fiddle, guitar, and violin. A sour smell rose from the clay floor when it was sprinkled between dances to lay the dust.

Tules sat beside the white wall in the row of women dominated by Doña Prudencia's black silk bulk. Pedro claimed her and whispered extravagant flattery as they spun around. Her hazel eyes were bright with triumph and excitement, and she smiled at everyone, including a handsome stranger standing with the men at the door. He smiled back at her, gestured for the next dance, and she nodded. He looked vaguely familiar, and she watched his thin young face with the straight nose and long chin. The light shone on his straight black hair, level eyebrows, and dreaming dark eyes. As he came toward her she heard a man call him Ramón.

"Are you Ramón Ortega from Santa Fe?" she asked with astonishment as they began to dance.

"Yes, señorita, at your orders," he smiled. "But how did you know my name?"

"You have forgotten me, but I remember you because you spoiled my trip to Mexico six years ago," she sighed. "I am Tules Barceló."

"You—you are Tooo-les!" he exclaimed and looked at her closely. "But of course. Your hair is still red even if you have grown tall and beautiful. I have thought of you many times and wondered what happened to you. But I thought you lived in Taos. . . ."

"Now, I live here," she said. Their eyes held each other in long, deep communication as they recognized each other's features, and they breathed faster as their bodies recognized the mysterious surge of love. They exchanged quick, searching questions about the past that linked their lives. Ramón's arms tightened around her, and pulses of joy throbbed through Tules at the touch of his hands.

She forgot Pedro.

But Pedro claimed her for the next dance and whispered jealous, passionate words as they bowed and swung other partners in the maze of the paso doble. His eyes smoldered, and she was glad there

59

was no opportunity for him to speak of the marriage letter. This was the triumphant moment she had worked for, and now she cast it aside.

She evaded Pedro and danced with Ramón time after time. Her face lifted to his like a flower turned to the sun, but they could only ask and answer fleeting questions as they met and parted in stately quadrilles.

"I leave tomorrow with the carretas," Ramón whispered during the last waltz. "I must see you again, talk to you, chiquita. There are words in my heart. . . . I long to hold you close. . . ."

"There is no chance tonight," Tules sighed. "Doña Prudencia marches us home and locks us in a bare room. But I will meet you in the little dawn tomorrow—in the orchard to the left of the road."

"I will sing under your window until then," Ramón promised.

At home Tules knelt by the barred window in the dark room, and Rosita joined her. They opened the shutter when they heard a man's deep voice sing under the stars:

> Tus ojos son estrellas,
> Tu boquita un coral,
> Tus rizitos en la frente
> Son dignos de amor. . . .

"That's my Antonio," Rosita sighed. "He says my eyes are like stars and my lips coral. . . ."

"That isn't Antonio. It's Ramón," Tules whispered indignantly. "You haven't curls on your forehead that are worthy of love."

"Por Dios, close that shutter! You will poison us with the night air," an older woman scolded.

When the serenade was over Tules crept to her pallet with spellbound ecstasy and hugged the thought of Ramón to her fast-beating heart. Bright, happy plans chased each other through her mind like butterflies in the sun. She would go to Santa Fe with Ramón, and they would be so happy. She remembered the warm kindliness of his home when she was a frightened child and the gaiety of the capital. Ramón might not be a rich caballero, but only aristocratic blood could have given him that supple grace and fine manners. She shut her eyes tight and vowed that she loved him with all her heart.

Before dawn she braided her hair and longed for perfume to scent her lips. She crowded her swollen feet into the tight red slippers so that Ramón would not remember her as a barefoot pelada. The moment the cook unlocked the door she slipped out into the silver grayness.

She jumped over the dark water of the acequia, ran into the orchard, and peered down the rows of bent trees. He had not come, but she held her breath to listen for his footsteps and watched a fresh world take shape in the first fan of light. It brushed the desert with gold, wakened the sleep-flushed red of the village, and tinted the pond with trembling pink. Small clouds floated against the tender blue sky, as rosy as the apple blossoms above her. She turned away impatiently to stare at the road. She closed her eyes against the fear that Ramón might not come. Perhaps she had been a poor country fool last night. Perhaps city boys made light promises.

"Tules! Chiquita!" he called, caught her willing body in his arms, and kissed her as she had dreamed. She lifted trembling lips to his, and her body quivered as his hand caressed the smooth skin of her shoulder.

Afterwards she could remember little of what they said. They tried to fill in the past six years, and Ramón clenched his fists when they talked of Bernardo. They laughed over the peso Ramón had rescued for her long ago and called it their first talisman of love. They confessed that they had loved each other since childhood, and their lips clung with the enchantment of finding each other again.

"When these apples are ripe I will come back with the fall caravan. Will you wait for me, chiquita?" Ramón asked. "Then I will take you home to live with me forever in Sante Fe. Ah, linda mía . . ."

They tore themselves apart when sheep bells tinkled near them and a shepherd drove his flock up the road to mountain pastures. The sun was dazzling radiance, and Ramón groaned that he must leave.

Tules clung to him as he kissed the tears on her cheeks and her trembling lips. "Be ready when I come in the fall, chiquita. Until then I shall think of you day and night," he said as he left her.

She hurried to the small plaza to watch the salt caravan leave. The carretas were lined with oxhide and heavy with dripping salt. Brine trickled into the dust, and the upper seams gleamed with dried white crystals. Men shouted and lashed the oxen to budge the wheels under the dead weight. A dozen horses nickered as the cavalry guard waited to protect the caravan along the desert where nomad Apaches lurked.

"Until next fall, Juanito," Cuca called to a soldier whose long spurs made his black horse rear.

"She'll bulge with a present for him next fall," the old crone, Chapita, cackled to a woman standing next to Tules. "Where a weed grows, there is an ass to eat it."

"Only the inexperienced cat counts her kittens," the other woman laughed.

Tules moved away from bitter old voices that gibed at love and watched Ramón's tall, graceful figure walk beside his carreta and drive his eight red oxen. The beasts moved ponderously, their heads lowered under the wooden yokes lashed behind their horns. Tules looked at him with pride as his long whip cut through the air to guide the lead oxen. He waved to her, smiled, and called, "Until next fall, Tules. Hasta la vista!"

"May the Mother of God protect you and bring you back," she cried and winked back her tears. She ran away quickly to be alone with her wonderful dream.

The miracle of love changed the world for Tules, but everyone else continued their stupid routine. They even forgot the Santa Fe caravan and counted the days before the fiestas of San Juan and San Pedro at the end of June.

The peóns endured hard work and poverty for the hard play and fun of the fiestas generously sprinkled through the calendar. The small settlements were two or three leagues apart in the foothills of the Manzanos; they struggled for bare existence and lived in lonely isolation except when they visited each other on gala days. In spite of the threat that Apaches might plunder the houses and kill the few men left on guard, everyone went visiting.

No family was too poor to share bread and blankets with friends, and the houses of the ricos were filled with guests. For this midsummer week each settlement offered its special amusement. The celebration started at Manzano on San Juan's Day with El Gallo, a chicken pull; moved to Torreón and Tacique for horse races; and ended at Chililí with a cockfight in honor of San Pedro. There were masses every morning, races, games, and gambling every afternoon, and dances every night. They warmed the blood and provided a setting for fights and love-making.

Early on San Juan's Day Tules and Rosita climbed up on the church wall to watch the chicken pull in the plaza. Doña Prudencia and her guests reigned like queens under the long portál of a house near the church. Over their heads a green vine left a shadow garland on the white wall. It was the only cool spot in the hot, glaring plaza.

Rosita bubbled with excitement, but Tules stared indifferently at the frieze of wide, peaked sombreros where men sat their horses at the far side of the plaza. Today every man was a caballero, a gentleman on horseback. Most of their mounts were small, strong mustangs whose heads drooped sleepily now, but they would leap into the race at a second's notice.

"There's my Antonio getting off to test his cinch! Por mi amor, get it tight, or you'll have a spill, chulo!" Rosita cried and then poked Tules, "Look, there's Pedro!"

Tules sat alert, scenting danger as Pedro rode toward them. Pedro had faded from her thoughts in the shining dream of Ramón. She had cautiously avoided the pasture and even given up the pleasure of watching old Celso train the palomino mare for the race. She wanted to keep out of the way of Pedro's jealous temper until Ramón returned. Now she watched Pedro's arrogant shoulders straighten as men shouted to him to win El Gallo. His proud eyes turned to Tules, and she smiled and waved. It was safer to be friendly with him. He nodded, dropped his red bandana on the ground, and swooped to retrieve it as the audience cheered.

"There are the rancheros from Torreón." Tules shifted her eyes to watch the men, women, and children pile out of carretas, shout gaily, and embrace friends.

"They are betting on who will win El Gallo," Rosita cried. "Look at the men hold up one finger, two, three. Por Dios, if we could have all the pesos that change pockets today, we'd never have to work again! I'll bet a cuartillo that my Antonio gets the first cock and brings me the wing. Then everyone will know we are pledged. Will you bet on Pedro?"

Tules changed the subject quickly by pointing to the men at the other side of the plaza. "Look, they're burying the red cock Juan Pérez gave them. There must be seven men named Juan to have given those seven cocks today. It will be a long fight."

She watched the squawking cock's head turn wildly above the place where it was buried alive in the sand. Its feathers shone with grease to make it harder to hold, but its neck would be wrung the minute it was snatched out of the ground. The big Indian drum began to beat, and the horses plunged into the race. Riders shoved each other for position and swooped toward the sand to grab the cock's slippery head.

Thick clouds of dust hid the riders, and the girls could only see the legs of plunging horses. The staccato beat of the drum stopped suddenly, but the dusty air still pulsed with the deep vibration. That was the signal that one rider had pulled out the cock. He waved it above his head and dashed off. The other riders plunged after him to fight for the carcass, and feathers flew in the air. The horses raced to the open fields beyond the plaza, turned, and raced back. People scuttled out of the way, and the girls pulled up their legs on the wall.

"That's Antonio's buckskin in the lead," Rosita shrieked. "He's holding the cock as high as he can reach. Look at that brute crowd him and grab his arm! The son of a pig!"

Tules's eyes widened as she watched the horses race neck to neck and the riders grapple with each other for what was left of the cock. Other horses closed in on them, blowing and rearing. One horse

64

jumped free from the scuffle, and the rider raced to the spot where the judges stood. The other horses halted as suddenly as they had started. The victor waved his trophy before the judges and cantered out of the dust toward the plaza.

"It's Pedro! He has the cock! Viva Pedro! Viva El Gallo! Bravo!" the crowd cheered. "Who's your sweetheart?"

Pedro's dark face was covered with dust and sweat, but he threw back his head and waved the broken wing in his hand. He pulled up his horse, bowed from the saddle, and tossed the wing toward Tules. It fell on the ground at her feet.

"Take it, girl. You have a brave novio. Invite me to the wedding," a man laughed as he picked up the wing and put it on Tules's lap. She drew back from it and would not touch it. She hid her blushing face in her reboso.

Pedro watched her and shrugged his shoulders. Then he hid his eyes behind his hand, mimicking her shyness, and got another laugh from the crowd. He settled his hat jauntily and rode off to be ready for the second race.

Rosita's envious fingers snatched the wing as she said, "My Antonio will pull out Pedro's cocky tail feathers in the next race. Even if he is the best shot in the country, Pedro can't have everything."

"Blessed San Antonio, don't let Ramón hear of this!" Tules prayed to herself.

She saw trouble ahead now that Pedro had publicly proclaimed his choice. Even if she didn't love him, he would force her to accept him to save his pride. She wished that she had remained away from El Gallo. Her teeth were gritty with dust, and she watched anxiously as men grabbed and fought over other cocks. Rosita's shrieks stopped until she was as silent as Tules. Her Antonio had not caught a feather

Now men planted long, slender poles in the ground. A live cock dangled from a rope between the poles, and the audience murmured in anticipation. To grab the swinging cock from high overhead required even more skill and courage than to snatch one out of the sand.

The Indian drum throbbed wildly again, and horses trotted single file around a trail that circled between the poles. Riders tried to time their horses' pace to the swaying cock and reached high from the saddles as they raced under the rope. Dust churned over the horses, and the drumbeat rolled on. No one had touched the cock, and the horses raced through for a second try. The drum stopped suddenly, and men shouted as they plunged after the winner. One pony stumbled, threw his rider, and the other horses veered sharply. They surged beyond the plaza and then back. One horse tore triumphantly between the poles, and the audience cheered. No one could see who he was in the thick dust. As he rode nearer they shouted, "Caramba, it's Pedro again! Qúe hombrón to win twice in one day!"

"Dios de mi vida, let me hide!" Tules cried. She dropped behind the wall hastily, fell, and twisted her ankle.

"He isn't coming this way. He's turned," Rosita hissed. "He will have two sweethearts, and the laugh will be on you."

Pedro rode straight through the plaza and pulled up in front of the long portál. He called loudly, "For Doña Prudencia! A sus ordenes! I kiss your hand, señorita!" and tossed the cock's head toward Doña Prudencia's astonished face.

"Viva Doña Prudencia! Viva Pedro!" the crowd shouted and laughed boisterously at this unexpected ending.

Tules peered over the wall with mingled relief and resentment. She saw Doña Prudencia beam like a full moon as Pedro rode away. "Come on," she poked Rosita. "It's over, and we have to help with dinner. I don't see how the ricos can enjoy chicken after this morning, even if it's stewed in wine."

"We don't have to hurry. Doña Prudencia will sit there for two hours receiving congratulations on the first cock she's ever had," Rosita grumbled. "Pedro is smart to flatter her. Someday he'll be an Alcalde. You'd better remember that at the dance tonight and not make him mad."

Tules clapped her hand over her dry lips as she remembered that Pedro would expect her to set a date for him to present the marriage letter when she danced with him tonight. Pedro would be furious if she repulsed him now. She would pray that Ramón would never hear

66

of this and hide in the house until he returned. "I can't go to the dance," she groaned to Rosita. "I've broken my ankle."

"But you'll miss the horse race this afternoon and the fun of all the fiestas this week," Rosita said.

"There is no remedy," Tules groaned as she limped along. "I'll wash your hair this afternoon, if you will tell Pedro that I am lame. Say I fell off the wall in the excitement of watching him and broke a bone. I'll loan you my new slippers to wear to the dance tonight if you will make him believe it."

Rosita nodded and said, "I'll tell Antonio."

# 8

In order to avoid Pedro, Tules stayed inside the kitchen and meekly submitted to Doña Prudencia's tired nagging after the fiestas were over. Doña Prudencia was a mountain of a woman. Bulging hips padded her full black skirt, and bulging breasts strained her tight bodice. She wore a knot of black lace in her gray hair like a crown, and her tapping cane even pounded commands to her gentle brother, Don José. She had been the neglected maiden aunt, but now her noiseless feet and small eyes pried into everything as she called on the saints to witness the servants' laziness. They hid from her on fast days and giggled over her loud struggles between gluttony and piety. Her days were divided by rich food, indigestion, and prayers.

"Get out to the salt pots, Tules. You have limped around the kitchen long enough," she ordered. "My brother is a simpleton to give the peóns a week off at the end of the dry season. The rains may come in another week, and everyone must hurry to finish the salt now."

Tules dreaded to work outside, but she went to the high ground west of the house where big copper caldrons were set above wood fires. She knew that Pedro passed by the caldrons when he returned with the salt crew, and she noticed with relief that four older women stood by the end pots. They would be good dueñas to curb Pedro's actions. Then she saw that Cuca stirred the salt in the caldron next to her.

"So the patrona sent you out to blister, too," Cuca grumbled as she ladled scum off the brine with a long wooden spoon. "The fires add to the sun and make this place as hot as hell."

Tules stirred her brine silently and looked from the hard porcelain blue of the sky to the houses squatted like panting red hens on the sandstone ledges of the loma. The pond had shrunk to a small

68

turquoise mirror with a broken, red rim. Its banks were choked with white water lilies whose heavy, sweet fragrance saturated the torrid air. At this dry season there was no water in the acequia to turn the stone grinding wheels in the log-sided mill or irrigate the drooping young corn. Small green apples littered the parched orchard.

"Ojalá that the rains will come soon, and cloudbursts will stop the work at the lagoons! My feet are tired from dancing, and the salt and fires make them burn," Cuca complained as she poured white salt crystals from her caldron into a deep willow basket.

"Don José is a kind patrón to give us a week off at the end of the salt season. He has a good heart, even if he is rich. No wonder they call him 'Old Salt of the Earth,' " Tules said and echoed the veneration of the peóns who prospered with Don José in his salt trade. The tang of salt ran in their blood and gave them the fatalism of seafaring people. Their talk was sprinkled with "sal Andaluza," the dry wit and proverbs of their long-cherished Andalusian homeland.

"You sound as though you were going to leave Don José," Cuca said suspiciously.

"How could I go? You know that I'm a bound peón like everyone else," Tules said quickly and tightened her wide lips over the secret that she planned to go with Ramón this fall. She longed to boast of Ramón and say that he was as strong as an Apache chief and as handsome as Saint John, but she was afraid of Cuca. She suspected that Cuca would sell any secret to Pedro to gain his favor and influence.

She looked over her caldron toward the east where the desert spread out in bleached desolation. In the hot, glaring light the ashen sand extended to the far rim of the faded sky. Alkali streaked the highest dunes whose only vegetation was tongue-cutting salt grass. In the central depression of the Salinas she saw the seventy shallow lagoons glitter like evil, rheumy eyes.

"I'd like to see Laguna del Perro," she pointed toward the largest lagoon. "Celso says the wind stirs the bitter water, and the salt is like a thick crust on the sides. Válgame Dios, I wouldn't want to work on that causeway and pry cakes of salt loose with a long wooden fork! You might fall and sink in the brine like Emilio Fernández, who was drowned there last year."

"The brine isn't as dangerous as the Apaches," Cuca said. "The salt crew makes a dark camp and keeps armed men on guard. For three days and nights they are afraid that the savages will jump out from behind every dune."

Tules nodded as she remembered stories of how the fierce Apaches pounced on caravans going to the salt lakes. Traders left the Chihuahua Trail and made a loop through the Manzano mountains to get the free salt, but many of them were killed by the Apaches. Don José sent an armed escort with his caravans, gathered the salt in dry weather, and sold it at his store. This year most of the traders had bought their salt at Manzano. That was cheaper than the expense of an armed guard to and from the lagoons.

The Apaches claimed the wide desert as their own domain, but they did not molest other Indians who followed the ancient tribal rites for gathering salt in the Salinas. The Pueblo tribes made long journeys to dance and chant beside the lagoons. They left prayer sticks for Salt Old Woman, their goddess who wore white boots and a white mantle and poured salt from a great white abalone shell for all her red children.

"Look at the lovely water," Tules cried and shaded her eyes to stare at a lake of fresh water in the desert. Tall trees rose from its banks, and its waters sparkled in sweet, lapping waves.

"False ponds!" Cuca mocked. "You'd die of thirst if you walked to that water. Don't let a mirage fool you, Tules. They are as false as love. They hold out beautiful promises and then—pouff—they're gone."

Tules rubbed her smarting eyes in unbelief. While she looked at it the lovely, fresh lake disappeared. She had seen many mirages, but today she would have sworn by San Antonio that she could have bathed her hot body in that cool lake. Perhaps the heat waves from the caldrons added to the burning sun to make the lake look so real and tempting. "María Santísima, there's a curse on this country," she muttered and crossed herself.

70

"Men perish from that curse," Cuca nodded. "They are lured into the desert with false ponds and false gold. Only a few men, like Don José, survive and get rich. Your Pedro will be a man of property too, someday. You have all the luck. Would that I could sleep in the bed of a rich man instead of rolling on a woolsack with a sheepherder for half a peso."

Tules turned her head away from the boiling brine and Cuca's searching eyes. She guarded her secret and tried to keep Cuca away from talk about Pedro. He was at the lagoons, and, if she kept out of his way until Ramón returned in the fall, she would leave this desert and its curses behind her. This summer happy dreams filled her heart, and she was no longer hurt by her mother's neglect or Doña Prudencia's, raging like a General. Her only worry was the fear that Ramón might forget her and not return in the fall.

"You're as freckled as a turkey egg," Cuca said at the end of the week. "You should have put on a bleaching mask before the salt crew comes home today. Look, you can see them coming back. The carretas look no bigger than chicken lice crawling over a buckskin hide. They'll be here in an hour."

Tules's hazel eyes darted in quick fear to the oxcarts beginning to climb out of the desert. She tried to laugh casually as she looked at Cuca's tanned, full-blooded cheeks and said, "You're as black as a heretic yourself. Maybe you are the Dark Woman who lives in the lagoons."

"She turned the sweet water to salt because she was an unfaithful wife. As long as I'm not married, I don't sin." Cuca winked and shook her head until the black strands of hair came loose under her red kerchief. "It would take a strong man like your Pedro to keep me faithful. Then I would be too busy to look around. . . ."

Tules knotted the blue cloth closer under her chin and looked at her bare, freckled arms. The evaporating brine left a salty crust around her curved nostrils and bleached light streaks in her red hair. She leaned over her caldron, jumped back, and cried, "Por Dios, I've burned my hand!" She sucked at the red welt on the side of her hand, and tears filled her eyes. They came more from her terror of facing Pedro today than the stinging burn.

71

"You'll burn all over if you think you can fool Pedro," Cuca guessed shrewdly. "If Pedro wants you, you'd better forget that gawky ox driver from Sante Fe. Oh, yes, I saw you in his arms in the orchard. After that you let Pedro give you the wing in El Gallo. He won't forget that! Don't be a fool, niña. Here come the carretas and Pedro now."

Tules saw the carretas turn into the corral through the wide gate in the red rubble walls. Men yelled and cracked their whips to steer the oxen to the proper dumping spots for the different grades of salt. They pulled the pins from the axles to tip the carts and the slither of running salt mingled with the thirsty lowing of the oxen. Pedro waved to a driver to go on to the farthest bins with his third-grade salt. It was coarse and heavy with red clay and only used to salt cattle or cure hides.

"No, no, not there, you half-witted bastard," Pedro shouted to another driver. "Put the second-grade salt on the other side."

That sulfur-tinged salt was Don José's staple of trade. Miners paid five pesos for three hundred pounds and used it to extract silver and copper ores. Almost every summer day burros loaded with this salt left Manzano for distant mines to the north or south. Months later the pack trains brought back goods, wine, food, or ingots of silver.

Pedro hurried to help unload glistening chunks of the first-grade salt near the gate. They shone with a thousand facets as he lifted them carefully into high bins. The women boiled this pure salt, and Don José sold it to the ricos.

Pedro turned to a heap of dull, chalky lumps and called to the corral boss, "Did you sell the paisanos any of this nice salt? A man could keep his wife out of mischief with a dose of this. Hombre, you're a poor merchant!"

The men guffawed and the women giggled at Pedro's old joke of tricking some country fellow into buying the nauseating medicinal salt. It was a violent purgative called "sal drástica" and used for bloated cows. It formed in the lagoons during cold weather, and every good salt gatherer took care not to mix his first spring load of good salt with its dull, bitter lumps. Pedro looked to see if the girls had laughed at his joke, and Cuca waved to him. He came toward them with a swaggering stride.

"Qué tal, Pedro? God has saved you from the Apaches to plague women's hearts again!" She laughed and rested her hand on her curving hip. She looked at him boldly and fanned her hot face with her wooden spoon. "Dios, I'd give any man a kiss for a long, cold drink! I'm as hot as Satan himself."

"You go to the salt lagoons, and you'll know what it is to be hot. My tongue is as dry as a lizard." Pedro appraised the curves of Cuca's figure and passed on to Tules's downcast eyes. "Your salt is ready, Tules," he said curtly and grasped her hand on the long spoon handle.

She stepped back as he lifted the caldron and poured the white crystals into the willow basket. She saw the sweat on his brown forehead and thick upper lip as he stooped over the fire. He wiped it off with the back of his hand and stared at her.

"Did you sleep with me last night that you can't say good day to me now?" he demanded with a flashing grin that showed his white teeth.

Tules flushed, but Cuca rewarded him with a ringing laugh. "I've just told her not to act like a novice taking the veil."

"Cuca, bring another basket from the house," Pedro ordered. When Cuca was out of earshot he stepped close to Tules, hungry desire in his burning eyes. "Have the Apaches cut out your tongue? I haven't seen you for weeks, yet you have no welcome for me. Your heart is as soft as granite, but—válgame Dios!—you are beautiful."

Tules kept her eyes lowered. This summer others had said her face was like an opening bud. She knew it came from the magic of love, and she intended to keep her fresh beauty for Ramón.

"You don't have to play shy with me, niña," Pedro said roughly. "I can remember your smiles and saucy talk this spring. You waited for me at the pasture, and God knows how you caught me. What tricks are you up to now? Are you trying to drive me crazy with hunger? You know that I am mad with love for you, even if you are a barefoot pelada. Everyone knows that I chose you at El Gallo, and

73

now they laugh because you run away from me. Remember that the loaf comes out as the oven wills. I am boss around here. What is the matter with you?"

Tules glanced swiftly at his unshaven chin and the mat of coarse hair showing above his open shirt. She shivered before the primitive passion in his eyes and whispered, "I hurt my foot. I couldn't go to the fiestas. . . ."

"Bien, but your heart should not limp. Válgame Dios, what you do to me! After these weeks the sight of you is like cool, sweet water in the desert. Never before have I felt this way about a woman. You stand there like the Virgin, and I am wild to hold you. . . ."

"Take care, Pedro. The women are watching you," Tules whispered, thankful that the women at the other pots were so close.

"Curse their eyes!" Pedro muttered. "I must see you alone. I have something to say to you—and to your mother. Does that satisfy you?"

"You say that I am a barefoot pelada. Others could give you more . . ." Tules murmured.

"Is that what eats you? Yes, I, Pedro Bustamente, could have any girl, but I must have you. I can't think of anything else. I will hold you close, kiss you until you laugh again, warm you with my fire. . . ."

"The women are listening," Tules warned.

"Let them listen!" Pedro said, but he lowered his voice. "Soon everyone will know. . . . I must return to the salt lagoons until the rains come. Be ready for me when I come back. Then I will go to your mother. Dios, how can I wait two more weeks?"

Cuca ran toward them with the basket and called, "Go to the pasture, Pedro. A wild stallion has kicked Celso in the head. Don José sends for you!"

"In two weeks, Tules," Pedro muttered as he stalked away.

The girls emptied their caldrons and started home in the twilight. Fiery color licked the far reaches of the desert, but the houses on the loma were already cool under the long shadow of the mountain. The high rock tower stood out in a dark silhouette against the flaming sky.

74

"The torreón makes a long face at the drought." Tules pointed to the loopholes in the red masonry, anxious to talk about anything that would stop Cuca's questions. "See the eyes and nose and long mouth."

"You will have a long face too if you give Pedro the squash." Cuca smiled slyly.

"If you think he's so fine, why don't you take him yourself?" Tules snapped, annoyed with her own fear and Cuca's curiosity.

"He won't have me," Cuca said bitterly. "I should run away from him, the way you do! But if I am a friend of his, he can help me—help you, too, if you're not a fool. He has money in his bag, and he will go far. What's come over you? Don't you want a new skirt instead of that rag that's patched like a rainbow?"

"Of course, but I'll buy it," Tules lifted her chin.

"With what you save out of your wages of one peso a month?" Cuca mocked. "Red cloth from Mexico costs six pesos the vara, and a decent skirt needs four widths. Twenty-four pesos is two years' work, child! And three pesos for a blouse, and another for ribbons for your braids. Will you buy a silk reboso with the hundred pesos you have left over this year?"

Tules felt her patched skirt with fingers that longed for finery. She had to have a new skirt before Ramón came. "Maybe Don José will give me credit," she faltered.

"Then you will be further in debt and under Doña Prudencia's thumb forever. If you do what Pedro wants, you'll be free and have everything. Dios, if he wanted me I'd run to him! You should go to him tonight before he leaves. . . ."

"No," Tules cried, sick with the fear that Pedro would come back soon and she would not escape him. If she could run away. . . . But then she would miss Ramón. She must think of some other way. She knew that Cuca would watch her and help Pedro. She stopped in hopeless despair outside the little door cut into the zaguán gate, leaned her head against the cool wood, and cried, "Why does God make life so hard for the pobres?"

"You make your own life hard with your stubbornness," Cuca's

75

loud voice insisted. "A pretty girl like you needs pretty clothes. You can work Pedro like a handful of dough. Men have given me silk and shoes and money. We can slip out tonight while that old she-devil is asleep. Doña Prudencia is not made for love but for lack of a lover. But if a lover came to her, he would think he had rolled on a feather bed. We can get away from her. Come on and . . ."

The little door jerked open from the inside, and Doña Prudencia loomed before them in the open passageway. "Get in here," she thundered, as she pulled Tules inside and turned her fury on Cuca. "You—you slut! You dare to brag of your indecencies right under my nose. I pace the floor and lift my soul to God with my evening rosary and these foul words came to my ears. Hail-Mary-full-of-grace . . ."

She pulled the door shut, and the beads slipped through her fingers as she stormed, "You can't fool me, Fruit-of-thy-womb-Jesus. I will have only decent women in this house, Hail-Mary-full-of-grace. You dare to say that I need a lover. I will put you on bread and water and lock you in a dark room for that, Hail-Mary-full-of-grace. You dare to call me a feather bed, The-Lord-is-with-thee. You brag of adultery and try to lead another girl astray, Thy-will-be-done-on-earth-as-it-is-in-Heaven. But I will cool your hot blood, Hail-Mary . . ."

Her eyes flashed like cedar sparks, and the bristles on her chin stiffened as she ordered, "Tules, go to the storeroom and bring me a sack of sal drástica."

"No, no, not sal drástica, patrona! It makes me so sick," Cuca cried.

Doña Prudencia took Cuca by the arm and marched her off to the servants' quarters as Tules ran to the storeroom. When she came back Doña Prudencia was saying, "You have done this before. Now you slip out to the men like a mare in heat. For a few nights you'll have another reason to run out."

"For the love of God, don't give me sal drástica," Cuca begged. "I promise to stay in. I'll never go out again."

"You need a purge for your vile tongue." Doña Prudencia poured the salts into a gourd cup of water and forced Cuca to drink it. "If

76

you go out again, I'll give you salts every night for a week. You will be so thin that any man would rather sleep with the slats on his bed. This is a warning to you too, Tules. Get to your work."

Tules ran out of the room before the patrona changed her mind. She was sorry for Cuca, but she sighed with relief. For a few days Cuca would have to stay near the backhouse and would be too sick to help Pedro. "Blessed San Antonio, let Pedro find another girl," she prayed fervently.

# 9

TEN DAYS later Tules pulled her reboso over her head to shut out the crashing thunder and lightning of the first summer storm. Drought followed by cloudbursts was typical of the violence of the country. She watched the needed water run off in swift flash floods and knew that Pedro would return as fast as his oxen could pull through the mud. She held her breath when she saw a man on horseback dash into the corral, but it was not Pedro. It was her stepfather, Rafael, who was in charge of Don José's cattle ten leagues north in the high mountains.

"What brings you home in such a hurry?" she called.

"Tell Luz to come here at once," Rafael shouted. "I must see Don José first. I have great news."

Tules sent a boy for her mother and joined the servants who had stopped their work to speculate on the great news. Refugia guessed that the Governor was coming to pay them a visit, but Magdalena said they must have found Doña Carmen at last. Cruz Tafoya thought it was a revolt against the Mexican Government, while Juan Pérez, the torreón guard, insisted the Apaches were on the way to attack the hacienda. Luz ran to them with the baby tucked against her back in the fold of her reboso and a small child held by either hand.

"Dios de mi vida, is Rafael hurt? Where is he?" she cried.

Tules pointed to Don José's room, and everyone talked at once. They only quieted when they saw Don José come through the passageway with Rafael. Rafael's eyes shone with excitement, but Don José's face was calm under his white hair and close-trimmed goatee.

"Take a rest until after siesta, and come to me before you return to the cattle," Don José said quietly and turned back to the house.

"Rafael!" Luz cried. "Madre de Dios, I thought the Apaches had scalped you!"

78

Rafael embraced her so hard that the baby cried. Then he turned to the waiting faces and said, "I have great news for you, amigos, but I had to report it to Don José first."

"But, válgame Dios, what is it, this news?" they cried. "A revolt? The Apaches? Doña Carmen at last?"

"Wait, amigos," Rafael held up his hand and turned his eyes to heaven. "I have the best news in the world. From this day on you can have all the gold you want."

"Gold? All we want? He's drunk or crazy!" Juan Pérez tapped his own temples.

"No, Juan, I speak the truth," Rafael gloated. "They found gold in the Ortiz mountains, there to the north. Gold as thick as dirt! Mountains of gold! They found one chunk heavier than lead and yellow as Spanish doubloons. Maybe it's worth ten thousand pesos. I know—I was a miner in Sonora."

"Merciful saints, gold! *Gold!* Where is it?" Juan cried, and everyone strained his eyes toward the distant peaks to the north.

"A vaquero from the Ortiz ranch told me about it first," Rafael explained. "Don Francisco Ortiz, who owns all that grant of land east of the Sandías, lives at Ojo de Dolores. They lost some of his cattle, and Don Francisco rode with his friend Don Jesús María to look for the prize bull. . . ."

"He's throwing us the bull. Otro toro!" Cruz laughed.

"May San Juan Nepomeneca strike you dumb!" Juan cried. "How can a man hear in this din? Go on, Rafael. . . ."

"Pues, they found the bull, but a cow caught her foot in a hole. They pulled her foot loose, and a heavy rock came up too. It shone yellow, and Don Jesús María looked at it. He knew it was gold because he came from Spain to mine gold in Mexico. It was solid gold and as big as my two hands."

"For the love of the saints, did you touch that much gold?" Tules asked.

"Pues, I didn't exactly touch it, but I know all about it," Rafael said. "I talked to the vaquero who was with Don Francisco when they found it. I left my cows with Simón Durán and went to Dolores

79

myself. Everyone is wild there. Men and women search arroyos, and children find nuggets the size of your thumb. There's enough gold for all of us to be rich. . . ."

"Gold! *Gold!* Let's go at once. How far is it?" men shouted.

"And my brave Rafael—you came back to get us!" Luz exclaimed and patted his hairy arm.

A cloud passed over Rafael's triumphant face as he shrugged and pointed with his chin toward the house. "Don José says I cannot go until I have worked out my debt."

"Jesucristo, must we work as slaves forever?" men appealed to each other. "He has no right to tell us we can't leave when gold is so near. I almost had my fingers on it! Por supuesto, we are all in debt. We expect to live and die in debt. But now we will go and find gold. Don José shall come with us and gather gold instead of salt!"

"I told him all that and more." Rafael shook his dark head. "He says it's fool's gold. He says real gold couldn't have been there all these years without men finding it before this. He says the Apaches will steal his cattle and sheep. He says his work must go on. He showed me my debt in his books. You heard him tell me to go back to the cows. . . ."

Rafael stooped to pick up his little son and took small Rafaela's hand as he started toward their home on the loma. Luz and Tules trailed close behind him. He shook his head in despair as servants followed them, shouting questions and arguing between themselves. The family huddled on the dirt floor of their room to decide what to do. Tules hugged herself with joy. San Antonio had sent her a chance to get away before Pedro returned.

Luz unwound her reboso to nurse the fretting baby and said, "Holy Mother, Rafael, is it really gold?"

"I swear by all the saints, it's pure gold," Rafael insisted as he stretched his tired body on the clay floor. "I . . . ."

"The shirt must be true to the master who wears it." Luz reminded him from her long habit of obedience. "You are responsible for Don José's cattle."

"What do cattle matter now?" Rafael sat up, rolled a cornhusk cigarrito, and lighted it with his flint. "A cow brings five pesos and a fat sheep one. I tell you, Luz, you can pick up fifty pesos in gold in one day. Let the sheep and cattle go. . . ."

"By the three Marías, I only taste meat once a month, but you would give the Apaches a whole herd like that!" Luz snapped her fingers and moved the baby to the other flabby breast. "Pobrecita, with all this excitement my milk has dried up. Tules, get the sugar tit."

"Have people come there from Sante Fe?" Tules asked, thinking of Ramón as she handed Luz the rag stiff with dried syrup.

"Of course. They come from everywhere." Rafael made a wide gesture. "Hundreds of men come on their fastest horses. Others come in carretas or on burros. Some walk in spite of the Apaches. A month ago Francisco Arballo didn't have money for beans. Now he clears one hundred pesos a day. Even children find enough gold for a rich dowry. . . ."

"I could have a new skirt. Let's start now," Tules cried.

"Holy Mother, help us!" Luz groaned as she rocked the baby. "What torture to put gold so near and then chain our hands! The law would bring us back for our debts. Don José has been kind and paid off my debts once. But we have to buy from the store, and we are slaves as long as we are in debt."

"But we can pay off our debts in a week," Rafael insisted. "I tell you this is the gold the Conquistadores came to find in the Seven Cities of Cibola. They passed near it, but they missed it in a strange country. My father told me that the great Cortés said, 'I come not to till the soil but to find gold.' Spaniards are not wretched farmers, satisfied to harvest a handful of beans. They are brave men, exploring new countries. They are soldiers, adventurers, miners. Have you forgotten the rich mines in Sonora? Pues, woman, you have lost your spirit in childbearing. . . ."

"No, no, Rafael, I want to go." Luz dashed at her tears with the heel of her hand. "But how far can I walk with three children?"

"Then I will go back to the cows this afternoon to please Don José," Rafael planned. "I will leave them in charge of Simón Durán, but you must say nothing. In two weeks I will find enough gold to pay all our debts. Then I will buy another horse and come back for you."

When Rafael left Tules looked at the distant blue mountains, torn between the joy of finding gold and the fear of missing Ramón.

Manzano burned with gold fever, and tales of riches soared with each telling. The poorest peóns planned to squander thousands of doubloons on food, wine, and silks. Each morning fewer men reported for work. They walked north by night to avoid the Apaches.

"Pedro has gone to the gold camp," Cuca whispered to Tules. "He told me to tell you that he would bring you the finest trousseau that money could buy. Come, niña, let's follow him. I am going with some men who leave tonight. New men, new clothes, and no more of Doña Prudencia's salts! Come on. . . ."

"I must wait with my mother for Rafael." Tules shook her red head and sighed with relief that Pedro had gone. "Don't forget me when you are rich."

"Anything that I have will be yours," Cuca promised. "When you are married to Pedro you will thank me for my good advice. I am older. . . . Wish me luck, niña."

The next day Doña Prudencia stormed loudly at her brother. "Why don't you send a warrant of debt to Dolores Springs and arrest these deserters? Now you have only enough men for one salt crew, and your cattle and sheep are lost. . . ."

"Pedro was my best foreman," Don José sighed. "Even my own sons have left me. The world is gold-crazy. Men leave honest work, honest pay, a home and care, for this false dream of quick riches. Pues, no good or ill endures a hundred years!"

A few listless men harvested the corn, and women husked it on warm, moonlit evenings. A melon hidden deep in the yellow, rustling ears speeded the work. Women and children picked the green chile pods in the fields, tied them in bunches on long strings, and hung them over the roofs. In the glowing September sunshine the chile turned scarlet and then crimson and looked like brilliant garlands garnishing the houses.

82

Tules's eyes glowed with happy hopes, but Luz fretted that Rafael had not returned with the extra horse and gold. She waited impatiently for two months and then moved back to the patrón's house. Her old job as cook gave her a little credit on her debt and her children free food.

Tules and Rosita picked apples in the famous orchard to store them for the winter. The mellow October air was heady with fruity fragrance as Tules reached for the apples that were the fulfillment of Ramón's spring vows. The caravan might arrive any day. A happy song came strangely from her stiff white lips. She had coated her face with bleaching clay for two weeks to remove the sunburn and freckles before Ramón came. Rosita's face was stained scarlet with her favorite remedy of alegría juice. They suffered any beauty preparation rather than have the disgrace of dark skin that implied Indian slave blood.

"Listen!" Rosita raised her red face. "Men are shouting on the plaza. Maybe it's the Santa Fe caravan!"

"Alma de mi alma, let's run, Rosita!" Tules cried as they lifted the basket of apples. "Let's go the back way and peel off these masks. Madre de Dios, what will I do if Ramón has not come?"

In the kitchen Tules soaked her face and pulled frantically at the bits of clay that stuck to her face and arms. Excited tears stood in her eyes as she wondered if Ramón had forgotten her. She rubbed tallow on her smarting face, buffed her cheeks with a mullein leaf, and powdered her nose. She stared at Rosita with wide eyes and trembling lips, afraid to go outside.

In the plaza her eyes peered through the shimmering dust at men in fringed buckskin. Was that—was that Ramón? Not so tall as she remembered him, but tall enough—and handsome. Her heart pounded as he turned and waved to her. She pointed to their trysting place in the orchard and ran to it.

"Linda, linda," he whispered when he held her in his arms. "For six months I've dreamed of you and longed for this moment."

"Oh, Ramón, I was so afraid you wouldn't come," she cried, as her arms tightened around his neck and her lips pressed his.

83

She lay with him that night in the shadow of the trees. His hands caressed her trembling body, and she was lost in breathless rapture. The stars wheeled above them, and they forgot the hard ground as they pressed close to each other.

The next morning Ramón bowed before Luz and asked permission to take her daughter with him. Tules looked from Ramón's shining, young eyes to her mother's thin, careworn face as Luz turned to her and said, "You must have permission from Don José. Can Ramón pay your debt?"

"No, Mamá, not now, but we will soon find enough gold to send Don José the money." Tules's voice lilted like a song.

"We will leave the caravan and go to El Real de Dolores where there is much gold, señora," Ramón explained.

"Then, válgame Dios, you can find Rafael! Tell him I wait," Luz exclaimed and forgot her objections in this chance to catch her husband.

Tules waited for Doña Prudencia's good humor after her second breakfast and then stood with her arms folded across her chest in the position the patrona required.

"What impudence is this?" Doña Prudencia scolded. "You would leave with a strange man without a marriage blessing! Holy Mother, God will punish you for such sin!"

"But, patrona, the padre will not come until Christmas. Besides, we cannot pay a marriage fee of twenty pesos now. We will be married at Dolores—or maybe Santa Fe."

When she escaped from Doña Prudencia's lecture she ran quickly to Don José. He was seated in his bare counting room with a quill raised over the ledger on the table. He looked shrunken with trouble, and his face was thin under his white hair. Tules swallowed hard to think that she was leaving his gentle hands, but she blurted out her story.

"Ramón says the mountains shine with gold. Soon I can send back enough to clear my debts," she pleaded.

"This gold drives men crazy like the false ponds," Don José sighed and turned to his ledger. "Let's see what you owe. One peso for white

84

cotton for a blouse. One real for a red ribbon. Half a real for brown sugar cone. One real for blue ribbon. Five pesos for a blue cotton reboso. That was two years ago. This year twenty pesos for red cloth for a skirt. Ten pesos for red slippers. One peso for white cloth. One real for green ribbon. Umm—about forty pesos, and you have credit for the last two years' work. You owe sixteen pesos. Another year would almost clear it."

"But Don José, I can't wait another year." Tules knelt beside him and caught his vein-lined hands. "Ramón leaves in three more days, and I must go with him. You have been kind to me, and Doña Carmen was kind too. She was like you. . . ."

"God have mercy on her soul!" the old man groaned. "No voice is strong enough to deny love. It is the greatest blessing and the most powerful force in life. At least for a few years Carmen was blessed with love. In her memory I will write off your debt." He reached into the money chest and brought up a handful of coins. "Here, take this silver as a wedding gift from Carmen. And tell Luz to give you my daughter's blue silk reboso. She does not need it now. Go with God, child."

While Ramón was away at the lagoons the days were full of happy preparations. Luz spread a cloth on the floor and packed Tules's patched skirt and blouse, the cracked mirror, wooden comb, and ball of powder. The servants added presents from their meager possessions: a creased red ribbon from Rosita, amole and oshá roots from the old curandera. Doña Prudencia relented enough to send a worn bedspread. The fifteen pesos from Don José were sewed in a bag and tied on a string Tules wore around her neck with the medal of Our Lady of Guadalupe.

"Here are beans, corn, a few loaves of bread, and dried mutton in the olla," Luz said, pointing to two sacks and the earthen cooking pot. "Feed your husband well. Love sours on an empty stomach."

Before dawn the next morning the women dressed the bride in the trousseau Ramón had brought her. His sister María had made the red skirt, stitched bands of blue and white above its hem, and smocked the blouse with blue. Luz draped Doña Carmen's rich blue

85

silk reboso over Tules's shoulders, and old Magdalena gave her a little wooden statue of San Antonio holding the Christ child on his arm.

"Your face shines like an angel hearing the words of God," Magdalena whispered. "Take San Antonio with you. He listens to the prayers of the heart. May the saints watch over you, niña!"

Ramón was stiff with embarrassment when the chattering women brought the bride to his carreta. He lifted Tules awkwardly to the pad strapped on the broad golden back of the lead ox and tied her bundles near his pack and two guns. She smiled at wreaths of wild purple asters and yellow chamiso twined around the ox's horns and over the high sides of the carreta. She caught at the ox's loose hide as he began to move, and the bells jingled.

"Adiós, Tules, don't forget us!" her friends called. "Wait for us at Dolores! Take care of her, Ramón! Good luck! Adiós, adiós, God be with you."

She threw kisses to her mother, the children, Rosita, and waved to Don José. She adjusted herself to the slow rhythm and the creaking song of the wheels. Her bare legs and red slippers clung to the ox's flank. She watched Ramón shyly, but he swung his long whip and called, "Step up there, Perdito! Hurry up, Flojo! Keep to the right, Juanito!"

After the first league the road curved into the open valley and away from rocks and shrubs where Apaches might hide. The garlands on the ox yokes wilted as the sun rose high. Tules turned for a last look at the red terraces of Manzano, the orchard and the turquoise pond and the golden billows of the desert. Now she would never look into the clear, bubbling depth of El Ojo del Gigante, talk to Celso, or whisper secrets with Rosita. She might never see her mother or Don José again.

She clutched the little statue of San Antonio fearfully and pulled the blue silk reboso tighter. A cloud hid the sun, and its shadow traveled swiftly over the dry yellow sand. She looked toward the distant purple peaks that were filled with strange people and strange ways. Even Ramón was a stranger. She looked at him in panic, ready

86

to leap off and run home. He turned his head to look up at her with adoring eyes and smiled.

She unfastened her slippers and kicked her feet free before she jumped into the sand and ran to Ramón. He caught her in his arms and kissed her.

"Come, linda," he said at last. "The oxen have left us. We'll have to run to catch up."

# Part Three:
# El Real de Dolores 1828-1829

# 10

Last year Dolores Springs had been a quiet water hole in the remote Ortiz mountains. This year the discovery of gold brought swarms of people to the springs to live in warrens on the side of the red gulch. A road twisted through the bottom and crossed level ground where oxcarts unloaded before the long adobe store, dance hall, and cantina. Above the springs Tules could see the flat roofs of the Ortiz hacienda and the chapel of Nuestra Señora de Dolores. They were withdrawn in haughty dignity from the new rabble.

Ramón put their bundles down and began to dig a cave in the sandy side of the gulch.

"But we can't live like prairie dogs!" Tules protested.

"We have no time or money to build an adobe room or even a cedar-post jacal." Ramón laughed and kissed her. "We must dig a cave quickly, stake our claim, and wash gold before it is carried away. You won't mind living like the other buscones for a few weeks. In a month we'll be rich. Then I'll build you a fine house, linda."

"All right, Ramón. A cave will be warm," she agreed, taking courage from the bright dream in his eyes. She helped him dig the cave and fill the front with mud-chinked cedar posts. He hung a cowhide for a door and built a crooked rubble chimney that smoked. Tules hung her wedding finery over a pole pushed into the rounded roof and set the earthen cooking pot to simmer on the hearth. She clapped her hands with the pride and joy of her own fire and watched the last coal glimmer as she lay on the sheepskin in Ramón's warm arms.

88

At the store she spent half of Don José's money on a whole chicken, a leg of pork, bread, eggs, goat's-milk cheese, and piloncillo, her favorite hard brown-sugar cone. Ramón shook his head over her extravagance but said they would soon find gold. She had no idea of the cost of food, but she discovered that the bountiful days of the patrón's kitchen were over. She raged the first time she had to buy salt and soap and learned to hoard their precious food, wood, and water.

Ramón carved bateas out of soft cottonwood, and Tules polished the inside of the shallow wooden bowls with stones and sand until they were so smooth that no grain of gold could escape her keen eyes. She found black sand under rocks, scooped it into the bateas, poured water over it, and shook the bateas around and around with slow rhythm. Her deft fingers flicked out the larger pebbles that rose to the top as she swung the batea to the right again.

"Look, Ramón! Gold!" she cried, when she found bright, shining grains at the left edge of the wet black sand.

He spooned the gold carefully into a gourd cup and told her to wash the sand again. As she shook the batea she dreamed of lavish riches, but her yellow grains were never worth more than a few reales. At the store the clerk weighed their half-filled quill of gold dust and grumbled about the expense of transporting gold to the mint at Durango. He cursed the taxes, the bandits, and the gold that was cached and never found after an Apache raid on the trail. He lowered the buying price and raised the cost of food. Their bill grew larger each week though they only bought beans and corn.

The gold at El Real de Dolores was so pure that Santa Fe gold-smiths had to add alloy to strengthen the delicate, twisted wires for their filigree. There was gold everywhere: nuggets found on the mountains; gold sifted into wind-blown dirt on the mesas; gold mixed with black sand in deep arroyos; gold sunk through the sand to the layer of red clay resting on bedrock. Through eons of time mountains of gold had literally washed and blown away.

But only a few grains were found at a time. Somewhere there must be a deep, rich mother lode, the original source of this gold dust.

Every day prospectors left the camp to search for it. Some packed a little food, picks, and canteens on sturdy burros and started for lonely cañóns; others tied a bundle to a stick over their shoulders, set out on foot, and were never heard of again.

Tules's stepfather, Rafael Sánchez, stumbled into their cave one night, bearded, ragged, half frozen, and starved. As Tules warmed food he babbled crazily that he had found the mother lode.

"My mother and the children wait for you at Manzano," Tules reminded him.

"Tell Luz to have patience a little longer," Rafael cried. "I have found the true vein, and we will be as rich as those miners from Zacatecas who buy capes for five thousand pesos and pave their doorsteps with solid silver blocks when the Bishop comes for a christening. Write to Luz and tell her to prepare a great fiesta for our marriage and the baptism of the children. Dios de mi vida, I will return to the mountains tomorrow and bring back sacks of pure gold. . . ."

"I will go with you," Ramón cried, his eyes shining like black opals. "We'll claim the mother lode together. . . ."

"No, no, Ramón, I am afraid to stay here alone," Tules pleaded, fearful that the gold fever would craze Ramón too. "Let Rafael go again and make sure. When he returns, we will go with him."

"Válgame Dios, if I was alone I could get rich!" Ramón grumbled.

He sulked as he watched Rafael leave the next day. That was the last time they saw him. In the spring a man found Rafael's sack and the bones the coyotes had left.

The talk with Rafael made Tules homesick. She had not seen a familiar face since she left Manzano. Some of Don José's peóns had been arrested for debt, and others had returned willingly, after they starved at the gold camp. She wished that she could give her mother news of Rafael and hear Rosita giggle. These buscones in the gulch were strange, bitter people who thought only of gold or eased their gold sickness in fiery aquardiente on Saturday nights.

And now Ramón was sulky because she had begged him not to go with Rafael. She decided quickly to buy a little meat with Don José's money, since they had had no meat for a month. After a good supper Ramón would love her again.

She ran down the trail to the store and looked out of the corner of her eye at the brothel across the road from the cantina. It was a long row of single adobe rooms, with names painted above each door in gaudy letters. She read quickly, "Lupita," "Adelita," "Pepita," and such alluring titles as "El Viejo Amor," "Siempre Para Ti," and "La Paloma Blanca." The upper halves of the doors were open, and women with hard, painted faces leaned out to call to miners. There were also laughing young girls with paper carnations against their dark hair. Tules heard guitars and men's voices and hoped that Ramón had not taken his disappointment to these girls.

In the store Tules resolutely turned away from tempting luxuries and spent half a peso for stringy mutton. As she hurried out the door she bumped into a well-dressed woman and stared in amazement at Cuca's bold, handsome face.

"Cuca!" she cried and threw her arms around her old friend. "Where have you been? You must have found the mother lode to wear shoes in the daytime! Dios, I'm glad to see someone from home! Doña Prudencia was furious when you left."

"It was my lucky night when I escaped from her dose of salts." Cuca laughed and winked a rolling black eye. Her face was crudely painted, and she rustled her silk skirt. "You should have come with me. Pedro Bustamente is here, and he is a man of influence now. Most of the time he is in Santa Fe with his cousins who are big politicians. He has claims staked all over the cañón in the names of those cousins. He didn't like it when he heard you had gone off with Ramón. . . ."

Someone grabbed Tules's arm, and she looked up to see Ramón's face, sultry with anger. She pulled away from him and said, "Stop, you're hurting me. Ramón, this is Cuca from Manzano."

Ramón bowed stiffly, murmured, "Con permiso," and dragged his wife away.

"Ramón, how can you be so rude?" Tules cried. "I worked with Cuca for years. She's my old friend from Manzano."

"You country simpleton!" Ramón growled. "Here she is the best-known harlot in the camp. She lives in that row. You can't be seen talking to her on the road in the daytime! Válgame Dios, people will say that you are one of those sluts from Manzano! Don't speak to her again. Get home now and keep out of mischief, or I'll . . ." He pushed her ahead and turned back to the cantina.

Tears streamed down her face as she ran up the trail. She loved Ramón so much that his displeasure hurt her. In spite of their poverty she was happy that she was his woman and no longer a peón. She comforted herself that this was the lot of every woman. Ramón only beat her because he loved her. She submerged her own quick temper to rally Ramón when he was gloomy and hold him down when he had some wild plan to find gold.

The winter was dry, and the buscones were only permitted to fill their jars with drinking water from the spring. All placer mining stopped until the first snow fell in January. Then Ramón built a small dam against the hillside, packed snow into it, and melted the snow with hot stones. They used the little pool of water to wash black sand, and Tules's arms ached again from swishing the batea around and around.

When Ramón was in a good humor he repeated the wild tales that ran through the camp like fire before wind. He told tales of a sheepherder on the opposite mesa who had seen the pale green fire that hovers over hidden gold. He said an old man had shown him a soiled map with the location of a lost Spanish mine; or he had talked to a vaquero who had crawled under a cliff in a storm and found he had slept on solid gold, but he could never find the cliff again. Another time a hunchback with second sight claimed that the Spirit of the Mines, the Padre Mina, had told him of solid galleries of gold below the San Lázaro Mountains.

Tules learned to sew her lips together, but she knew that most of these fantastic visions came out of a bottle of mescal and peyote. Every Saturday night the cañón roared with wild, drunken men, who sweated to wash gold all week and threw it away in one riotous night. Sunday they slept in sodden dreams, and Monday they broke their backs again. They were sure that next week they would find a heavy nugget, a pocket of pure gold, or even the fabulous mother lode. A few lucky ones found enough to fatten all their hopes. Tules made light of the tales to cool Ramón's gold fever, and tagged behind him on Saturday nights.

Gambling at monte had the same fascination as mining for gold. Ramón and Tules edged into the crowd around the monte tables beyond the dance hall and cantina. Their eyes looked hungrily at the stacks of gold and silver coins, and they watched every card the dealer turned. Tules remembered Tío Florentino's games in Taos, and her hands itched to get hold of the cards. She knew the plays and was sure she could win and quadruple her bet. They needed the money, and Ramón finally nodded for her to bet half a peso. She gulped with despair when she lost and looked at the dealer with flashing green eyes. He had so much money that he could have given them two pesos for bread.

One Saturday night Ramón's eyes gleamed with a new scheme. This time they would soon be rich through his partnership with Dionisio Silva in a crushing mill. Ramón explained that they would dig a shallow circle in the ground, build a low wall around it, and fill it with ore-bearing rock. Then a mule would drag a flat stone around and crush more gold out of the rocks than they could wash from sand in a year. Dionisio had the mule, and Ramón would bring the ore from the gambucinos who dug gold on the mesa. He reached for his poncho to settle the business with Dionisio, and Tules foresaw that their last reales would buy drinks in the cantina.

"Let me go with you, chulo," she coaxed and caught his hand. "There is a dance tonight, and we will celebrate this fine plan and our good luck. It is so long since I have danced with you. . . ."

She slipped into the new red skirt she had worn as a bride, hummed a song as she combed her red hair, and draped the beautiful blue silk reboso over her shoulders. She carried her slippers so that they would not be torn on the trail.

The air of the dance hall was heavy with dust as Ramón spun her around in a fast schottische and polka. Then he saw Dionisio and

93

left her in the decorous row of women against the white wall. She knew that he would come back from the bar tipsy and quarrelsome, but she shrugged her shoulders and looked at the crowd. She saw Cuca standing near the table where wine was served. Many times that winter she had been homesick and longed to talk to Cuca, but she remembered Ramón's threat. When they met Cuca nodded formally and lifted her skirt to show her silk petticoat.

She forgot Cuca in the pleasure of dancing every time the fiddler played. By custom any stranger or neighbor could ask for a dance, whirl her around, and return her to her seat. Cipriano Arballo, whose claim was next to theirs, asked her for the honor of the next quadrille, and they took their places on the dance floor. Tules caught her breath when she saw the couple coming to join them. It was Cuca and Pedro Bustamente. His stocky figure looked larger in the grandeur of the silver buttons down his tight black pants and the elaborate white leather scrolls on his short black jacket. She could see that they talked about her and watched her. It would be an insult to leave the floor now.

She smiled, danced toward them, and curtsied as the music started. When the corner couples danced, Pedro caught her in his strong arms and whirled her until her red skirt stood out.

"You witch!" he whispered. "You are more beautiful than ever. I am glad I came back tonight."

They were in the far corner of the room when the dance ended. and Cipriano took her to the table where Pedro bought glasses of red wine. Tules's heart pounded from the fast steps, excitement, and danger. She did not see Ramón and accepted the wine and Pedro's toast. Cuca laughed shrilly and flashed the rings on her fingers. Tules hid her rough hands and broken nails under her reboso.

The next dance started, and Pedro drew her toward the floor. She looked around the room quickly. Ramón had not come back. Pues, it was his fault; he had left her.

"Your heart flutters like a frightened bird, chiquita," Pedro whispered. "Or is it that you are so glad to see me?"

She smiled at him under curving bronze lashes. She forgot her

94

fear of him and was only conscious of the challenge of his primitive male strength.

He pressed her closer and whispered, "I shall be here often, now that I know you are my neighbor."

"Your neighbor?" she asked.

"You have the claim next to mine, chiquita. Cipriano works for me, but now I shall come there to be near you. Dios, I have not forgotten that you belonged to me first! Now that we are here together . . ."

A shot rang out at the end of the room near the cantina. Men stopped dancing and ran to see what had happened. Pedro left Tules abruptly, and she backed against the cool wall. She looked anxiously for Ramón.

"It's two gringos fighting. Let the heretics kill each other!" a woman shrieked. "Here comes Pedro Bustamente. He will stop them. Let the law pass!"

A strong hand caught Tules's shoulder, and she looked up to see Ramón scowl. He muttered, "Get out of here." He pulled her outside, slapped her, and shoved her toward the dark trail. "Go home and stay there. Getting drunk with harlots. All of you are a bad lot from Manzano. I'll teach you to behave. . . ."

"Please, Ramón, let me explain . . ." she begged.

"I know about you. How Pedro gave you the wing in El Gallo, and you were promised to me. Caramba, there's no truth in women!" He shook her and sent her sprawling in the dark. "Get up and go home. If I see you with Pedro again, I will kill him. And if you talk to that Cuca I'll beat you until you can't lie down. . . ."

Tules sobbed as she threw herself on the sheepskin in the cave. One minute she dreaded Ramón's anger when he came home, and the next minute she trembled for fear he wouldn't come. If he fought Pedro in the cantina, Pedro would put the law on him. Pedro was an officer now and a friend of powerful politicians. There was no recourse against such a man. She wrung her hands and wished that she had never gone to the dance.

She hid in the cave when she saw Pedro coming to the claim next

95

to theirs the next day. After that he must have gone away, although her frightened eyes watched for him for a week. To be doubly safe, she went further down the cañón to search for black sand and told Ramón that it was easier for her to wash gold near the spring. He shrugged and went back to his blindfolded mule at the crushing mill, though he was discouraged with the trifling amount of money they made.

They bought expensive potatoes to save the highly taxed quicksilver they needed to extract gold. Tules split the potatoes, filled a hole in the center of each with the gold concentrate, and bound the halves together. She baked the potatoes in the ashes and found a small gold button inside. Then she carefully squeezed the potato pulp to recover the quicksilver and use it again.

"For all our hard work we make no profit," Ramón complained.

He was sullen and restless, and Tules crept into the chapel at the end of each day. She knelt in the shadows, held her brown arms outstretched as Luz had taught her, and longed for a candle to light before the Virgin. Perhaps then Our Lady would heed her prayers and send a child to fill her arms and keep Ramón's wandering heart at home. She could not believe Doña Prudencia's warning that God would punish them. He must know that they were too poor to be married by a padre.

That summer wildfire news flamed through the gulch that a vein of rich ore had been found on the mountain at the head of the cañón. It might not be the true mother lode, but at least it was a concentrated deposit of gold. Don Francisco Ortiz started a shaft into the breast of the mountain, and stories of the mine's riches soared to fabulous heights.

Ten leagues south of Sante Fe a Spanish King had given the Ortiz family land that included mountains, valleys, and an ever-flowing spring. At that time a mountain range, more or less, was not important in the wilderness of New Mexico, but a dependable source of water was of the utmost importance for grazing cattle. Don Francisco had built a home near the spring and lived peaceably in his isolated kingdom until gold brought the buscones in like a plague

96

of grasshoppers. Although he owned the land, the buscones knew that the old Spanish code gave them a right to any gold they found on their claims. Don Francisco protected himself by staking and working claims under his own name and those of his numerous relatives.

The operation of his mine was in charge of his father-in-law, Don Damasio López, a Spanish grandee with long mining experience. The first month's profit from the mine amounted to several balls of solid gold, a sizable sum when it was sold to the mint at Durango for 17.30 the troy ounce.

Any mining claim in the Spanish colonies had been called a "Real," or "Royalty," since the King automatically profited by one-fifth of all royalties. But the gold of the Incas and the silver of the Mexicans no longer supported Spanish Kings. Don Francisco was willing to send the required 3 per cent tax to the chaotic Federal Government in Mexico City, but he maneuvered to keep the rest of his wealth out of the greedy hands of local politicians. He took his gold shipments to Sante Fe under an armed escort and often paid the necessary graft money to the politicians' sturdy henchman, Pedro Bustamente.

Pedro rode in and out of the camp on his important business, but Tules managed to avoid him all but twice. The last time he met her on the narrow trail, laughed at her, and twisted his black moustache insolently. "I have not forgotten you, chiquita," he said. "I wish I could forget you, now that I am a man of affairs, but your beauty drives me wild. I know that you run from me and that gangling ox driver curses me. Pues, when I am ready, I will come for you."

That night Ramón grumbled, "I am no better than that mule at the crushing mill, plodding around day after day. He gets hay. I get beans. Caramba, this is no way to make money! We'll go to the mountains and stake another claim near the mine. Andrés says there are gold nuggets up there."

"María Santísima, I would be terrified to live alone high up on the mountain with the wild beasts," Tules cried.

97

"Stay here and watch your fine Pedro's claim then," Ramón sneered.

"Oh, no, chulo, I go where you go," Tules said quickly, dreading Pedro even more than the high mountain.

Ramón laughed, his black eyes shining with the old faith in a new plan. He kissed her with passion for the first time since the dance, and her eager body answered his urgency with the rapture of fulfilled love. When he slept she touched his cheek tenderly, loving him as her child as well as her man.

Ramón dug another cave on the sloping ridge of the mountain, and the autumn sun distilled the pungent, fragrant cedars, piñón, and long-needled pine around their doorstep. Tules was obsessed with the secret fear that the mountains would smother her. The cordilleras had been blue saw-toothed outlines beyond the safe distance of prairies, but now she lived under the rocky peaks. She told Ramón that she was afraid of wild, prowling beasts, and he made her try out the gun that always rested beside the door. She was thankful that old Celso had taught her to shoot.

They were poorer in gold but richer in happiness in their mountain cave. Ramón was quiet and steadied by the work at the mine, and Tules was happy that the Virgin had heard her prayers and they would have a child in the spring. As usual, Ramón's mind raced with a dozen new plans. He said the baby would be a boy, and they would name him Fabián for his father. They would send to Santa Fe for his sister, María, to help when the baby came. She would live with them and stake another claim.

Late one evening they went down the trail to the store and saw miners talking in small, excited groups. Ramón asked what had happened, and Crespín Meléndez threw up his hands.

"Por Dios, haven't you heard the bad news? The Government confiscated the mine today. The politicians remembered that old Expulsion Law and gave all foreigners notice to leave the country at once. They did it to get rid of Don Damasio and force Don Francisco to take them in as his partners. They want the gold. . . ."

"But Don Damasio is Don Francisco's father-in-law!" Ramón exclaimed.

"Yes, but he had to leave this afternoon. Pedro Bustamente brought soldiers from the capital, and Don Damasio fled to the frontier. Governor Manuel Armijo won't leave a foreigner in the province. He will also drive out the Yanquis, English, and French who trap beaver and work in the mines. It's Mexico for the Mexicans now!"

"Ojalá that means more for the rest of us!" one miner said.

"Válgame Dios, did you ever know a politician to throw a scrap to a dog?" Crespín demanded. "We will work harder for less pay until they starve us out. Don Damasio knew how to mine gold, but these políticos only know how to dig gold out of another man's pocket. I'm going to leave."

"But our claims . . ." the miner protested.

"Don't worry about that. If your claim has gold, some político will grab it. If you demand your rights, you will be thrown in a stinking jail. We are not so smart as Pedro Bustamente. He was a peón, but now he is a friend of the ricos. Our robber is a splendid fellow, say the thieves. . . ."

"Come on, Ramón." Tules pulled at his sleeve, and they bought a small sack of freckled beans in the store.

"This is bad luck. We may have to leave," Ramón said as they started up the trail. Tules was silent, and the night veiled the fear in her eyes.

# II

THE PANIC over the Expulsion Law died down when the work at the mine continued under the new management. The miners' perennial hopes rose again. Tomorrow they would find a big nugget, a rich pocket of gold, or the true mother lode.

Ramón worked in the deepening mine shaft, and his small weekly wages gave Tules comforting security. He accepted the pittance for the winter but talked of finding someone to grubstake him next summer. The bright future still beckoned with its lure of quick wealth in spite of Rafael's tragic fate.

Tules tried to make the cave tidy and comfortable. She leveled the dirt floor, sprinkled and tamped it until it was smooth under their sheepskin. They slept with their heads toward the back of the cave and their feet toward the fire. Ramón had made a good rubble chimney this time and spread a weather-tight layer of mud over the cedar posts that closed the front of the cave. He built a doorframe and promised to hang a solid wooden door before winter. In the dry fall weather Tules was glad to have the sunshine pour through the open doorway. She was content with the cave except for its darkness. She hated the dark and the sharp, towering mountains.

They set the stakes for their new claim on the rocky slope in front of the door. There were other stakes below and around them, but no one worked at them now. Gold panning would not begin again until there was melted snow.

Their nearest neighbors lived at the foot of the long downhill trail. Tules's lonely eyes watched for the smoke from their chimneys, and she stopped to talk to the women before she started up the trail with the jar of water on her head. She missed the comfort of solid adobe walls and friendly, familiar faces. She felt deserted in the strange, high stillness and jumped when she heard a twig crack.

100

She held her breath for fear an Apache, a slinking mountain cat, or a wolf would creep out from behind a jutting rock. She kept within sight of Ramón's gun beside their door when she searched for black sand or pebbles of gold.

A light November snow had powdered the mountains during the night and left shreds of torn clouds between the peaks. The heavy frost had opened the piñón cones, and the tiny, sweet nuts had fallen to the ground. After midday Tules went out to gather nuts and raised her head quickly when she heard a rustling sound. She smiled when she saw a squirrel with quick, bright eyes and an arrogant tail.

"Get away, you thief," she called to him. "You want to steal my piñones and carry them off in your fat cheeks. You look like Doña Prudencia. Maybe some witch changed her into a squirrel. If you weren't so pretty, I'd shoot you and make a warm cap for my baby."

The squirrel frisked away, and she sang to herself as she stooped to gather nuts. The good sun warmed her aching back. She didn't mind the pain for the proud joy of carrying her child. Ramón, too, was happy with plans for his son. He had been kind and gentle since they moved up the mountain.

Her fingers were sticky with pitch and dirt as she picked the nuts out of the black loam. The piñones were as small and brown as coffee berries, and the afternoon shadows lengthened as she filled her sack. She wanted to store a large sackful to crack before the winter fire.

She reached eagerly for an unopened cone—there would, be many nuts in that. Her fingers picked it up, but it was not a cone. She felt it and thought it was a stone, but it was too heavy. She tested its solid weight and peered at it. Could it—María Santísima!—could it be a nugget? She weighed it in her hands, one trembling palm holding the other. She held it close and stared at it. Madre de Dios, it was so heavy it must be a nugget! She couldn't believe it, but she clutched it tight between her palms. Then she breathlessly opened her hands and stared at it again. Could that dark lump be solid gold?

She raced into the cave and slopped the jar of water over the rock. It was the size of a bantam's egg and heavy. She rubbed at the wet surface and held her breath. She scratched at the wet dirt and saw a yellow gleam. It was a nugget. It was gold! Solid gold! She pressed it against her pounding heart, threw herself on the sheepskin, and sobbed with delirious joy.

She sat up and stared at the nugget again, scratched it, weighed it, kissed it. Ramón—she must tell Ramón. But women brought bad luck to men underground, and no woman was allowed in the mine. How could she wait until Ramón came home?

How his eyes would shine at this wonderful find! They would have a feast. They would eat and eat—beef, pork, even chicken! They would have bread—loaves and loaves of crusty bread! And sweets— brown sugar, dried grapes, apples, custards with rich cream, cakes, wine!

And moccasins so that her feet wouldn't be frostbitten this winter—no, silly, fine slippers like Doña Carmen's! And warm, heavy shawls! And dresses—green silk and blue brocade and changeable taffeta the color of flame. And fine suits for Ramón and boots and a hat with silver tassels. And long white dresses with insets of lace for the baby! Dios, it was wonderful to be rich!

Maybe there was another nugget. Maybe the mountainside was thick with nuggets hidden among the cones. She ran out to the piñón shrubs near the door and scratched in the dry needles like a hungry dog. Darkness settled like heavy smoke as she sifted the dirt between her fingers.

"Hola, Tules!" Ramón called as he came up the trail. "Did you bury a bone?"

She ran to him, trembling with excitement as the words spilled out. He didn't believe her at first. He took the rock, felt it, rubbed it, poured water on it, and tested it with his teeth. He held it close to the flames in the fireplace and stared at the gleaming yellow facet.

"Jesucristo!" he breathed. "It's solid gold!"

They talked at the same time, hardly listening to each other, glutted with their find.

"Come, we will go to the store and weigh it," Ramón said at last.

"Dios, it gets heavier all the time! It must be worth a thousand pesos."

Ramón shouted their good fortune to everyone they passed. A horde of long-haired, excited miners followed them into the store. The eagle-eyed clerk scoffed at the news and let them wait while he measured out a poke of sugar. Finally he took the rock from Ramón, felt it, rubbed it, and squinted at it in the candlelight. Then he poured water on it and rubbed it on his pants. He looked at the uniform color and nodded. A long, released sigh escaped from the crowd.

While he balanced the weights for the two brass saucers used for weighing gold, Don Francisco Ortiz, Pedro Bustamente, and two men in fine military uniforms came into the store. The wildfire news of a big nugget had penetrated the patrón's thick walls.

The crowd made way for Don Francisco and the políticos. With accustomed authority, Don Francisco picked up the nugget and chipped at its surface with his long fingernail. He tossed it in his hand as he questioned Ramón. Pedro prompted him to ask exactly where Tules had found the nugget, the location of his claim, and how long they had lived on it. Tules watched Ramón's smiling face as he answered freely, convinced of his wealth by Don Francisco's interest.

"Do you wish to see it, General?" Don Francisco asked. He handed the nugget to a strapping, handsome man in a gold-braided coat. Someone whispered that he was General Manuel Armijo, Governor of New Mexico.

Tules watched the General like a cat as he weighed the nugget in his hand and nodded. She saw Cuca raise herself on tiptoe to look over his shoulder at the nugget. Other women with painted faces watched the men. The store was crowded to the doors. Tules breathed more easily when the General handed the nugget back to Don Francisco.

"Would you like to lock it in my chest tonight?" he asked Ramón. "It will be safer there. When you come tomorrow, we will weigh it and see how much it will bring at the mint."

"A thousand thanks, no, señor," Ramón smiled boyishly and held out an eager hand. "I—I want to keep it tonight."

"You're the first man who wants to sleep with gold," Pedro sneered. "Usually it's the women . . ."

"As you please," Don Francisco tossed the nugget to Ramón. "It would be safer here. Your wife had good luck. May it continue. Until tomorrow then. . . . Adiós!"

When the patrón and his friends left the crowd closed in around Ramón and Tules.

"They'll take your claim now, you'll see," an old man croaked.

"You're as cheerful as a buzzard, grandfather. This isn't the Day of the Dead when you rattle skeletons at a feast," the miners shouted. "Ramón's nugget is worth five thousand, maybe ten thousand pesos. It's good luck for all of us. Come, let's see where Tules found it. We'll find more nuggets. Gold, solid gold! Ay, qué caray, hombres!"

The ragged, chattering crowd clambered up the trail and trampled the dirt in front of the cave. Tules pointed to the spot where she found the nugget and repeated every detail again. The men built a bonfire and lit pitch-wood torches to search the ground, but they found nothing.

"We will come back with the first dawn," they laughed. "Tonight we will celebrate. . . ."

"We have no wine," Ramón apologized.

"Of course not, but tomorrow you will have plenty. Come, we will go to the cantina and drink to your good fortune. Lead the way, amigo."

"Ramón, I can't go. The excitement and all made me sick at my stomach. The baby . . ." Tules whispered and caught Ramón's arm. "You go, and I'll stay here. But let me have the nugget. Don't spend it tonight. . . ."

Ramón hesitated, annoyed with any halt to his excitement.

"Give it to her," Andrés said. "It's hers. She found it. Tonight the drinks are on us. Tomorrow you can buy us champagne."

Ramón shrugged, put the nugget in Tules's hand, and started ahead. Friends held his arms, singing, cheering, laughing. Tules watched the flaming torches bob merrily down the dark trail toward the orange light of the cantina windows. She looked up at the sharp, black peaks against the star-studded sky and the cold silver radiance of the full moon.

She went inside the cave and looked at the nugget in the moonlight that streamed through the open doorway. She kissed it, stroked it, and held it against her hot cheek. Then she slipped it down below her breasts to warm safety between her body and the tight fold of her sash. She stretched her trembling legs on the sheepskin and relaxed with deep thankfulness. She fell asleep saying an extra "Ave Maria."

She dreamed that she wore elegant bright green satin and sat at a table lighted with a hundred candles and laden with warm, savory food. When she started to serve herself, the platters were whisked away. She tried to order the servants to wait, but she could not speak. . . .

"Hola! Tules!" a man's voice woke her.

"Ramón?" she called sleepily.

"Por Dios, you live like a rabbit in a hole!" the man said. She saw the silhouette of a wide, peaked hat in the doorway.

"Pedro!" she gasped and scrambled to her knees.

"Of course!" he laughed. "I told you I would come. I saw you in the store tonight. I have something to tell you, chiquita. Come out where I can see your eyes in the moonlight."

"Go away!" Tules cried.

"Oh, no. Your brave husband is drinking in the cantina and talking more than he should. He swears that you have the nugget. Let me see it. Come out, or I'll come in after you. . . ."

Tules crept noiselessly over the dirt floor and felt for the gun beside the doorway. No, if she shot Pedro, she and Ramón would be thrown in jail. She must think of some other way. Trembling, she stood up and held to the doorframe. In the moonlight she saw the stocky outline of Pedro's figure, one foot in the shining black boots negligently propped on a tree stump.

"That's better, chiquita, though your beauty is lost in the dark,"

Pedro said, as he looked at her frightened face. "Never mind. I'll see you in the light of many candles from now on. We'll make a good pair, living in style in the capital."

"What?"

"But of course, chiquita. Don't you know that I own this claim? All these claims are staked for me or my cousins or Don Francisco. We must protect ourselves so near the mine. I let that pelado of yours dig the cave to see him sweat. Now he can go back to his oxen. With this nugget, I'll be a rich man. . . ."

"You haven't worked your claim here. The nugget is ours. . . ."

"Yes, ours. Yours and mine. I don't know why I share it with a barefoot beggar when I could have any rich girl in the Province. But I can't forget you. You led me on at Manzano, and I made a fool of myself. Now I will have you. . . ."

"No," she cried and backed into the cave as Pedro came toward her.

His strong hands pinned her arms as he rubbed his rough chin against her cheek and kissed her neck. She smelled strong brandy on his hot breath. She twisted and turned, but his hands were like a vise. She butted his head away from her breast.

"Quiet there, my wild mare. I'll have to tame you," he laughed as his hand thrust under the loose neck of her blouse. "Ah, skin as smooth as bishop's satin! And firm, round breasts."

"Stop, Pedro!" she screamed, trying to wrench away.

"What's this? The nugget so warm and happy against your heart? Now it goes into Pedro's pocket for safekeeping. Our beautiful nugget . . ."

"Thief! Bully! Coward!" she spat at him. She caught the tip of his ear between her teeth and bit savagely.

"That's enough from you, you fool! You forget your manners." Pedro jerked his head away and hit the angle of her jaw with his fist. She swayed with dizziness and reached for the wall of the cave.

He caught her to him and exulted, "I have you at last. You thought you could rouse me and then run off with a dumb ox driver. No one can laugh at Pedro Bustamente. I swore I'd have you and

106

now . . ." He strangled her limp body in his powerful arms and kissed her with passionate triumph. She moaned as he forced her to the floor.

She was dazed and helpless against his strength in the blind darkness of the cave. Out of the blackness she dimly heard a man's tipsy voice floating up the cañón. He sang the serenade in happy abandon, his high falsetto slurring the words. That was Ramón. Her mind cleared quickly, and her body stiffened with fright as she saw the danger ahead. Ramón would find Pedro here, kill him. Then they would arrest Ramón, hang him. She must get Pedro out.

"Listen," she whispered. "Ramón is coming. You must go."

"What?" Pedro mumbled, drowsy after brandy and passion. He raised his head and heard the wavering song. His body tensed as he jumped up and tightened his pistol belt. He sneered, "Your brave Ramón will soon sing another song. . . ."

"Pedro, Ramón will kill you if he finds you here," she pleaded. "Slip out the door and around the back. Hurry."

"Kill me?" Pedro scoffed. "I am the best shot in the Province. His aim is no good, and besides he is drunk. I will tell him to get off my claim now instead of tomorrow."

"Pedro, I beg you, wait until tomorrow. Go now. I promise . . ."

"Stay where you are," he ordered, as he stepped to one side of the door and looked down the trail.

Tules cowered on the sheepskin and begged the good God to send Ramón back to the cantina. Her heart pounded like thunder in her ears, and her throat closed. She pressed her hands over her ears, closed her eyes tight, and prayed. Then she heard Ramón's voice, thick with wine, shout, "It's a lie! She's my wife! This is my claim, my gold! Get away from my door, you swine!"

"You'll find out whose claim it is tomorrow, you drunken fool," Pedro called insultingly. "You can go peaceably now or . . . Don't touch your gun, cabrón! I warn you. . . ."

A shot rang into the still night. Tules clapped her hand over her mouth to keep from screaming and crawled to the door. Pedro stood below the door with his pistol in his hand. In the clear moonlight she saw Ramón's body twisted on the trail. His hand reached toward the gun beside him, and she heard him groan. He was wounded. She must get to him. She froze in horror and forced herself not to move yet, not to cry out. She must not tempt Pedro to shoot again. She looked wildly down the cañón, wanting to scream for help. But no one would dare arrest Pedro. He would shoot Ramón again, then turn on her. She must be quiet to help Ramón.

Ramón's body was still now. Pedro stood a little below her with his back to her. He was arrogantly alive as he watched and waited. His peaked hat shaded his eyes, and his hand held the pistol. Jesucristo! He had killed her Ramón, yet he stood there, gloating. . . .

She jerked erect with blazing anger. Then she stooped and reached for the gun inside the door. She lifted it noiselessly and took steady aim at the back of Pedro's head. She pulled the trigger. The noise reverberated in the cave, and the smell of gunpowder choked her. She slipped another bullet in the gun and looked out. Pedro sprawled on his face on the ground. His hat rolled away; the pistol had fallen from his hand. She watched the convulsive twitch of his shining boots.

She moved toward him, holding the gun with hands that shook now. He did not move. She shuddered as she looked at the blood oozing from what had been the back of his head. Moonlight caught the silver buttons down his dark, tight pants and the elaborate white scrolls on his jacket. He had been proud of his fine clothes and secure power. He had risen above them to jeer at their poverty, rape her, and cheat Ramón.

Ramón! She must save him. She dropped the gun inside the door and ran down the trail. Ramón had fallen on his back, one leg caught under him. His face was beautiful and clear in the moonlight. She caught his lolling head against her breast and kissed his lips. Her arms strained around him to push back death. "Ramón! Ramón!" she cried. "Don't leave me. You must live. Merciful God, save him. . . ."

She pulled open his shirt and felt for his heart. Her hand touched thick, warm blood. There was no heartbeat, no breath. She buried

108

her face against his lifeless shoulder and sobbed, "Ramón, Ramón, come back. . . ."

"Hola! Hola, Ramón! What is it?" she heard men call. Their anxious voices raced ahead of them as they ran up the trail.

They would see that she had killed Pedro. They would find her, and she would rot in jail. Ramón couldn't help now. She must run, hide. She kissed Ramón swiftly and ran up the dark mountainside like a hunted coyote. She heard the voices come closer, calling Ramón. She was afraid of making a sound as she crawled into the deep shadow under a jutting rock. The footsteps stopped, and she tried to make out what the men said. She heard them exclaim, "Ramón!" and "Pedro!" and then they called her name. They called again, louder, and the sound echoed against the mountain. An icy wave of terror shook her. She heard branches snap as they searched for her.

After a time they stopped calling and started down the trail. Their footsteps were slow now. They carried two bodies.

Mother of God, they are taking Ramón away. My Ramón. He will never come home to me again. They will bury him like a beggar without absolution. At least he should have a Christian burial. If I had the nugget he would have a decent grave. And I could buy my freedom. If I had only thought to take the nugget from Pedro's pocket. But I couldn't touch Pedro. . . .

A wave of sick revulsion passed over her as she thought of his shattered head. Murder. She had killed him. Then she burned as she remembered how he had forced her an hour ago. If he had lived he would have gloated that he had gotten rid of Ramón. After he had satisfied himself with her body, he would have kicked her out like a dog. She had avenged herself and Ramón. "Oh, Ramón, forgive me," she prayed.

But there was no time for grief or blame. They would send soldiers to search for her now. She must get away, leave before dawn. She would hide in the mountains, hide from soldiers and Apaches and wolves. Then try to reach Manzano? No, not Doña Prudencia again. She would go to María in Santa Fe. María would help her for Ramón's sake. Get to Santa Fe some way.

The moon had dropped behind the mountains. The cañón was black with a sinister, watching stillness. She listened for every small sound as she crept carefully toward the deserted cave. She felt her way over the doorsill and reached for the blue silk reboso hanging over the pole. She spread it out and hurriedly packed her other skirt and blouse and the little statue of San Antonio. She took a stack of tortillas from the fireplace and found the gun. She would need them for the weeks alone in the mountains.

What was that? Footsteps coming to the door? Was it already too late to run? Madre de Dios, help me! If they find me now . . . She froze still as she heard a woman's voice call, "Tooo-les! Tooo-les! Where are you?"

She crouched lower and held her breath. Her heart beat too loudly, and she tried to smother it. Who was it? A neighbor who looked for a reward? A friend of Pedro's?

"Tules, answer me, wherever you are," the woman called again, and a shawled head looked through the door. "It's Cuca. I am alone. I have come to help you. . . ."

"Thanks be to the merciful God," Tules gasped and wiped the cold sweat from her forehead.

"Hurry, Tules. You must get away before dawn," Cuca said. "They found that Ramón had not fired his gun. They say you killed Pedro because he took the nugget from you. Don Francisco found it in Pedro's pocket. No matter if Pedro stole it, they will throw you in jail for killing him. You know how they are. . . . They will scour the mountains for you as soon as it is light."

"Madre de Dios, help me! If I could get to Santa Fe . . ." Tules begged.

"That's what I planned. A caravan leaves for Santa Fe at dawn. Get what you need, but be quick. You must go. . . . I know the sergeant, and he will take you to girls I know."

"I want to go to Ramón's sister, María."

"All right. I didn't mean that you must stay in the house," Cuca said bitterly.

"Oh, Cuca, why do you do this for me?" Tules cried. "It is dangerous. If they find you helped me . . ."

"I can take care of myself. We were friends in the old days. You wouldn't believe it, but I always tried to help you. You were young. . . . Anyway, I'm glad you killed that upstart Pedro. Quick, put this dark shawl over your head. I'll take your bundle. Keep to the right and away from the trail. Hurry. Dawn is coming."

Light was rising like a mist as they slipped down the mountain. Tules darted from one dark shrub to another. Near the bottom Cuca whispered, "Wait under the bank of the arroyo until I come." Tules shuddered and tried to flatten herself out of sight against the sand bank.

"Come quickly," Cuca called. "This is a shipment of wool, but Don Francisco's gold is hidden in the woolsacks. It will be safe with the military escort. The sergeant's name is Julio. You can trust him. You will get to Santa Fe after dark. He will find the house of your sister-in-law. . . ."

"Oh, Cuca, you are so good," Tules sobbed.

"Quick. There is no time to talk." Cuca pushed her. "The fourth carreta. Climb in while the men are harnessing the mules. Get down between the sacks. Courage, child, you will soon be safe. Here are two pesos. Go with God. . . ."

Cuca boosted her over the solid wheel, and Tules climbed down between the woolsacks. She pulled one over her head and remembered how she had hidden in the Taos carreta. She was sick with fear when she heard men's voices close to her. Then the wheels creaked, and the caravan started. She shuddered and pressed both hands over her mouth to smother her anguish.

# Part Four: Santa Fe 1829-1846

# 12

MARÍA LIVED in one small room in a dark courtyard. She opened her door to the unexpected knock and welcomed the frightened girl calmly. María was small and thin and moved like a flitting shadow. Her brown face was deeply pock-marked and stamped with a serene resignation that made her seem older than her thirty years. Her dark eyes filled with sympathy as Tules sobbed out her story.

"We will pray for the souls of Ramón and Pedro," María said without reproach. "You must stay inside for a time. Dolores is far enough away for the políticos to forget about this, especially since they have gotten the mine. The neighbors are humble people, and you will be safe here with me. And in the spring, God willing, Ramón's child will bless our home."

María hurried to her stall in the market each morning, and Tules huddled beside the fire. The room was poorly furnished, but María had pointed out her two treasures—a red geranium in a pot and a saint's statue in the wall niche. Tules kept the fire going with one stick at a time, knowing that María's small earnings did not cover her generous hospitality. She watched the blaze, moaned for Ramón, and cried until her eyes were as dry as her heart.

At first she was terrified of being discovered, but no one came near the door. She did not go outside until February, when María insisted that she must go to mass and touch her sore throat with the water blessed for San Blas Day. The next night María peered into Tules's reddened throat and shook her head.

"Tomorrow I will bring the curandera to vaccinate you. The same medicine might have saved my family when they died of the black smallpox three years ago. Thanks be to God some colonists have come from Mexico with fresh scabs. Before they left Chihuahua the first man was vaccinated. Then they took the matter from his scab for the next man and the next until they brought this cure to Santa Fe."

In spite of Tules's protests María brought Tía Apolonia with the vaccine. She was the midwife and doctor of the poor, a small, energetic woman with gray hair pulled into a tight knot and cheeks as round and rosy as apples. Her bright blue eyes, fair skin, and high color made her look like an alien among her olive-skinned patients, but all of them confided in her and called her "Auntie."

She looked at Tules sharply but made no comment as she scratched the arm. María called her again when Tules's arm throbbed and she burned with fever. Tía Apolonia nodded with satisfaction, warned María to stuff the door cracks against the winter cold, and agreed to deliver Tules's baby in May.

The news of a relative in María's house brought a neighbor to the door the next week. Tules opened it fearfully to La Casimira, whose long nose was sharpened by curiosity. La Casimira retailed gossip with the hope of learning more news and found that her greasy pack of cards was the easiest way to gain confidences.

"Let me tell your fortune," she offered, scenting tragedy in Tules's pale face. "With your youth, good looks, and red hair you should have good cards. I'll wager the cards next to you will be a light man, love, and money."

She spread the cards on the floor, peered at them, and asked sharply, "Why should you have the death cards around you?"

The freckles stood out on Tules's cheeks as her face blanched, but she shrugged and shook her head. Her lips were sealed over her secret, and La Casimira left with mumbled incantations about the bad luck in the room.

"This black magic of running the cards belongs to the devil," María scolded gently when she heard of La Casimira's visit. "God does not intend weak mortals to guess at His will. La Casimira is said to be a witch. Anyway, she is malicious if she turns against you, and

113

it is best to keep her as a friend. But remember, child, that silence reaps what loose talk sows."

La Casimira made some neighborly excuse to come in every day, and Tules welcomed this diversion to her sad, monotonous thoughts. The death cards appeared every time in Tules's fortune, and La Casimira finally refused to lay out the cards. Tules was relieved, but she persuaded La Casimira to give her an old pack of cards. She practiced the card tricks Alfredo had taught her and soon astonished La Casimira with her skill. To all questions Tules only told of her days in Taos and let the neighbor believe that she had come directly from Taos this winter.

Tules filled in the lonely hours of each day shuffling, dealing, and laying out the cards for monte. She memorized where her fingers placed certain cards in the deck and drew them out with deft skill. She dealt over and over to imaginary bets and remembered her hungry anger when she had lost the tostón on the monte table at Dolores. The cards fascinated her, and she wished again that she could be a dealer.

At night she helped María prepare the tamales she sold at her stall in the market. Tules stirred the thick corn-meal mush, filled the cornhusk wrappers with it, and added chile and meat in the center. María tied them with a swift twist and boiled them for an hour. While they worked María told of the rivalry of petty vendors where bitter poverty brought out greed and cruelty one day and spendthrift generosity the next.

But María was more concerned with her devout religion than with market gossip. Tules listened with awe as María spoke of her strong, simple faith, so unlike the gluttonous lip service of Doña Prudencia. One night María pinched her earnings and bought Tules a candle to light before her San Antonio. "When a holy guest comes to live with us we must show him honor," she said. "Besides, you will need his help soon."

Tules nodded as she listened to the May wind. It swept the hard blue sky clean of clouds and denied them spring rains. Angry dust devils danced over the parched ground and sifted fine dust into every crevice. The cottonwoods had put out small timid leaves, and the peach trees were bright with pink blossoms, but everyone said that the drought and the late frosts would nip them. The birth of spring was a joyless travail.

For the humble people who lived close to the earth, no water meant no food. The irrigation ditches were dry, and only a few seeds sprouted in frightened patches in the fields. The pobres groaned that drought would bring high prices and starvation. Even the Government storehouse near the Palace, formerly filled with grain to be distributed in time of need, was now a customhouse for the important new trade coming over the Santa Fe Trail.

"Adversity is God's way of bringing people back to their faith," María said. "Tonight we will pray in the fields."

"In the fields?" Tules questioned.

"Yes, niña, tomorrow is May 15, the feast of the farmer's San Isidro. He brought the water to the roots of the sprouting corn and plowed the fields so the farmer could go to mass. We will take San Isidro to the fields to show him the drought and pray for rain. We will go to vespers now and join the procession later.

"Oh no, María, the políticos might find me," Tules shrank back and touched her swollen body. "I don't want people to see me this way."

"The políticos have forgotten everything now," María soothed her. "Besides, they don't go to the fields; but all the pregnant women must go. God has shown His love with their increase, and their feet bring fertility to the earth."

"No, please, María," Tules begged. "I haven't been out for so long. I am still afraid. . . . You know the baby should come this week. Today the pains have been worse in my back, and I am so heavy I can hardly walk."

"Tía Apolonia said the walk would be good for you," María said firmly. "She will march at the head of the procession. We can't pay her, so we must do as she says."

"María, you have been so good, and I have put these burdens on you," Tules cried. "If you would take that blue silk reboso to the

115

store, you could sell it for enough to pay Tía Apolonia and have some money left over for yourself. . . ."

"No, it was Doña Carmen's, God save her! It is all you have left. We will manage," María said. "This is very little for me to do for Ramón's baby, when I am to be his godmother, and he will have my father's name. It was a lonely room before you came, niña. There's the bell for vespers. Ave Maria, Madre de Dios. Come, we must hurry. Your shawl will cover you."

The sky was a clear green, and the reflected yellow sunset gilded the town as they hurried through the plaza to the parroquia. After vespers they marched slowly through the dusty streets. María nudged Tules to notice the bulge under the shawls of many women and whispered that at least there would be a good crop of babies.

Tía Apolonia marched ahead carrying the statue of the Santo Niño. The Christ child wore a velvet cape, a hat with a pink plume, and carried a tiny basket of flowers and the tiny shoes he needed for his many errands of mercy. Behind him four women carried a square board on their shoulders supporting the large figure of San Isidro and his diminutive oxen. The procession stopped before one house where Tía Apolonia sprinkled incense on a shovelful of glowing coals, and the aromatic fumes filled the evening air.

Beyond the chapel of San Miguel they came to the fields, and Tules stumbled over ground that had been plowed with a forked tree branch and planted in corn hills. The women lowered the saints to let them feel the parched earth. Then they marched across the rough fields chanting. The women's high voices rose and fell, and the men's deep bass carried fervent supplication. They beseeched the golden-bearded San Isidro to spare them from locusts and earthquakes and remind God to send them torrents of rain. They sang

San Isidro labrador
Liberta nuestros sembrados
De langostas y temblores.

San Isidro, barbas de oro,
Ruega a Dios
Que llueva a chorros.

116

Tules listened to the chanting and forgot her terror and the pain in her heavy, awkward body. They passed a large cross set up to bless the fields, and she looked up at the high, clear canopy of the evening sky. She breathed deeply of the fresh spring air, and for the first time in six months, she felt at peace. The child turned within her body, and a wave of exaltation passed over her. Soon she would hold her son in her arms. She had never owned anything in her life, but the baby would be hers. How she would work for him! She would give him an education, training, money, and he would become a great man.

At dawn she was awakened by strange pains. María built up the fire, heated stones to put at Tules's back, and ran for Tía Apolonia. The midwife brewed a hot herb tea and made Tules walk around. She sent María off to the market and promised to watch Tules during the day. Tules paced the floor as she counted the pains and dozed by the fire in the afternoon. She dreamed that the Bibirón was strangling her and screamed. She wept with relief when Tía Apolonia came in.

"Don't scare María with your long face," the midwife said cheerfully. "You are young and strong, and you will be doing the washing in four days. First babies take a longer time. You are no different from a million other women. It's God's plan for women to suffer. The Bible says 'in sorrow shalt thou bring forth children.' Drink a sip of this Pass brandy, and I'll give you atole to strengthen you."

Tules caught her breath each time the pains shot through her, but she managed to smile when María came home.

"Light the candle I brought for your San Antonio," María said as she pulled Tules up from the floor. "I sold all the tamales today, and that is a good sign."

"Dios te salve, María . . ." Tules screamed. "My body is breaking. It's tearing me apart. Oh, Madre de Dios. . . ."

Two neighbor women, Carlota López and Lourdes Tapia, came back with Tía Apolonia and shook their heads as they watched Tules bite her lips in agony. Her eyes closed as the pain caught her, and she opened them wide in terror of the next onslaught. María sat on

117

the floor, held Tules's head in her lap, and moistened her swollen lips. Tía Apolonia whispered to the neighbors, and they left hurriedly.

"Mamá! Mamacita!" Tules called. "Help me, help me! This is Pedro's curse. It is because he came to me. . . . Now he will kill me, because I killed him. . . ."

"Hush, niña," María put her hand over Tules's lips and turned to the midwife. "She is out of her head. This is some evil dream. . . ."

"I hear more than the Father Confessor, but no word passes my lips." Tía Apolonia made a tight mouth.

The neighbors returned carrying their statues of the Virgin of Guadalupe, San Ramón Nonnato, the Santo Niño, and San Isidro with his small oxen. They placed them on a box at Tules's feet so the saints could see how much their help was needed. Carlota took San Antonio from his niche and put him close to Tules's tortured body.

When the full morning light came Tía Apolonia's cheeks had lost their high color, and her lips tightened to a worried line.

"Shall we call the padre?" María whispered.

"He would let the mother die to save the baby." Tía Apolonia pushed back her gray hair.

"There's the French doctor who lives with Juan Escolle on the plaza." Carlota suggested the only doctor in the Province.

"What does he know about childbirth?" Tía Apolonia turned on her fiercely. "You could not have a man—and a stranger at that—take care of a woman at this time. It would not be decent. No man belongs here. María must hold her under the arms, and you two pull her hands. If that does not help, we will call the padre."

Tules cried out, "Let me die! Let me die! Take it away! Oh, Ramón, help me! Mother of God, help me!" Then she sank into exhausted stupor.

The women had been too busy to notice that clouds had darkened the noonday light, and they jumped when there was a clap of thunder. The wind and rain banged the door, and the roof leaked. They lifted Tules as gently as they could and moved her to a dry spot. A tremor shook her body, and she screamed. It was like the high, in-human cry of a mountain cat.

"Thanks be to God," Tía Apolonia said as she leaned over her patient. "But—quick, María. Help me work some breath into this boy."

She spanked the buttocks, moved the tiny arms and legs, and forced her breath into the baby's mouth. She listened for the heart and shook her head.

"We must baptize him quickly. You know the name, María?" She dipped her fingers in the bowl of water quivering in María's hand and made the sign of the cross, "Fabián Ramón, in the name of the Father, the Son, and the Holy Ghost."

Carlota and Lourdes began the death wail, but Tía Apolonia quieted them. She handed the baby to María and said, "Wash him while I take care of her. Lourdes, hand me the pot with the dedalera leaves. That will strengthen her heart."

After some time the stimulant took effect, and Tules opened heavy eyes. She stared at the women dully, and then an anxious question flickered over her drawn face.

María brushed the tears from her own thin face, knelt beside Tules, and patted her cheek. "A boy, niña. We baptized him Fabián Ramón. He was—dead. It is God's will. . . ."

Slow comprehension came into Tules's tired eyes. "Let me see him," she whispered. She touched the small, new body and turned her face to the wall.

"It is more expensive for pobres to die than to be born," Tía Apolonia said in a practical tone. "Shall we take him there—beyond the fields?"

"Not bury him in consecrated ground?" María was shocked.

"That will cost forty pesos," Tía Apolonia said.

"Forty pesos! Yes, I remember now. I will never have forty pesos in my life. But he must lie in the campo santo," María said anxiously.

"Leave him in the church," Carlota suggested. "The padres will have to bury him in holy ground if they find the body in the church, and no one claims him."

"That is best." Tía Apolonia nodded.

They told Tules what they planned to do, and she moaned and shook her damp head as she watched them bundle her son into a square of white cloth. She called feebly to María, "Get the blue reboso and wrap him in it."

"Oh, no, Tules . . ." María protested.

"Yes, get my blue reboso. He will be cold," Tules insisted.

"Dios de mi vida, how beautiful it is!" Lourdes exclaimed when María unfolded the lustrous sky-blue silk. "That will buy a dozen masses. The padres will think it is the son of some rica. . . ."

"Tules, I don't want to do this." María hesitated.

"Yes, yes, it is my reboso. I want my baby wrapped up warm. It is all I have to give him. Oh, Mother of God, why did you take my baby?" Her words ended in a high, stricken wail.

"Don't upset her. She is burning with fever," Tía Apolonia warned. "Next week she will regret it, but we must do as she wants now. She will never bear another child. It will soon be dark, and I will leave him in the church."

When Tía Apolonia opened the door the smell of clean, fresh rain rushed into the close room. A torrent of water had cut the road in front of the house, and brittle branches littered the ground. Tía Apolonia held the little body wrapped in the blue reboso under her shawl and stepped carefully over the shining pools of water as she started up the road.

# 13

Tía Apolonia's herbs failed to give Tules strength after long weeks of fever. She huddled alone in the one room, grieving over the loss of her baby and Ramón. María said the baby was "one more little angel," but that was no comfort for Tules's empty arms. She appreciated María's strong faith and resignation, but she could not accept it. The extra expense of the year worried her, but María petted her and told her to rest until her pale face filled out.

The ricos lived near the protection of the Palace, but the homes of the pobres straggled to the edge of town. Their houses were built close together on the narrow streets and opened into courtyards in the rear. María lived in one of these at the end of the Calle San Francisco and met her neighbors as they drew water from the common well. They were poor, friendly people who ran in and out to look after Tules and bring her small treats.

La Casimira came in every day, thankful to find a welcome fireside. People usually avoided her dark, brooding eyes for she was a solitary woman who was said to be a witch. Girls came to her for love potions and charms and more than once she was accused of bewitching some poor soul with her powerful brujería. María shook her head and said that La Casimira was half-crazed and possessed by a devil for some old sin. Carlota insisted that the slinking woman took the shape of a cat, prowled by night, and looked into windows. La Casimira always moved with the stealth of a cat and scratched with her malicious claws. She liked to bask with half-closed eyes by Tules's fire and mix her gossip with tales of witches, incantations, good and bad omens, charms, and potions.

Tules threw out the vile-smelling brews La Casimira brought and was not afraid of the witch. She believed that she had already suffered the worst of bad fortune when she lost Ramón and the baby.

She nodded silently when La Casimira said the bad cards meant the baby's death and predicted a good future. Tules thought she had never revealed her secret, but La Casimira's sharp nose sniffed at sudden exclamations or the expressions on the girl's face. With these she pieced out the story of the double murder at Dolores and locked it in her tortured mind until she had use for it.

Tules might have heeded María's warnings if it had not been for the fascination of the cards. She left the fortunetelling to La Casimira, but she loved to shuffle and stack her own deck. Her hands were long and supple and had an extra sense for sleight-of-hand tricks. She practiced by the hour and baffled La Casimira by bringing out four aces or four knaves or by slipping the winning card off the top when she was dealing from the bottom.

The witch tried the tricks, but her hands were not so quick and sensitive. Every day Tules laid out the cards for monte, dealt from the bottom, and won. They played with colored kernels of corn and wished that they had money to play at the monte tables on the plaza. Tules was sure that she could win and repay all María's expenses.

"But you should deal monte," La Casimira said. "You could make a fortune."

"Doña Carmen used to say that," Tules said ruefully. "But how can I deal when I haven't a tostón of my own? I could win if I had someone to stake me. Ay de mí, I'll never have a chance!"

La Casimira slunk out one day when Tía Apolonia walked in. She opened the door wide to let the fresh air drive out the evil spirits and shook her head. Her clear blue eyes looked straight at Tules, and her firm mouth set in a straight line.

"That bruja worries María and does you no good," she said. "You have shut yourself in this room for a year. You are well enough now to get to work. María has done enough. . . . She is spoiling you, as she did her brother. You said Doña Prudencia taught you to make soap. That is a good staple, and you can make it and sell it at the market."

Tía Apolonia bargained at the slaughter pens for tallow, helped Tules boil it with the lye from wood ashes and pat it into balls of

122

common gray soap. She arranged for a stall near María's and took Tules to the market the first morning. Tules had been alone so long that she was afraid of the noisy crowds. She kept her reboso drawn over her face as she sat on her heels behind her straw mat and hardly spoke to the two or three people who stopped to buy soap. After a month her sales were so small that she wept with discouragement.

"Stop sniffling," Tía Apolonia scolded. "No wonder you don't sell anything with your face covered as though you had the pox. Anyone would think your soap was mixed with La Casimira's snake poison."

"But if the Alcalde should recognize me," Tules sobbed.

"No one remembers your troubles. They have enough of their own. What happened in Dolores is no concern of the Alcalde here. You must begin a new life. You are young, strong, and not bad looking with that red hair. The soldiers have been paid today. Sell your soap to them. They need it. But don't act like the Mother of Sorrows with a backache. Smile. Soldiers will buy your smiles, and you can throw in the soap."

Tules was surprised at how well Tía Apolonia's prescription worked. It was a warm summer day, and she let her reboso fall to her shoulders. She smiled timidly at first, then gained courage to flatter the soldiers, and sold all her soap.

Her spirits revived with the fresh air, new surroundings, and busy, sociable life of the market. She watched the town and people with excited speculation and interest.

Each morning when she started to market she looked above the flat roofs to the massive green shoulders and bald pate of the Sangre de Cristo Mountains that seemed close enough to touch in the clear air. Santa Fe was at an elevation of seven thousand feet, and the mountains behind it were almost as high again. White clouds sailed with the wind across the flat prairie to the south and west and broke into moisture against the high mountain barrier. The town basked in the sun under these protecting slopes, and its little river trickled through the edge of the wide golden saucer rimmed with blue peaks. Tules had crossed that saucer coming from El Real de Dolores, but she had seen nothing of it, hidden under the woolsacks.

She went through the plaza to reach the market and remembered that this first royal city in the northern Province had been laid out in 1609 under Don Pedro de Peralta and named for the Holy Faith of St. Francis of Assisi. Don Pedro had followed the strict city plans sent from Spain to the colonies and built the church on an elevation at the eastern end of the plaza and the Palace and Presidio on the northern side. The soldiers' chapel, La Castrense, was opposite the Palace, and the homes of the ricos completed the hollow square. After two centuries of pioneer life, constantly menaced by hostile nomads, drought, and pestilence, the plaza still maintained its early Spanish character. Although the buildings were primitive adobes, the towers of the church balanced the long, low line of the one-story Palace and gave a sense of dignity and charm to the outpost capital.

During those hard centuries there had been neither time, money, nor inclination for outward adornment. In the glaring sunlight the plaza was a bare, sandy square where a rutted road circled the sundial and a few neglected trees. Slow oxcarts, pack trains of burros, or horses dancing under spurs filed around the plaza and sent up shimmering dust. Shade was provided by deep porches that faced every building and made a pleasant all-weather passageway. Even in the early morning Tules noticed that men with bright, striped serapes folded over their shoulders lounged against the walls in the shade, officials strutted through to the customhouse, and women wrapped in rebosos hurried home from mass.

She watched the sentries pace under the long portál in front of the Palace. Its walls were four to six feet thick for protection against sharp arrows; its windows were as deep and narrow as those of a fortress, and its flat roof was a high vantage point for firing down at savage raiders. In times of siege women and children scuttled through underground passages into the high walled compound of the Palace. This compound extended north for two blocks and included officers' quarters, barracks, corrals, and an acequia to bring in vital water. Tules looked at the Palace timidly and wondered what rich appointments gave luxury and beauty to the Governor's private apartments.

She watched the heavy zaguán gate open and close as couriers rode forth with orders to the far, sparse settlements. The Governor General ruled so large a Province that its boundaries had never been explored. New Mexico extended from the uncertain American frontier on the east to the narrow, ocean-rimmed province of California on the west; from the southern boundary of Chihuahua it included all the Río Grande watershed and on to the unknown north whose forests were hardly known even to the French-Canadian trappers. It was a tremendous wilderness area of mountains and deserts, inhabited by sixty villages of peaceful Pueblo Indians, raided by the nomad tribes of Navajos, Apaches, and Comanches, and held by the fortitude of a few thousand white men.

Its potential mineral wealth had lured these Spaniards north, and now its geographical position in the wave of westward expansion brought lusty American traders. Santa Fe was the capital of the fabulous Spanish settlements, the meeting point for trails from every direction and men of every race. It was the largest and most important town in the province, yet it was only a huddle of closely packed adobe homes that sheltered three thousand souls.

The long Palace portál ended in two-story towers. The officers' chapel was in the eastern tower, and the western tower enclosed a dungeon, a dirty jail, and an arsenal. It was ironical that the humble people, who were often jailed for petty thievery or some politician's whim, should swarm around the thick buttresses of the western tower with their open-air market. The market hugged the protection of the high adobe walls of the Palace and ran the two blocks' length before it ended in the field where horse traders met.

The favored stalls were nearest the traffic of the plaza, but María and Tules contented themselves with the cheaper rent of puestos at the farther end. Their greatest worry was having the money ready for the soldier who collected for the market.

"This is the day for the rent," Tules groaned one summer morning.

"I have only half a peso. If I don't sell my soap today, how can I pay?"

"You will sell it, niña. God will provide," María said patiently. And, to help God a little, she added, "If you haven't the peso when the soldier comes this afternoon, we will give him tamales."

Tules shook her head over her unattractive gray balls of soap that were only bought by lazy housewives. She had experimented with a few bars of white soap, strained through expensive Swiss, but no one had bought them. She held up her faded skirt and the ends of her black reboso with one hand and leaned over the straw mat to pile the soap into little pyramids. Suddenly someone pinched her buttocks. She whirled around to see a grinning soldier.

"How dare you touch me? I'll report you," Tules exploded, her green eyes flashing as she jerked her reboso around her.

"Too much temptation, señorita," the soldier snickered. "It was the grace of God that led me to touch an unknown back and find a pretty young face. I meant it as a compliment." He touched his cap and held out a grimy hand. "I have come for the rent for your puesto, señorita."

"But it's too early," Tules faltered. "I haven't sold my soap yet. If you will come at the end of the day . . ."

"The end of the day with a handsome muchacha like you! That's a bargain!" the soldier laughed, as his eyes ran from her red hair down her straight, slender body to her bare feet. "Your face is new here. I'll be back at the end of the day. Hasta luego!"

All day Tules waited desperately for purchasers, but the weather was hot, and few people drifted to her end of the market. She had only half a peso and did not want to impose on María again. When the soldier returned she lifted her eyes to him, lowered them, and sighed, "Business is poor. I haven't enough for the rent. . . ."

"No importa," the soldier grinned. "That will give me an excuse to come tomorrow and the day after. We can talk it over if you will take a small coffee with me now. . . ."

Tules trembled with nervousness but forced herself to laugh and chat with the soldier. He twisted the end of her reboso and smiled.

126

"Why worry about the other tostón for the rent, chiquita? My cousin is a político and the Mayordomo of the market. I can explain to him. . . . A pretty redhead like you should not bother about rent. . . ."

Tules learned quickly that a smile, a tilt of her chin, and a challenging flash from her green eyes softened the heart of the Mayordomo as well as the soldier. He reduced her rent and moved her puesto nearer the plaza. In a few months she forgot the lonely years of fear and illness and bubbled with vitality, hope, and high spirits. She laughed lightly over kisses or other favors that brought her help.

But to María and Tía Apolonia she talked seriously about building up her business. She remembered the French soap Don Miguel had brought from Mexico and determined to imitate it. She skimmed and strained the soap jelly until it was a clean white, added a pinch of salt to harden it, and ground melon seeds, bran, and romero weed to give it a smooth texture. Into one batch she mixed aromatic juniper juice and the yellow coloring from chamiso blossoms, into another the red stain of alegría leaves and cheap perfume. When the cakes dried in the sun they were bright yellow and pink and sold for three times the price of the plain white cakes.

"I'll give you herbs and roots for pomade and hairwash," Tía Apolonia offered, while her clear blue eyes twinkled with the success of this new business.

"But who can buy such costly things?" María sighed, knowing of the hard bargains to save a copper tlaco.

"Women will starve to buy love or beauty, comadre." Tía Apolonia spoke out of her long experience in assisting human beings in and out of the world. "Women haggle over gray soap because it only washes clothes, but they will offer three times the price if its scent will hold a lover. Pomade gives the sheen of hope to dull hair, and ointment smoothes the wrinkles of disappointment. Carmín is for courage when cheeks are too old to blush. . . ."

"Only the rich can afford to be vain," María mumbled.

"God put vanity into everyone." Tía Apolonia nodded her wise gray head. "Vanity only stops with the last breath. It is a woman's

127

strongest defense, even in her shroud. Tules will support all of us if she works with vanity."

Tules pounded the brown amole roots into a foaming hairwash and concocted pomade from beef marrow and roseleaves. She begged and borrowed precious bottles for the hand lotion thickened with quince seeds and made abayalde Mejicano from roasted eggshells soaked with rice and melon seeds and patted into hard white balls of powder. She liked to use her long, quick hands, but it was tedious work to make the other powder from deer horns soaked with corn-cobs and then baked, ground, and sifted through fine Swiss.

When she hinted that these recipes were used by famous beauties in Mexico, women went without bread to buy the bleaching masks, ointments, and powder. She used all the market tricks to cajole, flat-ter, or bully her customers. Her green eyes sparkled when she outsold her neighbors and outwitted stingy housewives.

During the bright, sharp winter days the ciboleros dashed into the plaza on their wiry horses. The men were hard muscled and sun-burned from their three months' hunt on the plains, and their eyes were woman-hungry. Colored tassels dangled from their lances, and their pockets jingled with money from the sale of buffalo robes, lard, and meat.

Their leader, Pepe Cisneros, stopped in front of Tules's puesto and threw up his hands in mock despair as he looked at her wares. "Compadres, don't come near here unless you are prepared to wash off your blackest sins," he called to the ciboleros behind him. "Dios de mi vida, pink and yellow soap sold by a red-haired beauty! Now I know I had reason to go for three months without bathing. How do you sell your jaboncillos, señorita?"

"With a smile, señor," she laughed, "and a recipe that calls for hot water."

"But we are as much afraid of hot water as the devil is of holy water," Pepe exclaimed. He touched one pink cake gingerly with his finger as though it would bite. "It's harmless, compadres. Come, señorita, give us a good price for all of it. I shall make a song of the

128

brave ciboleros who tilt their lances at the huge, fierce buffalo and return home to buy pink soap. Ay, qué caray!"

He pulled at the guitar that hung on a cord around his neck, strummed cords, and began to sing a rollicking, improvised song. Tules watched him with a fascinated smile. He was about thirty years old, tall and well built. He wore the hunter's fringed deerskin leggins and jacket and swayed on his moccasined feet with the easy grace of an active, outdoor man. His nose and jaw were strong in his full-fleshed, sunburned face, and his head was bound with a tight red kerchief and topped with the flat cibolero hat. His twinkling black eyes, white teeth flashing in wide mouth, and overflowing spirits of fun and good humor captivated her. She clapped enthusiastically with everyone else when he finished his song. He bowed, clutched his throat, and called hoarsely, "Soap, compadres, soap! How much for the lot, señorita?"

Before Tules knew it her stock was gone, and she was caught up with the gay, laughing crowd of ciboleros. Pepe led them from stall to stall, buying chile, sweet cakes and coffee, sweets, ribbons, brown earthen mugs, and small mirrors.

Later they danced, and Tules found that Pepe's light steps were part of the music. She abandoned herself to the carefree laughter that Pepe called forth with his buffoonery, good nature, and songs. He linked his arm through hers in an impersonal, comradely gesture. At the monte table he saw that her eyes shone with eagerness, gave her a tostón, and urged her to play. She studied the cards in the layout, watched the dealer's quick hands, and placed her bet. She laughed with joy when she won, bet again, and lost.

"Better luck another time when my pockets are full," Pepe laughed and turned up empty palms. "Tomorrow I return to my wife and children and my little ranch up the river. But I shall not forget you, my beauty."

With the first warm weather the mountain men from north of Taos brought in their packs of beaver and sold each pelt for ten pesos. They threw away their money on fufarraw with lavish gestures,

129

crazy for women, drink, and excitement before they returned to their silent hunting and trapping. When they were whooping drunk Tules thought it was charity to take their silver before some robber stole it. The money bought food for María and herself and a few coins to lose on the monte table.

Later in the summer the American wagons rolled in from the Santa Fe Trail with a new flood of silver for the market. Tules picked up American words and hard money from these blue-eyed strangers. Their manners were crude and boisterous, but she flattered them into staking her at the monte table. She had a never-quenched thirst for gambling. She seldom won, but she came to the monte tables so often that she met Santiago Flores, the manager of the gambling hall at La Fonda. She flattered and flirted with him, boasted that she could deal, and showed him how deftly her fingers handled the cards. He shrugged and said that it required money and other favors, as well as clever fingers, to deal for him. But he encouraged her to come to the sala and bring the traders with heavy pockets.

Tía Apolonia scolded Tules for flirting with strangers. She knew too much of human nature to be shocked by a lack of morals, but she reminded Tules that virtue was a marriageable asset and should not be squandered.

Tía Apolonia talked to María, who said gently, "I wish you would marry, Tules. I would feel safer with a man to watch over you."

"I don't sell enough soap to support a lazy husband," Tules teased her. "Look at Carlota and Lourdes with another baby every year and nothing to feed them. Their husbands only work to make children."

"But you are young and beautiful, child." María shook her head. "Ramón is dead, and all that is over. . . ."

"Yes, if Ramón had lived everything would be different. Dios, if I only had my baby. . . ." Pain darkened her eyes; then she shrugged and smiled bitterly. "Pues, what is in the heart does not cover the back. I can't go through life with no more pride than a burro tramping the threshing floor. Thanks to you and Tía Apolonia I am well, and I can take care of you. Why should we bring in a man to make trouble? I would take nothing less than a rico, and I can never have that."

The ricos were beyond her reach, but she found that the petty politicians could be useful. The market had taught her that, while everything had its price, politics meant power. The success or failure of politicians was the daily drama that provided the hot, spiced sauce for each man's tortilla. Sante Fe was a small, close community whose livelihood depended upon Government revenues. The money seeped down from the highest to the lowest in meager salaries fattened with graft and bribery.

Though the Governor was appointed by the fluctuating Federal Government in distant Mexico City he was always the target for betrayals, assassins' plots, and threats of a general revolt by opposing factions. His subjects criticized him with the strong Spanish individualism that resented anyone in authority. Every rico weighted this delicate political balance of power with funds for his own protection, and every pobre felt the shifting pressures on his humble daily life. The Governor and the ricos were unattainable dignitaries to a market girl, but their underlings who supervised the stalls could be approached and flattered. Tules succeeded in this so well that her puesto was moved to the entrance from the plaza, where she had the advantage of getting the first customers.

# 14

"WHAT A RAIN that was last night! Our roof leaked like a down spout," Carlota called to Tules as they spread their mats on the damp ground at the market.

"It always rains on those who are already wet," Tules laughed. The early morning air was fresh and clean, and the dazzling July sun was already drying the mud puddles in the road.

"Ave María Purísima, the rains have started, and now the Americans will come!" Carlota said. "They should get here today, and we shall have good business."

Tules nodded as she arranged her wares in bright patterns and remembered the saying that the American wagons brought the rain, each vital to prosperity at the end of the Santa Fe Trail. No one bothered about the practical reason that the Americans waited in Missouri until there was enough grass on the prairies to feed their oxen and mules, and the six weeks' journey ended when the summer rains began.

This year of 1834 torrential rains had flooded the prairie, and the wagon wheels had cut ruts that would mark the route for the next century. The news was relayed to Santa Fe that eighty wagons, one hundred and sixty men, and fifty traders had left Westport on May 24. They were protected by United States troops under Captain Clifton Wharton as far as the American border. For the last hundred leagues within Mexican territory the caravan had to depend upon its own guns to drive off hostile Comanches and provide buffalo meat. Yesterday two traders had raced ahead into Santa Fe to be the first to sell their goods and announce the arrival of the caravan for this afternoon.

Tules tingled with the general excitement of a good summer season, but she was anxious to sell her homemade cosmetics before the Americans brought in newfangled rouge and patent medicines. She sat on her sandaled heels and moved with lithe grace as she arranged her gaudy cakes of pink and yellow soap, balls of white powder, and odd-sized bottles of lotion. Her vivid face advertised her wares, for her full lips were scarlet with carmín, and the hated freckles on her long nose were hidden under white powder. Her cheeks were the same warm olive as her bare neck and arms, half revealed under the reboso loosely draped over her round-necked cotton blouse. For this gala day her curly red hair was held back with cheap, brilliant-studded combs, gilt crescents dangled from her pierced ears, and red beads fell between her high, firm breasts. She was careful not to soil her wide green calico skirt for she planned to wear it to the caravan baile tonight.

She looked eagerly at the busy market where square white canvas canopies protected each puesto from the hot sun. The smell of the damp earth mingled with that of spices and garlic in the simmering cooking pots. She wrinkled her nose at the odor of spoiling fresh meat and noticed that a few merchants had thrown pink mosquito netting over liver, tripe, and tongue; but flies settled thickly on hunks of beef and venison and the naked yellow carcasses of turkeys and chickens. As the sun rose higher she caught the stench of live poultry, squealing pigs, and bleating lambs. Thrifty women paused along the line of stalls to bargain over neat piles of firewood, newly cut alfalfa, silver pyramids of onions and garlic, sacks of freckled beans, stacks of sweet rolls, or a dozen varieties of chile.

The vendors' shrill cries echoed through the market, and Tules joined them to call her wares and wave a cake of pink soap. "Jaboncillos! Buy my fine soap! Pink like a rose, yellow for bleaching! Fine rice powder! Powder your nose, señorita, before the gringos come! Rice powder, carmín, pomade! Jaboncillos, señorita, jaboncillos!"

"Save your breath, Tules. They're holding their money for the gringo novelties. Let's rest and have a smoke," Carlota called from the next puesto. She had this favored position because she was a distant cousin of the Mayordomo, but she was too lazy to push her goods. She always said that tomorrow someone would need blue

133

denim, brown muslin, or the coarse white domestic cloth. Now she sat comfortably on the ground with her thick legs spread apart. Her bulging body reeked with garlic, and her round, greasy face smiled good naturedly as she passed the cornhusks and tobacco flask to Tules.

Tules drew in the first satisfying puff from her cigarrito and said, "I must sell more soap before the gringos come. With two more pesos I will have enough to buy the shawl for María's saint's day."

"Why do you work so hard, niña?" Carlota yawned. "With your gipsy looks you can pick the richest gringo on the wagons. You have all the luck. Here I get nothing but ten children from one husband, and he is not simpático. If I was young . . ."

"If I can get a trader to stake me at monte tonight, I'll win," Tules nodded. "La Casimira says my luck has changed, and I'll have good fortune. She told me last night that I would have a light man, a dark man, and lots of money. 'Mountains of money,' she said. Por Dios, if I have that much I'll deal monte! I've shown Santiago Flores how well I can deal, and he has half promised me. . . . His claw fingers make me shiver, but I itch to get hold of the cards. To-night I know I'll be lucky. Say a prayer to your Santo Niño for me, and tomorrow I'll bring you wine." She pointed to the small board crudely painted with the Christ child that hung from the support of Carlota's white canvas canopy.

"Look, here comes the rich patronas!" Carlota said and lumbered off the ground to kneel before her mat. "The young one is the bride, and the fat one is Doña Trinidad, the wife of General Armijo. She's here to visit her cousins. Look, look, they're coming to us!"

Tules glanced quickly at the six ladies approaching like a flock of twittering blackbirds. Their black taffeta skirts rustled, their black lace mantillas fell over black ringlets, and their black eyes sparkled with the adventure of coming to market. Stiff maidservants hovered behind them, and houseboys followed with empty baskets.

"The crow is only as black as his feathers. Watch me sell them. That Doña Trinidad will need perfumed soap if she's going to hold the General," she whispered and then called "Jaboncillos, señorita! Fine rice powder, carmín, señorita!"

The patronas picked their way daintily around the mud puddles with small shrieks about wetting their fine slippers. Tules looked enviously at their gold lockets and crosses, filigree earrings, brace lets, and rings. The bride wore a bowknot of pearls, but an emerald pendant trembled on the lace at Doña Trinidad's full bosom.

"There's the pink soap and the redheaded vendor they were talk ing about." Doña Trinidad's voice carried above the chatter. "She's the hussy that passes from man to man like a counterfeit coin. Por Dios, what do men see in her?"

"Shhh!" the bride cautioned and came nearer Tules's puesto. "Are you La Tules? Is this where Doña Bárbara bought the soap?"

"Si, señorita. At your orders, señorita." Tules's face burned from the insult, but she forced her voice to a humble plaint. "I am honored that you glance at my poor soap. It will suit your fair skin, señorita." She offered a cake of soap to the bride, while her voice rose and fell with the singsong lilt of the market vendors. "This will leave your skin as soft as a baby's, señorita. Like a bath of milk and carnations. . . ."

"I can't believe that Doña Bárbara came to this dirty market," Doña Trinidad interrupted. "I wouldn't touch that soap, cousin. The poisonous color might bring out a rash."

Tules lifted her chin and looked at Doña Trinidad defiantly. "These are secret recipes my mother brought from the court ladies in Mexico. I sell them to the gente fina. Only yesterday a beautiful girl told me a General admired the fragrance of my soap when he kissed her. . . ."

"A General, you say?" The bride giggled and nudged her cousin. "How much is this fine soap?"

"Two reales a cake, señorita. It is dear because of the French perfume. Por favor, let me try this lotion on your white hand. This is pomade for the hair. . . ."

"She uses Spanish henna on her hair." Doña Trinidad sniffed behind her lace-bordered handkerchief. "Let's go, cousin. This stuff

135

is spread on the ground and thick with flies and dust. We might catch the pox. . . ."

"My things are fresh, señorita," Tules insisted. "I made them only last night to sell to the American ladies who will come with the caravan today."

"You would sell to those gringa cows and not to us?" Doña Trinidad exclaimed. "Let me see the carmín, girl."

"I promised to save it," Tules said, even while she unpacked the carmín and powder from her basket. "With this fine rice powder your skin will be like your pearls, señorita. And carmín makes the cheeks glow. . . ."

The patronas vied with each other now to buy her entire stock. They bargained, compared the soap and powder, and motioned to their servants to fill the baskets.

"Señorita, glance at my denim, strong blue denim!" Carlota called. "Brown muslin, señorita? The white domestic is a bargain. . . ."

But the patronas left in a flutter to hurry home and experiment with beauty.

"The ugly snobs! May their teeth fall out!" Carlota cursed. "They wouldn't even look at my things. The Santo Niño has forgotten me. I'll fix him!" She reached for the small painted board and slammed it face down under the brown muslin.

"That Doña Trinidad is a bloated pig, curse her!" Tules's voice shook with anger. "Did you hear her call me a hussy? 'A counterfeit coin that passes from man to man. What do men see in her?' Válgame Dios, she is worse than I am! Lives in a fine house, spends her husband's money, and sleeps with any man she can get. If I was the wife of that handsome Don Manuel . . ."

"Pues, you held your tongue and made the vain fools pay twice over. You've sold out," Carlota shrugged.

"Thanks to San Ramón that I didn't spit at her," Tules said as she counted her coins and tied them in a rag. "I'll bet by the sundial in the plaza it's only two o'clock. Now I can buy María's shawl from the American wagons and have enough left for a new skirt. Luck is with me, and I'll win tonight."

"La caravana! Here come the American wagons!" someone yelled. The crowd in the market ran toward the plaza as they called, "La entrada de la caravana! Los carros! Los gringos!"

Tules hastily packed her basket, called good luck to Carlota, and ran to the plaza as the first white-topped wagon rolled in behind eight galloping mules. The driver cracked his whip, yelled at the mules, and waved to the crowds lining the narrow streets. Two men, wedged on the front seat with him, threw up their hats and shouted, "Whoopee! Viva Santy Fee! Hey, girl, save me a kiss!"

The white hoods of more prairie wagons flowed down the loma where the Santa Fe Trail entered the town and circled the plaza. Mules plunged in excited fright as pistols and whips cracked and leather-lunged gringos yelled. The sleepy plaza became a milling jumble where mongrel dogs barked, children screamed, and the crowd shouted.

Tules looked admiringly at the Conestoga wagons, three times as large and fast as the two-wheeled carretas of the Chihuahua Trail. Their wheels were as high as her shoulder with bright yellow spokes and wide iron rims. The red wagon beds sloped up to the back and front as though the weight of the goods within made the wagons sag to the center. Osnaburg sheeting, roped over the high wagon hoops, glistened in the afternoon sun like great puffed clouds.

She watched the gringos jump off the wagons and move stiffly in the rumpled suits they had unpacked this morning. Their long hair was rubbed up with bear grease, their cheeks were freshly shaved, and their blue eyes burned in their tanned faces. Old traders still wore their grease-spattered buckskins and hickory shirts unbuttoned over their hairy chests.

She smiled as she saw Mexican men twist their black moustaches and look scornfully at the gangling gringos. The men did not like these blond rivals because their women were already rolling black eyes at the staring strangers.

The French-Canadian drivers, who came with the caravan each year, shouted with abandon, threw their arms around old friends, and made themselves at home. Gringo travelers thrust their hands

137

in their pockets and surveyed the unpretentious adobe buildings, narrow streets, and chattering, foreign mob. They looked as though they couldn't believe that this dirty mud hamlet was far-famed Santa Fe. They pulled back in distaste as maimed beggars plucked at their sleeves. One man shouted that a pickpocket had already snatched his roll from the many pockets in his overlapping fustian coat.

Tules hurried to the customhouse, intent on her purchases. Goods had been inspected at Arroyo Hondo, two leagues from town. Now the interpreters rubbed their hands together between new traders and pompous government officials. Greedy eyes watched each other— the officials hungry for graft and the traders determined not to be skinned. The older traders, used to greasing palms, had already paid the diligencia and started selling. The first sales made the largest profit. If the traders had "mulas" of unsold stock after six weeks, they had to sell at the lower wholesale price or take their goods on the long, expensive trip to Chihuahua.

Tules elbowed her way into the low-raftered customroom and watched as bolts of pink, green, blue, and red calico emerged from the wrappings. Women fingered it, tested the corners, and admired the small print patterns. Then they began to bargain, calling on heaven to listen to the prices; pleading that they were poor; flattering, cajoling, whining. Tules selected yellow calico and ordered five varas. The trader measured the vara by stretching the calico from his nose to the length of his arm.

"Pues, señor," Tules rolled her eyes at him and used the English she had picked up from the traders, "your arm is too short. You would rob a poor muchacha?"

The trader grinned, let the calico sag, and added generous inches. "That makes a yard by our measure. For the extra length I want a dance with you at the baile tonight."

"Of course, señor." Tules laughed and nodded.

She darted to the counter where traders were unwrapping black cashmere shawls. The price was set by the fine weave and length of the fringe. She rubbed the cashmere between her thumb and

138

finger and inspected the fringe from short wool to long, knotted silk. A young giant with china-blue eyes and light hair falling to the open collar of his red-checked shirt helped a trader open the bales. Tules asked him the price of the shawls and drew in her breath when he said forty pesos. She picked up two shawls and started to carry them to the door where she could examine them in the light.

"Not so fast, ma'am," the young giant called and grabbed her shoulder with large, firm hands. "You didn't buy those shawls. Put them back."

Tules whirled on him with flashing eyes. "You theenk I wish to steal heem? Por Dios, you theenk I am thief? I only take heem to the door to look at the color."

The young man stared at her, confused by her swift, broken English and her flashing eyes. He was so tall that his sunburned face bent to listen to her. His blue eyes were young and innocent, and his big, spare body looked as though he had outgrown his flesh.

Tules thrust the shawls into his long arms. "Pues, take heem! Other traders with shawls are more polite than you, señor. Válgame Dios, I don't steal heem! I only wish to look at the color in the daylight."

The young man blushed and said, "Excuse me, ma'am. I'm new here. I didn't understand. I'll take them to the door for you."

Tules examined the shawls closely in the daylight. She smiled into his blue eyes and confided, "We wear the shawls muchos años. Some black gets brown, some green. You theenk thees one will remain good black?"

"I declare, ma'am, you've taught me something," the boy exclaimed. "I thought all black shawls were black. You must be a careful buyer."

"The shawl is for my sister this winter when it makes cold. It must be good black." Tules lowered her curving lashes. "But it is too dear."

"You want this shawl for your sister?" he pointed to the shawl with the longest fringe. "Come on, and I'll see if Mr. Collins will shave the price."

The older trader was less susceptible, but Tules bought the shawl for two pesos less than she expected to pay.

"You got a bargain, and now you give this young fellow a good time," Collins told her. "He's new out here. First trip away from home. His name is Jim Mathews. You teach him the dances at the fandango tonight."

"A sus ordenes, Jeem. Hasta tonight!" Tules laughed and kissed her fingertips to the staring young giant.

She ran home, delighted with her purchases and full of plans for the young gringo whose money would stake her at the monte table.

# 15

THAT NIGHT she danced with the young giant at the public baile at La Fonda. He danced stiffly, without the natural grace of the Mexicans, but she suited her steps to his. He flushed bashfully when she flirted with him and called him "Jeem."

"Your men get muy borracho on Taos Lightning and Pass brandy," she protested when a clumsy teamster stepped on her new slippers.

"Is that what you call the stuff, ma'am? We call it 'Oh-Be-Joyful.' " Jeem grinned. "You'll have to excuse them, ma'am. They've been layin' awake for six weeks plannin' on this fandango. We were short on rations the last week—flour and coffee almost gave out. Brandy hits 'em on empty stomachs."

"Peóns feel the wine when they have not eaten," Tules said, "but caballeros don't get drunk."

"We used up all our whisky back on the Trail when floods covered the prairie," Jeem explained. "It rained so hard the wagons were like Noah's arks. We crawled under, but the wagons dripped, and the ground was soaked. Our clothes were wet all through, and the fire wouldn't burn. That whisky saved our lives. First time I ever touched hard liquor, and I hope my ma doesn't hear about it."

"She permits you to come so far from home?" Tules teased.

"She didn't want me to come," Jeem confessed. "She'd be proper horrified if she could see me now. But my pa understood that I'd gone to school long enough. I had to stretch my legs before I settled down. Mathews men follow the sea, and I felt like I was sailin' when we hit that flat, green prairie. My pa got me the job with the caravan. Fixed it for me to get to California and sail around the Horn in one of our New Bedford whaling ships. New Bedford's my home town."

Tules studied the boy under half-closed lids. He boasted of being twenty, only four years younger than she was, but she felt old enough

141

to be his mother. For all his awkward ways, he must be a rico. Experience would harden his open, simple face before he returned home, and he might as well begin to learn his lessons now. She was eager to get to the monte table.

"Your men make too much the noise. There will be a fight. We should leave here," she suggested and guided him through the side door.

The small, sharp-eyed proprietor greeted her as they entered the gambling sala. Tules's hazel eyes flashed him a message as she stopped and said, "Permit me, Don Santiago, to present Don Jeem. How is luck running tonight?"

"Well enough." Santiago Flores nodded. "Por favor, pass inside."

Men and women jammed around a chuza table and watched avidly as three little balls spun around a wooden bowl with numbered slots.

"Roulette!" Jeem exclaimed. "My ma would call this a den of iniquity. I reckon we'd better get out."

Tules smiled up at him, took his arm, and urged him beyond the table. They passed the faro and dice players, and she stopped at her favorite monte table. Jeem would stake her, and she would win tonight.

The love of gambling was in her Latin blood, and her eyes shone as she looked at the stacks of gold and silver on the center of the table. Intent faces bent nearer to see the card drawn by the dealer from the bottom of the pack. If the new card matched in color and number the card covered by the bet on the layout, the lookout paid double the bet. Betting was high tonight, and exclamations of joy and low curses on bad luck mingled with the clink of coins. The gleaming stacks in the "bank" increased with the dealer's safe percentages.

Tules turned to draw Jeem into the game. He stood stiffly erect and frowned at the sombreros, mantillas, and greasy frontier hats bent over the table. She pressed his arm, smiled, and asked "You play now?"

142

"No. This is a gambling hell," he said sternly.

"But, no!" Her eyes widened in astonishment. "This is the best sala in Santa Fe. Everyone plays here. See, there's the padre from Taos. And the lady with the diamonds—she's Doña Trinidad, the wife of the General. And there's Don Augustín Durán from the customhouse. Peóns come here, too, but they have only a few cuartillos."

"Poor fools. They starve to come here and be swindled."

"No, this is an honest game. Santiago Flores has the best dealers in town. Try just once, Jeem, and you will see."

"No ma'am, I've heard about these crooks. I aim to save my money and go on to California with Sutter next month. Let's clear out of here. This is no place for a nice girl. I'll see you home."

He dragged his eyes away from her smooth olive shoulder when Tules hitched up the low round neck of her thin blouse. She looked at him in amazement. To have money and not play—what was the matter with him? She went unwillingly as he pushed her toward the door. See her home? What did he mean? He could not come into her house. María was there. If he wanted a trysting place, he could go to the willows by the river.

The plaza was quiet and deserted under the clear summer stars. Tules pulled her reboso around her and hesitated. How could she get away from him and go back to the monte tables?

"Which way do you live?" Jeem asked.

She pointed vaguely down San Francisco Street, and he started off, Tules hurrying to keep up with his long steps. She had never heard of girls being escorted home except by dueñas. Now that she had no patrona, she ran the streets alone day or night. Jeem acted as though Comanches were after them.

"This is all new to me. This is my first trip to foreign parts," he apologised. "It's different from New Bedford. I hope it's all right with your folks for me to see you home."

"I live with my sister-in-law. She will be asleep." Tules's voice was worried. What would María say if this gringo entered in the middle of the night?

"But your folks—your mother and father?"

"My mother is in Manzano. My father, my husband—they are dead."

"You're young for a widow." Jeem looked at her more closely.

"I help María. We are pobres. We have puestos in the market."

"Poor little thing!" Jeem's voice was warm with sympathy, but his arms hung stiffly at his sides. "So you work to take care of the old lady? And they told me there wasn't a decent girl in the town!"

Tules looked up at him uncertainly, trying to translate his strange, nasal words. The low adobe houses lined the narrow street. Their doors were fastened and darkly mysterious. Jeem wouldn't know which door was hers. She must stop him before he went too far. Her footsteps lagged, and she put her finger to her lips and shook her head.

"You live here?" Jeem asked. "And you want me to skedaddle? All right. Thanks for the dance, ma'am, and I hope I'll see you tomorrow. Good night, ma'am."

He raised his hat and marched up the street. Tules stared after him and finally ran down the dark road to her door. On this first big night when the caravan arrived she had missed the fun and dancing and drinks. Worst of all, she had missed the chance to play monte with a trader to stake her. She was tempted to run back to the sala, but she was afraid Jeem would see her and hustle her home again.

She shook her puzzled head as she crept in beside María. All gringos were queer, but this one was either a fool or too smart for her. He was not guapo, but there was something straight and clean about him. And he had money. One wasted evening might pay in the end. A finger doesn't make a hand, she reminded herself drowsily.

The next morning Jeem towered over her puesto and tipped his hat awkwardly. "So this is where you hang out! My, what pretty soap!"

"I make it." Tules smiled up at his fresh face. He was as tall and straight as the white trunk of a young aspen.

"Do you now!" he gulped. "Come to think of it, I need soap to wash my shirt. I'll take two cakes."

He was too shy to bargain and handed her a round "eagle dollar." She rubbed it curiously and untied the rag where she kept her money. She looked up to hand him the change in reales and saw that his mouth gaped open and his eyes were like blue saucers. She followed his gaze and realized that he was staring at her bare brown breasts, exposed where the loose blouse fell away when she stooped over. A hot wave of shame boiled through her, and she threw the end of her reboso around her neck to cover herself. They were too embarrassed to look at each other. Jeem clutched the two cakes of soap and his change, scraped his big feet in the worn boots, and left hurriedly.

"Por el amor de Dios, you've found a tower of gold!" Carlota chuckled as she watched Jeem stalk away, his blond head towering above the market crowd. "You will be rich with those fat eagle dollars."

"He's a good boy, but he's not used to our ways," Tules defended him. "He's saving his money to go on to California. . . ."

"If he isn't killed by Indians on that bad trail north of Abiquii he'll lose his roll in California. If those robber traders don't pluck him, the women will. He's too young. He would be in less danger if you kept his money here," Carlota winked.

"I don't need his money. . . ."

"Nombre de Dios, what's come over you?" Carlota cocked her dark head inquiringly, her hands akimbo on her wide hips. "Did you eat loco weed for supper?"

Tules shrugged her shoulders and bent to arrange her soap. It was hard for her to explain this new feeling, even to herself. Men set the game. They wanted pleasure, she wanted money. She had learned to twist them, rouse them, hold them off until they were willing to pay. It had nothing to do with love, the tender, protecting love she had felt for Ramón. Ramón had possessed her heart. Her body was no more important than the cornhusk around a tamale.

But this Jeem, he made her feel different. He thought she was decent and working hard to "support the old lady." He treated her as though she was above him, something good and precious. It was the first time a man had been respectful and gentle to her. It gave her a strange, new pride.

He came to the market every morning and followed her once when she was having breakfast at María's puesto. She translated Jeem's halting sentences into flowing Spanish so that María would think him galán. They laughed when he choked on the hot chile and offered him goat's milk to cool his throat.

"Your joven's blue eyes are as happy as the clear sky when he looks at you," María said that night. "Will you marry him, niña?"

"No, he is going away next week," Tules shrugged.

"You could keep him here, if you wanted him. He is a good boy. In a few years he will be a strong man. You should marry. . . ."

"Marry? With no money, no family? Who would have me? Don't molest me with this talk. I will take care of myself." Tules tossed her head.

Jeem drove off the other men with his fierce young pride. He danced with her every night, but he never mentioned love. His strange, stiff ways aroused her curiosity.

"María asked if your wife is waiting at home?" Tules said, watching him under her fringed lashes.

Jeem's fair skin flushed. "I don't have a wife yet—but I aim to get one."

"Yes?" Tules looked up, and her heart beat faster.

"I've been settin' up with a neighbor girl on the next farm. She's the daughter of John Bradford—name's Abigail."

"Abigail?" The name tasted bitter to Tules. It sounded like "abigeo," a cattle thief, a worse criminal than a murderer.

"We're promised to wed when I get back from this trip around the Horn. Abigail and my ma, they didn't want I should go. But I've got to see a mite of the world before I settle down. And the money I take home will give us a start on the farm her pa aims to give us."

"Is she pretty?" Tules asked. She was often puzzled by Jeem's expressions, but she knew what this meant.

146

"She don't look like the women out here." Jeem smiled slowly. "She's light-complexioned, and her eyes are gray like the sea. She's a good, careful housekeeper. She lives in a white wood house with green shutters and not a speck of dust. She'd have spells about how people live in the dirt out here. She'd never believe poor people could be so happy—singing, dancing all the time. She'd call it a sinful waste. And she wouldn't like the sun shining so bright it hurts your eyes. And blue skies that make ours look like faded wash lines. . . ."

Jeem went on talking about home, comparing the countries. Tules didn't listen. She thought of Abigail with a father and a farm. She didn't need Jeem's money. Besides, some strumpet in California might get away with Jeem's roll. She could make him forget that cold prude of an Abigail, loosen up with his tongue and money. . . .

But she couldn't. She was a fool, but she could not mar that clear, clean look in the boy's eyes.

One day he came to the market with a long cut down his cheek and a halting story about meeting a drunken teamster. Tules found out about the fight. A gringo had joked about Jeem's girl and called Tules a filthy name. Jeem's fist smashed the man's mouth. Tules lifted her head with new pride. A man had defended her.

Jeem was going away in two more days. She vowed to leave him alone, let him go. She would avoid him, get to the monte table, and find some other gringo to stake her. The summer had been—how did Jeem say it—"a sinful waste."

The next night she slipped into the gambling sala and sidled up to Santiago Flores. "Why don't you let me deal, Don Santiago? I can keep the men coming to your place. Now they are squandering their money on cockfights."

"I have other requirements, if you deal for me," Santiago insinuated as he flashed the diamond ring on his long yellow finger.

"I can deal." Tules ignored his suggestion. "Let me show you again. I've worked with the cards for years. My fingers know them."

He offered her a new pack of Spanish cards, and she dealt the layout two by two on the empty table while they talked of bets, percentage, payoff.

"Ah, Santiago, I could be the best monte dealer in the world," she coaxed, her hazel eyes flattering him. "I would bring you fame."

"Bien." Santiago twisted his black moustache and appraised her. "When you have enough money to open a bank, I'll give you a table."

"In our country we say, 'Lucky at cards, unlucky at love,' " someone said in English behind them. Tules turned to find Jeem watching her with a stiff, righteous frown. Santiago looked contemptuously at the stupid blond giant and strolled away.

Tules was angry that Jeem had interrupted her plan. In another minute she might have persuaded Santiago. Jeem had spoiled that plan, and now he could pay for it. Abigail should not have his money. She flirted and danced with Jeem in the stately quadrilles and taunted him into drinking a glass of red wine.

The gringos had taken the town tonight, the beginning of the farewell celebrations before the California party left tomorrow and the traders returned over the Santa Fe Trail next week. Men were wildly, uproariously drunk. They threw money to the orchestra to play American tunes and shouted verses of "The Mellow Horn" and "The Days When We Were Gipsying" in strident, nasal voices. They brushed Mexican dandies away like flies, grabbed dark-eyed girls, and charged up and down the room in boisterous square dances. A rawboned trader in a hickory shirt beat on a tin pan and yelled the calls:

> Up the river and round the bend,
> Right hands up and gone again.
> Break and trail home 'long that line,
> Ladies in front and gents behind.

> Back to the center and circle four.
> How do you swap and how do you trade?
> Your pretty girl for my old maid?
> She is pretty and so is mine,
> You swing yours, and I'll swing mine.

The caballeros, waiting at the end of the room, looked scornfully at these boors who did not drink like gentlemen. They fingered the pistols and daggers pushed into the bright sashes around their narrow hips. Women's eyes glistened with excitement, novelty, fright. Their feet followed swiftly in the mad new steps. The gringo's heavy boots stamped like a herd of buffalo. One trader loudly kissed his partner when he met her in a do-si-do. Fast as an echo, there was the sharp crack of a pistol.

At once there was wild confusion. Women scuttled away from the dance floor, hid behind chairs and overturned tables, and clapped their hands over their ears. Jeem pushed Tules behind him and protected her with his big body. Every man's hand leaped to his belt and pulled out a pistol, dagger, or long "Green River" knife.

A circle of hate-filled Mexican eyes watched the small band of traders swarm together in the center of the room. The gringos moved shoulder to shoulder toward the man who had fired the first shot. A gringo rushed him, shook the pistols from his hand, and tossed him against the wall.

Shots rang out, chairs hurled through the air, and women screamed. The large candelabra, swinging from the rafters, crashed to the floor, and darkness added to drunken battle. Jeem's long arms lifted Tules and held her tight against his chest as he forced his way out the door. She could feel his heart pounding as she clung to him.

After the noise and fighting, the dark deserted plaza was curiously quiet. Jeem stopped, put Tules down gently, and looked at her. "I—I guess you'll think I'm as wild as the rest of 'em," he stammered. "But I didn't aim to let them stampede and trample you."

Tules smoothed her hair, settled her reboso, and smiled. She felt like the Queen of Heaven.

"By heck, ma'am, I don't know what you do to me but . . ." Jeem gulped. "When I first came here, I couldn't get used to women goin' around half naked. In my country respectable women are covered all over in tight dresses. I thought—well, anyway, I like it now.

149

Seems like women here are warm and friendly like God made 'em, not just sawdust dollies. But it's so different. I've tried to picture you in my home, but you wouldn't like it. You'd die, like a tropical bird in a blizzard. . . ."

"You like it here?" Tules asked softly and looked up at him.

"I'd like powerful well to stay here always, ma'am. I'm not handsome and quick tongued like your men, but someday lots of fellers like me are goin' to live here. Something about this country gets 'em. But—well, I've promised to go with Sutter tomorrow, and Mathews men always keep their word. . . ."

Tules pulled at the fringe of her reboso. A word now, a kiss, his hand cupped over her breast, and he would stay here forever. She breathed faster and leaned toward him to catch his serious, young words.

"You—you're the grandest woman I've ever known. Young and beautiful and working your fingers to the bone to support the old lady. I'll never forget you, and I don't want you should forget me." He swallowed hard. His big hands fumbled in his pocket, and he held something toward her. "I'd be mighty pleased, ma'am, if you'd keep this ring to remember me by. My grandpa, he was a sea captain, and he brought it to my grandma from Spain. She gave it to me, and I brought it along for a luck piece. It ain't much, but I'd like to think it stayed here with you when I'm gone. . . ."

Tules peered at the ring in her hand. It was a carved gold band, worn thin and smooth. It was the first gold ring she had ever owned, and she slipped it on the third finger of her left hand. She turned it, caressed it, and started to thank him. He broke in nervously. "I guess Ma's right. Mathews men have the itching foot, they're always wanderers on land or sea. She says womenfolks only get half a Mathews man, 'cause even when they're old and bound to a chair their eyes are seein' strange women an' bright birds in foreign ports. When I'm old I'll see the sunlight in your hair, your eyes . . ."

"No woman has all of any man," Tules sighed. She could hold him, keep him here. But he would be unhappy, homesick for the cold sea and that bleak land. . . . He didn't fit in. . . .

150

She started on, and they walked in silence in the summer darkness. When they neared her door, Jeem halted and stood awkwardly on one big foot, then the other. "Winter's comin' on," he stammered. "I—I don't relish thinking you'll be cold. I'd like to buy you a shawl, but I don't know much about women's fixin's. I hope you won't take offense. I don't mean it thataway. But if you'd take this money and buy you a good, warm shawl, I'll rest easier this winter. . . ."

He thrust some money into her hand, and Tules looked at it —three heavy, twenty-dollar gold coins. A surge of shame scalded her. Other men had given her money—one, two, sometimes five pesos thrown like a bone to a dog. She had given this boy nothing. She could not take his money.

"No, no, Jeem." She held the money toward him. "I give you thanks, but it is too much. You will need it. . . ."

"I earned it, and I can earn more. I want you should have it. It'll make me happy." He hesitated, and then the words came in a rush. "But could you—would you let me kiss you just once before I go?"

Tules looked at him in the moonlight. She wanted to feel his strong, gentle arms around her, press her cheek against his clean, young jaw. If she kissed him as she wanted to, he would never go.

"You're so fine and good," Jeem said. "It would be just one kiss to treasure in my dream chest. But if you don't want to . . ."

Tules leaned toward him and lifted her lips. He took her in his arms, held her a moment, and kissed her unresponsive lips. She only allowed herself to pat his cheek.

"God A'mighty!" he cried. "I'll have to go or . . ."

He tore himself away and ran up the road. Tules listened to his long, fleeing steps and murmured, "Only the brave are not afraid to run." She was tempted to call him, bring him back. She turned the ring on her finger and rubbed the coins in her hand. She hid the money between her warm breasts and went into the dark house.

When Jeem rode out of town next morning, she waved to him, threw him a kiss, pointed to the ring on her finger. He raised his hat, but there was no smile in his blue eyes or on his set, young lips. She felt old and deserted for a moment and remembered the pain in her heart when Ramón left Manzano. But Jeem was young. He would remember her only as a symbol of this strange, vivid country after he married his cold Abigail. She sighed as Jeem and his young love vanished like a mirage in the desert.

What had Jeem said—"Unlucky at love, lucky at cards." She would play monte tonight, and Jeem's money would be her stake. She pressed the coins, hidden between her breasts, and called to Carlota, "I'm going to win tonight! I shall have all the luck; I feel it in my bones."

"Merciful saints, you sound like yourself again," Carlota laughed. "I began to think that rubio had bewitched you."

Tules ran to the monte sala that night, gay, laughing, greeting everyone. She called to Santiago, "Get my table ready. I'll have the bank. I'm going to win—this is my night."

Her full green skirt swirled around her supple body as she danced and raised her hands as though she was clicking castanets. Her eyes flashed, and bronze ripples gleamed in her hair as she tilted her chin and whirled on her toes. Men circled around her, laughing and clapping. She felt a strange power flow out of her, a wave almost as visible as smoke. She looked at the men's fascinated faces, took the wine one gave her, lifted her glass, and cried, "To good luck, señores!"

They called back:

"Salud y pesetas,
Mujeres y muletas,
Ay, qué caray!"

Santiago led her to the monte table and nodded to the dealer. She squeezed into the seat beside him and cut the cards. She rubbed Jeem's worn ring on her finger for luck and felt a strange tingle. She stacked all her money on a king and cried, "Alza! The blond king rides toward me." The matching king came "out of the gate," and the lookout pushed a pile of pesos toward her, paying the bet four to one.

Hours passed, and the stacks of pesos grew around her. Tonight she could not lose. Men talked of her streak of luck and followed her

152

bets. Her cheeks were flushed, and her eyes shone, but she watched carefully every play, every payoff. Men lost, shrugged their shoulders, moved away. Others sat in. At last all the money was divided between Tules and the "bank" in the center of the table. Men sucked in their breath and leaned over her as she continued to win.

"Time to close," Santiago announced finally.

"You're afraid she'll break the bank," men called.

"No, señores, permit me to invite you to come tomorrow night. There will be another table." Santiago bowed and waved his hand toward Tules. "Tomorrow night La Tules will deal from her own table."

"Viva La Tules!" the men cheered.

# 16

TULES WENT to the long monte table the next night, escorted by oily Santiago Flores and followed by curious onlookers in the cantina. The table was supported by two heavy walnut legs, and the carved trestle between them was worn smooth by the anxious feet of the players. Her winnings from last night filled the two cash drawers on either side. The light from a hundred candles fell on the green cloth marked in squares and on the stacks of silver pesos on either side of it.

Vicente Mares sat opposite her as her "lookout," prepared to take in the losing bets, pay the few winners, watch for cheats, and signal if rich men approached. His pistol was ready in case of trouble, and his dark watchful eyes also spied for Santiago on the percentage of profits for the house.

Tules smiled at Vicente and swallowed hard to relieve the tension in her throat. Now that she had reached her goal, her hands were icy with fright. She heard men joke that it would be easy to take money from an ignorant girl. Her "bank" might melt in an hour, and then Santiago would send her home. She twisted her hands nervously under the table and rubbed Jeem's ring. Her finger tingled, and an excited nerve flashed a message of good luck up her bare arm. It gave her courage to tilt her head and smile with shining eyes at the men watching her. Her heart pounded but she called gaily, "Bien, caballeros, let's see what the future holds."

As soon as she began to shuffle her hands steadied with the feel of the cards. The deck was thin with only forty of the narrow Spanish cards since the eights, nines, and tens were always removed for monte. She snapped the first four cards down for the layout and called, "Alza! Place your bets, caballeros!" She drew the cards from "the gate" at the bottom of the deck with cool skill, watched each play sharply, and heard the silver clink when Vicente stacked the pesos. Her hazel eyes burned with excitement as the hours passed and the silver mounted around her. Long after midnight, when the last disgruntled player gave up, she heard a man say to Santiago, "You're a smart fellow! La Tules is not only a handsome redhead, but she's a clever dealer. With this new attraction every man in the province will come to your sala. But you won't be able to keep all her smiles for yourself."

Each night Tules rubbed the worn gold ring on her finger. She was as superstitious as all gamblers, and the ring became her talisman. She thought of Jeem's clean blue eyes, wished him luck wherever he was, and waited for the sign. When her finger tingled she played for high stakes and watched the silver grow. When the ring was a cold, heavy band she played closely, passed long chances, and felt her heart trip as the "bank" dwindled with losing bets.

The players were also superstitious, and Tules soon learned which were the favorite cards of the aficionados, their habits of betting, and the weight of their pockets. She knew where the matching cards lay in the deck, and, if a run of desperate luck threatened the bank, her fingers moved too swiftly for anyone to watch the shuffle. That was seldom necessary with the odds of forty to one in favor of the house, and she took pride in an honest game and fair winnings. She used the old market tricks to flatter, cajole, and attract the players to her table, but when the play began her face was a set, impersonal mask. She trained herself to show no emotion whether the cards were running for or against her.

Months passed in a haze of excitement, shrewd play, and the challenge of running a better game than the men dealers. Tules's freckles faded during the long nights under the candles, and her skin took on the texture of vellum. The nervous strain sharpened the firm line of her jaw and the angles of her high cheekbones. The sensitive arch of her brows and the curve of her bronze lashes were feminine contradictions in the almost masculine strength of her handsome face. Her eyes could darken with mysterious seduction, but when she dealt they were a clear, sharp green.

As the winnings grew her shabby market clothes were replaced with the rustle of a taffeta skirt, whose color changed from red to green, and a fine silk reboso with stripes of yellow, purple, and cream. She enjoyed the tap of the high heels on her red satin slippers as she walked across the sala. Much as she longed for splendid jewelry, cheap brilliants still studded the combs in her red hair and her earrings. She hoarded her money against a long run on her bank, but she knew that gaudy clothes were a good investment. They whispered of success, money, and fame and drew an envious horde to her table.

She smiled triumphantly tonight as she marked off her first year with a good profit. She stood in the deep recess of the back door and looked into the gambling sala. It was early. Like an actress who knows the value of good timing, she would wait until later to make her flashy entrance.

On the opposite side of the long narrow room a large mirror reflected the crowd gathered around the bar. Tules watched the officers in brass-buttoned uniforms, American traders in open-necked hickory shirts, and rancheros in denim jackets. The bartender set bottles of whisky and Pass brandy before the gringos and poured red wine for the Mexicans. Peóns in loose, unbleached-muslin shirts and white pants stood silently at the edge of the crowd. Their dark eyes, under the shadow of their wide straw sombreros, glistened as they watched the rich men drink.

Tules knew that the men who drank now would gamble later. The traders would spend little money, since this was the end of the summer season and they were intent on collecting their bills and returning East; but the officers always played as long as they had one peso. All life was a gamble to them, whether they won silver at monte or a new office through politics. They filled the cantina every night to measure the unrest due to the recent appointment of the new Governor, Don Albino Pérez, and ease themselves into the next shift of power.

Tonight men crowded around Don Manuel Armijo, whose broad shoulders dwarfed the men beside him. Tules looked intently at this man who had been Governor, General of the Army, and now held

156

the lucrative office of Sub-comisario, Collector of Customs. He belonged to the powerful, rich Armijo family from Albuquerque and was the leader of the Río Abajo.

The sharp cliff of purple volcanic rock at La Bajada, six leagues south of Santa Fe, divided the Province into the Río Arriba and Río Abajo, the Upper and Lower Rivers. There had always been fierce political rivalry between them. There was a rumor now that Don Manuel of the Río Abajo had misappropriated funds, and the new Governor would replace him with Don Francisco Sarracino of the Río Arriba.

Don Manuel did not seem disturbed by this tonight. His hearty laugh rang out as he joked and slapped the backs of the compadres around him. He was a large, handsome man of about thirty-five with an arrogant nose, dark inscrutable eyes, and full, sensuous lips. He dominated every man in the room with his virility, sense of power, and shrewd raillery.

When Vicente beckoned to Tules to begin, she adjusted the reboso over her shoulders and let one end swing over her elbow as she rested her hand on her hip. She held her red head high, moved gracefully into the room, and preened with satisfaction as she heard people murmur, "La Tules! Here she comes! Look at the diamonds in her hair! No wonder she smiles with all her luck!"

She laughed as Pepe Cisneros called, "Qué hay, Tules? Your beauty blinds the luck of a poor man!" She stopped to ask him about his last buffalo hunt. She liked his good-natured face and jokes, but she had to move on to her table.

The officers proferred her wine and lifted their glasses to her with the usual toast of "Salud y pesetas!" She laughed and replied, "Y tiempo para gastarlas." Wine dulled the sharp wits she needed, and she never touched it until the evening was over.

An officer whispered, "Your head is as clear as a diamond, and you're as beautiful as the stars, but you have no heart." She motioned with her chin for him to come to her table.

Her finger tingled when she rubbed the ring, and she looked around to see who would challenge this good sign. The fever of gambling never reached its peak until midnight. Tules's fingers practiced through the evening with the first low bets. A peón sidled into a chair, bet his tostón, won, and lost. Tules watched his head droop and remembered her old despair when she lost her last tostón. She wished him better luck next week. She knew he would come back, for gambling was as much a part of life as breathing.

There was a little commotion as the peón slipped away and Santiago ceremoniously seated two people at the table. Tules looked at the priest with the curly brown beard on his jowls and the richly gowned lady beside him. She caught a whiff of expensive perfume and recognized Doña Trinidad Armijo, who had called her a hussy and a counterfeit coin at the market. She glanced into the cantina and saw that Don Manuel Armijo still talked to the men. She wished he had come to her table instead of his haughty wife. Doña Trinidad's bodice strained over her full bosom, and diamond rings flashed on her puffed fingers. She drew away from an ill-smelling paisano sitting beside her and complained to the padre, "We should have gone to another table. I don't see why you wanted to come to La Tules. . . ."

Tules's long eyelids tightened when she heard the "La." Its tone and emphasis suggested notorious ill fame rather than the familiarity used for children or servants.

The padre tried to hush her, but Doña Trinidad's face was flushed with wine, and her tongue hung in the middle. She said in a loud whisper, "She stacks the cards. I've heard that she marks them or roughens them with sandpaper to make them stick together. . . ."

Tules's face flushed, and her lips set in a hard red line. If Doña Trinidad expected shady tricks, she should have them. For the first hour luck favored Doña Trinidad and the padre. Tules dealt with cool, impersonal dignity as Doña Trinidad crowed over her winnings. Vicente stacked as much more money in the bank from the losing players.

"San Augustín, help me!" Doña Trinidad laughed and called on the gambler's patron saint as she bet five hundred pesos.

But San Augustín forgot her, and she lost. She whipped off the long gold chain around her throat and tossed it on the table. Vicente

158

counted out two hundred pesos and took them back after the next play.

"Give me five hundred pesos for this," Doña Trinidad demanded as she worked a diamond ring off her finger.

When she lost two more rings she cried angrily, "I told you this was a crooked game, Padre. I don't mind losing. I have a jewel box full of diamonds. . . . But to be cheated by a woman without decency!"

As she flounced away men murmured, "Even a peón has better manners when he loses."

Tules wound the gold chain around her throat, examined the diamonds, and slipped the rings on her fingers. She wondered how seriously Don Manuel listened to his fat wife.

It was never safe to incur the displeasure of powerful políticos, especially at this time when there was jealousy of the new Governor and talk of revolt. The fear of Navajo raids coupled with the new taxes led many New Mexicans to abandon their homes and settle in California. Governor Pérez stopped this with an order that no one should leave the Province.

A week later men gathered around a handsome boy who had defied this order. Nicolás Pino had taken fifteen thousand sheep to California, sold them at a big profit, and returned today with his herders. His defiance was backed by his father, Don Pedro Pino, who said that the rights of the ricos permitted no interference by a mere Governor, especially when that dignitary was an "outsider" from Mexico and foisted upon the Province against its wishes.

Tules watched the wild, headstrong boy drink with each friend at the bar. Black hair waved back from his slender, aristocratic face, and his long hands gestured dramatically as he pointed to a pearl-handled pistol stuck in the red sash around his narrow hips. She watched Santiago pilot Don Nicolás to her table and smiled as she thought that his money belt would be heavy. He protested that he had left his money at home tonight.

"With all the sheep you sold, your credit is good, señor," Santiago purred. "The word of a Pino . . ."

159

Tules saw the boy frown as his laughter rose to a high, nervous pitch. Perhaps Don Nicolás had gotten into a scrape in California like most young galanes or had taken too much wine. His cheeks flushed as friends teased him to play. Suddenly he stood up and pointed to the table.

"How much is in the pile?" he demanded.

"Perhaps ten thousand pesos." Santiago shrugged as he sized up the stacks of gold and silver on the table.

"Bien. I will bet my life on the ace of swords against the bank. If I lose, I will pay with my life." He threw his pearl-handled pistol on the card in the layout and folded his arms.

"But you don't have to wager your life," Santiago protested, as he looked at the boy's stubborn mouth. "I will give you credit."

"I have placed my bet," Don Nicolás said haughtily.

Santiago slipped behind the boy and shook his head at Tules. Her eyes flashed agreement that it would be bad business if the boy killed himself. Don Pedro might close the sala and throw everyone in jail. This might be a dramatic bluff, but a hotheaded young rico was dangerous.

She shuffled the cards calmly and looked at the money on the table. She loved the untarnished glint of gold. That was the money of her bank, the basis of her business. She thought of her favorite proverb, "With silver, nothing fails." Without silver she would have to return to the market. The ricos would destroy her for a whim; but Don Nicolás had also offered to destroy himself. He was foolish but young and warm with life. He must win.

The card opposite the ace of swords was the gold five. The bet depended upon which card was paired first. Tules's long memory ran over the cards in the deck; she was sure the matching ace was near the bottom, but she was not certain about the matching five for the bank. She dealt swiftly and turned up a four and a deuce.

"Jesucristo!" a man murmured, crossed himself, and looked at the pearl-handled pistol. Don Nicolás stood like a statue. Only his eyes moved as he watched the cards fall.

The third card was the blond queen, and everyone sighed with

160

relief. As Tules pulled the fourth card from the bottom men glimpsed the ace and sucked in their breath.

"Bravo! Bravo! Don Nicolás wins! What luck!" they shouted and reached toward the boy to shake his hand.

Tules watched Vicente stack the money in neat piles and push it toward the boy. An aftermath of resentment squeezed her heart as she looked at the empty table.

Don Nicolás bowed to her as he stuck his pistol in his sash and grinned. "I tell you God's truth, señorita, I didn't have a peso. I gambled in California and lost everything. Tomorrow I would have had to confess to my father, and I would rather take my life than face his displeasure. Now I can pay off my men and raise my head again. A thousand thanks, señorita. . . ."

As he started away Santiago offered hilarious congratulations. Tules lifted one eyebrow. Santiago hated to lose money as much as she did. She was tired from the strain, shrugged, and drew her reboso around her shoulders.

Don Nicolás's bet excited the men, and they crowded around her table, clinking the silver pesos they tossed between their hands. Santiago nodded slyly toward the cash drawer. Tules hesitated, wishing she could force Santiago to set up the new bank. There was no time to argue with him, and she unlocked the drawer and spread her reserve money on the table. If tonight's bad luck continued, she would be ruined. She was puzzled by the earlier tingle of good luck from her ring.

Men sat close together around the table, and others stood three deep behind them. In the clamor she and Vicente kept a sharp watch on the silver and gold thrown on the cards and settled disputes over where the bets had been placed. She dealt for an hour, noticing that a gringo won many bets and had a stack of silver in front of him. He wore a black coat, and a diamond stick pin sparkled in his wide cravat. His eyes were shifty, and his hands had the supple quickness of a dealer. He was probably a professional gambler who made a crooked living in St. Louis or New Orleans. She straightened her shoulders as she recognized this rival and saw with concern that he

161

continued to win. She looked sharply at Vicente, but he seemed unaware of any crooked play. Santiago shrugged. Tules's lips tightened as she realized that Santiago would sacrifice her rather than start a row in his sala. He boasted that pretty girls were cheap and plentiful.

Tules's face was a pale mask as she waited for bets to be placed, but her inner terror brought the cold sweat to her palms. Men threw their money away in the contagious excitement, but the gringo played coolly and added to his pile. When it amounted to as much as the money in the bank he announced that he would bet all of it on the knave against her three spot. It was too late for another shuffle, but her memory counted back over the cards in the deck. When she drew the winning three for herself a suppressed sigh escaped from the crowd.

"You're a damned cheat! I saw you pull that card from the top instead of the bottom," the gringo shouted and drew his pistol.

"Put that down!" a big voice called above Tules's head. Another pistol cocked above her and pointed at the gringo. She glanced up swiftly to see that Don Manuel Armijo held the pistol. Vicente grabbed the gringo's wrists and forced his gun down. Santiago pushed in to help him, but Don Manuel ignored the proprietor and took charge himself.

"Get out of here and don't come back," Don Manuel ordered. "I watched you, and I know your crooked tricks. All gringos are crooked, and we don't want you in our country. Get out, or I'll have you thrown in jail. . . ."

"You dirty greasers! You don't know what fair play means. This is a den of cutthroats," the gringo shouted, as Santiago took him by the arm and the crowd pushed him to the door.

"Good riddance! Our country would fare better if we kept every gringo out," Don Manuel said.

Tules stood up and held out her hand to him. "How can I thank you, señor? You saved my life. Though it is worthless, I pledge it to you. You are so brave, wonderful . . ."

"It was nothing, señorita." Don Manuel smiled and bowed gal-

162

lantly over her head. "Any man would consider it an honor to defend a beautiful girl. I know a little of the cards myself, and I watched his crooked ways. Allow me to congratulate you on outplaying him."

"Viva Don Manuel!" Santiago cried. "Thank God for such a bold, handsome defender. We can never repay this debt to you, Don Manuel! With your permission we will offer our gratitude to you in wine and pledge your good health. Come, caballeros, let us drink to Don Manuel and this happy ending."

Tules raised her glass to Don Manuel and thanked him again with glowing eyes. "You are so brave, so handsome, so wonderful! I have heard of you so much, but even your fame dims beside the real man. . . ."

The answering flash in his black opaque eyes made her heart pound. Some deep current of like natures, ambitions, passions passed between them, but before he could answer the men crowded around him with noisy cheers.

Santiago followed when Tules went to the back room to get her shawl. "You'd better light a candle to San Augustín for saving you tonight," he said. "Dios de mi vida, I thought you were about to give up when Don Nicolás cleaned you out. . . ."

In the flush of triumph over Don Manuel's gallantry Tules had forgotten the Pino boy, but now the memory of her empty table goaded her to say, "That was a fine play between you and Don Nicolás! You would ruin me for a joke. He wouldn't have killed himself!"

"No, my men were prepared to grab his arm before he touched his pistol." Santiago smiled like a cat licking cream. "But he was young enough to hurt himself or someone else. With all the unrest stirring now with this strict new Governor, it was well that you avoided trouble. . . ."

"But I lost ten thousand pesos!" Tules voice shook with exasperation. It was like a man to be so cocksure he was right. Santiago had not lost anything. She had had to dig into her hoarded reserve.

"Caramba, you drool over money like a miser!" Santiago sneered. "You don't know the rules of the game yet. Don Nicolás will lose

163

all that money and more next week. He thinks he is a big gambler, now, muy hombrón! This is the best advertising we could have—an honest game, a big loss for the house. People will talk of nothing else. Everyone will come to your table. We'll win it back a thousand-fold."

"You should have put up for the second bank," Tules insisted.

"We have delayed the settlement for these jewels you took last week." Santiago eyed her diamond rings, stepped closer, and fingered the gold chain hanging between her high, pointed breasts.

In the excitement Tules had forgotten them. She wanted to keep them to flaunt before Doña Trinidad. She said sweetly, "Ah, Santiago, you're the smartest man in the Province. You're so clever to plan every move. No wonder you're rich. . . ."

"Gamblers don't gamble. They are men of business." Santiago threw back his shoulders and stuck out his thin chest while his fingers fondled her arm. "This time you may keep the jewels for having sense enough to pull the right card against that crook."

"Don Manuel was magnificent!" Tules smiled. "And so brave! Dios, what luck! My fortune is made. But will he be angry that his wife lost her jewels to me?"

"He doesn't give a fig for her jewels or her virtue unless they reach into his pocket," Santiago winked. "He grew up as crooked as a lamb's hind leg. He was a peón sheepherder and stole the ewes from his patrón until he had a herd to sell back to the old man. He taught himself to cipher with a piece of charcoal at a campfire. He made his way to power in the Río Abajo with every low-down trick. His greed for power will make trouble for this new Governor."

"But he is one of the great Armijo family from Albuquerque." Tules defended her new idol and repeated the legends of his life and exploits. "Some say he was the eighteenth son of Don Vicente Armijo by the second wife and was cheated out of his patrimony by an elder stepbrother. Por supuesto, a man as handsome and daring as Don Manuel must have the blood of the Right People. He is the greatest leader we have. He should be the Governor again."

"You have much to learn." Santiago ran his jealous hand along her

164

bare arm. "Beware of dust in the eyes, lest it choke the heart."

He let her go reluctantly, and as she hurried down the dark road she wished she had her own sala. She hated the musk-scented pomade Santiago used, his yellow skin, and snaky fingers. If the money flowed back to her as Santiago promised, she would set up her own sala and not share her bed or money with any man. Don Manuel could come there without meeting Santiago's jealous eyes. Ah, she had had the best of luck to meet Don Manuel tonight!

# 17

POLITICAL CRISES drained or fed everyone's life and marked the two years of Governor Pérez's rule as a time of bitter scarcity. Don Albino tried to install an honest and just government and ousted former suspicious officials, including the Customs' Collector, Don Manuel Armijo.

When Tules heard that the Armijos had wrathfully returned to Albuquerque, she was pleased that Doña Trinidad had been humbled but disappointed that her exciting first contact with Don Manuel should be allowed to cool. Whenever he came to the capital, rumors grew that he had strengthened opposition in the Río Abajo and would either have Governor Pérez recalled or lead a revolt against him.

The winter of 1837 was as lean as a cow after a drought. Navajos raided the colonial settlements and the towns of the peaceful Pueblo Indians. Rancheros were afraid of attacks on lonely roads and stopped bringing their never-abundant produce to the market. Terrified settlers moved into the town, but they had no money for shelter or food. High prices and new taxes increased starvation to the panic rumble of revolution. The pobres fought for a cuartillo and cursed the growing horde of Saturday beggars.

One Saturday Tules found a beggar child asleep by her fire. He was a hunchbacked orphan named Victorio whose parents had been killed in a Navajo raid. He roamed the streets with other wild, abandoned children and had come to beg for alms. María fed him, let him curl up by the fire like a stray dog, and pleaded for the hungry waif.

"Let him stay," Tules nodded as she looked at the humped shoulders and the strange smile on his wizened face. "There's a Catalán saying that a merry fool brings good luck. He will be company and protection for you, María."

She had persuaded María to give up her tamale stand at the market

166

and move into the luxury of two rooms. María missed the sociability of the market and lavished motherly care on Victorio. The boy's twelve-year-old face was drawn with pain, but his tongue had a droll twist, and the neighbors called him an "inocente." Tules knew that his half-witted drollery was the hard wit and courage that had kept him alive. His body was dwarfed, but his long arms hung to his knees and had abnormal strength. He could help protect María and the buried pots of gold in these troubled times.

Tules remembered her own bitter struggle with poverty and always had coppers ready for the Saturday horde. When a woman pulled at her reboso one night at the cantina, she thought it was the usual whine for help. She looked into the woman's hard, deep-lined face and was shocked to recognize Cuca. Her face was old and coarse, and she must have seen hard times since the prosperous days at El Real de Dolores.

"Un momentito . . ." she whispered. She finished the deal, excused herself to take a short rest, and motioned to Cuca to follow. Her mind raced back through the years to the gold camp when Pedro had killed Ramón and she had killed Pedro. She would have been thrown in prison or hanged if Cuca had not helped her. The sight of Cuca stirred the ghosts of fear and grief she had trained herself to forget.

In the small back room she threw her arms around Cuca and cried, "How are you, comadre? Can it be eight years since I saw you? Por Dios, you've gotten fat! You didn't take enough of Doña Prudencia's salts."

Cuca's grin showed two front teeth missing. Her hair had the metallic tinge of black dye, and her face was heavily caked with paint and powder. The penetrating odor of cheap perfume mingled with that of stale sweat from her plump body and shabby purple sateen skirt. She looked twenty years older than the saucy girl who had defied Doña Prudencia, but her bold black eyes still rolled with audacity and earthy humor.

"I came from Dolores last week," she said. "Everyone has left the gulch. The camp looks like a deserted prairie-dog town."

167

"But the mine? The gold?" Tules exclaimed.

"There was no gold after they drove Don Damasio out. The políticos don't know how to mine gold from the earth!" Cuca shrugged. "They say an English syndicate has bought the grant. You were lucky to leave. . . ."

"That was not luck but your help, Cuca. You might have brought trouble on yourself. What did they say when they didn't find me?" Tules asked.

"The soldiers searched everywhere." Cuca made a wide gesture. "They went to Manzano, but Don José said you were not there. To save their faces and further work, they reported that you had been killed by the Apaches."

"Then I am dead—and safe," Tules grinned.

"No one is ever safe." Cuca shook her dyed head. "Políticos can hold an old murder over a man until he shivers into his grave clothes. But Pedro was not important; he was forgotten in the new murders that celebrated every Saturday night. Pues, to bathe with thieves is to lose the soap, no, niña? I heard you were a soap vendor, and now I hear you are the best monte dealer this side of Chihuahua. What good luck!"

"Yes, luck turned, but I starved at first." Tules nodded and unlocked a cupboard to pour wine for Cuca.

"Fortune belongs to the one who goes after it." Cuca sipped the wine and shrewdly appraised Tules's gold chain and diamond rings. "You were always handsome, Tules, but now you're smarter than the políticos. You have more to offer than any of my girls."

"Your girls? Were they the new girls who wriggled their hips around the cantina tonight?" Tules demanded.

"They had better do more than wriggle." Cuca nodded, and a whine crept into her voice. "I am too old for hard work, but I have ten pretty girls. Santiago wants a big cut if they come here. I have a house, but I need money to get started. If you would loan me two hundred pesos, Tules . . . Help me for the sake of old times. You are rich. . . ."

168

Tules drew back at the mention of two hundred pesos. She was not rich. The money on the table belonged to her bank, and she had to give Santiago a fat percentage. She hoarded her profit in order to have her own sala someday.

"A whole peso was riches at Manzano, but now one hundred pesos scatters like dust," Cuca sighed. "Ojalá that you still had the gold nugget!"

Tules remembered her delirious joy over the nugget, her grief for Ramón, her blazing hatred of Pedro, the terror of men hunting her on the dark mountains. Unaccustomed tears blurred her eyes as she said, "You saved my life, Cuca. Anything that I have is yours. . . ."

"Ah, niña, I knew I could count on your good heart. I'll pay you back ten pesos a month—or more if I find rich old men." Cuca's grasping hands took the money Tules counted out to her.

Tules was glad that she could help an old friend, but the loan cut into her thrifty budget. Her bank had shrunk since that night, two years ago, when Don Nicolás won ten thousand pesos. All that money and more flowed back to her, as Santiago predicted, but when that flash flood was exhausted the silver stream dwindled to a thin trickle. Now it was a big night when any man bet a hundred pesos. This summer even the American wagons failed to bring the annual prosperity. There was no cash, and the traders were forced to sell on credit.

During the plentiful years Tules and María buried four pots of money in the dirt under the hard clay floor of their room. In spite of Cuca, Victorio, and the constant demands of the pobres, Tules filled one more black Indian jar with pesos in the first six months of this year. She urged María to help her bury it with the excuse that they must hide it from Victorio. She did not want to frighten María by her own fear that revolution might break out any night. Robbers would kill for that pot of money, or it might be lost in riots and looting.

After the last trace of loose dirt was swept from the floor Tules swung up the road in the late July twilight with an easy stride. She was safe, in spite of the rumors of revolution that blew around the plaza like dry leaves in a dust storm. In the plaza she saw men holding a pine-knot flare to read some notice posted on the wall of the customhouse and went close to see what it was. In the wavering light it was hard to make out the shaded script, but she read aloud:

| | |
|---|---|
| Vehicles bringing in foreign merchandise, per month ........... | 2 pesos |
| Cutting timber for lumber, per month ...................... | 5 pesos |
| Foreign permanent merchants, per month .................... | 2 pesos |
| Each animal engaged by foreign merchants, per month .......... | 2 reales |
| Horses and mules for sale, per head ..  ............... | 2 pesos |
| Driving sheep or goats through Santa Fe, per head ............. | 2 reales |
| Theaters, per performance ................................. | 2 pesos |
| Dances, per night ....................................... | 4 reales |
| Gambling tables, per night ............................... | 2 pesos |

"Two pesos a night for each monte table!" Tules exclaimed. "Nombre de Dios, we can't pay such taxes!"

"You have reason to be dismayed, señorita, but no one will have money to play monte anyway," Flavio Martínez said bitterly. "There are taxes on chickens, on bread, on chile, on beans, on soap and fat, besides the old taxes on tobacco, candlewicks, paper, and cloth. And, on top of that, tithes for the church! The pobres should dig their graves now, while they have some strength left. . . ."

"We sweat blood for the wine our fine Governor drinks," another man muttered. In the group around him dark faces nodded under their tattered straw sombreros. "We freeze in our rage to buy gold lace for Don Albino's coat, red velvet curtains for his windows, silver and linen for his table. He brings carretas from Mexico loaded with brocade, tapestries, furniture, solid-silver picture frames, and casks of wine. María Santísima, our children starve while he eats white sugar!"

"Sí, señor, and he says Santa Fe is a filthy town, full of beggars and robbers." Flavio doubled his fists and shook them at the Palace. "He says our children are lazy and ignorant and must go to schools he will open or pay a fine. They will be no help at home or with the sheep. Don Albino has a fine education, but does any sheepherder

170

need to read or write? As for counting, I can count all the pesos I've ever had on one hand. . . ."

"You have reason, señores. These new taxes will kill us," Tules said as she started for the cantina and made a face at the lighted windows of the Palace. Now her monte table would buy candles for those glowing chandeliers. She thought resentfully of the long pier-glass mirrors, soft rugs, imported food, and the retinue of servants which filled the Palace with the pomp and formality of a long-forgotten court. She had no sympathy for Don Albino, even if he was a sick man and often confined to his apartment with his homesick wife and child. His motives might be honest, but his reforms were too sudden and drastic.

The Federal Government should recall this aristocratic "outsider" and allow New Mexico to be governed by her own men. A man like Don Manuel Armijo was brave and smart and would benefit the people. Of course he knew how to grease palms. That was the custom of the country and made things run smoothly.

She told herself that Don Albino had blundered when he discharged Don Manuel as Customs' Collector. A Texan named Fox charged that Don Manuel falsely appropriated the gringo's money and proved that Don Manuel had not accounted for taxes collected from the settlement of Los Padillas. Only a bold Tejano like this Fox had the courage to bring charges against the most powerful politician in the Río Abajo. Don Manuel denied the charge and swore vengeance on Fox, but Governor Pérez found this a good excuse to dismiss a Tax Collector who had lined his pockets with public funds. Don Albino was unpardonably stupid if he did not understand that a fair portion of public funds was a legitimate addition to the meager official salaries.

When she reached the cantina she saw that men were too upset by the list of new taxes to play monte but stood in tight groups grumbling to each other. Tonight Tules recognized the open criticism of Governor Pérez as the "grito," the first step of revolution. It would be followed by the formal complaint in a "pronunciamiento," and a few days later a "plan" from some locality would bind the signers into decisive action. Constant revolution in Mexico had produced a punctilious pattern, as closely observed as the precise steps of a bullfighter pirouetting before a charging bull.

She shuffled her cards idly at her deserted table, then edged along the bar to hear the comments of Don Juan Rafael Ortiz and the former Judge, Don Juan Esteban Pino. They were leading Insurrectos and loyal supporters of Don Manuel Armijo. She was always alert at any mention of the gallant General, and her heart fed the secret hope that someday she could charm Don Manuel to return her warm interest. The memory of his magnetism, bravery, and commanding presence stirred her imagination with bright dreams.

Don Juan Rafael Ortiz adjusted the fine serape over his shoulder, and the Judge fingered the gold chain around his paunch. They listened to the grumbling men and prodded them like the picadores who stabbed at the bull to infuriate it before the matador came into the ring.

"Times were bad enough before this," one man complained. "No more money from the trappers. They say men don't wear beaver hats any longer, and it doesn't pay to trap and cure the pelts. Qué mala suerte!"

"Yes, we lose more revenue every day," Don Juan agreed.

"Soon we will have no sheep," another man added. "Válgame Dios, Mexicans without sheep are like dogs without teeth! How can we eat without food or money? The few sheep the Navajos haven't run off are dying from scab. . . ."

"And humans are dying from the pox and this typhoid fever," a third man said bitterly. "Por Dios, God has cursed us! My wife died only last month and left six little creatures. . . ."

"I am sorry to hear that, amigo," the Judge said sympathetically and then shrugged. "But you will have to give up your wives anyway —or pay a tax for sleeping with them."

"What?" the man exclaimed. "A tax for sleeping with our wives! By the Holy Virgin, that's too much. . . ."

"But it's the truth! You'll see . . ." the Judge insisted.

"Caramba, it's been no pleasure to sleep with my old woman for

172

years. Should I be taxed for my duty?" a man spat. "This is more than I can swallow from that fellow. . . ."

"Then we must have a change, amigos," the Judge counseled. "Don Albino does not comprehend our needs. He is a sick man and an outsider. He attempted to punish the nomad tribes but he only killed men and good horses. Navajos plunder the north, Apaches and Comanches plunder the south, and no one stops them."

"Yes, Don Albino is helpless," Don Juan mourned. "It takes all his funds to keep up his court. Soldiers are never paid and have to forage for themselves. A hungry soldier can't fight. The ricos are tired of being milked for this foolish pomp. Don Albino forced the foreign merchants to give him supplies on credit, but soon their stores will be empty. . . ."

"Hola, compadres!" a hearty voice called, and every eye turned to watch Don Manuel Armijo's large, majestic figure come toward them. "Qué tal, Juan? Cómo te va, Rafael? Qué hay, Felipe, Andrés, Cruz, Benito!" He embraced friends, called laughing greetings across the room, and ordered Santiago to set out wine for everyone. The crowd at the bar fused into a warm, admiring audience.

Tules's eyes lighted with pleasure as she looked at his handsome, vital face. He made the other men seem puny and impotent. Although he had lost his office, he still wore the resplendent uniform of a General. A pale-blue broadcloth coat covered his deep chest and shone with gold braid and buttons. Tules edged closer, pretending to play with the deck of cards in her hand.

"We were talking of the hard times that break our backs, Manuel," Don Juan said in a loud voice that silenced the chatter. "There is much distress among our people, unhappiness, unrest. . . ."

"It ferments with the wild ideas brought in by the gringo traders," an old man declared. "Those Texans stir up sedition and heresy. They supply the Navajo raiders. . . ."

"Yes, the Texans are traitors," Don Manuel's voice deepened with righteous wrath. "They were colonists who were given good land in the Department of Texas. As soon as they raised crops they wanted to claim the whole country for themselves and withdraw from the Mex-

173

ican Federation. Two years ago they had the impudence to declare their independence as the Lone Star Republic. But there are only a handful of the traitors, and they will soon be punished. . . ."

"Didn't the Texans capture General Santa Anna when he took a siesta under a tree?" someone snickered.

"Another piece of infamy!" Don Manuel snorted. "They don't even follow the fair rules of war. But the United States could not overlook such disgraceful action. This spring the United States returned our illustrious leader to his honorable place in Mexico City. Now we can count on General Santa Anna to snuff out the Texas bonfire and restore our country to its proud prestige among the great nations of the world."

"Aren't the Texans also Americans?" a man questioned.

"The Tejanos are ruffians, outlaws, boors." Don Manuel shook his large finger at the man. "The Americans are bad enough, but the Texans are insufferable braggarts. They look down on us, who have proud Spanish blood in our veins, as though we were their own black slaves. I tell you, amigos, if we had a man in the Palace instead of a dummy he would prohibit any Texan from crossing our frontier."

His wrathful voice reminded Tules that Don Manuel had bitter, personal reasons to hate Fox and the Texans now.

"It's the fault of Don Albino. He is weak, helpless and can't prevent this suffering," the old man cried. "We should appeal to the great Santa Anna. . . ."

"You speak with wisdom, grandfather," the Judge said smoothly and threw his arm around Don Manuel's broad shoulder. "Our compadre Manuel and General Santa Anna are in close touch with each other and have profound mutual admiration. I see the dawn of a prosperous new day coming when 'outsiders' will vanish and our Province will be governed by our own good man."

"Viva Don Manuel! He will be our Governor. Qué hombrón! May that dawn soon come!" the crowd cheered and lifted their glasses to Don Manuel.

Tules's eyes shone with the mounting excitement, and she cheered and raised her glass high. Don Manuel smiled broadly as his dark eyes

174

traveled from face to face. When they reached Tules they stopped a second and stared. Then they warmed with recognition, and he bowed slightly. A thrill ran through her, and her heart pounded a warm flush to her cheeks. She leaned toward him to smile into his eyes, and her red lips opened to invite him. . . .

"Take care, Manuel," Don Juan exclaimed. "A fox comes with a firebrand in his tail."

Tules turned quickly to see what he meant. A tall, lanky gringo had come to the other end of the bar and ordered a drink. She recognized him instantly as Fox, the Texan who had charged Don Manuel with fraud and caused his dismissal. Don Manuel had sworn revenge. Now he would kill the Texan.

"Get out of here if you value your life!" Don Manuel shouted to Fox. "You would like to sneak up on my back the way you sneaked to Don Albino with your dirty lies about me. This place is not large enough for both of us. Get out. . . ."

Fox smiled under his broad-brimmed hat and held his glass of whisky in a steady hand. The other hand rested on his hip beside his gun. He was known to be a dead shot. He drawled casually, "I'm enjoying my drink. If this place is not large enough for both of us, I reckon you had better get out."

"You swine!" Don Manuel roared. "You have no breeding. You stay where you are not wanted. We won't have peace until we drive every one of you out. You come here to fatten on us, spy. . . . Curse you! Santa Anna will fix you!"

"Your Santa Anna won't stick his finger in the fire again," Fox sneered. "A handful of Texas Rangers whipped his whole army. They kept him prisoner as long as they could stand his stink. They should have burned him, the way he burned those pore fellers at Goliad. After this your Santa Anna will play safe in Mexico. Texas is free of him, like your country ought to be. . . ."

Fox drawled his insults across the twenty feet that separated him from Don Manuel. He stood at ease, but the cords showed in his neck above his unbuttoned collar. In the shadow of his wide hat his gray eyes were bright, alert, wary.

Men cleared out behind him and also slid away from Don Manuel. Both men were good shots, but there would be a stray bullet from the one who was hit first. Don Juan and the Judge cautiously moved out of range. Tules pushed to one side with them, one hand clapped over her mouth and the other gripped on her deck of cards.

Don Manuel's jaw sagged, and his full lips opened. He hunched his heavy shoulders and thrust his head forward. Tules watched his hand move uncertainly toward his gun.

"You damned Tejanos! You dirty skunks!" he bellowed. "Get out now before I. . . ."

Tules saw the sneer deepen around the Texan's mouth. His tall body was easy, loose like a mountain cat's, ready to spring. Don Manuel's big hand fumbled. The Texan's slight movement was quick, sure. He would shoot first and kill Don Manuel. Nombre de Dios, that must not happen. . . .

She darted into the cleared space between the two men and whirled so that her full skirt stood out. She stopped with her back to Don Manuel and held the pack of cards high in her hand. Then she lowered them toward the Texan and cried, "You disturb a pleasant evening, señores. Let us cut the cards and see who goes out first."

She looked at the Texan's cold gray eyes and knew that he watched Don Manuel behind her. She held her breath as she saw the sneer whiten his nostrils and mouth. He drawled, "I'll take on any number of men, but I don't fight women. If he has to hide behind your skirts, ma'am, you win."

He turned on his heel and walked insolently out of the cantina.

The muscles in her knees jerked now that the danger was over. She saw Don Juan and the Judge rush over to Don Manuel and slap him on the back. Don Juan cried, "Bravo, Manuel. In another moment you would have killed the skunk. Your patience was magnificent. It was too early to kill gringos tonight. More important business needs your hand. . . ."

"But La Tules!" a man shouted. "She took the big chance. I thought she would receive the Tejano bullet through her heart. Por Dios, she was brave! She saved our good Manuel!"

176

"Yes, válgame Dios, she had courage," another cried. "Viva La Tules! Viva Don Manuel!"

"I give you a thousand thanks, señorita." Don Manuel bowed ceremoniously. "In another moment it would have been too late to save the Texan. And, quién sabe, you may have saved my life as well. Or someone might have been hurt. . . . I offer my profound gratitude, señorita, and place myself at your orders. Wine, Santiago! Wine to drink to the brave senorita!"

"To the finest things in the world—" Don Juan proposed the toast —"a woman's beauty and a man's courage!"

"Viva Don Manuel! Viva La Tules!" the men cheered.

The wine trembled as Tules lifted her glass to Don Manuel, and her glowing eyes met his. For a second she was held by the powerful magnet of those resentful black eyes. Then a spark flamed in them and sent her some deep message.

"It is late. We have grave matters before us. . . ." Don Juan's voice broke the spell. He took Don Manuel's arm, and the three men bowed and went out together.

Tules held her red head high as she returned to her table and patted the cards still gripped in her hand. They had served her well tonight. She dealt automatically as she thought of Don Manuel, and exciting visions surged through her.

# 18

"The indians have declared war! They're fighting now!" men shouted as Tules ran up the dusty Calle San Francisco that hot afternoon of August 4, 1837.

"Who? Where?" she called.

"All the northern Pueblos have joined the Insurrectos at Santa Cruz. That's only ten leagues to the north. They'll be on us by sundown tomorrow!"

"María Santísima!" she cried and stopped at the edge of the crowd to listen to the news. "What happened?"

"Pérez had the Alcalde at Santa Cruz, Don Diego Esquibel, thrown in jail," Felipe Durán said. "Pérez wanted to put in his own man, Don Ramón Abreu, but the Indians wouldn't have him. They said Don Diego was the people's Judge and he had protected their land. They mobbed the jail, freed Don Diego, and locked up Don Ramón. They'll march on the capital to finish Pérez and his Judges."

"God knows what will happen now that the Pueblos have joined together," Evaristo Tafoya cried as he threw up his hands. "My father says the only other time the Pueblos fought together was in the Rebellion of 1680. Then they drove every Spaniard from the Province and kept them out for twelve years."

"You mean the Indians will rule in the Palace now?" another man exclaimed. "We wouldn't permit that. . . ."

"You wouldn't say much if the Indians had taken your scalp," Evaristo reminded him. "You think the Pueblos are harmless because they don't like to fight, but when they go on the warpath they're as fierce as the other savages. When each Pueblo stands alone they can't protect themselves from the Navajos, so now they have united under the Taos chief, José Gonzáles. They are furious because they have had no protection from the raiders, and their land will be confiscated for these new Pérez taxes. They will kill every Christian. . . ."

178

"But if the Indians only have lances and bows and arrows, our guns will defeat them," Felipe said.

"This time the Indians have **guns** and ammunition." Evaristo swelled with importance as he saw the consternation on the faces around him. "Verdad, hombres. The traders have supplied guns. They are at the bottom of this trouble. It's a gringo plot to arm the Indians, urge them to kill us, and then take the country away from the Indians."

"What a story!" Felipe cried. "How could a dozen traders defeat our Federal troops? The Insurrectos lead this Indian mob, and the Insurrectos are our own people. It's a fight for power between the políticos, and, as usual, the pobres will die for it. Manuel Armijo is the leader of the Insurrectos and wants to be Governor. He started to make trouble for Pérez as soon as he lost his fat job as Sub-comisario and Francisco Sarracino was put in his place."

Tules pushed closer to listen to this talk of Armijo. She knew this was his plot from hints that she had heard about his troops in the Río Abajo. If he added the southern forces to this northern insurrection, Pérez would be banished, and Armijo would be governor. She pulled her reboso over her mouth and drew in a deep, exulting breath as she thought of Don Manuel riding in to the capital as Comandante Militar. She would find ways to reach him, if he was only across the plaza in the Palace.

She listened intently as young Santiago Ulibarrí spoke. He was one of Armijo's top men. "You forget, amigo, that Armijo was governor ten years ago and did not bleed us with taxes." Ulibarrí's voice carried authority. "If we stand together, we can control the Indians and the gringos. We must fight for the 'Plan of Santa Cruz' that was adopted yesterday. It guarantees that we may govern ourselves as a department and decide on our own taxes."

"Viva the Plan!" a tipsy fellow shouted.

"Callate, hombre," Ulibarrí silenced him. "Don't shout now. There are alien ears in the Palace."

"Yes, Pérez has the militia and supplies," Felipe muttered.

"Pérez thinks this is only a minor squabble that can be squashed by

179

a handful of militia. He will find out." Ulibarrí pounded one fist into the other palm. "The whole country is up in arms against him. He called for volunteers and less than fifty men answered. Will any of you risk your life and provide your own horse and guns for a man who calls you dirty, ignorant peóns?"

"Not I. My family needs my head," Evaristo cried. "If Pérez has only a few hundred men in the militia and fifty volunteers, the Indians will wipe them out the first day."

"You speak the truth, amigo. You see the wisdom of the Plan. I will remember your words next week." Ulibarrí shook hands warmly and went on.

Tules hurried through the plaza and saw Federal soldiers staggering under armloads of goods they carried out of the gringo stores. The American merchants dared not refuse a Government order. Governor Pérez quieted their protests by signing worthless bills of sale. The merchants looked on helplessly as their stock disappeared into the Palace compound to outfit Pérez's militia.

In the cantina Tules glanced quickly at the close groups of men who whispered and watched to see that no enemy overheard them. Everyone was too excited to sit still at a table.

Santiago Flores beckoned to her from the back doorway. His pomaded hair and mustache were as black as crape against the frightened yellow pallor of his skin. "You're late," he scowled and pushed her through the door.

"No one is at the tables," Tules protested.

"There will be no play tonight. Do you think I would put loose money before this wild crowd? But you should have been here an hour ago to help protect this place against a saqueo."

"Saqueo!" Tules's eyes widened with fright and she clapped her hand over her mouth. If the rabble sacked the town everything would be lost.

"Yes, saqueo, tonta! The Indians are in their war paint and yelling, 'A lanzas!' Tomorrow their lances may stick through our ribs. Can a hundred of Pérez's little puppets hold back five thousand savages thirsty for Christian blood?"

"But our men are their leaders! They wouldn't let the Indians attack us," Tules cried.

"The Indians outnumber us a hundred to one!" Santiago's mouth twisted. "If they take the town, they'll kill and loot. . . ."

"María Santísima, I must go home! María is alone," Tules gulped and remembered the horror of the Taos massacre.

"She can go to the neighbors. I need you here." Santiago's fingers tightened on her arm, and he whispered, "We must hide the money before the barbarians come. . . ."

He pushed her into the money room where Vicente waited, shivering with fright. Santiago locked the door, thrust a lighted candle on a high wooden safe, and jerked open the lid of a long carved chest. It was filled with shelled tithe corn. Santiago credited it against gambling losses and held the corn for high winter prices.

"Put the corn in these." He threw sacks to Tules and Vicente.

"This is no time to s-save corn," Vincente stammered.

"If you're hungry, corn is better than gold. Get to work." Santiago went out and locked the door behind him.

Tules turned up her silk skirt, fastened it around her waist, and began to ladle double handfuls of corn into the sacks. She sneezed with the sweet dust, and Vicente jumped. "There will be a s-saqueo, but S-Santiago only thinks of s-saving corn," he muttered.

Tules thought of her own pots of money buried under the floor at home. If they were lost, she would be a beggar.

"All the women should leave now," Vicente mumbled. "My wife and children have gone to her father's ranch in the mountains. I s-should have gone to protect them."

The Navajo raid flashed through Tules's mind again. María might be scalped like old Caterina. She must find some way to get home.

They had filled five large sacks with corn when Santiago came back. He pulled a bunch of keys from inside his fine cambric shirt and went to the high money safe. Its thick doors were bound with heavy iron straps and fastened with seven locks. The wooden sides and back were studded thickly with nailheads that would have ruined any ax used against it. Santiago cautiously fitted his keys into the seven locks, and Tules heard the doors creak open.

"Here, Vicente, help me lift these. Be careful. Thieves can hear the clink of a peso a league away." Santiago helped lift out heavy buckskin sacks filled with silver pesos and smaller almueres, the standard measure of 1,000 doubloons. Gold doubloons spilled out, and Tules helped stuff them back. She counted twenty almueres filled with gold at sixteen pesos the ounce. Santiago was rich. All these years he had mourned over his losses, haggled over her pay, but he wouldn't lie again.

Inside the safe drawers were labeled "Dollars," "½ dols." "Gold dols." "Pesos," "Marcs," and "Francs." Tules looked enviously at the tiny gold dollars as Santiago emptied the drawer. She longed for a handful to dangle on her chains and bracelets. Then he took out a lacquer box inlaid with mother-of-pearl and fragrant with sandalwood. It slipped from his nervous fingers, and jewels spilled on the floor—brooches set with diamonds, emeralds, rubies, gold chains and watches, black pearls gleaming on enameled bracelets. Tules drew in her breath and reached for a diamond ring that rolled to one side.

"Put that back," Santiago barked.

"Cómo no?" She replaced the ring. "But, Santiago, where did you get such treasure?"

"Not every bite is from a mad dog," Santiago quoted as he picked up the jewels. "Put your trinkets in here, too. For safekeeping. A thief might kill you tonight for your rings. Vicente is my witness that I'll give them back—if we live!"

Tules hesitated but handed Santiago her rings, bracelets, and gold chain. He took the jewel box to the grain chest, fumbled inside, and slid back a secret panel. It revealed a space deeper than a hand span between the false floor and the bottom boards of the chest. He shoved the jewel box far under the panel, fitted in the almueres of gold, and pushed the panel into place.

"Fill it with corn again," he ordered. "I will leave some of the silver and gold in the safe. If thieves break in, they will think that's all I

182

have. If the Indians come, let them take the corn, but if they move the chest shoot them."

"But if they s-shoot first," Vicente protested.

"The mob may kill me at the front door." Santiago turned up his palms. "You and Tules will stay here and relieve each other every two hours. You can go home, Tules, but get back quickly if you want to keep your table after this is over. If either of you talks of what you have seen here tonight. . . ." His thin fingers pointed to the pistol at his belt.

Tules ran through the plaza where torches flared and soldiers hurried in and out of the Palace. They would march at dawn. At home, María opened the door a crack, pulled Tules in, and exclaimed, "Your jewels, niña! They've robbed you already?"

"No, no." Tules gasped from running. "They are safe. But there will be a saqueo. You must leave."

"No, I will stay here, niña. God will protect us. To each his own house, but God lives in all. We have brought in food and water for three days. You must stay here. There is too much danger in the cantina."

"I must go back, or I'll lose my table. Give me your black skirt and shawl. Thieves don't molest pobres." Tules threw off her gay clothes, put on María's somber cotton, and twisted her red hair in a tight knot. She tried to joke as she scrubbed off the rouge and powder, but she almost sobbed when she thought that she might never see María and Victorio again. She pulled the black shawl over her head, kissed María, and cried, "Lock the door and stay inside. May God protect you!"

She relieved Vicente and sat on a folded blanket in the small dark room. She thought of the night she shot Pedro and wondered if she still knew how to use the gun across her lap. She felt for the dagger strapped below her knee. If the soldiers threatened her, she would tell them she was Armijo's girl. He had more power than anyone in the Province and would lead the Insurrectos. If she could get word to him. . . .

At dawn she watched the troops march out of the Palace, led by Governor Pérez on his black horse. His face looked ill and pinched above his dark cape, and he turned north toward Santa Cruz de la Cañada. Mules drew the one cannon, and the soldiers proudly carried their English muskets. They counted on these superior arms to overcome the rusty flintlocks of the Insurrectos and the Indian's bows and arrows.

An ominous quiet settled over the deserted plaza. Merchants fastened heavy wooden shutters over their windows and worked behind barricaded doors to hide their remaining stock before the saqueo. Carretas passed, piled high with household furnishings, and the wheels whined as they turned in the dusty road. Families trudged beside them, bound for the comparative safety of the mountains. Rumors grew that Indians and troops from the Río Abajo would camp in Santa Fe on their way north.

At nightfall a runner reported that Pérez's militia had marched six leagues and camped beside the river at Pojoaque. "They are well but tired from marching in the sun. Dios, it was hot! But we saw no one. The Insurrectos have vanished, frightened by our Federal troops. Governor Pérez will find the traitors and bring them here in chains tomorrow."

"This is only the first day," Santiago mumbled.

That night Tules paced the floor to stay awake while she was on guard. She worried that no word had come from the southern troops. Had Don Manuel's plot failed? Had troops from Mexico subdued the southern "canton" before they could start? She counted so much on Don Manuel's bravery and shrewd strategy. What had happened to him? When she went into the cantina men boasted of Pérez's strength. Armijo's followers bought wine to warm their faith.

"A massacre! Rout!" a terrified runner gasped the next day. "All is lost. They met at the foot of the Black Mesa near San Ildefonso. Governor Pérez led his troops in the open, like brave men. Indians jumped out from every rock, every bush. Madre de Dios, what a defeat! Our men started to set up cannon. Before they had it in place the Indians killed six. . . ."

184

"Who? Ay de mí, was it my Chato? Luis? Meliton?" women shrieked and began the death wail. "Where is the army? Where is Pérez?"

"He fled. Everyone ran to save their lives. They had no chance against the thousands of yelling demons. The Indians are searching every mountain, every cañon for Pérez. They will drag him from the Palace and kill all of us. The women and children must hide."

"God save us! Where can we go?" the women cried.

On the heels of the fleeing soldiers the first Indians rode into the plaza on foam-flecked horses. Their naked brown bodies were painted with red ocher and sweat ran down their glistening backs like rivulets of blood. Their faces were hideous with stripes of black-and-white paint. The fading sunset caught on the sharp ends of their upraised lances.

People scurried away like rats and let the Indians take over the plaza. Inside the cantina Tules peered through a crack in the shutter. The plaza swarmed with Indians holding their bows and arrows ready as they watched every doorway. A few Mexicans walked among them and greeted the Indians as comrades.

"Where are the troops from the Río Abajo and General Armijo?" Tules asked the question that had been on her tongue all day. "They would protect us from a saqueo. . . ."

"They will get here when the trouble is over," Santiago sneered.

Tules reluctantly went back to the money room where Vicente handed her the gun. She felt for her dagger and planned how she would use it before the savages attacked her. She remembered the bloody heads of the massacre at Taos and poor Doña Carmen bound to her horse. Why didn't Don Manuel come? What had happened to him? He was a tower of strength. His courage and valor could turn the vengeance of this mob. Madre de Dios, send him soon!

She paced the dark room that was like a dungeon and shook with a nervous chill when she touched the cool, thick wall. Her hand froze on the gun, and she held her breath as she heard a sound at the door. It passed on. At last Vicente came in with the latest report. "The Indians have made camp down by the river by San Rosario. They may attack tonight or wait until dawn. More Indians are coming all the time. They want to catch Pérez first. They have sent trackers in every direction."

"Padre Jesús, save Maria and Victorio down there near the Indians!" Tules prayed.

The night passed in sinister quiet. Inside the barricaded buildings people crouched in the dark, ready to run at the first war whoop. But where could they go? At sunup the Indians filled the plaza. Tules rubbed her tired, smarting eyes as she watched them through the shutter. They stood there in a silent, sullen mass. They were waiting for some signal. Then the saqueo would begin.

Suddenly a high, terrifying yell cut the suspense. Every hideously painted face turned west where the war whoop had sounded. Every bow and arrow, every lance was raised and ready. At a signal, answering war cries roared from a thousand throats, and the Indians surged toward the Calle San Francisco.

"What is it?" Tules cried between chattering teeth. "María! Victorio! They're in the path of the Indians!"

Now the Indians surged back into the plaza. They yelled and stamped in a wild dance as they brandished their lances. They ran after something, like dogs after a rabbit. A round object flew through the air above their heads. They ran after it, kicked it again.

"Jesucristo!" Santiago's voice cracked with fear as he pushed Tules aside for a better view through the shutter. "They found Pérez! That's his head they're kicking like a football!"

"María Santísima! Pobrecito! God have mercy on him!" Tules clutched her dry throat.

"Look! That's Pérez's body!" Santiago muttered.

The Indians hurled a headless body into the plaza. As it rose above their heads the legs and arms dangled inertly, and blood oozed from the stump of the neck over the dusty uniform. Half a dozen lances stuck in the lifeless body. The Indians pounced on it and stripped off the Governor's clothes. José Gonzáles, the Taos chief, stepped back from the mob wearing Pérez's fine striped vest over his naked chest. Other Indians thrust Pérez's head on the point of a lance and danced around it in wild orgy.

186

"God have mercy on us if they break in!" Santiago gulped.

"Pepe has come," someone whispered.

Tules ran after Santiago into the back room to find Pepe Cisneros. His ruddy face was grave with bad news, and he seemed older than the gay, singing cibolero Tules had joked with in her market days. He had escaped from the rout at the Black Mesa and made a long loop to bring news to Santa Fe.

"They have been told so many lies that they are wild," Pepe said. "They caught Pérez at Agua Fría at dawn, but his wife and child are safe. Don Miguel Sena, Don Marcelino Abreu, Lieutenant Hurtado, and two soldiers were lanced and mutilated. They caught Don Santiago Abreu at Los Cerrillos and took him to Santo Domingo. They put him in the stocks, cut off his hands and feet one at a time, gouged out his eyes and tongue. . . . God pity him! They are a mob without reason now. They will do anything. . . ."

"May they burn in hell!" Santiago muttered and ran out to tell the news.

"María Santísima!" Tules gasped and shut her eyes.

"You should not be here." Pepe tried to quiet her and pressed her shoulder with his firm hand. "I hoped to find you. A woman is in greater danger with these savages. Pérez did them no harm, but they have been fed lies until they are crazed. You must leave here. I can hide you, help you get away."

"Santiago says I must stay on guard," Tules shuddered. "I can't leave María and Victorio, and I can't get to them. The Indians are at their door. They need help more than I do. If you could help them to get away, Pepe. . . ."

"Come, Pepe, look at the plaza," Santiago called.

Tules followed them to look through the crack in the shutter. She heard the deep beat of drums and the fury of a war dance. Mutilated bodies lay where they had been pierced with lances. Santiago muttered that the Indians would attack after dark and set fire to the houses.

"I came back to help you. Come with me now," Pepe whispered, but Tules looked at Santiago and shook her head.

187

Again that night the town shivered in the foreboding quiet. Satiated with bloody rites, the Indians returned to their camp at San Rosario but left a strong guard in the plaza. They killed the dogs who sniffed at the corpses.

Tules sank into exhausted sleep in the dark room and dreamed that María was scalped, Victorio mutilated, and the money pots gone. When Vicente wakened her she rubbed her stiff neck and asked resentfully, "Where is General Armijo? Are we to be tortured with no one to help us? He could save us. . . ."

In the morning the Indians filled the plaza again but made a wide circle around the corpses. They believed that death waited in lifeless bodies to snatch another victim. They ignored the Palace and the stores as though the adobe walls were mounds of dirt in the desert. They were plainly waiting for orders. Whose orders? Were the nomad Indians coming to join them? What would they do? Only General Armijo could prevent a massacre now.

At midmorning Tules heard guttural cries and saw every savage face turn toward the west. Something had happened. The orders had come.

"Listen!" Santiago whispered fiercely. "Horses! Federal troops from Mexico to help Pérez!"

"No, they are shouting as friends," Felipe said. "The Navajos have horses. If the Navajos and Comanches have joined the Pueblos, God have mercy on us!"

"It is General Armijo!" Tules cried. "Look, look! He has come at last! Thanks be to God!"

As soon as Santiago saw that it was General Armijo he threw open the shutter for a better view. The General rode ahead on a large sorrel horse followed by an armed guard. He was triumphant in his pale-blue uniform. Red, green, and white plumes nodded from the gold lace at the top of his helmet. He brandished a shining saber and saluted the Indian chiefs. His hearty voice rang out with the cry of the Insurrectos, "Viva Dios y la nación!"

People ran from their barricaded doors to echo this cry and follow the General up the street to the parroquia. The Indians let the horsemen go by and fell in behind them. Men crowded into the church to give thanks for deliverance.

After mass Santiago opened all the shutters and pulled the barricades away from the doors. "I knew Don Manuel would come and that the Indians were only waiting for him," he boasted. "It takes some time to come from the Río Abajo. Now Don Manuel will be Governor, and we shall have peace. No more 'outsiders.' Our own man knows how to rule the country."

The plaza came to life, like bees flying after a long winter. Merchants opened their stores, and people greeted each other excitedly. No one dared to touch the bloated corpses for fear they might be accused of loyalty to Pérez. They could only be given a decent Christian burial on General Armijo's orders.

Tules ran home with the good news and hugged María. "Thank God you are safe!" she cried.

"And you, niña," María nodded. "I knew that Our Lady was watching over you when Pepe Cisneros came last night. He said you were worried and offered to help us get away. He is a fine, brave man, that Pepe!"

"It was brave of him to come here where the Indians might have caught him," Tules said. "But the danger is over. You should have seen Don Manuel ride in this morning. They are meeting now to make him the new Governor. There will be a great celebration tonight."

She slipped on an embroidered blouse and silk skirt and threw a magenta shawl over her shoulders. "Do I look my best?" she laughed and cocked her head at María. "I must be beautiful for the new Governor. Another life begins for us today. Ah, María, kiss me and wish me luck. Now I must go. . . ."

The cantina was filled with men drinking wine and exchanging experiences. She smiled at them and repeated the cry of the Insurrectos, "Dios y la nación!" Pulsing new hopes made her face radiant and attracted every man's eye.

"This will be a big night," Santiago said as he returned her rings and gold chain. "All those soldiers from the south. Get ready to play.

189

They will come here as soon as the junta is over. Don Manuel will be the new Governor. I have asked him to honor us. . . ."

"The junta is over. They are coming out of the Palace now," someone shouted.

Men crowded around the first soldiers to hear the news. Tules's eyes sparkled, and she repeated to herself, "Mi General! Mi Gobernador!" Other endearments for Don Manuel would come later.

"Caramba!" a tipsy man laughed. "Don Manuel rode up the hill, and now Don Manuel rides down again!"

"What?" Tules demanded, astonished by the sullen looks of Don Manuel's soldiers.

"Don Manuel didn't have enough compadres, even with all his army," the man leered. "The Indians outvoted him. They elected one of their own men Governor—the Taos chief, José Gonzáles!"

"An Indian as Governor!" Tules exclaimed. "You mean they will turn us out and take the town?"

"Take care!" the man laughed. "Their chief is already resting upon Pérez's bed in the Palace. Don Manuel signed the papers."

As Tules dealt the cards she listened to the talk around her. Armijo's soldiers looked sullen and stood by themselves. Men gossiped of how Don Manuel had had to sign the agreement making the Taos chief Commandante Militar.

Late in the evening Don Manuel himself came into the cantina. Men pressed close to him and asked questions. His heavy face was stern, but he announced loudly that he and his troops would give every aid to José Gonzáles and the Indian administration.

Love and pity for Don Manuel filled her heart as Tules watched him in this hour of disappointment. She was confused, upset by this unexpected turn. She wanted to go to him, share his pain, comfort him.

She made an excuse to leave the monte table and moved toward him. She was afraid of his stern face and haughty bearing, but she yearned to touch him, help him. This was the first time she had seen him since the night she had whirled between him and Fox. She re-

190

membered the deep look they had exchanged then. It made a link between them.

She came close to him and laid her hand on the sleeve of his blue uniform. He turned sharply to see who had touched him. She smiled, lifted her glass, and said in a low voice, "To your good health, my General! May success await you tomorrow!"

"Tomorrow be damned!" he cursed and drew away. He scowled at her as though he had never seen her before and turned his back.

# 19

TULES WAS torn between her secret worship of Don Manuel and his stinging rebuff. Her vanity was wounded because her love and sympathy and the message exchanged by their eyes meant nothing to him but everything to her. She reminded herself that a monte dealer was beneath the notice of a haughty General and tried to throw off the one-sided infatuation. But no other man was large enough to blot out the bright image of Don Manuel.

She had no chance to forget him. The men around her table argued endlessly about the curious twist of fate that had tossed the Governor's cane of office into the hands of an ignorant Indian. They said General Armijo had accepted the lesser appointment as Chairman of the Committee to Ask for Federal Aid. Ten days later he announced that the Indians no longer needed his advice and returned at the head of his troops to the Río Abajo.

"Don Manuel will never forgive this humiliation. He'll get even," Santiago said. "He follows the strategy of his idol, General Santa Anna, who 'withdraws' from Mexico City to hatch plots in seclusion. Don Manuel won't throw his house out the window."

"He signed the agreement to support the Taos chief as Governor," Tules said.

"Yes, but don't count on it," Santiago winked. "He will ride up the hill again."

With everyone else in the capital, Tules was shocked that an Indian was their Governor and occupied the Palace. In the warm September sunshine she saw Indian braves in breechcloths pass in and out through the middle doors. After the punctilious pomp of the Pérez court their bare bronze bodies seemed indecent. But the garments worn by the chief, Governor José Gonzáles, were a greater insult. They were Governor Pérez's personal clothing, brazenly exhibited as triumphant spoils of war. The long black braids of the chief

192

fell over Don Albino's fine striped vest, and the broadcloth dolman flapped awkwardly over the blanket around his hips.

The chief had a strong face with an aquiline nose and firm jaw, but his dark eyes looked puzzled by the strange business he tried to direct. In Taos he had been a famous hunter and an honest chief with a well-earned Indian name. As a Spanish subject his baptismal record was easier to transmit with a Spanish name, but that did not help him now with devious politicians and an exhausted treasury.

Tules heard that the Indians were baffled by their empty triumph. The headmen of the Pueblo tribes held their Council in the formal halls of state in the Palace, moved out the ornate tables and chairs, squatted on the floor in a blanketed circle, and smoked native punche. The Elders recited long, word-of-mouth histories about their prior claims to the country, but they had no practical plans for its government. Few could read or write, and they had to call in Mexicans to inscribe the official decrees and add figures.

The peaceful Pueblo tribes had united in desperation to save themselves from two perils that were about to destroy them. Their enemies, the nomad Navajos, took Pueblo women, sheep, and crops, and Pérez's taxes threatened to confiscate their tribal lands. The Taos chief abolished taxes but found he had no money to run the Government. Pérez had left large debts, and the soldiers refused to serve unless they received back pay. With even the weak militia disbanded, the Pueblo Council knew that the Navajo raids would be worse than ever this fall.

"Válgame Dios, the gringos are the cause of this Indian blunder!" Tules heard Evaristo shout to men in the cantina. "Today the Indian Council declared that the Mexican Government had given them no protection and agreed to turn this country over to white men who would stop the Navajo raids. The gringos are plotting with the Indians for our downfall."

"This is our country, not theirs," men cried. "Down with the Indians! Kill the gringos!"

Men stopped playing monte, rushed over to hear the news, and Tules followed them.

"The Indians say we have no money, no arms, no sense." Evaristo waved his arms. "They say we fight each other and let the Navajos slaughter the Pueblos. Their legends prophesy that white men from the East will rule the country. They are ready to save themselves and the country by joining Texas now!"

"Texas! The Indians are traitors," men shouted. "What insult, blasphemy! We will never give in to the Tejanos. We would be slaves, fools. For more than two hundred years we have ruled the Indians. They have power for two weeks and betray us. The election was a mistake. We should drive the Indians out of the Palace tonight."

"We killed the dog and took on the fleas," Santiago mumbled.

"We must send for Don Manuel," Evaristo cried. "He is the only man who can save us. We must work together against the Indians and Texans. We must fight. . . ."

"Viva Don Manuel! He should be in the Palace tonight," men yelled.

Tules could not escape the contagious hero worship of that week. No one talked of anything but Don Manuel. Since the common people pardoned no fault in any man, they invested their new hero with every virtue. With Latin fervor they lauded his bravery, his leadership, his majestic presence. They boasted that he was one of themselves. He understood the bitter poverty of the pobres because he had been a poor sheepherder; but he could also govern the ricos because he had achieved wealth and power. In another year they might crucify him, but, this September day, they hailed him as the savior who would rescue them from Indians and Texans.

The grito and pronunciamiento of the new revolution crystalized in the Plan of Tomé, signed by General Armijo and Padre Madariaga in the little settlement below Albuquerque. General Armijo dispatched a letter to his friend General Santa Anna denouncing the Indian revolt and asking aid from Federal troops. He added that he had recruited troops from the Río Abajo at his own expense and would lead them to Santa Fe to hold New Mexico for the mother country until a new governor could be appointed.

After this swift news the capital seethed again with the prospect of

194

becoming a bloody battleground. But the Indians left the Palace overnight and set up their own headquarters twelve leagues to the north at Santa Cruz de la Cañada. They did not understand this new strategy, but they would wait until General Armijo was ready to work with them again.

For the second time in a month Tules watched General Armijo ride into Santa Fe. This time he came as an undisputed conqueror and installed himself in the Palace. A strong bodyguard protected him day and night from the smoldering hate of the Perezistas and the resentment of the northern Pueblo tribes. For so large a man he moved delicately to ward off another uprising until he was reinforced by Federal troops.

In January Colonel Justiniani and four hundred soldiers marched in from Zacatecas and Chihuahua. The town crier commanded everyone to assemble before the Palace for an official announcement. The winter sunshine was bright, but the air was cold and sharp, and Tules and Cuca pulled their shawls closer as they waited in the plaza with the throng.

When the church bells stopped ringing Colonel Justiniani stepped out from the door of the Palace and read the letter from General Santa Anna. He commended his illustrious friend, General Manuel Armijo, for his personal valor in protecting the honor and glory of the mother country and appointed him Governor and Comandante Militar of New Mexico. Colonel Justiniani's small, dapper body shrank beside the large, powerful figure of General Armijo, who stepped forth to receive the congratulations of the officers and the ovation of the crowd.

"Viva Don Manuel! Viva Armijo! Viva Dios y la nación! Viva Mexico!" they cheered, their voices shrill with relief after the past five months of fear and anxiety.

"Viva Don Manuel!" Tules cried and raised her hands high. She forgot her smarting hurt and was caught up in the wild tumult and enthusiasm of the crowd. As they cheered she hugged the thought that this great man was closer to her than to these bystanders. She magnified their chance meetings and gloated that Don Manuel had thanked her for saving his life. If she had not whirled in to protect him that night, he might not be here today to save the country. That gave her a special hold on him, and she identified herself with his life and success.

"Your man won!" Cuca nudged her slyly. "Your stallion came in first on the second race, even though he fumbled the first. Pues, where the wolf finds one lamb, he seeks another."

"This is best for the country. We need a strong man." Tules tossed her head. Her eyes shone, and a flush of personal triumph warmed her cheeks as she listened to Don Manuel begin his acceptance speech. He stood under the portál of the Palace, his dark, handsome face glowing with magnetism and vitality. Her blood raced as she heard the deep, resonant tones of his fiery oratory. She was drawn to him by a bond that held and twisted her heart. In spite of her cool practical sense, some inner knowledge told her that her destiny was forged with his and that someday her ambition would be fulfilled. She did not heed the words, but her eyes never left his proud bearing, his keen eyes, his dramatic hands. The mad desire to touch him, throw herself in his arms, press against his hard, male strength ran through her body like a flame.

"You're in love with him," Cuca mocked. "You should know that a woman pays too much for love. You had one hard lesson. This fine General is another Pedro."

"Your tongue wags at both ends, Cuca," Tules said furiously. "How can you compare an ignorant vaquero with a magnificent leader like Don Manuel? You don't know him. He is a great man—smart, shrewd, brave. He is above anyone in the Province—or even in all Mexico!"

"He is Pedro on a larger scale," Cuca insisted. "Pedro would have climbed up too, if . . . No importa. I am only thinking of you. Don't sell your heart cheap."

Tules looked at the crowd around them and realized that she was only one of the lowly pobres looking up to the mighty Governor. "I have no chance," she sighed. "He would not look at a monte dealer."

"With your good looks you can have any man you want," Cuca said. "You were born lucky. See where you are now—the most famous

196

dealer in the Province! Don't throw that away! You know how to rouse men and turn their heads. Bien, use them but don't let them use you. Any woman is lost if she entrusts her heart to one man— especially a man who looks at women as though he was the only stallion in a spring pasture filled with mares!"

The Governor raised his hand in a final salute to his cheering people, took Colonel Justiniani's arm, and led him into the Palace. They would feast at a regal banquet spread on Don Albino's fine linen and silver.

"He who does not pay for it can give a fine feast," Cuca snorted as they turned to leave. "But there are debts to settle before this is over. The General still has to subdue the northern Indians and Insurrectos at Santa Cruz."

The capital celebrated the inauguration with a week-long fiesta. One night Don Manuel brought the visiting officers to the cantina, embraced his friends, and ordered wine for everyone. Tules joined the admiring crowd around him, and he nodded to her in high good humor. She was not sure that it was a personal greeting, but it renewed her hope that he could be reached if good luck continued to smile on her.

She took it as a favorable sign when soldiers piled new Zacatecas silver on her table every night. Even in the far south they had heard of this famous woman dealer and eagerly bet their money against her skill. They gaped at her vivacious beauty, grace, and wit and the mystery that surrounded her. They tried to discover the magic in her supple fingers and the strange sorcery by which her eyes read the cards. She dealt steadily for two days and nights, while Vicente pushed stacks of silver and gold back and forth across the table. The tingle of success ran up her arm from Jeem's gold ring. By dawn of the third day she had won all their money. Now she could afford to have her own sala where Don Manuel could come as a favored guest.

The caciques from the southern tribes had come to swear allegiance to Governor Armijo, but the northern tribes and the former Insurrectos stubbornly maintained their dual authority at Santa Cruz. The Federal troops were cold and restless. When the January snow melted

General Armijo was forced to lead his followers against the pretenders at Santa Cruz.

Santa Fe shuddered again with the terror of another Pérez massacre. They knew that the five hundred men under General Armijo were vastly outnumbered by the Indian hordes, who were now armed with new guns and ammunition. If the Indians routed Armijo, they would not leave one Mexican alive. Once more shutters were fastened over the windows, and every door was barricaded. The American merchants were in double danger. The Mexicans cursed them as traitors who were in league with Indians and Texans, and the Indians suspected them for the arms and supplies they had been forced to give Pérez and then Armijo.

Two days later the church bells rang with delirious joy as a runner brought news that the Indians had been decisively defeated. The next day General Armijo returned in triumph, and everyone followed him to the parroquia for a victory mass.

The northern tribes had fled from Santa Cruz, but General Armijo demanded the punishment of the rebel leaders. That afternoon a dozen captives were brought to the Garita, the prison on the eastern foothill overlooking the town. Among them were General Armijo's former lieutenants, the Montoya brothers, and the Alcalde, Don Juan José Esquibel. The Montoyas were a powerful clan and used every pressure to beg for reprieve, but all the captives were shot at dawn.

Then the news spread over the plaza like wildfire that the Taos chief, José Gonzáles, had been captured and brought to the Garita. The excited crowd followed General Armijo and his escort when they rode to the prison to interview the vanquished chief. Tules ran with them, ruining her thin slippers on the stones and mud as she climbed the hill.

She pushed into the bleak enclosure that was surrounded by high adobe walls and guarded by two square towers at the north and south corners. Beyond the walls rocky foothills led up to the high, snow-blanketed mountains. Storm clouds shrouded the sun and diffused the light into a cold, brooding gloom.

She shivered with the foreboding that Don Manuel's future hung on his wisdom and generosity today. If he condemned the Taos chief, as he had the other captives, he would always be threatened with unrelenting enemies in the north. She felt sure that he would make a magnanimous gesture, forgive his foe, and win over the Taos tribe as a strong ally. She swung with the pendulum of his destiny as though it was the breath of her own life.

She stood with the front spectators and noticed that the military escort shivered in their heavy uniforms. Don Manuel pulled his long blue cape closer around him, and his shining black boots stamped nervously in the bitter wind.

A murmur escaped from the crowd as the tower door opened and the Taos chief came out. He held himself erect and drew the scarlet-and-blue chief's blanket around him as he walked toward his former commander. He held out his brown hand and said calmly, "How are you, compadre?"

The Governor ignored the outstretched hand but turned to a lieutenant and said, "Give him chocolate and buñuelos."

As the chief drank the hot chocolate and munched the crisp pastry, a man beside Tules whispered, "Bien! Now Don Manuel will free his friend and make peace in the north."

"Ojalá that you are right!" Tules nodded.

She watched breathlessly as Don Manuel's lips set in a stern line. He looked directly at the Taos chief for the first time. His voice barked sharply, "Confess yourself." Then he beckoned to the soldiers and ordered, "Shoot this man."

Tules gasped and crossed herself as she saw the Priest go to the condemned man. The chief looked steadily at Armijo's averted profile. Only the pinched nostrils, blanched against his brown skin, showed that he had taken a deep breath. Not a flicker of surprise, anger, or rebellion passed over his stoical face. His dark eyes lifted slowly from Armijo's helmet to the Taos Mountains far in the north. He made no protest as the soldiers bound his hands behind him, led him twenty steps, and ordered him to kneel with his back to them. The firing squad stepped forward, and their guns cracked. As the

199

blanketed figure jerked upwards and then tumbled to the ground, a moan seeped from the crowd.

"Pobrecito!" a woman groaned beside Tules. "He thought Armijo was his friend. He was alone. He had no chance."

"It is the rule of war. The Governor's life would not be safe if his enemy lived," Tules defended Don Manuel, but her eyes filled with tears.

"What a waste to give chocolate and buñuelos to a condemned man," a fat fellow muttered.

Tules felt sick and shaken as she stumbled down the muddy hill. She knew that the Taos pueblo would never forget that their chief had been betrayed and murdered. They would avenge this ignominy. She kept hearing Don Manuel's stern voice pronounce the chief's doom, "Shoot this man."

A childhood memory flashed into her mind as she thought of the conquerors of her country. Spain had conquered the Indians, and Mexico had freed herself from Spain. Don Manuel was the new conqueror. Would he in turn be vanquished? God forbid!

Her eyes lifted to the west to look into the Jemez Mountains rimming the town. Under the threatening clouds they were a purple mass tipped with triangular white peaks. They were solid, indestructible, changeless. From long ago she heard Tío Florentino say, "The puny cries of men in this land are like the wind that travels swiftly before the sun but leaves no shadow."

# 20

IN THE SPRING new hopes unfurled as thickly as the tender green leaves in the willow thicket by the river, and life settled into its accustomed ways. There were still whispers of plots to avenge the death of the Taos chief and the Montoyas, but the loudest critics mysteriously disappeared, and the weaker tongues kept quiet.

Tules watched Don Manuel's rise to power with mingled pleasure and irritation. He had risen above her reach. He was like the sun; every eye lifted to him, but he shone impersonally in his high place.

She listened enviously to gossip of the magnificent balls and dinners in the Palace. When Don Manuel's rich friends from the Río Abajo came to the cantina to play monte she studied their hair, their clothes, and manners. She combed her red hair into the same ringlets and dug into her hoarded money to buy a fine shawl like theirs. Her "mantón de Manilla" was of jade-green silk, lavishly embroidered in crimson roses and flying white birds. When she draped it around her shoulders and swished the long fringe, she felt as beautiful as any of the gente fina. Her body was as straight and graceful as a flower stem, and she held her head proudly. But her long green eyes watched for an opportunity to focus Don Manuel's attention.

One night he came into the cantina, closely followed by his bodyguard and the toadies who ran at his heels. He did not come to the monte tables but stopped at the bar to talk with the men. His long blue cape hung from his shoulders in luxurious folds, only showing the red-and-gold stripes on the collar of his uniform. His face was flushed and beaming, and everyone smiled at his hearty, good-humored laughter. Tules decided to try her luck while he was in this expansive mood and signaled to Vicente to watch the table. Her heart beat faster, and her hips moved with sensuous grace as she sauntered toward the bar.

When she was halfway across the room a laughing voice called, "Hola, Tules! You are more beautiful each time I see you. I have a song for you tonight."

She stopped to smile at Pepe Cisneros whose guitar and comic songs always drew a crowd. She had not seen him since last fall when he offered to take her away from the Pérez massacre. "I owe you a thousand thanks, Pepe," she called and hoped that he would understand that she appreciated his courage in going to help María and Victorio that night.

He spanked his guitar with a final whack and grinned at her. His black eyes twinkled, and his cheeks were like firm, ripe plums above his black moustache. He wore the buffalo hunter's deerskin leggins and shirt with careless grace and swept off his flat cibolero hat with a flourish. "I dedicate this song to La Tules. Ay, qué caray!" he announced. His lusty voice rang out above the rollicking cords as he sang:

> All the girls love me, they do,
> The single and married ones too.
> Young or old, dark or fair,
> Fat or thin, I'm aware
> That all the girls love me, they do.
>
> But the middle ones please me the best,
> With a curve to the hips and the breast.
> Not too old, prim and cold;
> Not too young, when I'm bold.
> Yes, the middle ones please me the best.

Tules laughed and applauded the song. Pepe's jolly exuberance always made her feel young and gay. He loved to play the country buffoon and make the crowd roar with his naive questions His quick fingers on the guitar mimicked any sound, and his quick wit improvised verses that made fun of sham and pretense. With typical Mexican humor, he sang of graft and chicanery and carried it off as a bold jest. Other men would not dare whisper what Pepe sang as a ribald joke.

She waved to Pepe and turned away, impatient to reach Don Man-

202

uel. She glanced over her shoulder and saw him coming toward Pepe, attracted by the songs and laughter. She caught his eye and flashed her most inviting smile. At that moment a man grabbed her elbow and whirled her around to face Pepe again.

"Un momentito," Pepe called to her. "Por favor, listen to my gambling song." He rolled his eyes and sang in mock despair of betting on his favorite deuce and losing his last centavo. He nodded to the laughter and cheers, and, hardly pausing for breath, he started another song:

> Don Albino's striped vest was too short,
> Don Albino's striped vest was too fine.
> To keep off all the fleas
> Taking bites from his knees,
> He needed a cape that was long,
> He needed a cape wide and strong.
> Qué caray! a cape that was long.
> Cuándo! a cape wide and strong!

·Tules caught her breath at this bold joke and the implication that Don Manuel's long cape hid the "little bites" of graft better than Don Albino's striped vest. Her eyes darted to the faces near her to watch their reaction to this raillery at Don Manuel. Someone pushed her roughly, and she almost fell. "Stop pushing, cabrón," she cried, "you almost threw me. . . ." She looked back to see that she had jabbed her elbow into Don Manuel's thick waist.

He pushed her aside, stepped into the space around Pepe, and defiantly tossed the end of his long blue cape over his shoulder. "That's enough from you," his big voice shouted. "Your croak is only fit for the buffalo wallow. See that you stay there." The crowd made way for him as he strode out of the cantina, trailed by his followers.

"You'd better leave tonight, or you'll spend the summer singing in jail," a man warned Pepe.

"What's wrong with my little song?" Pepe asked innocently and strummed chords. "How would a poor buffalo hunter know that a rich politician can't afford a fine vest?"

"I wish the buffalos would teach you some respect," Tules said

203

angrily. Her eyes blazed at him because he had ruined her chance with Don Manuel.

She stamped into the back room, powdered her long nose with vicious dabs, and rouged her pouting lips. She frowned into her little mirror and told herself that she had been a fool to stop before Pepe. She had liked him, but now she cursed him as a brazen clown. He should know that Don Manuel was too great a man to insult him by singing such a verse to his face. But she acknowledged that Pepe had courage. . . .

There was a knock at the door, and Cuca came in. She was now the prosperous madam, as plump and satisfied as a strutting pigeon. Crude circles of rouge on her cushioned cheeks belied the imposing respectability of her rustling black silk. She reached into the ample pocket of her petticoat and counted ten pesos into Tules's hand.

"The last of my debt to you, niña." Her black eyes lingered greedily on the silver. "May you receive tenfold blessings for your loan to an old friend."

"Business must be good," Tules said.

"Por supuesto!" Cuca chuckled. "I sent my prettiest girl to the Palace last night."

"For Don Manuel?" Tules demanded. Rage burned her again that she had muffed her chance tonight.

Cuca winked and rubbed her thumb and finger. "He pays in gold!"

"He must be tired of the gente fina he gets for nothing," Tules said resentfully.

"I thought you would know how soft the beds are in the Palace by this time." Cuca cocked her head and studied Tules. "You would give him more pleasure than my timid, squawking girls. If you want him, you should go after him. . . ."

"And be thrown off like the rest of the fleas?" Tules's green eyes flashed with scorn.

"Your luck at monte has made you too hard." Cuca rested her hands on her round hips and stuck out her bristling chin. "You used to know that a man only wants a warm body, sweet words, and caresses. . . ."

204

"That was when I was young. . . ."

"You are not thirty yet. You have years ahead for love. With your figure, your beauty, you can give any man pleasure that is the strongest wine of life. You and I could go far. You have what men want. I know how to make them pay. Let me send word to our fine Governor. . . ."

"I am not one of your girls," Tules said sharply.

Cuca shrugged her plump shoulders. "You want him so much you can taste it, but you are too proud. You stand off too far. After just one night you could hold him. . . ."

This was the chance Tules had longed for, but now she turned away. An inner hunch told her that the position she wanted with Don Manuel would never come through a procuress. She shook her red head and sighed, "Too many run after Don Manuel. He will only be held if he does the running."

"But he is not like the ordinary men who come to my house every night," Cuca insisted. "Now he is a dictator with absolute power. He can lift his hand and a man disappears as though he had sunk into the quicksand. You can't reach him in the Palace, unless he sends for you—as he does for my girls. I can tell him of your beauty, your charm, make arrangements. If you will go to him once, rouse his hunger, our fortunes will be made!"

Tules shook her head, rolled and lighted a cigarrito, and handed the tobacco flask and corn shucks to Cuca.

"La Casimira passed your handkerchief over the cards, and they give you a great future," Cuca sighed. "She says you will rule with a dark, handsome man. You know the people, you hear the plots against him, you will help him. Together you will go far. But you must reach him first. She told me to tell you that there was also danger. . . ."

Tules stared at Cuca as she heard this echo of her own thoughts, but she still shook her head and started back to her table. "If it's in the cards, we will win," she smiled. "A burro balks if you drive him, but he runs after a load of hay."

Don Manuel showed his displeasure by not patronizing the cantina for a month. Pepe left town a few days later, but men still snickered and hummed his song. Everyone knew that more "little bites" came out of the treasury for Don Manuel's pleasures than for Don Albino's reforms, but at least Don Manuel was their own man. They accepted graft as a customary perquisite and would have suspected any Governor who lived within the frugal legal salary. They took pride in Don Manuel's fine horses, colorful uniforms, and luxurious living. They praised him when he abolished direct taxes and promised that American imports would pay all Government expenses.

He accomplished this by a surprise manifesto issued the day before the first American wagons rolled down the Santa Fe Trail to open the summer trade. It stated that henceforth each wagon must pay five hundred dollars duty on its cargo. The American traders loudly protested this sudden raise and pointed out that it was unfair; some wagons carried cheap staples such as denim, muslin, and calico, while others were loaded with such luxuries as silks, velvets, laces, perfume, and jewelry.

The first customs inspection took place at Arroyo Hondo, two leagues from Santa Fe. The officials smiled blandly, explained that they were powerless to change the official decree, and forced the traders to pay cash for each wagon in order to proceed to Santa Fe.

The traders always raced over the last fifteen leagues from San Miguel's trying to beat each other into Santa Fe. This year a man named Jackson had put a light load of novelty goods into a carriage and dashed ahead with his fast team to be the first to sell his merchandise and get the top price. He cursed loudly when the officials stopped him at Arroyo Hondo and declared that he did not have enough cash to pay the full duty. They confiscated his novelties but allowed him to go on to Santa Fe to sell his horses so that he could redeem his goods. He drove around and around the plaza to the titters of Mexicans who thought this was a good joke on the shrewd Yankee traders. His chestnuts were fine Kentucky horses, but no one wanted to buy them.

When Jackson failed to get an offer he drifted to Tules's table like a blind, angry moth. Other traders made room for him and urged

206

him "to win enough in this den to get your stuff out of that crooked Governor's clutches."

Tules looked at them scornfully. The gringos made insulting remarks with the assumption that Mexicans were too ignorant to understand their Missouri English. She noticed that Jackson had had too many Pass brandies already and signaled Vicente to be on guard. Jackson's hickory shirt was open above his hairy chest, and he mopped his red face with a dirty bandana. He cursed the Governor, the people, and the country as he stacked silver on the corner of a card. He won four times over and swept the money into his hungry hands.

The traders laughed, pounded Jackson on the back, and shouted that his luck had turned as he continued to win. Men stood around the table clinking the silver pesos between their hands as they waited to play on their favorite cards. Then Jackson's luck failed, and his stack melted.

"Damn it, I've got to win," he shouted. "What'll you give me for my horses? They're worth a thousand dollars to a white man, but tonight I'll let them go for five hundred. . . ."

Santiago held up two fingers to Tules, and she said, "I'll give you credit for two hundred dollars on them."

Jackson cursed as he signed his name to the paper Santiago handed him, and Vicente pushed over the two hundred pesos. After three plays these were gone. Jackson pounded the table, got up, and yelled, "You're God-damned dirty thieves!" and left.

"Los 'goddamnes' are poor losers," Tules said coolly as she dealt again. She was hardened to taking a man's last tostón.

When they divided the winnings into a pile for Tules, one for Santiago, and one for the house that night Santiago slyly rubbed his hands and mentioned that Tules must pay back the two hundred pesos for the horses.

"They're your horses," she protested. "I only spoke when I saw your fingers. What would I do with fine horses? If they eat, I starve. Take them yourself; you can sell them. . . ."

But Santiago insisted that Tules had made the bargain and the horses were hers. The next day she went to the Leitendorfer corral to see them. Several men were there, admiring the chestnuts' glossy coats and long, slender legs. They had received good care on the Trail and were ready to race. Tules patted their soft noses. Ever since the days at Manzano she had loved good horses, but she had never hoped to own a pair as fine as these. She saw herself driving around the plaza in style and wished that she could afford to keep them.

"What will you do with them?" a man asked.

She shrugged her shoulders and ran her hand down the mare's silky brown neck.

"My patrón might like to have them," the man suggested. "Don Manuel likes fine horses. If you made him the right price . . ."

"Don Manuel Armijo?" Tules demanded. When the man nodded a light flashed in her eyes, and she slipped a peso in the man's hand. "There's more for you, if you bring you patrón to see the horses. Tell him they are the finest horses in the Province. Tell him they would win for him. Tell him to come to talk to me about them. We shall make a good bargain, señor."

She was not surprised when the Governor sent a young lieutenant and then his brother to inquire about the horses. She flattered the brother but insisted that she could not discuss so delicate a matter with anyone but Don Manuel himself. She knew this was a bold answer, for the Governor expected everyone to cringe and comply with his slightest wish. He might send word that he had no time to talk to a monte dealer. But she gambled on the hunch that her refusal would interest him more than a servile reply.

A week later he came into the cantina. Her heart beat faster as she saw him circle the other tables and come toward her. Por la vida de quién sabe quién, he was a fine figure of a man—so big, so handsome, so commanding! Her bright eyes widened, and fire ran through her body. Santiago pushed people aside and ordered a man to give up his chair to His Excellency.

"You know I never play. . . ." Don Manuel waved empty palms.

"Por favor, if you would sit here just once, my General," Tules begged, smiling into his eyes. "It would be the greatest honor that could come to me and my poor table."

"Muy bien!" Don Manuel smiled and seated himself with the air of humoring a child's game. The chair creaked under his heavy body, and his shoulders towered over the men beside him as he watched the cards. A ragged peón lost his last centavo and started to slink away from the table.

"What bad luck, hombre." Don Manuel's voice rang with sympathy. "You shouldn't throw away your last copper."

"But I wished to m-make enough m-money to pay my debts, señor," the peón stammered.

"Like the rest of the world," Don Manuel laughed. "Get yourself something to eat." He tossed two silver pesos to the peón and made the familiar gesture of putting a tortilla into his mouth.

The crowd, standing three deep around the table, grinned at the Governor's generosity. Tules's face was radiant. As a dealer, she had reached the height of success when the Governor sat at her table. As a woman, her heart raced with hope. She had heard that Don Manuel had dealt monte long ago, and she believed it as she saw him study the layout. By long habit she rubbed Jeem's ring, and the tingle sent a flash like lightning up her bare arm. Don Manuel dropped a stack of silver on the queen of cups. Tules forced herself to deal coolly, but she was happy when the matching card came "out of the gate," and the Governor won double his bet.

"Never push good luck too far," he said, as he pocketed the silver. He rose from the table and turned to Tules. "If you have time for a word, señorita . . ."

Santiago nodded for her to go, and she led the way to one of the private rooms. She heard men whisper, "El Gobernador! La Tules! God showers her with luck!"

Santiago followed with a decanter, glasses, and a plate of sugar-coated biscochitos. Don Manuel waited until Santiago lit the candles and reluctantly withdrew. Then he seated himself at ease at the table. The candlelight caught on his gold epaulets and shining boots. Tules's hand trembled with excitement as she poured the red wine and lifted her glass. "To your eternal happiness and success, my General! And to the happiest moment of my life!"

"Salud!" He sipped the wine and smiled broadly as he repeated the old proverb, " 'A woman's hair draws more than a team of oxen.' Your hair is as beautiful as your chestnut horses, señorita. My brother said you would not discuss them with him."

"I do not sing to the moon when the sun is in the sky." Her low voice caressed him, and she leaned toward him and smiled into his black eyes. "Ah, my brave, beautiful chestnuts! What luck they have brought me that at last I may talk to you!" She was so happy that she wanted to give him the horses, herself, anything he wanted.

"They are good horses." Don Manuel moved back and looked at her with cool, appraising eyes. "They are purebreds, but I doubt that they are strong enough for a long journey."

His cool voice was like a snowball in her face and roused the old market instinct. Bien, if he wanted to bargain, he could pay instead of accepting a fulsome gift. She sat back, raised the fine arch of her eyebrows, and looked at him under lowered lids. "Of course, you have reason, my General. For long journeys you need mules, but a caballero takes his pleasure in race horses. These are of the best. They are a bargain at one thousand pesos."

"Válgame Dios, one thousand pesos, señorita!" Don Manuel cried in mock horror. "I am a poor man. This is a poor country. . . ."

"You have a fine carriage, and you need fine horses, señor. How handsome you would look behind such a pair! When I consider that, I would be ashamed to let the other ricos or the gringos have the chestnuts. Though I will lose by it, I will let you have them for five hundred pesos. . . ."

"You are beautiful but hard, señorita." Don Manuel sipped his wine and looked at her vivid face and the warm seduction that darkened her eyes. "Your beauty tempts me to forget that my purse is light but . . . I know that you gave the gringo two hundred pesos' credit for the horses. I will repay that."

"Two hundred pesos, señor?" She mocked him with laughing eyes and soft red lips. "You have no mercy, my General! I will lose money. I have fed the horses for two weeks. . . ."

He threw back his head and laughed. The fragrance of her perfume came to him, and he looked at the provocative curves of her body, the tender flesh of her breasts rising and falling with each quick breath. His large hand closed around her smooth, bare arm as he said, "You can keep the carriage to pay the feed bill. If you draw another pair of horses from monte next week, I will drive with you in your carriage to Taos for the fiesta."

"Oh, for the love of God, don't go to Taos, señor," she cried, her eyes wide with alarm. "There is too much danger for you."

His heavy body stiffened, and he looked at her sharply. Her coquetry was gone. Her eyes pled with him as her low voice told him of a plot brewing against him in Taos. He cross-questioned her and finally nodded his large head. Her story confirmed some rumor he had already heard.

"I hear many things, my General," she confided softly. She caught his hand in both of hers and pressed it until he could feel the hot intensity of her desire. "Ojalá that I could help you. You are a great man, and we must protect you. This country needs you so much. I need you. . . ."

Don Manuel looked at her adoring eyes, her inviting red lips, her warm breasts, and murmured, "If we could be alone . . ."

"Yes." Her breath fluttered as she swayed toward him. The beating of her heart carried its rhythm into the warm, low caress of her voice. "But how? Everyone watches you here or at the Palace. If I had a place of my own, you could come and go as you pleased. Ah, what happiness we could have then. . . ."

"A place of your own?" Don Manuel studied her.

"A place for both of us," she breathed. "For so many years I have dreamed of my own sala. Then you could come to me. Get away from spies, assassins . . ."

"I need that." Don Manuel nodded as though this fitted into some plan of his own. "You have a wise head and a warm heart. After the cares of office I need relaxation. Quién sabe? You are generous, beautiful . . . With your warm body in my arms . . ."

"Ah, mi alma!" She lifted her eager red lips to him.

His powerful arms caught her to him, and his mouth bruised hers. Years of longing flamed through her as her supple body pressed hard against his in a passionate embrace.

# 21

"Niña, you are so beautiful," María said with wonder. "A candle is lighted behind your eyes. You look as happy as though you had just come from confession."

"Better than that," Tules laughed. The gold heels of her slippers danced over the dirt floor, and she gave María a quick hug. María's poor, bony shoulder had never known the delirious joy of love.

"Nothing is better than the Blessed Sacrament." María shook her head gently. "The love of God . . ."

Tules danced to the other side of the room and only heard the word "love." She could think of nothing but love. She loved the whole world—the sunshine, the trees beyond the window, the small white room, patient María, droll Victorio. The miracle of Manuel's love transformed the whole world into a shining, radiant place. The thought that Manuel had chosen her from all the women around him lifted her into glory. She had never been so happy as this last month when she had been with him.

She danced back to María and caught her shoulders in warm, eager hands. "I have a secret to tell you, María. I wanted to surprise you, but I'm too excited. You know that house at the end of the street that runs before the Palace? It faces on the road to Tesuque. . . ."

"Doña Luarda's house." María nodded.

"Don Manuel has gotten it for us. It will be our house, our home, María. In the front I will have my own monte sala. Dios de mi vida, did you ever hear anything so wonderful?" Her hazel eyes shone and her white teeth flashed in a wide smile.

"But that is a big house!" María exclaimed. "We haven't enough money for a rich house like that!"

"You know the family were Perezistas," Tules shrugged. "The

Government confiscated it. Don Manuel has arranged for me to buy it at a bargain. . . ."

"Blessed Mother of God, how can I clean a house as large as that?" María protested.

"I told you that someday I would get you many servants." Tules laughed and threw the end of the jade-green shawl over her shoulder. She whirled so that her full skirt billowed out above her trim ankles, hugged María, and whispered, "Tomorrow it will be ours."

Before dawn, while Victorio was asleep, María helped her dig up the Indian jars and count the gold pieces.

"For the love of God, niña, this is a fortune," María whispered. "Should you spend all this money to buy a house? Most men never see fifty pesos at one time in their whole lives."

"We have skimped to save this." Tules nodded her red head. "We will make it back from the house a thousand times. Besides, I will only pay one thousand pesos, and the house is worth much more."

Her voice was confident to María, but she had some misgivings as she counted out the gold to the Alcalde. Her fingers were cool and agile when she dealt monte, but when she took the unaccustomed quill her fingers trembled. She was proud that she could write, but the signature, "María Gertrudis Barceló," looked like a child's wavering scrawl.

At home she made María light two candles as she frowned to decipher each formal word of the deed. She read it aloud slowly to María's blinking eyes. At the end she pointed to her own name. "It's ours," she cried. "No one can take it from us." Tears sprang to her eyes as she kissed the paper, fondled it, and thrust it between her firm, warm breasts.

"Bien de mi vida," she said to Manuel that night as she stroked his cheek, "I am rich in your love, but my pocket is as empty as that house. It has fallen into ruin since the Perezistas left. How can I pay for all it needs? The roof leaks, the walls must be plastered inside and out, the well cleaned. Have you some idle fellows to help me?"

Manuel agreed to commandeer the workmen, and Tules spent her days supervising the dirt tamped into the roof and the mud spread over the cracks of the outside walls and the gleaming white yeso within. She ordered the men to tear out a partition to make a large room for her monte sala at the front.

Manuel strolled the block from the Palace to watch the remodeling. At first, in her happiness, Tules thought that he was interested in the house as his own home, but she found that he intended to use it for secret plans. He selected a small room off the sala where he could have juntas away from the spies at the Palace. Tules welcomed this arrangement to keep Manuel near her where she could watch over him, love him, and help him.

"I want this to be an exclusive sala, only open to those we invite," Manuel said. "Then I can get away from my enemies. There are certain affairs I can handle here better than at the Palace."

"But of course, querido," Tules agreed with glowing eyes. "It is more dignified to invite only the gente fina, those with heavy pockets, and a few poor friends. What a mind you have to think of it!"

Manuel's suggestion for a select and exclusive sala completed her dream. She had heard gringos tell of the fine gambling halls in St. Louis and New Orleans, and she determined that hers should be equally luxurious. But luxuries cost money. While Manuel was in this pleasant mood she coaxed money out of him for one of her most cherished plans. He was not pleased when he found she had spent the money to put a plank floor in the sala.

"Válgame Dios, you will ruin me with this extravagance!" he blustered. "Boards sawed and planed by hand! A board floor is like walking on gold. Not even the Palace has a plank floor!"

Tules knew as well as he did that there was only one other plank floor in the Province. That was in the store of Juan Escolle, an Irishman whose name had been John Scolly when he came to Santa Fe years ago. She sniffed delightedly now at the clean odor of pine boards and knew that she had a greater luxury than any of the ricos. But she lowered her eyelashes and murmured, "Forgive my extravagance, alma de mi alma. Dancing raises such a dust on a dirt floor. I thought you would like this. My house is at your disposition, and nothing is too good for you."

215

"You will want glass windows and Indians' ears next," Manuel laughed.

"Ah, yes, querido, glass would be wonderful, but you can keep the Indians' ears," she shuddered. These were the two things the country people gaped at when they came to the Palace. The sinister garlands of dried human ears had been paid for as bounty to show that prisoners, mostly Indians, had not escaped alive. Panes of glass, brought with great care and expense on the wagons over the Santa Fe Trail, had replaced the panes of mica in the Palace windows.

"You will have to be content with mica." Manuel pinched her cheek. "But see that there are strong shutters to fasten at night."

The sala was divided by a long beam and posts to hold up the heavy roof. One side would be used for monte and the other for the bar and dancing. Tules bought the largest mirror she could find to place behind the bar. A high platform for the orchestra flanked the bar, and near it there was a high seat for the spotter who would watch for crooked plays or fights. Tules was disappointed that the room looked so big and bare. It needed good furnishings to give it the luxury she wanted.

"Have you thrown away those old Pérez things at the Palace?" she asked Manuel one night, smiling at him as she played with the gold epaulets at his shoulder.

"No, they are still there," he said.

"But, querido, you should throw away the secondhand Pérez stuff and refurnish the Palace to show how much better your taste is than his."

"New things cost too much." Manuel shook his large head. "A politician never has money. Too many hands in his pocket."

"Then how does General Santa Anna get the fine things he orders from Paris?" she asked. "I want you to have things that are worthy of you, too."

"Santa Anna is a great man," Manuel said reverently. "He is my good friend and would give me anything I want. You have reason, linda. I will throw out the old Pérez things and order my own. I'll make those cheeky gringo traders pay for them."

216

She nestled against him while he talked of Santa Anna, finally raised her head from his shoulder, and asked, "What will you do with the old Pérez stuff?"

"Burn it. Destroy all traces of Pérez," Manuel said, acting on the idea now, as though he had thought of it first.

"We could put some of it in the sala. The room looks bare . . ." she suggested and ran her fingers through his hair.

Before the house was finished all the Pérez furniture had been moved to the sala. Long, narrow mirrors rose from low white marble shelves almost to the rafters and reflected the red velvet curtains at the windows and the carved chairs, tables, and trasteros. A great chandelier holding a hundred candles hung from the center of the room. Tules drew in her breath as she looked at it. Ever since she was a child, a chandelier with sparkling candles had been her symbol of wealth. Her heart beat with pride now as her eyes traveled over the room, and she stamped her heel for the pleasure of hearing it ring against the board floor. She hugged herself to think that this was all hers.

She lavished every luxury that she could beg or borrow on the sala, but her own room at the end of the patio portál was simple and bare. She treated herself to a mirror and chest of drawers, but the pallets for María, Victorio, and herself were still rolled into daytime seats against the white walls. María put the saints' statues in the wall niches and lighted ever-burning candles before them and set the red geranium in the window.

Next to their room there were small rooms for relatives. As soon as news spread that Tules had purchased the house, she was besieged with relatives. Even her mother made the long trip from Manzano and brought her three children.

"When we were poor they left us alone," Tules grumbled.

"No importa," María said. "Remember when bread is broken God increases it. You can't turn away relatives when your hand is always open to the Saturday beggars."

"What comes in the front door goes out the back." Tules shrugged. "Good luck follows me if I take from the rich and give to the poor."

"Bien, we will feed all who come," María nodded. "But we will make them work."

Tules was glad to turn over the supervision of the kitchen to her mother, "Nana Luz," whose harsh voice was more effective than María's gentle smile. The oldest child, Trinidad, called "Chico," was seventeen and a lazy scamp who always escaped to the plaza. The next one, Rafaela, was a plain, pock-marked girl of fifteen and a faithful drudge. The youngest girl, Lucita, had shy, winsome beauty. Tules was delighted with her big brown eyes and soft hair. They looked upon Tules as another mother, and she accepted Lucita as her own, planned that she should have the best of everything and grow up as one of the gente fina.

It was mostly on Lucita's account that Tules refused to rent Cuca and her girls the empty rooms in one wing of the house. Tules warned Cuca to leave Lucita alone.

"Maldita sea!" Cuca cursed. "Only the price makes you different from any other harlot. Our fine Governor has turned your head, but he may kick you yet. Then you'll need your friends. . . ."

Their shrill voices rose like market shrews. Finally Tules agreed to rent the house next door, on the Callejón de los Burros, to Cuca and allow her girls a percentage on the drinks the men bought them in the sala.

Tules set the gala opening of her sala for the fiesta of the Virgin of Guadalupe on December 12. She worked feverishly to have everything ready, and now she stood in the doorway for a last nervous glance at the empty rooms. What if the gente fina snubbed her and did not come tonight? What if the dealers cheated her? If there was a run on her bank, she was ruined. She could count on Manuel's help only so long as she could hold him. What if he tired of her and turned to a younger woman? At least tonight all this was hers. She rubbed Jeem's gold ring and smiled at the answering tingle of success.

She stopped before the long mirror for a last pat at her red hair under the black lace mantilla. Her long green eyes smiled back as she remembered how she had exchanged the short red market skirt for the black silk of respectability. She touched the fine lace ruffles

218

at her sleeves and low-cut bosom and adjusted the gold chain and diamond brooch. The tight bodice was flattering to her supple figure with its small waist and high, firm breasts. She pinched her pale cheeks to give them color and moistened her wide red lips.

The outer door opened, and she invited Santiago Flores to have the first drink to the success of her sala, though he was a rival proprietor. The bartender proudly offered him Pass brandy, Taos Lightning, tequila, native and imported wines, and champagne. There was also hot, foaming chocolate to warm the stomach on a cold winter night.

People filled the room, and Tules moved gracefully among these carefully chosen guests. Happiness and pride warmed her low voice as she welcomed the leading families—the Delgados, Pinos, Senas, Bacas, Romeros, Chávez, Ortiz, and López. Then she turned to Alcalde Rubidoux, the Vicario, and several padres from out of town.

Her hazel eyes sparkled with triumph as she greeted the ricos from the Río Abajo. She looked at the fine face of Don José Chávez and wished that she had a peso for each of his million sheep. She laughed as he teased Don Augustín Durán about the time when he pawned everything in a three-day monte game and finally pawned himself. He had to stay in jail two days until he could confiscate enough goods as Customs Collector to bail himself out.

She almost pinched herself when she saw that even the wealthy Don Pedro Perea had come to her open house. Don Pedro sniffed at the silver stacked on the tables and boasted that they played for real money in the Río Abajo. He rolled a cigarrito, and a younger man murmured, "Con su licencia, señor," and proferred his flint and steel. Don Pedro pulled out an American fifty-dollar bill, held it to the wick, and lighted his cigarrito with the burning bill.

"Bravo!" men called enviously. "Don Pedro has money to burn!"

Tules laughed with delight and clapped her hands. These men would bet high. She prayed that her bank would hold out. If her sala made money tonight, she was safe.

The blue haze of smoke from the many cigarritos drifted toward the sparkling candles. Tules looked over the crowd, picked out the few gringos, and graciously welcomed Juan Escolle, Baptiste La Lande, Eugene Leitendorfer and his wife, James Collins and his wife, Doña Juana Ortiz. They were the resident gringos; the summer traders had returned to the States months ago. The mountain men from above Taos were busy with winter traps, but they would come next summer, make fufarraw, and spend money here.

There was a buzz of excitement as Governor Armijo and his wife came through the door. Their well-fed figures showed off their best clothes, but Doña Trinidad's diamonds outshone her husband's gold buttons. The three-piece orchestra accompanied the singer in his flowery verses of welcome to the Governor. Tules swept toward them with smiling greetings and nodded to servants to bring hot mistela, fine spongecake, and empanaditas filled with spiced mincemeat.

"Salud, Doña Tules! Good luck to your new house!" Governor Armijo toasted her in the hot, spiced brandy and exclaimed at its excellence.

Doña Trinidad's double chin dropped as she looked around the room and recognized the Pérez furnishings. Angry tears glistened in her eyes at this brazen display of her husband's favor. She drew herself up haughtily and said, "I see you have the old red curtains we were about to burn for rags. Of course we could not use such faded, shoddy things. Our furnishings were ordered by General Santa Anna from Mexico. As a special gift he sent us a French bed like his own. It is of the finest brass with a beautiful canopy. But you don't know of such luxuries in a monte sala!"

She turned her back on Tules's flaming cheeks and greeted friends effusively. The Governor talked to another group; he had not listened to his jealous wife. Tules tossed her head and crossed the room to speak to the orchestra. She discovered Pepe Cisneros seated there with his guitar.

"Welcome, Pepe," she cried with relief. "It's good to see you. I was afraid you might not return from the buffalo hunt in time. . . ."

"There isn't a buffalo big enough to keep me from you," he laughed. "I have made a special song for your fiesta."

"Por Dios, don't make trouble tonight, Pepe!" Tules warned.

"This is my love song for you. Does that make trouble?" The twinkle in his eyes was replaced by a look of steadfast devotion. Then he shrugged and began a long corrida in her praise. The extravagant flattery of likening her eyes to evening stars, her lips to coral, and her teeth to pearls was customary, but tonight it was balm to her hurt pride after Doña Trinidad's scorn.

After the song the guests toasted her health and success in voices warm with wine and brandy. Don Manuel offered the first official toast, but his fat wife turned away.

Tules's eyes burned with hatred as she looked at Doña Trinidad's averted profile. The guilty knowledge that the wife had reason to be jealous fanned her anger. Doña Trinidad was childless and helpless to stop her husband's flirtations. She took lovers herself, but Don Manuel remained indifferent. Tules thought passionately of the warmth and love she would give Manuel if she was his wife.

She laughed and chatted with the crowd, but her glowing happiness was gone. She knew that these ricos still looked down on her as a market woman and courtesan. She vowed that she would make them come to her, respect her, invite her to their homes.

At dawn she counted the profit from her tables and found that her bank had doubled with the success of her fiesta. As she unfastened the gold filigree flower from the silk threads of her mantilla she nodded at the old proverb, "With silver, nothing fails." She had enough silver now to buy a position of honor, and, as long as she held Manuel's love, she would have happiness and power.

He came to the sala almost every evening, talked with friends, and met strange men. Sometimes he locked the door of the small room they used, sprawled on the pallet like a tired sheepherder, and held Tules close in the simple, primitive desire of man and woman. They forgot the world in happy, satisfied fulfillment. Tules was skilled in ways to give him sensuous pleasure, but now her body quivered with ecstasy, and she slept beside him in warm, contented peace.

Like all lovers he spoke of the first time he saw her at the monte table. He had heard of her beauty, sorcery, skill and wanted to attract her by ordering the gringo gambler to leave the sala.

"You don't remember, but we saw each other long before that, querido," she said and stroked his dark cheek. "It was in the store of Don Francisco Ortiz at El Real de Dolores, and you were so grand and handsome. I was afraid you would keep my nugget. . . ."

"Nugget? Were you the girl who found that big nugget? Wasn't there some trouble over it? Two men killed, as I remember." He heard her gasp and felt her stiffen with fear. He added shrewdly, "So you were the girl they searched for. . . ."

"But, Manuel, I had to do it," she cried. She sobbed against his shoulder as she told him of Ramón and Pedro. "You don't know what it is to be poor, hunted, starving. To have no recourse against the ricos and políticos, no justice! They would never have punished Pedro for killing Ramón and stealing my nugget!"

He soothed her and drew her close in his arms. "That was a bad dream, but now you are safe. I will take care of you. . . ."

"Oh, Manuel, I love you so much," she sobbed.

"But you must never tell this to anyone," Manuel warned. "I, too, know what it is to be poor and have every boot kick me. I fought to get to the top. Even now there are enemies who would use this against you and me. Don't trust anyone with secrets. If no one has suspected you, it is probably forgotten. Bien, we will forget it too and enjoy our happiness, linda."

But her lover was temperamental and scowled at her when his enemies plotted against him. Sometimes he was arrogant and took delight in humiliating her to build up his own self-esteem. He taunted her about the beautiful women who made love to him at Palace dinners.

To satisfy her own pride, she resolved to spend at least one night in the Palace in the fine, brass bed Doña Trinidad had boasted about. She had never enjoyed the red velvet curtains since Doña Trinidad called them "rags." Each day they reminded her of Manuel's newer luxuries which she could not enjoy.

She questioned Manuel about the new furniture from Mexico and hinted that she would like to see the Palace, but he laughed at her curiosity. For the next week she avoided his embrace, saying that she must watch the sala and bar.

"You said this house was at my disposition," he scolded her one night. "Now you are too busy. You have no time for me."

"Ah, lindo, without you my time is worth nothing." She kissed him lightly. "You honor my poor house. But a pallet on the floor is not good enough for you. Let me come to you at the Palace."

"There are spies and servants at the Palace," he objected. "That is why I got this house for you. And there is my wife . . ."

"She goes to the south tomorrow," Tules said quickly.

"There are no spies like you," Manuel laughed. "This morning Trinidad decided to go to Albuquerque, and you know it tonight. . . ."

"Then I will come to you tomorrow, querido?" She kissed him with warm, seductive lips when he nodded.

The next day Tules was as excited as a bride. She laid out her finest black silk dress, her black satin slippers with the high gold heels, her mantilla, rich reboso, jewels, and fan. There was one item she had heard of but never possessed—a nightgown. They must be useless and clumsy, but fine ladies wore them, and she must have one. She hurried to the Leitendorfer store and bought a high-priced nightgown of white muslin with lace ruffles at the high neck and long sleeves. Small diagonal tucks were set into a long panel where it buttoned all the way down the front.

María brought a copper pot of hot water to her room, and Tules scrubbed her ivory body, washed her hair, and arranged it in flat ringlets. She spent an hour before her mirror, trying earrings and necklaces, powdering her long nose, and dabbing French perfume on her throat and breasts. At midnight she knocked on the door of the Palace and gave the guard the password.

The Palace was like a dark sepulchre—not gay with lights and music as she had always pictured it. She passed through one dark cold room after another until the guard knocked at a door.

"Who comes?" Manuel's deep voice called out.

He opened the door, and she passed into the room. After the darkness she blinked at the many candles burning in wall sconces, on the tables, and in the deep windowsills. It was a large whitewashed room, carpeted in black- and white-checked jerga and filled with heavy furniture. Her wide eyes traveled quickly over the high, ornate black walnut wardrobe, the table with the sprawling claw legs and the one with the white marble top, the sofa and chair covered with red plush. A solid silver washbowl and pitcher stood on the stand under the large mirror.

Her eyes stopped when they came to the resplendent huge brass bed. It was a worthy gift from one General to another. At the head and foot the shining brass curved into sumptuous whorls. Four embossed brass posts upheld an elaborate canopy that was crowned with an intricate brass floral piece and almost touched the rafters. Pink china silk lined the canopy and hung down in deep ruffles. The bedspread was pale-blue satin embroidered in delicate Chinese designs of flowers and birds. Beneath it on the floor Tules saw a solid silver chamber mug. She drew in a quick breath at such luxury.

"Did you come to see the Palace or me?" Manuel teased and lifted her chin to kiss her. She had been too awed with the room to greet him. Now she closed her eyes and pressed tight against his chest.

He seated her on the red plush sofa and said, "We shall have a little supper to celebrate the first time you come here, vida mía." He removed napkins from silver trays of pastry and cake and poured wine from a crystal decanter.

Tules sat stiffly on the edge of the sofa and sipped the red wine. She was overpowered with this magnificence. Manuel was no longer her familiar lover but the Governor, the Military Commander of a vast Province, the trusted friend of General Santa Anna, the great and mighty dictator. She could think of nothing to say to him and twirled the stem of her glass between cold, nervous fingers. Suppose Doña Trinidad should walk in!

Manuel's big body sprawled at ease in the chair beside the table where he had been writing. His long legs stretched in front of him, and he reached often for the cake and pastry beside him. He always

224

had a large appetite. He told her of trouble that had come up with one of his officers. The wine began to warm her, and she settled a little more easily against the sofa.

"Pues, it's time for bed." Manuel yawned and finished the last of the wine. He got up, stretched, took off his fine cambric shirt, and struggled with his boots.

Tules nervously unpinned the black lace mantilla and played for time as she sniffed the spicy red carnation she had worn over one ear. She folded her black taffeta skirt and bodice and laid them carefully over a chair. She shivered in her cambric petticoat and wondered desperately what to do with the nightgown she had unwrapped from her bundle. She did not know how much to take off under it. After the fine ladies Manuel had known she did not want to betray her peón ignorance by taking off too much or too little. She had never been embarrassed when he admired her lithe, bare body, and she thrilled to his exploring hands on her breasts and firm, curved buttocks. But the nightgown was a disturbing question of etiquette.

She put on the nightgown, buttoned it, and caught sight of herself in the mirror. It looked like a stupid, long white bag. She was relieved when Manuel blew out the last candle. She let the petticoat drop and climbed into the high brass bed.

"Válgame Dios, how many clothes you women wear!" Manuel teased. "I don't want to sleep with a bolster. Take off that pillowcase."

She jerked off the nightgown and felt free again as Manuel drew her supple body close to his. Later Manuel snored, turned heavily, and a protesting spring gave a loud "ping!" Tules jumped and wondered uneasily if the bed would cave in. She felt suspended in air on these unaccustomed bedsprings and mattress. It was a senseless style to prefer this noisy, silly contraption to the comfort of a good, hard pallet on the floor.

She was wide awake now and peered at the room in the light of the ever-burning candle before Our Lady of Guadalupe. The white walls extended on and on, and the furniture loomed in dark, heavy masses. Something creaked, and she hid her head under the covers. She shivered at the thought that Doña Trinidad had returned home unexpectedly. When there was no further sound her knees relaxed, but she resolved to slip out before dawn.

A faint breath of air stirred the pink silk ruffles of the canopy, and she watched them with delight. She stretched her toes down luxuriously between the smooth white sheets and put out one hand to stroke the pale-blue satin bedspread that had once belonged to some Chinese princess. The candlelight caught on the brass bedposts. She smiled with deep satisfaction and curled her body around the warm comfort of Manuel's back. They had both come a long way, she thought drowsily, from dirty sheepskins to the luxury of this fine, soft bed.

# 22

A FASHIONABLE drive in the late afternoon with Lucita beside her was one of the luxuries Tules enjoyed with the success of her monte sala. Six strong, swift mules were now stabled in her corral. An adjoining shed protected the light carriage she had taken from the gringo and a heavy coach that was sturdy enough to withstand bad country roads when she drove to a fiesta.

It had been profitable to her and to Manuel to accept the Alcaldes' invitations for fiestas and set up her monte table in various little settlements up and down the Río Grande. The mozos guarded the oxhide chest filled with gold and silver for her bank and staggered under twice the weight when they returned home. Manuel provided a military escort in return for her confidential reports on political maneuvers. Tules enjoyed the fulfillment of her ambitions in the double role.

This afternoon only three mules drew the light carriage with the gaudy red-and-yellow spokes. They were harnessed in single file with an outrider on the lead mule and the coachman, Rómulo, on the front seat. Tules and Lucita were comfortably cushioned against the maroon upholstery inside. They were dressed in their best silk and rebosos, their hair carefully arranged under mantillas, their faces properly painted and powdered. They drove out for the world to see them as much as to see the world.

The ricos of Santa Fe had purchased new carriages from the American traders and now imitated the afternoon promenade of Mexico City. There the promenade extended down the length of the tree-shaded Paseo, but in Santa Fe it shrank to the dusty Alameda running from the plaza to the grove of cottonwoods planted by García Condé of Chihuahua.

As they drove around the plaza a man doffed his wide beaver hat, and Alcalde Rubidoux called, "I pass you good evening, Doña Tules—and your charming niece!" Two young strangers beside him stared with open admiration at Lucita. Tules nodded pleasantly.

"Gringos!" she commented. "They must have come with the last caravan. Now the Alcalde will bring them to the sala tonight. How much trouble these gringos cause! But we need their money!"

A youth dashed past them, showing off his curvetting horse, silver spurs, and bridle. He was young Antonio Chávez from Albuquerque, and Tules approved of his firm seat and his admiration for Lucita. She glanced at the girl, whose eyes followed Antonio, and coughed discreetly.

The dust raised by the carriage was enough to make anyone cough. It drifted above them in a golden cloud as they approached the glorieta. The cottonwoods made a grateful shade in the hot, glaring sunlight, and the green leaves hung motionless in the drowsy air. The mountain peaks seemed to rise directly behind the cottonwoods and were violet silhouettes against the turquoise sky. A luminous cloud peered over them, puffed with the promise of an evening shower.

When they drove back to the plaza, Tules was gratified to hear respectful voices greet her as "Doña," after long years of the condescending and unsavory "La." She smiled behind her black fan, enjoying the sparkle of its sequins as much as the perfume it gave off, and made sly comments on the friends they passed.

Near the Palace a sentry held up both arms and cried, "Halt! Halt! The Governor comes!"

Rómulo jolted the carriage as he stopped the mules, and Tules looked out to watch the sentry clear a lane between the people. Then he escorted the Governor and his lady to an elegant black equipage drawn by high-spirited sorrel horses. Tules knew how much Manuel loved this fanfare. He had clapped a paisano in jail for not removing his hat when the Governor approached. Manuel insisted that such ceremony taught people to respect law and order, but Tules suspected that it also fed Manuel's vanity.

"Don Manuel looks like a king in his blue uniform," Lucita said.

228

"It will soon take four horses to pull Doña Trinidad's weight," Tules shrugged.

She snapped at her fan as they waited for the regal pair to settle themselves in the carriage and start their evening drive. Her jealous hazel eyes watched Doña Trinidad's affable smile at the vivas for "El Gobernador! La Gobernadora!" She touched the long gold chain at her bosom that Doña Trinidad had lost to her at the monte table years ago. Doña Trinidad suffered more from losing a chain than a husband. She cared nothing about Manuel, except to demand that he give her the best of everything.

As the carriage rolled away Tules called to Rómulo to return home. She wanted to forget the regal pair, and her foot tapped impatiently as she thought of the opportunities Doña Trinidad threw away. If she was sitting beside Manuel as "La Gobernadora . . ." But that was impossible in this country where marriage was only severed by death.

She seldom went to Manuel's room in the Palace now. Its ornate pomp left her frightened and uncomfortable, and she was surer of herself and her man in her own surroundings. Manuel accepted the little room as his own and commanded her house as its master. The servants scuttled at his orders and cringed when he rebuked them. He used her house and wine with a free hand.

He teased her about the large bets she won in the sala, but she always made a poor mouth. She moaned over the heavy expenses—the servants, mules, candles, food, wine, the percentage to the dealers, lookouts, and Cuca's girls. Manuel brushed off these household worries like an old married man and often succeeded in "borrowing" money from her for some urgent plot of his own. The corners of her mouth sagged as she thought that this cost her more than Pérez's taxes; but it was worth it if she could hold Manuel's favor.

He was highhanded lately, arrogant with success, and merciless toward his enemies. His fawning subordinates dared not disagree with him. Tules shook her head as she thought of the unrest in the country, the hatred and revenge that still inflamed the ousted leaders.

229

She had helped to break up plots to assassinate Manuel; she loved him and tried to protect him. But he turned away from her now if she gave him anything but flattery.

Rómulo stopped at her door, and Rafaela startled her by calling, "Come to the kitchen. Women are crying and waiting for you."

Tules hurried across the patio to find half a dozen women huddled near the door and as many ragged children clinging to their skirts.

"Por favor, Doña Tules," one woman cried in a high, singsong voice, "we have come to beg your help. We are starving. We have nowhere to turn. God will bless you, if you help us. Ah, Doña Tules, you are the good friend of the Governor. Ask him to hear us."

Tules had become used to such pleas in the last two years. Someone always asked for her help with the Governor; young men whispered to her of political promotions, old men groaned that their property had been confiscated, mothers pleaded for their sons, others brought her petitions for land or water rights. Their pleas were always sugared with flattery for her position of honor as his accepted mistress and her strong influence with him.

She listened now to the woman's story of how twenty soldiers had been thrown in jail for refusing to accept their pay in the corn the Governor issued to them. "He would pay us in corn at four pesos the fanega, señora, when we could buy it at any store on the plaza for a third of that," the woman cried. "Our men are in jail, and we have had nothing to eat for a month. Ah, kind señora, ask the Governor to release our men. They have done no wrong. . . ."

Her voice rose to a high wail, and she wiped her streaming eyes and nose with her reboso, while the other women sobbed and the children screamed. Tules quieted them, promised to speak to the Governor, and gave them money. The women dropped on their knees, kissed her hand, and called on God to repay her.

The women's story gnawed at her mind as she dressed for the evening. She had heard reports before of the soldiers' refusal to take the high-priced corn as pay and hinted to Manuel about it but had only drawn his anger. He insisted that the treasury was bankrupt and he had to pay the soldiers in corn. He did not explain that he and his partner, Adolf Speyer, were the only merchants the Government paid, and they set their own price on corn.

It was dangerous for Manuel to add the soldiers' grievances to the rebellion that was ready to break out at any time. She must get him into a good mood and persuade him to release the soldiers. Woman-wise, she went to the kitchen to order Manuel's favorite food—chicken stewed in white wine, rice, sweet corn, squash, and those purple grapes from the Río Abajo.

That night the sala was full of gringos, and Alcalde Rubidoux presented the two tanned young strangers who had been with him in the afternoon. Their eyes bulged at the stacks of gold doubloons and silver pesos on the tables. The taller one watched Cuca's girls sauntering around the room and asked boldly, "Where is the beautiful girl who was with you this afternoon?"

"She is too young to come here," Doña Tules reproved him but called to one of Cuca's girls who wore a red rose in her hair. "Adelita, see that the young man enjoys himself."

She moved gracefully across the room, smiling and greeting friends. She stopped beside Santiago Flores, who was her manager and gave her respectful deference now that their positions were reversed. She watched him as carefully as he had watched her, but she counted on him to run the sala smoothly. She seldom dealt monte now, but she superintended every detail of the establishment. She whispered to Santiago, "We have good business tonight. Make the most of the rich gringos, but keep things quiet."

As she moved on a familiar voice called, "Hola, Tules!" and she greeted Pepe Cisneros and the Taos men with him. One was dignified Don Carlos Beaubien, and the other was the famous scout, Kit Carson. He was a small, slight man whose thin legs did not fill his worn leather pants. His long, sun-bleached hair was a strange contrast to his tanned skin. His brown eyes looked mild, but she knew that they recorded every person and movement in the room. She asked them about Taos, sympathized that the price of beaver had dropped, and wished them a pleasant evening.

She turned away to meet the cold, calculating eyes of Padre Martínez, who was also from Taos and a bitter enemy of Don Carlos Beaubien and Kit Carson. He was with the Vicario, Juan Felipe Ortiz, and Padre Leyba from San Miguel. As she talked with them, she thought of the latest friction between these rival factions over a grant of land Don Manuel had promised to give Don Carlos Beaubien. She suspected that each group had come to exert pressure on the Governor and sighed at the jealousy, selfishness, and greed that constantly pulled at Manuel. She would soothe him tonight, help him keep a firm hand and use good judgment to settle this rivalry.

The outer door opened, and the usual excitement stirred the crowd. Men called, "El Gobernador!" and quickly surrounded him. Tules swiftly appraised Manuel's mood. The air was sultry, and his large face looked hot and puffed, but every gold button was fastened on his heavy blue uniform. Gold epaulets dangled from his shoulders, and his sword hung at his side.

Her body swayed with sensuous grace under her rustling silk skirt as she moved across the room to welcome him and said in a laughing voice, "You put us to shame, my General! We wilt in the warm weather, but you stand as straight and handsome as the canes of St. Joseph!" She leaned closer and whispered behind her fan, "It is cooler in the patio. I have prepared supper—when you are ready."

She hurried to the patio to check the supper table and smelled the fragrance of honeysuckle twining over the portál. A full moon flooded the patio and left a deep shadow in the corner near the lattice where she had placed the table. Her foot slipped on a half-eaten melon rind that gave off the heavy, sweet richness of late summer as she tossed it toward the well.

"Shut up! Shut up, cabrón! Damn fool! Damn fool!" a hoarse voice scolded.

"Be quiet yourself, Pancho," Tules laughed as she stopped beside the perch to soothe the parrot who had wakened with ruffled feathers and angry red eyes.

"Por todo mal, mescal; por todo bien, también. Damn fool!" the parrot chattered. The mockingbirds in their bent amole cages began to whistle.

232

"Quiet, Pancho. You'll have the whole garrison out here," Tules scolded, as she filled his saucer with sunflower seeds. His words stopped in greedy cracking.

It was almost midnight when Manuel joined her in the cool dark-ness. She coaxed him to take off his heavy coat and made him com-fortable on a seat against the wall. He never exposed his back to a stray bullet or knife. He objected to lighting a candle that might make him a target in the darkness and ate his supper by the reflected light of the moon. Rafaela ran back and forth from the kitchen, bringing trays of savory food, and Tules filled their glasses with champagne. When Manuel finished the chicken, he belched, pushed back the table, and stretched out his long, heavy legs. He kept the champagne and the bowl of cool grapes beside him and spat the seeds and skins into the patio.

The glowing ends of their cigarritos were red embers as they re-laxed comfortably in the fragrant dark. Tules dreaded to disturb this happy peace. At last she mentioned the women who had come this afternoon to plead for their husbands.

"Let them rot in jail!" Manuel dismissed them lazily.

"But the women and children are starving!" Tules said.

"It's a good lesson for them. You listen to too many people. You have spoken of this before. Don't molest me with it again. Dios de mi vida, don't you know a man needs a woman for relaxation?" He reached for the second bottle of champagne and filled his glass.

"Bien de mi alma, forgive me." She leaned toward him and stroked his large hand. "I only thought that a little kindness to the soldiers now would shut the mouths of those who talk against you."

"Who talks against me?"

"You could send these soldiers to stop the Navajo raids," Tules suggested. "Every fall the ranches and pueblos suffer and say the Navajos are never punished. . . ."

"Válgame Dios, can I capture a thousand savages who ride like the wind with a dozen farmers on burros? Nothing would give me more satisfaction than to have the ears of the whole Navajo tribe hung on my walls. My people know that I have fought for them and lamed myself for life. The great Santa Anna gave his leg for his country, and I received a wound that will trouble me until death. What more do they want?"

"I know that the wound bothers you, mi vida. Haven't I rubbed your leg with warm, sweet oil? God forbid that the savages should attack you again! But if you sent the soldiers to protect the ranches this fall . . ."

"I have other uses for the soldiers now. Caramba, you know so little, yet you tell me what to do!" Manuel belched, drank his champagne, and turned his large body restlessly against the wall. "Next week I shall march at the head of my army and kill every gringo in the Province. They do more harm than the Navajos."

"Shhh, Manuel," Tules warned and pointed with her chin toward the lighted door of the sala. "You say that the customs duties are your only revenue. . . ."

"Yes, I have made good my promise. I have taken off all the taxes from our people and made the gringos pay. But they still triple their money every summer with the prices they charge us."

"Then if they bring business . . ."

"I have encouraged our people to get the trade and have gone into business myself with Speyer. If I could handle everything . . . I wish I had a dozen heads. I can't trust anyone. The Customs Officers make diligencia with the traders and put the money in their own pockets. I made my brother Jefe of Customs, but he will cheat me if it is to his profit. . . ."

"You can't be everywhere at once," Tules agreed.

"I will be where I can catch the gringo thieves." Manuel pounded the table and made the dishes rattle. "I put a reasonable duty of five hundred dollars on each wagon, and the traders unpack their wagons before they reach Arroyo Hondo and pile two loads on one wagon. They burn the extra wagons or give them to our people for graft. I require duty on all gold and silver taken out of New Mexico, and the traders hide their cash in the axles of their wagons until they cross the border. Then they brag about how they have outwitted me. . . ."

234

"Their tongues hang in the middle and clatter at each end." Tules nodded as she lighted another cigarrito for herself and one for Manuel. He drank more champagne to wash down his grievances.

"Dead tongues are silent. When the gringos have fled we can settle down to peaceful ways. Spain was right to prohibit them. We've had trouble with them for the last twenty years. It's a good thing Santiago Kirker and Dryden and their gang went to California. They were fomenting rebellion, working on the Indians and discontentos. But Santa Anna won't let them get away with another Texas. The Texans and Americans will stay on the other side of the border where they belong. . . ."

"But if there is war . . . The United States is strong. You are a great man, Manuel. You can make the traders do as you wish and still keep peace and good business. . . ."

"You think of nothing but business and money. Válgame Dios, have you no patriotism, no love, no honor for your country? I saw you flirting with the gringos tonight—that little runt, Kit Carson, the Frenchman from Taos, and that loudmouthed buffalo hunter. From the way you fill your place with them, ogle them, talk for them, I sometimes suspect that you have taken a gringo lover. If you have . . ."

"Manuel, you know no man has touched the toe of my slipper since I came to you," Tules cried.

"Then why do you wear that gringo's ring?" Manuel demanded.

Tules breathed sharply and quickly covered her left hand.

"At night you take off all the diamonds I have given you," he growled, "but you never take off that cheap gold band. If it means more to you than . . ."

"I told you the story of the ring, mi alma. The gringo boy meant nothing to me, but the ring—brought me luck."

"If you are true to me, give me that ring." Manuel grabbed her wrist.

Tules winced with pain as he crushed her hand. The sour smell of champagne blew in her face as he lurched toward her. He was stubborn and wild when he had too much wine. She let her arm hang limply in his grip and whispered, "We will talk of it another time. It is late. I must go in. . . ."

"Curse you, give me the ring!" Manuel twisted her arm.

Tules thought of calling the servants, but Manuel would never forgive that, and a scene would injure the sala. Tears filled her eyes, and she bit her underlip to keep from crying out. He could break her arm, but she would not give up the ring. It was her luck, her talisman, all the good fortune she had won since she began to deal monte. If she lost the ring, she would lose everything. She could hardly remember Jeem's face, but his ring was endowed with strange power. It guided her life. "Manuel, vida mía . . ." she pleaded.

A blinding flash of lightning shot through the sky, followed by the boom of thunder. The sharp crack of a gun cut through the thunder. Rain pelted the dry gravel in the patio. A woman's high scream came from the sala, and Santiago called, "Tules!"

"Damn fool!" a voice said at Manuel's shoulder.

Manuel released her wrist and crouched against the wall. "Who was that? The Texans have come already—they are here."

"No, Manuel, that was the parrot. But there is some trouble in the sala. Stay here. I will find Santiago. . . ." She sighed gratefully as she ran to the sala.

She looked into an empty room where the tables had been knocked over and wine and money spilled on the floor. In the candlelight she saw only one person in the room—a man lying on the floor, the stain of blood on his coat. "Santiago, what happened?" she called.

As Santiago came to her, heads popped up behind overturned tables and above the bar. By the time she reached the man, people were coming out from corners and doorways. A woman peered from behind the red velvet curtain and screamed, "The gringo started it. Drag out the gringos and kill them!"

Tules knelt beside the wounded man and recognised him as the tall young stranger who had stared at Lucita only this afternoon. Santiago felt for his heart; then he got up and dusted his hands.

"How did this happen?" Tules demanded as she looked into the young, lifeless face.

236

A dozen voices answered her, all talking at once. A fight. All the gringos had gone, except this young Texan. He drank at the bar and bragged that the Texans were coming to clean up this damned country. Matías answered that he alone would scalp every dirty Texan. They pulled their guns at the same time, but Matías was quicker. Served the gringo right. Throw him in the heretics' cemetery above the Garita. Bury the rest of the gringos with him or drive them out of the country. Down with the gringos.

"You are right, amigos!" Don Manuel's voice boomed behind Tules. He had put on his uniform and towered above the excited crowd. His wine-flushed face thrust out from his heavy shoulders like an angry bull. One of his lieutenants from the north, Santiago Ulibarrí stood beside him.

Don Manuel held a printed paper and letter in his hand and shook them at the crowd as he shouted, "Only this minute my lieutenant brought me these papers. They are the printed proclamations of the Texas Jefe, General Lamar, ordering New Mexico to become a vassal of Texas. We will avenge such an insult. Matías did well to get rid of one Texan. They are sending their army against us."

"We will be killed, raped, tortured. They'll run their lances through our children. The heretics will burn our churches. Ay, Madre de Dios, save us . . ." women screamed.

"Quiet, you fools," Don Manuel bellowed. "Time enough to cry after you have been hurt. We will turn our guns on the Texans first. We will burn those who dared to make this proclamation. We will save our country with the help of God."

"Viva Don Manuel! Dios y la nación!" the crowd cried hysterically.

"To arms, amigos!" Don Manuel flung up his arm in salute. "We march in two days. I will lead our army. I expect each man to volunteer. Come to me tomorrow at the Palace. Vámonos, hombres! We will win, with God's help!"

With a martial stride the Governor and his men hurried out of the sala. The wild enthusiasm subsided as the crowd faced the reality of war. Women sobbed, and men talked in grave voices as they started home.

# 23

DON MANUEL nursed his displeasure and sent Santiago Ulibarrí to Tules the next day with a curt demand for money.

"He said to send him the ring or two hundred pesos," Ulibarrí said and added, "He said you knew which ring. . . ."

Tules's eyebrows lifted with the knowledge that this was twice the amount Manuel would demand from any man, but she said coolly, "I will give you the money, but why do you need it this morning?"

"We offered a reward for the first news that the Texans had started," Ulibarrí explained. "We must pay the man today who intercepted a letter from Céran St. Vrain at Bent's Fort saying that they are on the way and will be here in a fortnight."

"But I hear this is only a trading caravan," Tules suggested. "It is not the Texas army. . . ."

"Look at this proclamation from the Texas General Lamar and judge for yourself, Doña Tules." He handed her the proclamation printed in English and Spanish which promised New Mexico protection, freedom, and a sister's share if she would join the Lone Star Republic.

"Texas claims the land to the east bank of the Río Grande on the strength of the old boundary dispute between France and Spain," he said. "She pretends that she has been invited to come here with this offer. If she has, it was by the Perezistas and the Insurrectos around Taos who would use the Texans to set themselves up and overthrow Don Manuel. For twenty years the traders have been the advance guard who filtered into our country to weaken our people with promises, business, bribery. Now they have sent an armed invasion. We will call their bluff and drive them out for good."

Tules handed Ulibarrí the money and said, "Por favor, tell Don

238

Manuel I am happy to help him. I must see him before he leaves. Say that I pray for his safety and success."

When Manuel did not come to her, she sent Victorio with a second plea. The little hunchback hated Don Manuel and took satisfaction in growling the message as he had received it. "He said, 'Tell Doña Tules I am occupied with military preparations. She can pray for the Texans. They will need it.'"

Tules watched Manuel as he left the plaza at the head of his tattered army. He rode a large, dun-colored mule, and his dark poncho gleamed with silver-and-gold embroidery. He ignored the cheering crowd and looked straight ahead, his stiff military bearing proclaiming his heavy responsibility as the defender of his country. Tules turned away with a heavy heart, troubled that she had not been able to wish him success, plead with him to protect himself, and assure him of her love.

A week after the army left wild rumors surged back and forth over Santa Fe. The first rumor claimed that part of the Texas army had been scalped, and the others had fled across the border; the next rumor insisted that the Texans had triumphed and Don Manuel had been captured like Santa Anna.

Tules anxiously questioned Don Santiago Magoffin, who had passed through San Miguel with his trading wagons a few days before. He assured her that he had talked to Don Manuel and had seen the Texas prisoners who were in jail in San Miguel. Don Santiago was an American, but his wife was from Chihuahua. He had conducted his large trading operations in New Mexico for so many years that he was not regarded as a "foreigner." His courtesy and Irish wit made him simpático, and he was welcomed on either side of the border at any time.

Hatred flamed against all other gringos. They were under suspicion as spies and traitors and forbidden to leave the country. Some were stealthily murdered, others shackled in jail after they resisted looting mobs.

The Spaniard, Don Manuel Álvarez, who had been the United States Consul for many years, was attacked in his office. Tomás Martínez, swollen with authority as the Governor's favorite nephew, led the attack, and the rabble screamed, "Drag Álvarez out! Kill the traitor! Down with the gringos!" Álvarez escaped with an ugly knife wound down his cheek and sought refuge with thirteen Americans who barricaded themselves in their house. They sent out word that the United States would avenge them.

Their house was only a little way up the road from Tules's sala. She twisted her hands with anxiety as she saw the mob gather in front of the house, stone it, and taunt the men inside. She knew that the traders were not Texans but Americans and that it was dangerous to arouse the wrath and might of the United States. If that strong nation was insulted and sent its army to subdue New Mexico, there was no hope. She wished that she could disperse the mob, but she was afraid of appearing disloyal to Don Manuel. His spies watched everyone and reported every suspicious action.

Each night men gathered in the sala to repeat rumors, boast in loud voices, and eat her free supper. They had no money to play monte, and Santiago Flores grumbled over mounting expenses. He would have grumbled louder if he had known of the alms and food Tules gave the beggars at the back door.

María kept in touch with their old neighbors, and Tules gave her money for Carlota, her ragged brood, and La Casimira. María said, "La Casimira says she must talk to you, niña. The devil who possesses her has grown stronger. Pobrecita! She looks hungry and wild. I gave her food, but she says she must see you. I sent her to our room. Have patience with her, Tules, and take care. . . ."

Tules was tired and worried but went to find La Casimira. The witch had huddled beside the fire and reminded Tules of distressing scenes in earlier days. Then she had been sick, poor, and frightened, and La Casimira mumbled over death cards. Now the witch looked haggard, her hair hung in disordered wisps, and her strange catlike eyes gleamed with fanatic light.

"I have come to run the cards for you," La Casimira croaked and laid out the cards on the floor. "Bad. Bad. Someone will betray you. I see a dark man—he menaces you. He is evil. Danger. Here is a woman

240

with him—she will defeat you. Beware! Black clouds hang over you. You must use a powerful charm against them, or they will destroy you. . . ."

"You're as cheerful as a buzzard, comadre," Tules laughed, and tried to joke La Casimira into good humor. "Let me cross your hand with silver. Find me good luck. The world is black with war clouds, and I need good news. . . ."

"You laugh at me now, but you will not laugh long. I came to warn you. Evil spirits are after you. I have had bad dreams of you. I bring you spirit messages, and you make fun of me. . . ."

"No, no, comadre, a thousand thanks for the warning. I worry over this war and bad times and need good fortune to encourage me. Por favor, find me some good cards . . ." Tules coaxed her.

"I don't make your fortune. I only tell you what I see. Years ago, before you were rich and haughty, you believed in my second sight. Now you have no time for me, but others—as rich as you are—come to me, value my messages. I see their fortunes, and I see yours. You will beg me for love charms, potions. . . ."

"Here's a peso. Give me the charm now, comadre," Tules smiled. She remembered how many times María had given this woman money.

"A peso won't buy my charms." La Casimira's eyes glittered. "Keep your money. It isn't clean. You had death cards around you. I remember how Pedro was killed. . . ."

Tules caught her breath sharply. How did La Casimira know that? She was suddenly afraid of the witch—not afraid of her spells but of her tortured mind and venomous tongue. She must quiet her, offer her anything, get the old story out of her mind.

"You were a good friend when I was alone and sick," she said gently. "I am sorry I have been so busy. Tell me now what I should do. Give me a powerful charm against this evil."

La Casimira mumbled of charms, potions, the evil eye. Tules gave her five pesos and took in exchange a dried cat's claw giving off a sickening odor of decay, musk, and penetrating medicine. A second five pesos bought powdered coral wrapped in a capsule of gold leaf, rat-

241

tlesnake fangs, and a bit of clay crudely molded in the shape of a man. La Casimira said she would bury this image and the enemy would die, but Tules must tell his name and add a hair from his head or a nail paring. Tules said she had no enemy, and La Casimira was angry again. She left mumbling of danger, bad luck, and Tules's ingratitude.

María said she would pray for the witch's tormented soul, but Cuca scolded Tules. "You should know better than to anger that witch. You should have given her some name—any name—and kept her tongue busy with her charms. Everyone knows she is crazy, but they repeat what she says. I have even seen this new rica, Conchita Mondragón, and her dueña come from La Casimira's hovel."

"You mean the heiress from Mexico who has come to look for her father's mine?" Tules asked.

"That is the story she tells," Cuca sniffed. "She is invited with the gente fina, and she was the toast of all the young galanes before they went off to this silly war. She is young and pretty and acts as though she belongs to the Right People. Quién sabe?"

"You're as suspicious as a cat at a mousehole," Tules laughed.

"Pues, we'll see." Cuca shrugged her plump shoulders. "The girl may be all right, but that dueña she calls 'Tía Lola' sticks too close. She only leaves enough room to pass a ten-peso bill between herself and her charge. If she gets the money, I'll bet she leaves the girl alone in the house. . . ."

"Has she interfered with your business, Cuca?" Tules teased.

"See that she doesn't interfere with yours," Cuca warned but refused to explain. "Don't go to sleep on your luck. You may lose it."

"Dios de mi vida, what do you mean by my luck?" Tules stamped her foot angrily. "Everyone comes to me for help, but no one helps me. La Casimira puts the evil eyes on me, Santiago grumbles, you scold, María prays. . . . This war is driving us crazy so that we fight, quarrel over nothing. I wish it was over."

"And you were snoring beside the General in the brass bed!" Cuca snorted.

After these vexations Tules was doubly glad to see Pepe Cisneros

242

in the cantina that night. He was the only person who was unconcerned with war, rumors, or revenge. His eyes twinkled as he sang comic songs, and Tules laughed as she listened to him. She was always a little uneasy about his bold political jokes, knowing that Manuel would hear them and blame her. Manuel hated ridicule even more than Texans. But tonight Pepe's songs were merry and without sting. He strolled close to her and whispered, "Will you give me a few minutes in the little room alone?"

When he closed the door behind him, his face lost the merry grin, and his thick eyebrows drew together in a frown. He said slowly, "I have come to ask a favor, but you may not like it. I have a friend who needs help—food and medicine."

"But, of course, Pepe . . ." she said.

He held up his hand and added, "You do not understand. He is a gringo—shut up in that house, dying. You know the feeling in the town now. But I must get help for him."

"Why do you do this, Pepe?" she asked. "The gringos are against us. The Texans are traitors. Why are you disloyal to your own people?"

"Because I love my own people and believe they would have a better chance with honest men." Pepe looked at her frankly. "I know these gringos and Texans. I have hunted with them on the buffalo plains. They are good men. They keep their word, and I can trust them. Can you say the same for any of our políticos? You know that they lie, steal, knife each other in the back. There is no justice, no equality, no chance. The ricos steal all they can and grind the pobres under their heels. I believe that the gringos would give each man a chance to live his own life, support himself, raise children to be something more than bound peóns. Don't you want that too?"

"Of course." Tules nodded. Her childhood fear of being sold and her mother's long peonage haunted her. She knew the injustice, cruelty, poverty the pobres suffered. She had held high hopes that Manuel would be the great leader to change the corrupt ways and develop a better country for everyone.

Pepe came close to her and took her hand, "My wife had no chance, and my children have no chance under this rotten system. My wife

243

died last year and left two motherless girls. I wanted to tell you this before, Tules. . . . I am free now. . . . I have wanted you so long."

Compassion filled her eyes, but she drew her hand away. Pepe was a merry clown, a carefree troubadour, but she could never think of him seriously. Though tonight he had taken off the clown's mask and spoke to her of his deep convictions with dignity, faith, and courage. . . . She turned away from the question in his eyes and asked, "You say the gringos are sick and need help?"

Pepe quietly accepted her refusal and said, "One man, shut in that house, has fever and dysentery. Another, who was captured at Antón Chico, was brought to the jail today and is dying from his wounds. No one will sell to them, but if you give me supplies from your storeroom you may save their lives. . . ."

"They are traitors," Tules said. "Why should I help them? Our men have gone to stop this invasion. Our men may be killed."

"This is a small trading caravan of one hundred and eighty men," Pepe said. "They are lost in a strange country and separated in three bands. There is no danger to your men from small unarmed bands of traders. . . ."

"The buttons on their coats were stamped with 'Texas,'" Tules argued. "Traders' coats don't have military buttons. I read the proclamation offering to make New Mexico part of Texas. They came here to invade our country, offer false promises to get us to join them. No, Pepe, this is our country and must be governed by our people. You would do more good if you helped our leaders make it a strong, honest country. . . ."

"What will be, will be," Pepe shrugged, unable to change her blind faith in Manuel. "Within five years the American army will come, and we will be better off. Even now Texas has been recognized by the United States, France and England. If we were part of Texas we would be adopted that much more quickly by the United States. I tell you this in confidence, and I know I can trust you, no matter how you feel about Don Manuel. But the sick gringos can't hurt you. Won't you help them?"

She nodded reluctantly, unwilling to deny Pepe again. They

planned the supplies and medicine and a way for Pepe to take them with him.

That week the news of a decisive victory crowded out every other thought. All the Texans were killed or captured. At the victory fiesta at San Miguel, General Armijo had publicly burned the Lamar proclamations with a dramatic speech against future insults or perfidy. The Texas prisoners started on their two-months' march to Mexico City under Captain Damasio Salazar, whose reputation for brutality left no doubt of their treatment. Men said that Salazar had already shot the weak prisoners who were too ill to keep up and had sent their ears to the Palace to claim his bounty. He had starved and beaten the others and marched them through the snow in chains. Pepe's eyes signaled his contempt for such cruelty, but Tules turned away from him to hide the anxiety on her own face.

Don Manuel and the army had left San Miguel to set up outpost headquarters in Las Vegas but would return to the capital the following week. Santa Fe immediately made elaborate plans to give Don Manuel a triumphal ball when he returned.

"We must have new gowns," Tules told Lucita, glad to make happy plans after the distress of the past weeks.

"They say this new girl, Conchita Mondragón, is the most beautiful in the Province," Lucita sighed. "All the men are mad with love' for her. Even Antonio. . . ."

"We will put her in the shadow with our new styles." Tules tossed her head. "I have the latest colored fashion plates that came from Paris to New York this summer."

She patted the sagging muscles under her chin as she thought of this new girl's youth and beauty. Then she sent for the seamstress and looked through the materials she had thriftily laid away. She selected a fine cream taffeta with a pattern of rosebuds on a brown satin trellis for herself and a heavy yellow taffeta with broad blue stripes for Lucita.

"I can't breathe," Lucita objected when Tules insisted that they must lace themselves in the new American corsets.

"You must learn to breathe from the top," Tules said. "You can

245

stand those whalebones for a few hours if they give you the fashionable straight front and small waist. A bulge at the stomach is vulgar now, but it is ravishing at the bosom. Our latest styles will be the envy of the ball."

They stood for hours while the seamstress fitted them. Tules twisted before the mirror and finally nodded approval that the full looped skirt showed off her small waist and fine figure. The fichu with the deep lace flounce was an innovation after the old-fashioned rebosos and mantillas and becoming to her creamy throat and shoulders.

The night of the ball Tules powdered her glowing face and sprinkled perfume in the enticing hollow between her high breasts. The rich brown satin in the pattern of her dress emphasized the warm copper lights in her hair. She jerked out a white hair, combed the ends into finger curls, and held them in place on each side with roses and diamond-studded combs. After she wound gold chains around her throat and put on all her diamonds, she turned to Lucita. For a moment she felt the sharp sting of envy for the girl's tender, unfolding beauty, a young radiance that was more priceless than a crown of diamonds.

María offered her the lace mantilla, but Tules pushed it away and said, "No, it's too old-fashioned. It would hide the new way I've fixed my hair."

"You will be the most beautiful woman at the ball," María sighed, with a loving touch for Tules's rich taffeta skirt.

Tules smiled into those faded eyes whose admiration always made her feel young, gorgeous, successful. She turned for a last critical look into the mirror and felt satisfied that Manuel would be proud of her style and good looks and would show her special favor. Dios, she had not seen him for so many weeks! She pushed back the memory of their last quarrel and assured herself that any unpleasantness would be forgotten in his high good humor over this significant victory.

La Fonda was ablaze with candles, and the hum of gay voices filled the long rooms. Most of the men were in uniform, and the ladies displayed their laces, embroidered shawls, and heirloom jewels. Don Santiago Magoffin was the only "foreigner," but he did not seem disconcerted that his countrymen had been excluded. Santa Fe had returned to the haughty isolation of the old Spanish settlements.

In the reception room Tules's eyes turned quickly to where Manuel stood alone holding court. He looked regal in his pale-blue uniform with the red on the collar and the shining gold of his epaulets, heavy braid, and buttons. Her heart went out to him when she noticed the deep, tired lines that ran from his curved nostrils to his jutting chin. His handsome face was dark and stern, and he accepted the fulsome compliments with the bored, unsmiling expression of a war-weary emperor. He held his large body stiffly erect and thrust his hand between the buttons of his coat.

"He is posing like Napoleon," someone whispered behind Tules.

"More likely he has five aces hidden in his palm," another sniggered.

Tules and Lucita took their places in the long line. Lucita motioned slightly to the back and whispered "Conchita!" Tules glanced back to see a ravishingly pretty young girl whose black gown and filmy mantilla were a foil for her velvety black eyes, red lips, and softly rounded figure. She was obviously aware that the eyes of all the men followed her and raised and lowered her long black lashes with alluring coquetry. She whispered into the long, severe face of her dueña, whose black reboso enfolded her with strict decorum.

Tules shrugged and moved on toward Manuel. She wished that he would smile, warm his people with encouragement, and bind them to him with loyalty and devotion. They needed heart-warming recognition if they faced future wars. She did not understand this new pose but excused it as fatigue. She stood before him, smiled, and said, "Permit me to congratulate you, my General, on this magnificent victory. We are happy and proud of your success. But you have been away so long. . . ."

Manuel looked down at her with lofty condescension and ignored her hand. "Your tune changes with the drums of victory, Doña Tules, but I notice that you still admire the gringos. I dislike the intrusion of these foolish American styles in ladies' dresses. We have banished the gringos and their ideas."

247

"No doubt you have been too occupied to inform yourself that ladies' styles come from Paris, señor." She raised her head defiantly and looked at him with flashing green eyes. She still could not believe that he intended to insult her publicly.

"It is unpatriotic to flaunt American styles tonight." Sardonic humor twisted his mouth as his eyes passed over Lucita and beamed at Conchita Mondragón behind her. He said loudly, "Ah, señorita, your style belongs to our country and proclaims a loyal heart. Your fine mantilla brings out the beauty of your eyes, your charm. . . ."

Tules's cheeks flushed, and her angry eyes lashed at Manuel's admiring profile as he bent toward the girl. Tules longed to slap his pompous face. She heard the girl pour out flattery and adulation and saw Manuel's eyes gleam with anticipation, pleasure. Tules opened her fan to hide her burning face and moved on. The girl would brag of this, and everyone would laugh tomorrow, but tonight Doña Tules would show a gay face. She held her head high and presented Lucita to the older ladies. It was some solace that Lucita was modest and beautiful and her good manners brought invitations from the gente fina.

That night no one was gayer than Doña Tules as she danced quadrilles before Manuel's eyes and sipped wine with the caballeros. Under her laughter her fury mounted that, in spite of everything she had been to Manuel, he should accuse her of disloyalty. He had used that Conchita as a means to discredit her, cast her off. She had dreaded this moment when he would turn to a younger face. She was no longer a novelty and mystery to him. But her maturity and intimate knowledge of his character gave her other ways to hold him and her own position of honor and power. As she danced she planned a dozen schemes for revenge.

# 24

TULES HAD trained herself to show no emotion at the monte table when luck ran against her. She used that discipline through the long winter to present a calm face and inscrutable smile. Her furious resentment of Manuel's ill-mannered rebuff had time to cool as months passed and he ignored her. Her profit dwindled, but she upheld the prestige of her sala with the free suppers, her rustling black taffeta, and Manuel's rose-cut diamond necklace. She often dealt monte, not only to attract men from rival salas but to give her anxious mind absorbing employment.

Santiago Flores complained that business had fallen off because Don Manuel and his followers did not patronize them and suggested a big fiesta to draw the políticos. Tules studied that plan and a dozen others to bring Manuel back but turned them down. She had learned to play a hard, patient game and knew that she would lose everything if she showed a timid hand. Any day Manuel's mood might change and bring his request for the aid and sympathy he needed at this critical time. He liked to sell honey without keeping bees.

The poor business was due to more than Manuel's absence. There had been no money in the Province for a year. The pobres were starving, and the ricos hoarded their wealth against future calamities. If Manuel carried out his threat to prohibit the traders this summer the pobres would perish, or there would be another revolution. Either would open the gates to the Texans.

In this crisis the traders were permitted to come with the July rains, but Tules heard them grumble about the exorbitant duty, the diligencia necessary to grease every palm, and the lack of protection for their lives or goods. They brought cash to the tables again, but their complaints increased the growing discontent in the country.

Like everyone else in Santa Fe, Tules heard daily reports of Manuel's official activities. He was on the alert to block plots to overthrow or assassinate him. Some enemies disappeared, others were exiled, and Manuel finally surrounded himself with only those advisors who flattered and praised him. He was away from the Palace much of the time, strengthening outposts in Las Vegas, Taos, and San Miguel against another invasion. In the Río Abajo he recruited additional troops and stopped for a long rest at his ranch at Lemitar. He took Doña Trinidad on a triumphal trip to Mexico City where they were regally entertained by General Santa Anna, who was again in power.

Tules heard Conchita Mondragón's name linked with Don Manuel's, but it was never more than a sly joke, and she dismissed it as idle gossip. The girl and her dueña left Santa Fe frequently on some mysterious business. During the spring she met Conchita at the home of one of the ricos and watched her young beauty. The seduction of her velvety black eyes and ripe lips fascinated every man and made every woman jealous. In public her manners followed the formal Spanish pattern which permitted no freedom to women but gave every man license to seek pleasure outside his home.

Conchita returned almost too quickly to her dueña after each dance and had none of Lucita's innocent flutter. She and "Tía Lola" sat close together like conspirators, and Tules saw them nod and whisper over herself and Lucita. She decided that the girl lacked a good dowry and was using her beauty to lure some young rico into a rich marriage. She forgot Conchita in the worry over her own problems.

During sleepless nights she fretted over the future and Manuel. Her mother, "Nana Luz," had returned to Manzano, but Tules still took care of María, who was thin and ailing, Chico, Rafaela, and Lucita. At least she could protect Lucita by arranging for an early marriage for her with young Antonio Chávez. He had often hinted of his love, and Tules won the father's consent by offering a large dowry for Lucita. The sala was cleared out for the wedding reception, and Tules sighed with satisfaction as she looked at the exclusive ricos holding their lighted candles and toasting the bride and groom in her champagne.

That spring Pepe Cisneros came to warn her again, his ruddy face serious and his eyes full of devotion. "There will be war this summer, and you must be prepared to leave at any time," he said. "The Texans who survived the death march under that brute, Damasio Salazar, were freed and returned home to stir the whole country with stories of the atrocities they suffered. They demand revenge. . . ."

"Isn't that Texas talk, Pepe?" she asked.

"No, it involves the United States as well as Texas," he insisted. "The newspapers in the United States and the statesmen in their Congress openly demand war against Mexico. The hunters on the buffalo plains showed me the printed speeches. They say the Texas army will come this summer. They will defeat us."

"Dios de mi vida, you would lose your ears if anyone heard you say that, Pepe!" Tules exclaimed. "You know the feeling against the gringos now. . . ."

"Yes, and I know how the gringos feel," Pepe said heatedly, trying to make her see the other side. "If the traders are attacked, nothing is done; but if a Mexican is accidentally shot, the traders are thrown in prison and not allowed to defend themselves. Last summer word was passed that the country needed the gringo goods and money, but if the gringos failed to return . . ." He shrugged and made the sign for cutting throats. "You know what happens on the Chihuahua Trail. . . ."

"Take care, Pepe." She shook her head to warn him not to repeat the dark rumors that Governor Armijo furnishd guns and ammunition to the Apaches. His messengers and the wagons of his partner, Adolf Speyer, crossed the southern desert safely, but the Apaches raided all other caravans.

"I only say these things to you." Pepe caught her hand and gazed at her with troubled eyes. "If you knew how many times I think of you each day, worry for your safety. . . . I come to warn you. This will not be a child's battle with a small, unarmed bunch of helpless traders. It will be worse than the Pérez massacre."

Tules thanked him and watched for signs of trouble. While Manuel was away plots flourished against him like hardy weeds. If any leader had had the courage to start a revolt the army would have mutinied and deserted their Comandante Militar; but the leaders were afraid and gave Manuel the usual lip service when he returned. He balanced his power shrewdly, set one thief to catch another, and threatened both.

Tules tested the plots by questioning one of Manuel's best lieutenants, Diego Archuleta. He had a fine, sensitive face and inspired his men with his sincere devotion to New Mexico and loyalty to the Mexican Republic.

"There was more to the affair of the Texas traders two years ago than we said," he confided. "Their spies were everywhere, ready to start a general revolt with guns and bribes. We cleaned them out. Shrouds have no pockets."

"Is there danger for Don Manuel now?" she asked behind her fan.

"Of course," he nodded. "The bodyguard has been doubled. Manuel is busy with plans. The Texans threaten to march on us this summer, but we will whip them again."

Tules watched him under her lashes to see if he believed this boast. Manuel needed honest, trustworthy friends now who would tell him the truth and warn him of danger. In spite of the hurt and humiliation in her heart, the old urge to help him and protect him was too strong. She said quickly, "Por favor, ask Don Manuel to come to the sala. Tell him I have important news."

Lucita was visiting her, and as they returned from their drive the next afternoon Tules saw the Governor striding under the portál of the Palace. Her heart beat faster as she watched the majestic figure in the long blue cape swing his gold-headed cane. The crowd made way for him and bowed except for one old, shrunken piñón vendor. Don Manuel almost stumbled over him.

"Out of the way, you bastard," he thundered, raised his cane, and cracked the old man over the head. "Válgame Dios, I have given orders to clear the streets of beggars! Throw this one in jail."

Rómulo stopped the carriage, and the crowd gathered in front of the mules. Tules leaned forward and saw the blood spurt from the old man's head. A woman stooped to pick up the small brown nuts that spilled from his basket. The old vendor groaned and begged for mercy as two soldiers dragged him away.

"Pobrecito! He is blind. He could not see the Governor," Lucita cried. "Tell Don Manuel he is blind."

"Por Dios, sit still!" Tules jerked her back. "You will make things worse. Don Manuel would not listen now, before this crowd." She motioned Rómulo to drive on and cautioned Lucita, "It would not help to have you punished too, child. The old man will rot in jail, but what can we do? The pobres have no rights. The courts are closed for lack of funds, but even when there were judges bribes weighed more than justice."

"But that was cruel," Lucita said. "What has happened to Don Manuel since he came back from San Miguel? He treats the people like dogs, and they run from him and hide. . . . No one would help him in another revolution."

"Hush!" Tules warned. "Never say that word. Spit it out like burned beans. He is drunk with power since he defeated the Texans. No one can talk to him. If we displease him, he can ruin us. . . ."

When Manuel strode into the sala that night her heart pounded, and she held her hand to her bare throat to hide the beating vein. She looked at him swiftly—he was heavier, his eyes had dark pouches of dissipation, and the lines had deepened into stern brackets around his mouth. She nervously rubbed her ring, but it was heavy and dead with warning. She shook off the bad omen and hurried toward him with a radiant smile.

"Bien venida, my General! My poor house has been dark without you, but now the sun shines again!" As she touched his shoulder in the customary embrace she whispered, "My heart has been desolate. You look tired, querido. Can you find rest and peace here tonight?"

"I can give you an hour, but I have important business later," he said indifferently.

She met him in the small room, poured wine, and smiled at him with the old intimate devotion. She raised her glass and said, "To your

253

eternal happiness and success, mi alma. I have been lonely without you. . . ."

"You know the affairs of state," he shrugged. His large body relaxed with the wine, and he drew in a satisfied breath from his cigarrito. "I spend my time weeding out one man, pleasing another. There is too much work. . . . But what is your important news?"

Her low voice told him of the reports in the American papers and speeches in Congress. He used to check each detail of such reports, but now he hardly listened. She minimized the Texas threats as she sensed his displeasure.

"You call this news?" he scoffed without looking at her. "I have no fear of the Texans. I taught them to stay on the other side of the border. They threaten to come again. Pues, if they do, we will kill every soldier this time. I will drive all the gringos out of the country. . . ."

"Then you will need every man," she urged. "You could strengthen the army by promoting the young officers who are dissatisfied. Make them loyal. There was talk of mutiny while you were away."

"You need not coach me in army discipline." His mouth hardened. "I can handle a few puking boys who know nothing of battle or my responsibilities. They will obey me when the order is given to defend their country. I do not like your suggestion that my officers would mutiny. You listen to too many traitors. You are jealous. You talk like a virtuous, nagging wife. . . ."

"I have no claim as a wife, and I do not pretend to have virtue." She lifted her red head and looked him in the eye. "Everyone knows that I belonged to you, Manuel. I was proud of it. I fought for you, worked for you. I still offer any help I can give. . . ."

"A man must manage his own affairs," he said and looked away from her. "A woman should give him pleasure, loyalty, relaxation. . . . Perhaps you have forgotten that."

"No, I have not forgotten. I remember our happy years when we loved each other." She leaned to him and caught his hand. "Por Dios, what have I done? What is the matter, querido?"

He drew his hand away as though her display of emotion bored him and raised his eyebrows. "Age changes us whether we are willing

254

or not. But time brings other satisfactions. You were ambitious and wanted this sala. Its success should satisfy your later years."

"You mean that I am too old. . . ." She jumped up to face him and drew her body erect with a deep, angry breath. The bitter truth that he had scorned her, discarded her, seared her mind and body.

"We are both older and should recognize practical values," he said as his lips set in a hard, cunning line. "We can still work together if you show loyalty and good sense. You may keep the sala for the present and reserve this room for my appointments, but I require discretion and quick service. I forgot that a man is waiting, and I must see him now. Con permiso. . . ."

He smiled impersonally, held the door open for her, and walked into the sala. She burned with shame at such a dismissal.

Her furious eyes saw him greet a gringo with a blond moustache, take him into the small room, and close the door. Afterwards she remembered that the man was Captain Lewis, who had betrayed his fellow Texans into surrender at San Miguel. Lewis had been in and out of Santa Fe since then to sell his information.

She stared with tragic intensity into the sala. A hundred candles twinkled in the great chandelier hanging from the dark rafters, flames danced in the fireplace, and the long mirrors reflected the red velvet curtains against the white walls. Shining money was stacked on the tables, and more would be added to it before the night was over. Manuel had threatened all of that, but he would not dare confiscate it without a good excuse. She knew too much about him, and she had too many friends.

She realized now that he intended to scorn her, tell her to her face that she was too old for his embrace, save himself from further quarrels. The bitter truth writhed in the pit of her stomach and nauseated her. She burned with humiliation that she had humbled herself again, begged for his love. She had been a blind fool over and over, and she cursed her own stupidity for offering her heart for this final insult. She started for the door to go to her room, sick with rage and shame.

"Qué tal, Tules?" Pepe's laughing voice called to her. "Can you spare a cigarrito for a poor buffalo hunter?"

Tules controlled the fury that shook her knees, forced herself to stop and smile as she handed Pepe her beaded case of cornhusk wrappers and her small copper tobacco flask.

"A thousand thanks, but I don't need the flint and steel." He laughed and waved it aside. He turned to the men standing near them and called, "I wish to display my magic to Doña Tules. Come, caballeros, I will give you a quicker way to make money than by playing monte. What will you bet that I can light my cigarrito without the flint?"

"You will draw a coal from the fire," one man laughed. "You have lived at the buffalo camp too long, Pepe."

"No, this time I will not use a coal, amigo. I will make magic before Doña Tules's eyes and light my cigarrito with it. Who will bet? Don't be misers!" He grinned and struck his elbow with his other fist in the sign for avarice. "Bien, if you won't bet more silver I will give my money to Doña Tules to cover your bets."

"No cheating, Pepe!" the men laughed. "Let's see the magic."

Pepe began an elaborate search through his pockets, pretending he had lost something and was ruined. Then he pulled out a rough plug of wood, broke off a small stick, and cried, "Now watch the magic!"

He showed the crowd the painted end of the stick and quickly drew it across the bottom of the wooden block. A yellow flame blazed, and the strong smell of sulfur filled the air. Pepe made a wide gesture as he lighted his cigarrito and grinned. Men gaped in unbelief and shouted. "What is it? What did it? It smells of sulfur and must be the devil's magic. What a wonder! Where did you get it, Pepe?"

"From the gringo buffalo hunters. They call these 'matches' or 'lucifers.' They are better than our flints. A thousand thanks, caballeros." He raked the bets from the bar, took his money from Tules, and presented her with the wooden block.

She passed it to the men to examine more closely. They carefully lit two or three matches, and the heavy sulfur fumes hung over their heads.

"These gringos can invent anything!" one man exclaimed. "They are too smart for us. Their guns shoot a mile. Verdad, hombres. No wonder their cannon can blow up our presidio if they have these sulfur flares to light the fuse!"

"Who talks of cannon and fuse?" a voice bellowed, and Don Manuel towered over them. He shouted angrily, "Who gave you permission to use your guns? I smell powder. . . ."

The men hurriedly gave him the wooden block, explained its wonder, and lighted a match. They said Pepe had brought it from the gringo buffalo hunters.

"Another trick of those cursed gringos!" Don Manuel growled. "Are you children to be dazzled by a toy? You should throw it in their faces. You believe any gringo trick or lie. I shall prohibit these sticks that stink of the devil."

He thrust the wooden block in his pocket and turned to Pepe. "As for you, cabrón, I know your traffic with the gringos. You will not have a second warning."

He marched out of the sala, followed by his bodyguard and the Texas traitor. The men slunk against the bar like whipped dogs, but Pepe grinned broadly, picked up his guitar, and began to improvise verses. Over the strummed chords he sang:

"Said the flint, "I am poor,
I'm old and I'm sick,
Men have to work hard
To kindle my wick."

Said the match, "Now behold
There are thousands like me.
I give a bright light,
And I'll set you free."

Tules shook her head and whispered, "Sing something else. We have had enough trouble here tonight!"

"I saw trouble in your eyes," Pepe nodded. "Whenever you need me, I will come."

Tules started again to go to her room. She needed to be alone. Her knees still shook with the shock of Manuel's open scorn. But Cuca stopped her at the door, cocked her head, and rested her hands on her plump hips.

"You look tired," she said and sniffed the sulfur in the air. "Don Manuel did not enjoy the devil's smell."

"Maldito sea!" Tules hissed. "This time I am through with him. He has gone too far at last."

"So you have found him out, have you? Everyone knew but you. I wanted to warn you about that girl but . . ." She shrugged.

"What girl? What do you mean?" Tules turned on her.

"That Conchita!" Cuca spat out the name. "He is wild for her. I told you he was a stallion and you couldn't keep him from the mares. I suspected from the beginning that this Conchita was only a high-class slut. I knew she lisped with the wives in the afternoon and entertained their husbands at night, but I thought it was a good joke on those high-toned ricas. Now it makes me mad that I pay an honest tax on my business while she . . ."

"That little harlot! That sly hussy. I could kill her," Tules choked.

"Oh, no, Don Manuel would cut off your ears. She drives him wild, gives him just enough, holds him off for a better bargain. He's lost any sense he ever had, the old fool!"

"María Santísima, I am the one who has been a fool," Tules cried. She clutched her dry throat, and the candles began a wild dance before her staring eyes. Cuca took her arm, guided her to her room, and made her lie on the pallet.

"Don't take it so hard. Manuel is only one man," Cuca said as she held a glass of wine to Tules's pale lips.

"I am finished." Tules shivered and pulled the jade shawl closer around her. "I know him. I have worked for him too long. I tried to help him and now he only wants youth, flattery."

"You have the sala, and that's more important than one man." Cuca's black eyes snapped. "Any woman knows that she must have patience with middle-aged men. They are my best pay, chasing false youth; but when they are worn out they are glad to go home. Enjoy your rest while you have the bed to yourself. Be ready to smile and please him. He will come back."

258

"I won't take him back," Tules muttered. She would not confess to Cuca that Manuel had cast her out tonight.

She tossed on her pallet, and her eyes stared into the dark, but she saw her life and herself more clearly than she had in years. She wrenched Manuel out of her heart, but that also pulled up the roots of her life. He was no longer the gallant, good-natured leader she had loved. Absolute power had turned his head, and flattery had increased his vanity to cruel disregard of everyone but himself. He might ruin her, but she would never go to him again. It was poor consolation to know that he did not want her.

Scorn and jealousy prodded her pride, and she vowed that she would not be made a cheap joke by Conchita. She would use her long training under Manuel to humble him and the girl. Her memory sifted the men of influence, their habits and desires, and the baits she would need to mold them to her plans. She speculated on the serious risks she would have to run and decided to gamble on the unrest of the country and the growing resentment of Manuel. In time he would change his ways and come back to beg her help—or be replaced.

Pepe believed that the American conquest was certain and that it would bring better government, but she was not willing yet to hand her country to the gringos. New Mexico needed a strong, just man to unify and defend it. Diego Archuleta was the only man whose patriotism was deeper than selfish interest. He should take Manuel's place.

The next morning Tules studied her face in the mirror for signs of age. She was thirty-three and old by the Latin standard that banished brides of fifteen to the obscurity of home, children, and eventually the strong background power of the mother. The contours of her pale face were sharply chiseled, and lines had deepened around her wide mouth and across her forehead. But her green eyes looked back at her with high-spirited challenge, and she lifted her red head with the courage to meet it.

"Competition has put new life into you," Cuca nodded the next night. "You haven't looked so handsome in years. Your eyes flash with the old lightning, and your face is turned in the right direction at last. You're lucky, and I will back you. . . ."

259

"We shall need good luck," Tules said grimly. Now that the suspense was over her eyes glittered, and she carried herself with the spring of determination. If the Texans were coming there was no time to lose, and she started at once to put her plan into action.

She took Diego Archuleta into the small room, turned her sorcery on him, and said with confiding flattery, "God forbid that any calamity should come to Don Manuel, but if it did, you would be the man to take his place. You know the danger and plots better than I do, Diego. Has Don Manuel ever planned for such an emergency?"

"His thoughts have been otherwise occupied lately." Diego smiled slyly.

"Yes, but the girl is only the whim of a middle-aged man." Tules's voice was tolerantly amused. "Though I agree that this is no time to sing to the moon. I admired your good judgment when you spoke of the Texas threat last week, Diego. Our first thought must be the defense of our country."

"Don Manuel does not take it seriously enough," Diego agreed slowly. "You know he only wants to hear good news and praise. He should give me more help in the east where the Texans will break through. Instead he sends help to Santiago Ulibarrí in the north."

Tules counted on this jealousy between the subordinates and used it to push her plan further. "You should have more help, more recognition, Diego. I will do all I can. You are the man to lead us if anything happens to Don Manuel."

"I would give my life for my country." Diego spoke with sincere conviction. "If the Americans conquered us it would be worse than death. As for the Tejanos—their boasts fill me with shame."

"You have true patriotism, Diego. Let us work together."

"If you were a man you would be a leader, Doña Tules. But the world would lose your beauty and charm," he said gallantly.

Night after night Tules wove the different threads into her net. She knew the constant struggle for power between the clergy and army and led the Vicario to discuss it. He was the titular head of the Church, though the brains of Padre Martínez in Taos planned every move. She spoke of her concern for Don Manuel's safety and asked who could take over if Don Manuel was lost on the battlefield. Among the younger men she mentioned Diego Archuleta and nodded as the Vicario praised him as a devout son of the church.

She waylaid the young officers who had threatened mutiny and listened sympathetically to their grievances. They complained that they had been exiled at distant outposts on suspicion that they were friends of Perezistas. When they told her that the expense of Don Manuel's retinue reduced the army pay to starvation wages she slipped them bags of silver and reminded herself that "With silver, nothing fails." She learned that favoritism and family had promoted new recruits over veterans and destroyed army morale. Manuel could never hold the army in a battle against the Texans. Even Diego Archuleta would need time to restore its faith and discipline.

She conferred with Diego often and strengthened his belief in himself. She was not ready yet to suggest that he should overthrow Manuel. Her advice was always hidden under the assumption that some calamity might befall the General and the second-in-command would have to step in. But she knew that Diego's own ambition, coupled with his real patriotism, would ready his hand to grasp the leadership when the time was right.

When Diego worried over the defense of the strategic northern gateway and Santiago's Ulibarrí's plans she offered to go to Taos for him. She would deal monte, investigate the rivalry between Padre Martínez and the "foreigners," and test the resentment that always smoldered against Manuel in the northern pueblos.

Her proposed trip met with opposition at home. Santiago Flores grumbled that this was no time to leave the sala.

"You will not have a military escort this time," Cuca warned. "The bandits or Navajos may kill you for your money chest. Stay inside your own doorstep, and protect it. You don't know what that girl might do if you were away. . . ."

When María added her plea, Tules agreed to take Victorio with her for protection. She gave María money for Carlota and La Casimira, but María sighed, "La Casimira is tormented by her devil and still curses you. Pobrecita! Evil has settled in her empty mind. Yet the ricos go to her—she runs the cards for that Conchita and her dueña almost every day. I will pray for her and remind her of all you have done for her."

"Tell her to put the evil eye on Conchita," Tules said scornfully. Her eyes narrowed with satisfaction as she thought that her own plans would bring the girl more ill luck than all the witch's mumbled incantations. As for Manuel—he ordered wine, but he would drink vinegar.

# 25

THE NEXT day Tules and Victorio left in the lurching coach for Taos. A hamper of wine, chicken, fresh loaves of bread, silver, and linen rested at their feet. Beside it there was a knee-high oxhide money chest, decorated with narrow thongs woven around squares of blue and scarlet flannel and secured with three heavy iron bands and a strong lock. Under the seat Tules had hidden a long, narrow buckskin bag, the regulation measure for twelve thousand pesos. Now it was stuffed with gold coins for her bank reserve and for any "gifts" that would help her plans.

Two trusted mozos, who always accompanied her to carry and guard the money chest, rode the lead mules. Her lookout, a strong, stolid German named Augustus de Marle, crowded the outer seat with Rómulo. The back pockets of the four men bulged with knives and guns. Two armed outriders rode ahead to scout for the coach.

Victorio sat beside Tules on the maroon upholstery fondling the shining steel of his big pistol, and she smiled at his intent eyes. She counted on the ability of his dwarfed body to slip into secret places and the abnormal strength of his arms more than his marksmanship. She knew that he would defend her to his last breath, but the dagger that was always strapped to her knee was her greatest protection. The dust rising above the coach made them an obvious target for bandits or Navajos, and Tules's lips moved with the silent prayer that the saints would protect her.

She had urged Rómulo to make the trip in two days to shorten the danger. The mules ran under his whip, and the heavy coach lurched from side to side. Tules amused Victorio with the story of how she had run away with the caravan and Bernardo had discovered her and driven her home with the burros. In telling it she relived her childish terror of the mountains, the Bibirón, Bernardo, and the agony of her bleeding, frozen feet.

The warm spring sunshine and clear blue sky made this a different scene from the snow-covered mountains of long ago. In the afternoon they reached the banks of the Río Grande, whose water tumbled in a muddy torrent from the spring rains. Where the valley widened there were plowed fields and low adobe houses huddled close together for protection against the Navajos and the lonely country. The smell of the good plowed earth and the fragrance of pink peach blossoms on the dark, gnarled branches drifted into the coach and replaced its musty odor.

They stayed overnight in the lush greenness of Los Luceros and left early to get through the narrow gorge where the river had cut a deep channel through mountains of bare red granite. This was a favorite hiding place for bandits, and Tules was relieved when they climbed out of the cañón to the high mesa. She drew in a deep breath of the crystal-clear air and smelled the aromatic scent of the new gray-green leaves on the sagebrush. The broad valley basked in the sparkling sunshine, except where the deep chasm cut through it in a twisting purple shadow. Across the wide expanse, massive blue mountains tipped with snow piled up against the vast dome of the turquoise sky. She looked thankfully at the white houses of Don Fernández de Taos nestling against the base of the mountains in the distance. The journey had been peaceful, and she was encouraged by this good start.

She made herself comfortable in her house at Don Fernández and arranged for the mozos to take turns guarding the money chest. As in any Spanish settlement, the cream-colored houses of Don Fernández clustered around the plaza and church and were built flush with the narrow streets. Though she had been there many times to deal monte for fiestas and spy for Manuel, she always associated the place with her childhood memories. She passed the blue doorway where Tío Florentino had lived until his death ten years ago and drove down the river to look at the crumbling adobe ruin that had been the Salazar hacienda.

She gave Victorio money to buy candles to take to the church in memory of Doña Carmen. Don Miguel had searched for her for five years but had finally given up hope. Each time that Tules saw him he looked older and more desolate. It was hard for her to believe that this haunted man was the same gay young patrón who had set off so hopefully for Mexico twenty-two years ago.

Tules was glad that Don Miguel was not involved in the whirlpool of intrigue in Taos. It had been a famous rendezvous for the French trappers and gringo mountain men who packed in their beaver pelts from the far northern streams. Later one fork of the Santa Fe Trail led to Taos and brought settlers and traders to the custom-house and military outpost. Now it was also the strategic gateway the American army might use if it invaded New Mexico. These changes had brought in new people and ideas who clashed with the old families and customs. The new ideas were vigorous, but the old ways had deep Spanish roots and the tenacity of two centuries of hardy growth.

This spring the smoldering antagonism had flamed into a fiery public dispute between Padre Antonio José Martínez, representing the Church and the old families, and Don Carlos Beaubien, the leader of the "foreign" settlers. Governor Armijo had given Don Carlos Beaubien and Don Guadalupe Miranda a huge tract of land north of Taos. Padre Martínez claimed that the land belonged to the Taos people as common grazing land and hunting range. His attack grew more vehement as he realized that his long autocratic power would recede if the "foreigners" brought in new industries, settlers, and democratic education.

Tules dealt monte every night, studied the rival leaders, and pieced together information. She hid her fears of the future under gaiety, beauty, and flashing diamonds. She encouraged the gossip that no one was rich enough to break her bank, and she played for higher stakes than any man. She laughed when a man gasped that she threw a fanega of silver on the table at one time and added that this bushel measure of money was too heavy for two mozos to carry. Success was a powerful magnet, and she wanted to dazzle everyone with her wealth. No one knew that she had broken with Manuel, and she let them think that she was still his confidante. It strengthened her plans when they revealed their grievances and ambitions to her.

Everyone came to the monte sala for a sociable visit as well as the fascination of gambling. When the beautiful Jaramillo sisters sat at her table Tules was glad she had worn her black velvet and diamonds. By old Spanish usage the daughters retained their father's name though they were married to "foreigners." Doña Josefa Jaramillo was the wife of Kit Carson, and her sister, Doña Ignacia, was the wife of Charles Bent. They were in a family party with Don Carlos Beaubien and his daughter, Luz, who was soon to marry the blond young gringo, Lucien Maxwell.

Tules nodded a smiling assent when Don Carlos whispered that he and his friends would like to talk with her, knowing that they expected her to carry their messages to Don Manuel.

The next evening Don Carlos, Céran St. Vrain, Charles Bent, and Kit Carson came to her room, and she searched their faces as she poured the wine. St. Vrain was a wealthy trader who knew every settlement between St. Louis and Chihuahua. Don Carlos had come from Canada many years ago, and his name had been Charles Hypolite Trotier, Sieur de Beaubien. His face was thin and nervous, while St. Vrain's was round and jovial, but both Frenchmen used their hands with quick, emphatic gestures.

The Americans were less talkative. Charles Bent was one of the four Bent brothers who were among the first traders over the Santa Fe Trail. William ran the great trading post at Bent's Fort, and Charles had a store in Santa Fe as well as Taos. His broad forehead tapered to a small chin, and his eyes held a kindliness and faith in his fellow man rarely seen in hard, frontier life. Kit Carson looked small and insignificant, but his fighting spirit had won him fame as a fearless scout and the respect of Indians, Mexicans, and gringos alike.

The Frenchmen began at once to praise Governor Armijo for granting them the land to the north. They said much of it had never been seen by a white man since it included a million acres of mountains, streams, forests, and meadows. The boundaries were confusing landmarks with an indefinite limit of "three days' ride" from the original homesite. In spite of Padre Martínez's loud protests they had taken formal possession last month. They were unaware that this lavish gift was as large as a European kingdom or that the vague title of this future Maxwell Land Grant would puzzle American courts for the next fifty years.

The Frenchmen were enthusiastic about the opportunities the land offered young, adventurous men. They spoke glowingly of schools and steady employment which would help the pobres, the increase of cattle and sheep on this range, and the prosperity that would come with woolen mills, lumber operations, and farms planted to sugar beets.

"That will be good for trade, Doña Tules," Charles Bent said. "We will be able to sell our native products to the States instead of sending the wagons back empty. It should bring prices down and produce good revenue for New Mexico."

"If we can avoid war. . . ." Kit Carson spoke quietly, but everyone turned to look at his watchful brown eyes. "Governor Armijo made a bad mistake when he marched the Texans to Mexico in '41 under Damasio Salazar. The ones who survived have gone home to curse this country. There's bad feeling against us in Texas and the United States."

"We have heard reports that the Texans threaten to come this summer," Tules said. "Don Manuel cannot be on two frontiers at once, but he has trusted lieutenants—Diego Archuleta at San Miguel and Santiago Ulibarrí here. . . ."

"Archuleta is an honest man though sometimes mistaken." Don Carlos tapped his long fingers together and added in an acid tone, "Ulibarrí has trouble here with all the unrest Padre Martínez stirs up—though he pretends to keep his hands clean for his great literary endeavors."

"The Padre can't believe the old days are over." St. Vrain waved his short, quick hands. "But new ideas have blown in, and he can't banish them across the frontier."

As they talked Tules realized that they longed for an American Government and would not help Manuel if the American army marched in.

It was a more subtle task to question Padre Antonio José Martínez. He belonged to the large Martínez family whose numerous members and wealth made it a powerful clan. He was a parish priest but so distant from Rome and the Bishop at Durango that he made his own rules. In a few years he would be unfrocked for lax morals and stubborn defiance and would conduct his own church, but now he was the brains of the clerical party and one of the most influential politicians in New Mexico. He maintained the only school for boys and had printed the first newspaper, though the press was only used now for his primers and catechisms.

His shrewd mind and good education made him the leader of Río Arriba and the chief contender for clerical power against the army faction. He had worked secretly with Don Manuel before and after the Pérez revolt. As long as they aided each other, they were firm friends. Padre Martínez's public censure of Don Manuel for giving away the northern land was a two-edged sword, one edge slicing the army power and the other that of the "foreigners."

When Tules called on the Padre she knew she was no match for this learned, crafty man. His face was austere, with its high bald forehead and stern mouth and chin. He began immediately to reproach Don Manuel like a grieving father.

"Manuel's ambition has blinded him to his true advisers," he said sadly. "He gave away land that belongs to the poor people of this valley. It will cause trouble and hardship for generations. The pobres will starve to fatten a few rich land speculators."

"But if the pobres can pay their debts and cease to be peóns . . ." Tules said, thinking of her mother's long bondage.

"Do you know any happier people than the peóns?" he asked. "The good patrón takes care of his peóns as his children. He gives them homes and food, work to keep them out of mischief, and cares for them when they are old or sick. They can't look after themselves. They know nothing of money, and their new employers will let them

268

throw it away and starve. This talk of turning these ignorant people loose in a democracy is criminal."

"But, Padre, you have a school," Tules said. "If there were more schools and education for all . . ."

"Education is not for the masses," he said sternly. "I am educating forty boys to be priests to guide the ignorant. I have chosen them carefully from old families. Every country must be governed by men who have inherited the proper ideas and responsibilities with their blood. It is the ignorant upstarts who harm us with their common notions."

Tules glanced at him swiftly, knowing that he referred to Manuel's humble youth and his rise above the old ricos.

The Padre answered the question in her eyes as he continued, "Manuel should correct his mistakes before it is too late. These foreigners bring in sedition, heresy, and corruption in exchange for a few import taxes. Manuel should banish them, close the doors before they steal the country. . . ."

"There is danger from the Texans this summer," Tules said. "Our frontiers are far apart, and Don Manuel must depend upon his lieutenants—Santiago Ulibarrí here and Diego Archuleta in San Miguel. . . ."

"Diego is a good man. He knows the danger of this foolish American talk and the greed of the foreigners." Padre Martínez nodded, and Tules was satisfied with his support.

She knew that each faction was trying to win over the Taos-pueblo Council. Padre Martínez said mass in the adobe mission church near the wall around the pueblo, but the Indians' real worship was concentrated in fervent pagan rites in underground kivas. The French and Americans promised them prosperity, but the Indians remembered the white man's greed. Any incident could swing them to one side or the other or incite them to general riot.

Tules took Victorio and went to see the Taos chief in the pueblo a league from the village of Don Fernández, where two large communal houses rose in terraced mud pyramids on either side of a clear mountain stream. The chief's bronze face was stoical as he pulled his blanket tighter around his hips and said scornfully, "Your men do not help us fight. They do not protect us from the Navajos. They lie. They break promises with our chief, José Gonzáles. They take him to Santa Fe and shoot him. We do not forget."

Santiago Ulibarrí returned from an inspection trip to the frontier that week and came to see Tules. "What news do you bring from Santa Fe?" he asked. "I wish you would tell Don Manuel that there is serious trouble here and I must have more money for reenforcements. Some of the Indians threaten to kill all the white men and take the country for themselves. If they get enough aguardiente there will be a riot and massacre. We must win them over, pacify them. That takes money."

After Ulibarrí left Tules sat by her fire, since the mountain night was chilly, and waited for Victorio to come in. She was satisfied with what she had found out in Taos and felt confident that, if she had enough time, she could build up strong support for Diego Archuleta and overthrow Manuel. She grew restless when Victorio did not come and paced the floor. When he had not come by dawn she was frightened that something had happened to him.

As soon as it was full daylight she searched for him in the plaza and deserted monte sala and sent the mozos and Augustus de Marle to look for him. She stopped people to ask if they had seen the little hunchback and went to the Alcalde and Santiago Ulibarrí. No one had seen him since yesterday morning when he had been with a group of boys. She questioned the boys, but they knew nothing. Tules was frantic. She loved the droll little fellow, and she knew María would be brokenhearted if any harm came to Victorio.

She went back and forth to the plaza all afternoon, and toward evening she saw Pepe Cisneros ride by. She called to him and was thankful for his quiet, steady help. That night Pepe brought the bruised and battered Victorio home. He had fought the boys who made fun of his humped back and had been thrown in jail.

"But I asked the Alcalde about Victorio. He knew nothing," Tules cried.

"Perhaps he told you the truth," Pepe said. "Some petty officer

270

put Victorio in the juzgado. He thought it wasn't worthy of a report since Victorio was only a misshapen pobre."

"But this is terrible, unjust, cruel." Tules's eyes flashed. "Victorio had done no harm. He might have starved there for weeks."

"You have known this system all your life, but now you see what it means when it touches your Victorio," Pepe said. "You know the pobres will never have any rights, any justice, any chance as long as we are governed by these corrupt politicians. I told you that was why I wanted the Americans to come."

As Tules bathed Victorio's swollen face and cuts and helped him to bed she thought of the long, hopeless struggle of the pobres. She had been a pobre, and she might be one again if Manuel dared to confiscate her sala. She drew in a sharp breath as she suddenly questioned his right to confiscate it. She had paid for the house and had the deed. Was there no law to protect her property? Then she remembered that Manuel had confiscated the house first from the Perezistas. There was no law, no protection, as long as the whole Government from high to low was rotten with bribery, murder, greed, and selfish jealousy.

She walked back slowly to Pepe and said, "I begin to think you have reason. If the Americans are honest and just, the pobres might have a chance."

"You know the gringos who talk and drink too much in the monte sala," Pepe smiled. "But I know them on the plains, where a hunter shows whether he is a brave, true man. I know the worth of these gringos. You hear much talk that the Texans brag, but the ones I know are modest, good friends who would risk their lives for me if I was in danger."

"But, Pepe, why do our people fail? We are all human. . . ."

"We don't have freedom. We have been treated like children too long. Children don't learn to govern themselves until they have knowledge and freedom to choose their way. Our people have no loyalty because each man only works for himself—and his family—to give him more power. We fight each other like the boys who attacked Victorio. If one man climbs a little above the others, a pack

271

is after him to drag him down. We never pull together as a team. Our army will fall apart if they meet the Americans in a battle."

Tules thought of this month she had spent in Taos and the examples of selfish interest that had been each man's price. She was sick of the corruption, greed, and petty intrigue. She was sick of her own part in it too. If Pepe knew how selfish and jealous she was, a spy, a traitor. . . .

"I told you the Texans were coming," Pepe said. "I am on the way home from Bent's Fort, and they say every man in Texas has volunteered to punish us. Fighting has already started with a skirmish at Mora."

"Then they are already in New Mexico!" Tules exclaimed.

"Yes, and this time there are five thousand armed men who swear to take the heads of Manuel Armijo, Damasio Salazar, and the traitor, Lewis. You must go to Santa Fe at once. This is no time to be here or on the road."

"All right, Pepe, I will start tomorrow," Tules promised.

"Then I will ride beside your coach." He took her hand. "I care for you so much, Tules. If you would only believe . . ."

There was a loud insistent knock at the door. Ulibarrí hurried in and frowned when he saw Pepe. Pepe laughed and said, "I must go. But no matter how early I get up, I can't hurry the dawn. Adiós."

"Don Manuel sent word tonight that the fighting has begun," Ulibarrí said quickly. "He told me to bring him two hundred fighters from Taos pueblo tomorrow. Caramba, am I a witch to pull two hundred Indians out of a hat? I must have money to pay them, outfit them, but Don Manuel forgot that. I have come to you to advance the money. Don Manuel will repay you."

"Don Manuel has to strengthen the other borders as well." Tules stalled for time. "Diego Archuleta is in charge at San Miguel, and he also needs help."

"Diego always wants twice as much as anyone else." Santiago clenched his fists jealously. "But that does not help me get the fighters Don Manuel demands now. I must have the money tonight."

Tules realized that she was caught in her own net. If she refused to advance the money, Ulibarrí would report her disloyalty to Manuel. She did not want him to suspect her or her plans yet. She needed more time to perfect them. While she thought this out, she argued over the amount of money with Ulibarrí and finally gave him three hundred pesos from her money chest. She knew it would never be repaid and smiled grimly to herself that this was another bad bargain to charge to Manuel. Ulibarrí crossed his first finger over his thumb to make the Penitente cross and swore that he would start at dawn with the Taos Indians.

# 26

WHEN TULES reached Santa Fe two days later everyone told her the Texans had invaded New Mexico and looked at her with the curiosity of antelopes. Even Santiago Flores's black eyes questioned her as he made his report. Considering the unsettled times, business had been good in the month she had been away. María kissed her with extra tenderness, brought the dress she had pressed, and lit a votive candle to San Antonio.

Tules had washed off the dust of the trip and was combing her russet hair when Cuca came into her room. Cuca, too, looked at her with alert curiosity and stuck her elbows out over her plump hips.

"The way everyone looks at me, I feel as though I had been away ten years," Tules laughed and began to wind the ends of her hair in curls. "Did you expect my hair to turn white because I went to Taos pueblo?"

"No, niña, you will always be a rubia," Cuca said. The curiosity in her small, shrewd eyes turned to concern. "I came to help you dress. You must look your best tonight."

"Por qué?" Tules asked. "I am not sending a sweetheart away with the army tomorrow."

"No, but Don Manuel sent word that he would come to talk to you tonight. He leaves with the army at dawn."

The fine arch of Tules's eyebrows raised as she asked, "Why am I honored with this sudden interest?"

"He heard that you interviewed many leaders in Taos . . ." Cuca began.

"Yes, that is part of my business." Tules smiled with satisfaction. So Manuel was afraid of her power! He had an intimation that her mind was not too old to outwit him. Did he expect to dangle her

274

heart again, persuade her to work for him while he fondled that girl? She would show him in time.

"Things have been bad while you were away. The young officers threatened mutiny, and Don Manuel had them shackled in the dungeon. Everyone was wild and cursed his fat back. But our fine Governor forgets the danger to our country while he jumps like a monkey when that Conchita crooks her finger. The stupidest thing in the world is an old man with a young fancy. The people of the town love you, and Don Manuel will go too far if he installs that Mexican slut in your place."

"What do you mean, Cuca?" Tules demanded angrily.

"He has promised to confiscate this house. Conchita wants to live here, and the Governor will take the money from the monte tables. Young love and easy money were too much temptation for the silly old peacock."

"But he can't take it. I have the deeds. Is there no law?" Tules cried.

"You know that a dictator makes his own law. I told you to stay here and protect your property. While you were away that girl and her sly dueña worked on him to get what they have been after all the time. They spread lies about you. . . ."

"But Manuel won't dare do this! I have powerful friends, plans. . . . I know too much about him."

"He knows too much about you, too. You should have kept still. Word has been passed in the plaza that you killed Pedro."

"Pedro!" Tules gasped.

"If there is a murder charge against you, Don Manuel can take this house with a show of righteous respect for the law. . . ."

"Madre de Dios, I knew he was vain, mean, cruel, but I never thought he would stoop to betray me!" Tules's cheeks burned, and her eyes filled with bitter tears. "That is why everyone stared at me— to see how I would take it. Did they expect to see the new favorite reigning here? I'll show them. I'll fix Manuel. The liar, cheat, bully. . . ."

"You can do nothing," Cuca reminded her. "You are not his wife.

275

You can't tell him where to sleep. All you can do is to flatter him and persuade him to forget this and let you keep the sala."

"Válgame Dios, I won't take this and flatter him!" Tules screamed and pounded Cuca's arm. "I know ways to make him suffer. I won't kneel to him and kiss his hand and have him kick me out. I'll kill him first. . . ."

"Hush, niña." Cuca tried to quiet her and made her sit down. "Guard your tongue, even in your own house. You can win him over. He knows he has gone too far, and he is afraid of what the people will do if he takes this house. He is glad to have an excuse to go with the army tomorrow."

"He is a devil, a dirty cheat, a damned liar!" Tules cried. "To think that he would dare mention Pedro, bring that against me. . . . I hate him! I hope the Texans will gouge his eyes out!"

"Bien, let the Texans do it, but you stay away from him. You have enough trouble to face now," Cuca advised. "Stop crying and wash your face. You must look your best. People will watch you. If you carry it off tonight, they will back you and scoff at that girl's lies. . . . Your sala is more important than any man. Use your wits and hold on to your future."

While she dressed, Tules's thoughts darted desperately around this new twist of fate. Not only her sala but her life was in danger. Fury burned through every tingling nerve as she realized that Manuel had betrayed her early confidence and would charge her now with Pedro's murder. She had almost forgotten it. The events of fifteen years ago belonged to another life, another girl. But she knew Manuel could revive the charge, find witnesses, and force the judges to sentence her. She pressed her throat, choking at the thought of the prison, the gallows. She must think, find some way to save herself. She retched at the prospect of humbling herself to Conchita, begging Manuel. . . . He was a filthy toad who tried to be as big as an ox. If the Texans had not come so soon, her plans would be ready to overthrow him by now. He could not harm her if he was out of the way. Her mind was a tumult of rage, shame, terror; she could not think what was best to do.

276

An hour later Cuca was satisfied that Tules was ready to enter the sala. Her dress of brilliant green silk stood out with a ruffle around the stiff, wide hem and showed off her supple figure. Fine lace, as creamy as her skin, edged the short sleeves and bare shoulders, and a gold necklace set with emeralds gleamed above her high, firm breasts. Her eyes were as green as the emeralds and flashed with feverish excitement. A crown of brilliants sparkled in her red hair as she tilted her head and greeted everyone with smiling vivacity.

She laughed as she told the news and gossip from Taos, waving the small golden tongs that held her cigarrito. Through the smoke she watched the frank curiosity on men's faces change to amazement and admiration. She breathed quickly and called for favorite songs from the orchestra. The dagger strapped below her knee did not interfere with her fast, light steps as she danced a mad schottische. She tried to watch the door, dreading the moment when Manuel would come, but missed his entrance. She caught her breath when she saw his large figure across the room and swept toward him with her head held high.

"Bien venida, Don Manuel," she called gaily and forced herself to touch his shoulder in the fleeting embrace. "What good fortune that the army has not carried you away already! I have many messages for you from Taos."

"Your trip must have been successful, Doña Tules. The mountain air has added to your beauty." He bowed slightly as he looked at her vivid face. "Will you honor me with the messages tonight? I leave with the army early tomorrow. . . ."

She nodded and turned to greet Santiago Ulibarrí who stood beside him. Later Manuel caught her eye and motioned toward the private room. She let him wait half an hour before she went to him. She closed the door behind her and turned the key in the lock.

His black eyes smoldered with impatience as he surveyed her brilliant figure. The half-emptied wine bottle stood at his elbow on the bare table and he drained the wine from his glass as he grumbled, "Caramba, do you think I have time to wait for you all night? I leave at dawn, and I have much to do. Santiago Ulibarrí is there at the door waiting for me. Tell me what you found out in Taos."

She shook her head as he motioned to the other wineglass and seated herself at the edge of the round table. She held herself stiff with dignity. Her voice was cold and formal as she said, "Santiago brought you the two hundred Indians from Taos pueblo because I advanced him three hundred pesos of my own money. I was glad to help you out in an emergency, but I expect to be repaid."

"Bien," Manuel said curtly, his black eyes watching her. "Santiago told me all this. But what were you doing in Taos?"

Her icy fingers opened her black lace fan and she lowered her lashes to look at the sparkle of the sequins before she said, "I dealt monte for a month, enjoyed myself, talked to my friends. . . ."

"Among them that Pepe Cisneros," Manuel added.

"Cómo no, Pepe Cisneros." She lifted her green eyes, and they burned into his. "All my friends told me of the serious trouble that faces you at this bad time. But that is not enough. You must make more trouble here. . . ."

"You mean the squawking of those silly boys who talked of mutiny?" He smiled scornfully. "They are spoiled children who should be spanked. They still have their mother's milk on their lips."

"Next time they will start a real mutiny, and it will be too late to spank them. The Texans have vowed to take your head. The Taos Indians would like to kick it around as they did Pérez's. If the army also turns against you . . ."

"Who says the army is against me?" he demanded. "It is my army. I am the Comandante Militar. Those boys are where they will make no more trouble. You always make a volcano out of an ant heap."

"In this time of danger, do you dare turn the town against you? The people will rebel if you keep the young officers in the dungeon—and other things they say you plan to do."

"You roll gossip on your tongue like a sweet," he sneered. "But then you were always jealous. . . ."

"No, I am not jealous," she said coldly, and her nostrils curved with contempt. "I would not lower myself to be jealous over a cheat and a liar. . . ."

278

"What?" Manuel rose from his chair, and an angry flush spread over his dark face. "Even you should be careful of your words."

She sprang up to face him and knocked over the chair behind her. Her eyes blazed, and her lips twisted with rage as she cried, "I know what you planned while I was away. You plan to give this house to that Mexican strumpet and take the money from the sala for yourself. I built up this business, and this house is mine. . . ."

"You ate loco weed in Taos," he shrugged.

"No, I have been warned of your plans. You betrayed me. . . . I was a blind fool and worshiped you for years. I believed in you and thought you were the great man who would save this country. I worked for you, loved you, endangered my life for you. But you spurned me and told me I was too old! You would turn me out of my house for a vain little chit who flatters you for what she can get out of you. . . ."

"Enough!" he warned.

She forgot everything except the mad urge to hurt him, taunt him, make him burn with anguish as she had burned these last hours. She sucked in her breath and let the words rush out. "You have gone too far. People laugh at your conceit and vanity and call you a silly old peacock. They will not swallow your injustice, your cruelty, your betrayals. . . . They will kick your empty head around the plaza. . . ."

"Stop, you filthy slut!" Manuel thundered. "You have lost your mind, and you should lose your vile tongue. I took you as a common harlot. I loaded you with diamonds, money, power, luxury, and this is my thanks. Maldita puta!"

"You dare to call me that!" she screamed, as she heard him use the coarse term and curse her. She drew her body straight, and her voice shook with rage. "You are no better than I am. You took me and used me for your own purposes. You took the money I earned, the information I dug out of the sewer for you. I risked my life for you many times, and now you call me names, threaten me. I wish I had let the assassins stab you. . . ."

The walls of the small, thick room echoed with their frenzy. They

279

faced each other across the narrow space, their eyes intent as they watched each other move. Manuel stealthily drew back from her violence. She followed as he moved toward the protection of the wall and doubled his fists across his large body. His dark, heavy face thrust forward from his neck, and his crafty black eyes watched her as though she was a spitting rattlesnake.

"Who are you to talk of murder, condemn me? I know too much about you, you fat swine, you bully, you damned coward!" The words hissed out as her face twisted with rage. Suddenly she stopped and reached under her full green skirt. Her body straightened up swiftly, and she clenched the dagger in her hand. Her arm raised with strength and skill as she aimed the shining blade at his heart. His long arm shot out, seized her wrist, and twisted it. The dagger flew over his head and buried itself in the adobe wall. His other hand caught the wine bottle and swung it against her head.

"Ay—Madre de Dios . . ." she shrieked as she fell to the floor.

"Santiago!" Manuel bellowed for help. He backed away from where she crouched on the floor, watching him with hate-filled eyes. Wine and blood stained her bare shoulder. She held her head with one hand, and the other pressed her heart.

Manuel's bravery returned when he heard a knock at the door. He looked at Tules and gulped, "You have no decency, no morals, you dirty slut! You killed one man, and now you have tried to kill me. You will pay for that. If I did not have to leave tomorrow, I would start your punishment at once. But I shall return in a few days. Then I will take over this house, strip you of everything, let you repent in jail. After that, with other charges against you . . ."

Someone knocked again and tried to open the locked door.

"Bien, Santiago, I am coming," Manuel shouted. Then he looked at Tules crouched on the floor and sneered, "With enough time in jail, you will take back all these things you have said. Prepare your confession before I return." He straightened his coat, pushed back a lock of hair, unlocked the door, and walked out.

She hardly knew that he had gone. She was only conscious of the terrific pain below her breast. Her head fell forward as she crouched

280

on the floor, and she pressed both hands to her breast. She moaned as an enormous hand squeezed her heart. She dared not move but waited in terror for the vise that turned within her body. It squeezed, squeezed until her breath stopped in black blind agony. She lost consciousness and sank into the blackness.

Her eyes rolled vaguely as Cuca fumbled at her dress and Santiago Flores tried to raise her. "Don't touch me," she groaned. "The pain will come back if I move. Let me die in peace."

Chico and Victorio came, and the four of them carried Tules to her bed. Cuca undressed her, took off the tight corset, and rubbed her limp arms. María wiped the cold sweat and blood from her face and moistened her blue lips. She wrapped a hot stone and put it at Tules's icy feet.

"The pain! The dark! I am afraid . . ." Tules moaned. "Light more candles, María, and fix the fire. Ay de mí!" Her teeth chattered in a violent chill, and María brought more hot stones and blankets. The terrific pain lessened, and the cold hand of death withdrew. Her body relaxed with returning warmth, and her breath was easier. Cuca tried to question her, but Tules's eyelids closed with exhaustion.

Ten days later she stared at the white walls of her room and wondered drowsily why the afternoon sun was shining through her window. Her body ached when she moved, and her fingers groped at the poultice on her head. Then her heavy eyes opened wide as the memory of her fight with Manuel rushed through her mind. She groaned and called to María, sitting quietly beside her.

"Thanks be to God that you know me again," María said as she knelt beside the pallet.

"Oh, María, what have I done?" Tules began to cry. "I am ruined, condemned! Everything is lost. . . ."

"Nothing matters now that the cloud has gone from your mind," María soothed her. "Even Tía Apolonia feared for your life, but she gave you dedalera tea and put the hot poultice of leaves to your head. God has heard our prayers, and He will provide."

"But Manuel . . ." Tules moaned. "He said he would take every-thing, even my life."

"When you are well, linda, we can start again." María patted her hand. "We can go back to the market. We were happier in those days. This money, this house has not brought us peace. I am always afraid for you. It was better when we were poor and thanked God for His blessings. . . ."

"But, María, you don't understand. He will hang me for Pedro. He won't forget—because I tried to kill him. I should have died then. I have brought this disgrace on all of us, and I will pay with my life. Oh, María, forgive me."

María looked at her quickly. She had not wanted to believe the feverish raving of the last ten days nor the evidence of the dagger they found in the wall. Now she knew it was true, and her faded eyes sank further into her wrinkled face. She knew too well what punishment such an offense brought and shook her head. The sad lines around her mouth deepened, but she said firmly, "No matter what happens I will go with you, niña. We must pray to God to forgive you."

Tules sobbed and covered her face with her long hands.

"Thanks to God's grace, you were spared from worse sin," María's gentle voice insisted. "You must go to confession, pray for forgiveness. The Mother of Our Lord will help you. You must pray, have faith. . . ."

Cuca stuck her dyed head through the door and marched in. "It's a good day, now that your mind is clear again," she said briskly. "Put your black shawl around her shoulders, María, and another pillow at her back. You look better already, Tules. Manuel gave you a bad crack with that bottle, but now you will be all right."

"I wish I had died then," Tules moaned.

"No, when a man beats you he feels better." Cuca's painted face grinned cheerfully. "He has been gone for ten days. He will be so pleased with himself when he brings home another victory that he will forget about this."

"He is too much like an Indian to forget." Tules turned her head from side to side in anguish. "He won't hurt his vanity by charging that I tried to kill him, but he will hang me for Pedro. I lost my mind

282

when I realized that he had betrayed the secret I told him and spread it over the plaza. . . ."

"Don Manuel did not tell it," Cuca muttered. "It was that girl."

"What!" Tules sat up. "You told me it was Manuel."

"I was afraid of what you would do to her if I told you Conchita had spread the story," Cuca said. "I told you they had lied about you, warned you to stay here. Conchita and her dueña wormed the story of Pedro out of La Casimira. . . ."

"La Casimira! That sly, evil creature!" Tules exclaimed. "But I never told her. . . ."

"Maybe her devil told her," Cuca shrugged. "Half her crazed wit mumbles spells, and the other half smells out scandal. Ojalá that I had kept my big mouth shut one more night! I tried to help you, prepare you. . . . I never thought that you would lose all sense and throw away years of work, your money, your house, your position in a jealous fit over one man. You were a fool and deserve a beating. If you go, he will put me out too. You must think of some way to save us."

"The house doesn't matter now. He will hang me," Tules cried.

"Then you must go to him, beg his forgiveness, promise . . ."

"No, never, I would rather die. . . ."

"You never learn," Cuca hissed. "Some time you told your secret and put the rope around your throat. I will go to Santiago Flores, and you will do as he says to save all of us."

Tules's jaws clenched with this new shock—that La Casimira had betrayed her. How had that slinking cat found out about Pedro? She remembered now that La Casimira had spoken of Pedro a few months ago, threatened her. She should have paid more attention instead of laughing at the witch's spells. But she had fed La Casimira, helped her with money each month. How could she guess that the demented creature would turn on her and sell the story to Conchita? María had told her that Conchita and her dueña were going to La Casimira's hovel, but even that had not aroused her suspicion. She hated La Casimira and Conchita, but at least Manuel had not betrayed her until his hand was forced.

283

She cursed herself for being such a blind, dumb fool. If she had come to her senses last year, she would have had time to work out her plan to strengthen the support for Diego, and Manuel would have been out. The Texans had come sooner than she expected, and now it was too late. With the country at war anyone would be shot who criticized the Comandante Militar. Tules cursed her own stupidity again, twisted her hands, and heard Manuel say, "Prepare your confession."

Santiago listened to the whole story and shook his head hopelessly. "Don Manuel will never forgive this. His hands have itched for the money from your sala. The only chance is to escape before he returns. We will all go to my home in Chihuahua and start another sala. But why did you throw away everything?"

He said they would have a week to get ready since Don Manuel had ridden almost to the Texas line. Tules packed her jewels and counted her money. She sent for Céran St. Vrain, who was in town, and gave him ten thousand pesos to invest in St. Louis. It was dangerous to carry too much money across the desert where Manuel's Apaches waited.

Late that night she wrapped herself in a black shawl and crept into the dark, silent sala for a final "Adiós!" to all she had treasured. Moonlight shone in silver bars through the narrow windows and made ghostly reflections in the long mirrors. Her bare feet moved noiselessly over the plank floor to her old monte table. Her hand caressed the green felt cover and lingered over the slick places where thousands of pesos had been stacked. She sat in the dealer's chair and pulled out the empty cash drawers on either side. Her cold feet rested on the carved stretcher between the heavy walnut legs, worn smooth on the side where men's anxious feet had ground against it. Memories of exciting nights trooped through her mind. She rubbed Jeem's ring, and her finger tingled. She sighed thankfully over that good omen for the Chihuahua move.

The next morning a messenger raced in with news that changed all plans. "Our army has been routed by the Texas Avengers under Colonel Jacob Snively," he cried. "They defeated the advance guard,

284

who were mostly the Taos Indians under Captain Ventura Lobato. The Indians didn't want to go ahead, and Lobato had to tie them to their horses. Eighteen Indians were killed, more wounded, and the entire company surrendered. We heard all this from a prisoner who escaped. He says the Texans have cannons, guns, and thousands of soldiers. . . ."

"Where was General Armijo?" Tules asked through set lips.

"He had led five hundred men forty leagues beyond the battle ground. He was in danger of being cut off from aid from Santa Fe. When he heard of Lobato's surrender he ordered instant retreat. Dios, it was terrible! The soldiers fled and left all their equipment, even spurs and lariats. In their panic they didn't know where to go. General Armijo left them and raced ahead, riding relays of fast horses to escape. He will reach here after dark tonight."

"María Santísima, we have delayed too long!" Tules cried to Santiago. "Now we are caught, and he will finish me. . . ."

"You will have to go to him and promise anything," Cuca snapped, "if you want to save your life. It is too late to get away now."

But Don Manuel was only concerned for his own life. He knew that the Texas Avengers had sworn to take his head, and his one desire was to get beyond their reach. He rode into the Palace under the cover of darkness that night. Before sunup he left secretly to hide in the safe wilds of the Río Abajo. That morning his deputies announced that on account of the "grave infirmities of health, increased by a former battle wound and the hardship of the present campaign, the Comandante Militar has been forced to retire to his ranch."

When Tules heard the official announcement, she thanked God for the reprieve and turned to Santiago. "We will stay here until he plans to return. There would be more danger if we tried to cross the Río Abajo now where Manuel is hiding."

"You know Don Manuel's favorite proverb, 'It is better to have the reputation of bravery than to be brave.' " Santiago hunched his narrow shoulders. "If the Texans conquer the Province and take Santa Fe, Don Manuel will not bother you again."

"Ojalá that the Tejanos will come!" Tules exclaimed.

The capital made desperate plans to defend itself and waited the onslaught of the Texans. It did not relax until a week later when a messenger reported that the Avengers had been disarmed and ordered back to their Lone Star Republic by Captain Philip St. George Cooke and his United States dragoons. The United States had sent the dragoons to protect the American traders on the Santa Fe Trail from raids by either Texans or Mexicans. The Texans dispersed, but the traders had to turn back anyway. After the Avengers' attack, General Santa Anna closed all New Mexican ports of entry to foreign commerce.

# 27

Tules listened for every echo of news that would warn her of Manuel's return and give her time to start for Chihuahua. She saw his "retirement" as the opportunity to push Diego Archuleta. She talked to Diego, told him this was the crisis they had planned for, urged him to take the leadership now to unify and strengthen the country. She praised him to other men as the staunch patriot they needed, the second-in-command who should take over since Don Manuel had collapsed. All of them agreed with her, but no one was willing to risk an open stand. Even Diego shrugged helplessly, said the country had no voice in its own affairs and would have to accept any appointment General Santa Anna made. He was Don Manuel's friend and would follow that advice. Tules saw that all of them were still afraid of Manuel's power. They were more worried now that he was planning unknown schemes in the Río Abajo than they had been when they could watch him in Santa Fe.

Tules was disillusioned by their hopeless feeling of defeat and inertia. They were fearful, wary, and anxious to save themselves with any excuse. They had been trained too long by lies, bribery, jealousy, and cowardice. She remembered that Pepe said each man worked for himself and never pulled with others in a loyal team. She wished that Pepe would come, so that she could tell him that she agreed with him at last. She grew more sure that the only hope for her country and herself was a strong, fearless American Government.

Conchita returned to Mexico when Manuel left, and the story of Pedro's murder died down. Tules was nervous with suspense, but she smiled friendly greetings at everyone in the sala. She soon found that people were too concerned with their own troubles to bother with hers. After hot words with Cuca and María she was persuaded to ignore La Casimira's evil tongue.

Manuel stayed in safe retirement, far away from the Texans and the Taos Indians who were enraged over the deaths of their sons under Captain Lobato. They turned on the "foreigners" at Don Fernández, sacked the tithe granaries and the home of Beaubien, and vowed they would take the scalps of Armijo and Lobato.

In the fall Governor Armijo formally resigned, and General Santa Anna appointed Don Mariano Martínez as Governor in spite of protests that he was an "outsider" like Pérez. Tules knew that he was a weak, temporary substitute for Manuel and still listened for any hint that Manuel would return. She contributed willingly when Martínez asked for "funds for defense," though she did not expect them to reach the army. The country had never been so stricken with graft and poverty. Even the ricos besieged Doña Tules for money, which she loaned at 2 per cent interest per month.

The year of bad luck for Tules reached its climax when María coughed and tossed on her pallet with a high fever. That was in March, when the winds tore the ragged clouds and covered the ground with sleet. Everyone sneezed and ached with vapors in the head, but Tules was alarmed when she looked at María's small, shrunken figure. She had forgotten the toll of time in the swift years and suddenly realized that María was frail and old.

"Do everything you can to save her, Tía Apolonia," she begged. "Get anything you need, no matter what it costs. María is dearer to me than anyone in the world. She has been more of a mother than my own mother, 'Nana Luz,' who died last year in Manzano. I can't live without María."

"It is as God wills." Tía Apolonia shook her white head. "I will do what I can, but María is good, and God may give her rest. Her breath only comes from the throat. Keep out the night air and put these wet cloths on her head to cool the fever."

Tules watched beside María all night, brewing herb teas on the trivet in the fireplace and changing the cloths that steamed on María's burning forehead. She listened to María's breath that rose as though she was climbing weary stairs and then sank and almost stopped. In those seconds Tules held her breath and prayed as she watched the

288

old, wrinkled face. She held María's thin, hot hand between both of hers and tried by her own will to hold on to the flickering life.

Tules had been the flame and María the shadow, but each was essential to the other. María faded into the background, but she was always there to give Tules love, devotion, and encouragement. Tules thought now of María's care the year the baby died, their happy companionship in the market days, María's delight in Tules's fine dresses and jewels, her loyal support when Manuel threatened them. She had needed the support of María's patient, quiet strength at every turn of her destiny. She could not let María go.

In the morning María roused, opened her sunken eyes and murmured, "Confession—Sacrament . . . Get the padre, niña."

Tules sent word to the Vicario, but she refused to admit that María was dying. When she heard the little silver bell ringing up the street, she knew that the padre and his acolytes carried the Blessed Sacrament, and men and women dropped to their knees as it passed. She covered her ears to shut out this heraldry of death, but the bell stopped before her door. María's old eyes lit up with pride that the redheaded Vicario himself had come to hear her confession and give her absolution. Tules thought rebelliously that María had nothing to confess. She was a saint.

After the Vicario left María seemed easier and motioned Tules to come close. The deep strength of her spirit shone in her eyes as she whispered, "Now I will go in peace, niña. You must not cry. I have received God's forgiveness and love. I have prayed that by His grace you will find faith and peace—know His love—His mercy and blessing. . . ."

Her eyes closed, and her spirit slipped away with a gentle sigh.

Tules grieved like a lost child as she arranged for the funeral mass. She had money now to give María every cherished rite, but this brought no comfort. She was lonely and distraught and filled with remorse for her neglect of María. These last years she had been too concerned with her own selfish triumph and power and her mad passion for Manuel. She wished now that she could exchange those vain days for one hour of María's selfless devotion. Her greatest

289

solace was Victorio, whose withered body turned to her in his grief for the gentle soul who had loved him.

Cuca also missed María, but she lived by harsh fatalism. After a month of mourning she bustled in to Tules and said energetically, "No hay más remedio. Crying will not bring María back. You must make haste and get the sala clean and shining. General Santa Anna has opened the ports to the American traders, and they will be here in six weeks. After a year of starvation, we will eat again."

In July one hundred and sixty sunburned traders swarmed into Santa Fe. The hoofs of seven hundred mules and sixty lowing oxen cut into the dirt road around the plaza and filled the hot, clear air with sparkling dust. Mexicans in peaked sombreros lounged against the adobe walls in the deep shade of the portales and smiled scornfully at the gringo fools who sweated in the glaring sun as they unpacked their white-hooded wagons. But the idle men, as well as their black-eyed daughters, were secretly glad that the traders had returned. One year without the American trade had taught them that not only Government revenue but cash for the peóns at the market and for the rancheros and sheepherders depended on the business brought over the Santa Fe Trail.

Tules welcomed the traders with a baile and supper at the sala, but she shook her red head as she heard them grumble.

"Why, this here Martínez is even worse than that scoundrel Armijo," one trader declared as he rolled a wad of chewing tobacco to his other cheek. "Martínez has raised the ante on us to seven hundred and fifty dollars a wagon. Besides that we have to pay 'diligencia' to every slick official who inspects us. That ain't just or right. We won't come next year, if he's agoin' to stick us this way. This country needs some honest men and good, plain American laws."

"You're right, man," Juan Escolle agreed hotly. "Martínez has taken all the taxes off the Mexicans and loaded 'em on the gringos. He tried to tax me five hundred pesos, but I told him my name used to be John Scolly and I was a British subject. I've lived here for more than ten years, and I've got a Mexican wife and children. Last year

290

I brought the first steel plows that ever came to this country, and we raised good crops over at my ranch on the Mora. Armijo gave me that land to develop the valley. For all his faults, Armijo is a better man than this crook Martínez. We ought to get Armijo back. I hear he's coming to take over soon."

As Tules moved away from them her heart pounded with fear, and she clenched her hands until her knuckles were white. She looked around the crowded, smoke-filled room to find Santiago Flores, tell him what the traders said, and ask if they should leave for Chihuahua at once.

"Dios de mi vida, have you no welcome for a poor cibolero? Por favor, Doña Tules, give me one word, one smile." The deep voice rose and fell as it mimicked the plaintive singsong of the market vendors.

Tules turned to smile at Pepe Cisneros's merry, handsome face. His cheeks were red above his black moustache, and his black eyes twinkled under his heavy brows. He pulled off the red bandana that had been knotted over his curly black hair and flourished it as he called, "Permit me to sing you a copla de amor, and do not answer with a verse of disdain, señorita. This is a verse from the heart, a song from one who has journeyed far from his love." He bent over his guitar, plucked the chords, and sang impassioned verses. His elbow knocked the broad end of the guitar like the hoofbeats of a trotting horse, and his full, rich voice carried the simple melody.

As Tules watched him her tight hands relaxed, and she felt comforted for the first time since María died. Pepe was honest and simple like María. His lusty love of life gave her confidence and filled her with a wistful longing that was like a half-forgotten song. She looked from his cheerful, healthy face to his sensitive hands and wished that she, too, could laugh at the world and meet it without fear.

He leaned toward her and whispered, "Will you permit me to speak to you alone in the private room in half an hour?"

She nodded and looked at him sharply. She tried to take courage from his grin, but her hands tightened again. For all Pepe's clowning, he knew the plots and undercurrents of the whole country. He had warned her and worried over her many times. Would he tell her now that Manuel was coming back and she must leave? She sighed as she looked at the crowded monte tables, the long mirrors, the glowing candelabra, and the row of colored bottles beyond the heads of the men at the bar. She hated to give it up.

She waited restlessly for Pepe, and when he came in she smelled the odor of damp leather. His leather pants had been soaked in the summer rain, dried as he rode, and were now curved at the knees as though he was about to jump. His fringed deerskin hunting shirt was open and showed his strong, sunburned neck. He rested his guitar in the corner of the room and came toward her with a serious face.

"What is it, Pepe?" she asked anxiously as she poured the red wine. "Have you come to warn me again? Is Manuel coming back? Must we go?"

"Martínez does not give satisfaction." Pepe nodded. "Armijo may come back for a while, but he will have to fight the Americans."

"Ojalá that they will come soon!" Tules exclaimed. "I know you are right, Pepe. I wanted to tell you that I am with you. . . ."

"That is the best news I have heard." Pepe's eyes glowed. "Now everything will work out. . . ."

"But if Manuel comes before the Americans . . . Should we leave now? How much time do we have?"

"If he comes, he will be too busy defending himself to molest you, if . . ."

"Dios de mi vida, I have lived in suspense for so long! You don't know him, Pepe. He will not forget. He will take everything, throw me in jail, sentence me to hang. . . ."

"Not if you have a strong man here."

"You know what I have—Santiago Flores, Chico, Victorio. He would brush them aside like flies."

"He would not brush me aside." The cords stood out in Pepe's throat as he took another sip of wine. "I want to stay here. I want to protect you as your husband. . . ."

Tules's unbelieving eyes stared at him. Husband? Did he mean marriage? He had often spoken of his devotion for her, but she took

292

it as a light, careless love. She thought he wanted to be her minstrel lover, making gay fiesta, joking with his comic verses, singing to her. It had never occurred to her that, even in serious moments, he thought of marriage. Long ago she had given up the hope of a husband. For such as she, there was no blessing of marriage.

"I chase buffalo and live 'on the hump' the rest of the year," Pepe explained. "If you would marry me, I could be here most of the time, fight for you, protect you as a man protects his wife. . . ."

Tules blinked her hazel eyes as she stared into his frank, honest face. No man had ever offered to fight for her, protect her, except that simple gringo boy, Jeem, and Pepe. As she thought of Jeem she rubbed her ring, and her finger tingled.

"You take my breath, Pepe," she murmured. Quick thoughts raced through her mind. Pepe might save her. He would fight for her, and they might outbluff Manuel in this time of stress. An honest marriage would also soothe her hurt pride, though Manuel would make fun of marriage to a poor cibolero. Under her lashes she looked at Pepe's worn moccasins and stiff leather pants. She had aimed for the ricos and their fine clothes and silver that would buy everything. She shuddered as she thought of the gold epaulets and stretched out her hand toward Pepe's honest, sturdy leather.

He took her hand and said, "I have had no home since my wife died. We had three children, but my eldest, the boy, was gored by a buffalo last summer. I have two little girls—Raillitas and Carmel. I want you to teach them, help them. . . .

"I miss Lucita. They could take her place," Tules nodded.

"Compared to what you have here, I have little to offer." Pepe turned up his empty palms and looked at her fine black silk dress. "I can't give you diamonds, but you were happier when you had only one red skirt. How well I remember the first time I saw you at the market, wearing the red skirt! You were gay, beautiful, happy. You were a bright flame that warmed my heart. You lived in one room with María. . . ."

"Ah, Dios de mi vida, if I could only bring María back," Tules cried. Tears filled her eyes, and she moved restlessly around the room.

293

"I know your grief, linda." Pepe followed her and put his arm around her shoulder. "You are alone now. Let me take care of you. I had no chance before, but now . . ."

"If Manuel comes back, he will show no mercy. He might kill you too. You would not want to run," she faltered.

"We will not run." Pepe threw back his shoulders. "Manuel has threatened me before, but it was a bluff. He could not even stop my songs. He was afraid because I laughed at him. He is a coward and a bully. We will only have to stand up to him once. My hands itch to get hold of him for the way he treated you. . . ."

Tules drew away from him as she remembered the vile names Manuel had called her. Pepe would not want that shame. "You know what I was?" she questioned him. "Would you want a wife who has had my life?"

"That is past. We will never speak of it again." Pepe's steady eyes looked deep into hers, and he caught her in his arms. "I have loved you all these years. I thought of your eyes those nights when I lay on the wide prairie and the stars were so bright and close. I sang to you, dreamed of you. . . . I tried to tell you, but you would not listen. . . . I want you. I love you with all my heart."

His lips sought hers in a long-denied kiss. Her lips were quiet under his, but her body leaned against his strength, and she relaxed in his arms.

"I will make you happy, my little bird," he murmured against her hair. "Tomorrow I will arrange for our marriage. Ah, Tules, mi alma. . . ." He kissed her again and held her off to search her pale face.

Pepe was as excited as a boy over the wedding. In spite of his talk that he could not give her fine clothes, he insisted that he would follow Spanish custom and provide the best trousseau he could buy in Santa Fe. He coaxed the seamstress to finish the white satin wedding gown in three days. When he saw Tules dressed in it, just before the wedding, he drew in his breath and said, "Alma de mi alma, you have never been so beautiful! You look like snow in the sparkle of the sun. My poor hunter's hands are almost afraid to touch you." He

294

fingered her white sleeve and leaned over to brush her cheek with a shy kiss.

Tules was amazed that she was the bride and had acquired the dignity and respect of a married woman. She looked around the sala at the guests who toasted her with new admiration and counted the ricos, the officials, and even Governor Martínez. The pobres hovered in the background, but Tules and Pepe had given orders that they too should be served with champagne and rich food. She smiled at Pepe's happy face with deep affection and touched his arm to assure herself of his strength and love.

The household settled into new ways as Rafaela took charge of the shy little country daughters and Victorio followed Pepe with the worship due a mighty hunter. Pepe's joking refusal to take any part in the management of his wife's sala soothed Santiago Flores and brought relieved satisfaction to Cuca's shrewd eyes.

The gringos knew that Pepe was their friend and flocked to the sala. One trader presented them with a wedding gift—a large clock to hang on the wall, ornately framed in a gilt garland. Everyone gaped and admired it as much as the other marvelous clock Dr. Josiah Gregg had installed in the tower of the parroquia. In that clock the painted wooden figure of a little Negro came out of the door and bowed as the hour chimed. But when the Vicario refused to pay Dr. Gregg the full price for the clock it stopped, and the little Negro did not come out again. Tules's clock also stopped, with its hands pointing to twelve and six. She said it would wear out and they should only let it run on holidays, and Pepe joked that they did not waste time. The town decided that exact time was only gringo foolishness and reverted to the pleasant habit of occasionally consulting their one timepiece, the sundial in the plaza.

Tules spent the evenings now listening to the gringos talk freely to Pepe. They predicted that the American army would soon take over New Mexico and read aloud the speeches of Senator Thomas Hart Benton to the United States Congress in Washington. He urged the United States to grant Texas statehood and occupy all of northern Mexico and California. He painted glowing visions of the future nation that would extend from ocean to ocean. His speeches were based on the reports of the Western explorations of his son-in-law, Colonel John C. Fremont. Tules and Pepe remembered that Kit Carson had been with Fremont in Santa Fe and nodded their approval.

They were often puzzled by the hot arguments between the Americans from the North and South. The Southerners insisted that when New Mexico became part of the United States it should have the same slave-owning laws as the South, but the New Englanders vigorously objected. Tules hoped that the Americans would put an end to peonage, which was much like Southern slavery, and sided with the New Englanders.

For years the sala had been a hotbed of political intrigue that reached from the Palace into the scattered settlements. Now the talk in the small room where they received their friends stretched the horizon to Washington and even across the Atlantic to England and France. Tules knew little about those distant nations, but she listened to the babel of French, German, Spanish, and English and soon perceived that the human motives for power and possessions were the same whether the struggle extended across an ocean or the Río Grande.

One night a Frenchman named Leroux said volubly, "Texas and all this country should be a French colony. We were poorly advised when we ceded our land west of the Mississippi to Spain and sold Louisiana for a song. Texas is bankrupt, and we will loan her money and regain our influence."

"You're too late," the Englishman, Gaines, spoke up. "All these years Britain has been looking after her vast mining interests in Mexico and has watched every move of the battle for independence in Texas. She has already loaned the Lone Star Republic a million pounds and will establish a permanent colony there. In a few years all the land from Texas to the Pacific will be a British protectorate, and the California ports will be vital links with our East India trade."

"I think you have forgotten the Monroe Doctrine," Don Santiago Magoffin said with his Irish smile. "That agreement was signed by your countries twenty years ago to prevent any European power from

296

setting up new colonies on the American continents. Texas will not need European loans. We will finance her. Her people are Americans, and Texas will soon be one of our states."

"That will mean war," Gaines declared. "Last year Mexico warned the United States that the annexation of Texas would be cause for war."

"We will accept war rather than allow European influence to gain an opening wedge on our borders," Magoffin said.

"But even your foolhardy politicians will hesitate before they go to war on two fronts that are two thousand miles apart," Gaines reminded him. "Are you ready to fight with Mexico over Texas in the south and with Britain over Oregon in the north? Britain will fight for her rights over the Oregon boundary and have the help of Canada and the colonial troops. Your Senator Benton would be wise to leave Mexico and Texas alone until the Oregon boundary is settled."

"But Mexico doesn't want a Texas Republic that would soon enlist all of northern Mexico under the Lone Star flag," Magoffin explained. "Nor does Mexico want Texas to become a British colony where British goods could be smuggled across the border and ruin Mexican manufacture. She would not grieve too much if the United States occupied the deserts of northern Mexico."

"And we will make the desert blossom as the rose," a New England boy spoke up, as though the words flowed out of the dream in his blue eyes. "I thought of that when we came over that high mountain pass last month and saw this country shining golden in the sun as far as my eyes could reach, shimmering in blue and rose and gold and just waiting for us to come. We'll bring water to it, build dams, make it blossom like the Bible says. Why, there's room for everyone here. A man could live free and proud. The clear air makes me lightheaded with the vision of what this country will be when we own all of it from ocean to ocean."

"Ojalá for the vision of youth!" Pepe smiled at the boy and added, "When the wind spreads the fire, there is no need to fan the flames."

When they were alone Tules asked, "What is this plan for the British to loan Texas money? The debtor always loses the land. The English and Americans talk as though it was a race between them to see which will claim Texas and New Mexico first."

"Nothing will stop the Americans, and they will be here soon," Pepe said. "There is yeast in them that pushes them on. You heard that boy tonight. They follow a dream. They will bring us honest men, good laws, safety. . . ."

"Safety!" Tules repeated the word that was the deep prayer in her heart. "We must do all we can to bring them soon."

"Every time you say that, linda, you put new heart into me." Pepe smiled as he kissed her.

She discovered how much she loved Pepe when he left for the buffalo hunt that fall. Cuca laughed at her long face and said, "You look as triste as a lone lovebird. Válgame Dios, you always depend too much on one man!"

"But Pepe has gone north where he may be attacked by the Utes," Tules explained.

The Ute chiefs had come to the Palace to sign a peace treaty, but Governor Martínez suspected their sincerity and protected himself by hiding a dozen armed soldiers behind a sheet hung over the end of his office. When the head chief fumbled in his blanket as though he might draw a knife, Martínez felled him with a chair, and the soldiers jumped out and killed eight other Utes. After that, every Indian tribe from north to south turned against the Mexicans and were ready to help the coming American invasion.

Before Christmas Pepe came home safely with a wagon load of buffalo robes, tongues, meat, and wooden pails of lard. He was full of good health and deep laughter and brought in the clean, free air of the prairies. His curly head seemed as carefree as a tassel of corn blowing in the wind. He was like the corn that grew in tall, straight stalks out of the soil, absorbed the deep, fecund power of the warm earth, and matured in sun and rain. Tules had known intrigue and petty jealousy all her life. Now she was surprised, and sometimes baffled, by this deep-rooted, elemental man who was her husband. She listened to the rumblings of war and politics and thanked God for Pepe and his strong, protecting love.

# 28

THE ADMISSION of Texas as one of the United States in July, 1845, was considered a preliminary declaration of war between the United States and Mexico. As a last hope to save New Mexico from following Texas, Governor Martínez resigned, and Manuel Armijo was again appointed Governor.

When Tules heard the news she paced the floor and cried to Pepe, "Now Manuel will be here with all his power. He will do as he threatened. Ah, Pepe, let us start for Chihuahua now. . . ."

"Do you still believe in him?" Pepe asked her sharply.

"No, Pepe, you know how I hate him. But I married you, and that will be one more reason for Manuel to humble me. He will hang me. . . . Oh, Pepe, we would be safe in Chihuahua."

"We will not run. We only need to face that bully once." Pepe straightened his shoulders. "No one else has brought charges against you, and Manuel will find it best to forget. He will have his hands too full with his own enemies and the American army. We will stay here, my little bird."

She bit her lip to keep from repeating Manuel's name again, but the old terror shook her. At last Pepe's calm strength reassured her, and her panic lessened when Manuel postponed coming to the capital until after the gringo traders left in the fall.

Pepe brought her a gift that he had ordered from a trader the year before. It was a Brussels carpet with red roses splashed over a rich, red ground, and he stretched it on the floor of the private room where they received their friends.

"Oh, Pepe, it is magnificent!" Tules cried and felt the thickness of the carpet with her thumb and finger. "It is the only carpet in all the Province. But it cost too much!"

"Only one load of buffalo robes," Pepe grinned. "I will bring more loads this fall."

"You can't go away and leave me this fall, Pepe." She caught his arm. "Manuel will come. . . . Please don't go, Pepe. If you go, I will go with you."

"Bien, linda." He kissed her with deep satisfaction. "The Arab proverb says a man finds happiness on the back of a horse or in the heart of a woman. I will stay at home."

The traders left, and Tules counted off the last short days of November before Manuel returned to the Palace. Even then he stayed inside the thick walls, and his friends explained that he felt the cold in his lame leg.

"Some night Manuel will come here," Pepe said. "You must be prepared."

"I have caught courage from you, Pepe." She smiled, and her eyelids drooped slyly. "I have thought of a plan. I will face him as though nothing unpleasant had happened. We will invite him to use the sala in order to watch him. That is one thing I can do to help you and the gringos. . . ."

Pepe laughed and pinched her cheek. "When you make up your mind, you try to put the ocean in a well. Bien, this will be a good joke."

Tules laughed with him, but inside she felt the same tremor that tripped her heart when she bet more than she could afford to lose on the monte table. She knew Manuel, his treachery, his cunning, his long memory. If she could bluff him this time, she might save herself and bring the day that much closer when the gringos would ensure permanent safety.

Every night for a month she dressed her red hair with special care and wore the new black velvet dress with the looped skirt, diamond earrings, and a gold chain around her throat. She studied her face for telltale wrinkles, powdered it, and added a new perfume. She was anxious that Manuel should see that her marriage was successful and happy.

The night when Manuel strutted into the sala she caught her breath sharply but nodded to Pepe's signal. They crossed the room together, Pepe's strong fingers sending reassuring messages to her bare arm. She saw at once that Manuel's extra weight strained the gold buttons on his uniform and made the collar with the red-and-gold braid look too tight.

The sardonic lines around his mouth deepened as he acknowledged their greetings and said sarcastically, "Permit me to congratulate you on your marriage, Doña Tules. I was surprised when I heard of it. Your tastes used to be—ah—richer."

"You know we change with the years, my General," Tules lifted her head, looked at him, and smiled calmly. "The years have brought me good fortune. I hope they have been as kind to you—and your health."

He raised his eyebrows at her dignified composure and shrugged. "I hope your temper has also improved. I recall certain incidents when you were angry. . . ."

"Does any man understand a beautiful woman's temperament, señor?" Pepe laughed, balanced himself at ease on his moccasined feet, and looked squarely at his adversary.

"In court such temper might be considered a serious offense," Manuel said sternly.

"Oh, no, señor, judges are human like the rest of us. What chance would a judge have against a woman who is beautiful, successful, and has many friends? My wife also has strong defenders, among them my good arm that has killed many buffalo." Pepe spoke in a joking tone, but his eyes defied Manuel and stated plainly how he would defend his wife.

Manuel looked away from his direct eyes, glanced over his shoulder, and saw that the crowd watched and listened. "You know only the rules of the buffalo wallow," he muttered.

"You are right, señor, and the first rule is to drive the lance in at the vulnerable spot. Then the mightiest buffalo falls. . . . But I did not intend to give a lesson on the buffalo hunt." Pepe raised his hands as though he had been too serious and offered Manuel an easy way out. "Of course, in this time of danger, you have more important things to consider. . . ."

Manuel took it with a haughty nod. "For the present I have no time to consider past incidents, but I shall remember them. I must overlook personal irritations in the responsibility that rests on my shoulders again." He turned to Tules and said loftily, "I shall need the private room for certain conferences. See that it is kept in readiness for me."

"Our house is always at your disposition, my General. We are honored that you will use our poor room." Tules nodded graciously, glad that her skirt hid her shaking knees. "May we offer you wine to welcome you and wish you good health? Santiago, give everyone wine to toast the Governor."

The men crowded around Don Manuel, and he used the opportunity to show that he was superior to Pepe's joking defiance. "My only concern now is to save our country from the grasping Americans," he said dramatically. "Our clever leaders in Mexico have led the gringos into a good trap this time. Their stupid President Polk sent the army south to Mexico instead of north to Oregon. The real war will be with England in the north, but, by that time, the American army will be in their graves in Mexico."

"What is this Texas claim to our land?" someone asked.

"It is ridiculous." Don Manuel shook his fist. "Their claim to all the country east of the Río Grande is absurd. If it was true, Santa Fe would be in Texas. You know that Santa Fe has been the capital of New Mexico for more than two hundred years. Would you give up your glorious heritage?"

"No! Never! Down with the Tejanos!" the men shouted. "But will the American army come here?"

"How can an army march four hundred leagues without food or water?" Don Manuel scoffed. "Even the few wagons of the traders have a hard time getting through. If the dry jornada doesn't finish them, we will. We can cut them off from their supply base at the back and wipe them out with our army in the front. I have no fear, my

302

friends, if all of us unite to defend our country. With God's help, we will wipe out this gringo scourge forever. Dios y libertad!" Don Manuel raised his large hand in salute and marched out of the sala, calling attention to his martyred leg with an exaggerated limp.

Tules sighed with relief as she watched him go, unfurled her black fan, and looked at the sparkle of the sequins as its perfume drifted on the air. She laughed and talked with her guests as though this was an uneventful, pleasant evening. Cuca, who had watched every move of the drama, came over to her to whisper, "Your luck never deserts you, niña. You handled him well tonight but watch him."

When they were alone Pepe grinned. "We won the first race, linda. I was proud that the big cat did not swallow my little bird."

"It was only because you were there to defend me, Pepe," she smiled.

"He will not trouble you again. You'll see. . . ." Pepe nodded. "But we have work to do before spring. He suspects me, but you can find out his secrets. Manuel and his partner, Adolf Speyer, plan to bring in guns and supplies. Discover all you can about them. If we can stop them, the army will be helpless and Manuel will have to surrender without bloodshed."

Even Tules was astonished by Pepe's knowledge, plans, and preparations. He sang to his guitar, joked lazily with everyone, but, behind his clown's mask, his wits were alert and his moccasined feet moved as stealthily as a mountain cat's. He met secret emissaries and left one night for Bent's Fort where messages were relayed to the Americans. The traders knew every water hole on the Trail; their experience was now vital for the long hazardous march of the American army.

The next day Tules learned that Don Manuel and his escort had also gone north. She was terrified that Manuel's spies had discovered Pepe's mission and might catch him. There were spies everywhere. The details of any plot in Santa Fe or Missouri were carried by fast runners to either end of the Trail. Other messengers went south to plead for help from President Paredes, but his troops were fighting their own battles with the Americans at Corpus Christi. Mexico was in the usual state of revolution and bankruptcy.

A week later Tules threw her arms around Pepe and cried, "Thank

God you are safe! When Manuel went north I thought he was after you!"

"I saw him yesterday, but he did not see me," Pepe laughed. "He tried to win over the northern Indians, but they reminded him that he had killed their chief. They said nothing could stop the Americans. . . . If they lost one battle, more and more gringos would come until they overran the country."

"There was a rumor that the Utes would help Manuel," Tules said.

"No, the Utes would kill every Mexican for the dirty trick Martínez played when he killed their chief last year. All the Indians are ready to help the Americans now."

Manuel returned, stalked in and out of the sala, and used the private room for secret meetings. Though he was suspicious of Pepe, he preferred to meet men casually at the bar and agree with a nod to plans that he did not want to reveal at the Palace. He bowed formally to Tules but never referred to his threats. She saw that Diego Archuleta was often with him as the second-in-command. She respected Diego's loyalty and strong convictions, and after their many conferences in the past it was easy to regain his confidence.

"What is this talk of the faction who opposes Don Manuel in the Assembly?" she asked. "They say the Americans will win anyway and we should surrender and save needless bloodshed."

"Válgame Dios, they are without one drop of courage." Diego pounded his fist into his palm. "Who wants to live without honor? We won't give up without a struggle. The supplies for the army will reach them in plenty of time. With a hundred well-armed men at Apache Pass, we will slaughter the Americans."

Tules hurried to report this to Pepe, and he left immediately to warn the Americans that Speyer and his ammunition wagons must be stopped on the Trail.

When the news reached Santa Fe that war had been officially declared on May 13, 1846, there was wild excitement on the plaza, and Rafaela ran to Tules with tears streaming down her pockmarked face.

"Madre de Dios, let us run to the mountains before these barbarians come," she begged. "Everyone on the plaza says the gringos will rape the women and brand their cheeks with a hot iron. They will mutilate the men and burn our holy churches. For the love of our mother, let us run before it is too late."

"These are lies spread to frighten you," Tules said sternly. "You know the Americans. You have seen them each summer. Have they hurt you? They will not harm us if we behave ourselves. Stop crying and put these lies out of your mind."

"Rafaela is a poor fool," Victorio said importantly. "I know that the gringos had a sign from heaven and they cannot fail. When the traders returned last month they saw the image of a great eagle on the setting sun. Everyone saw it and knew it was a sign sent by God. Pepe says we shall be saved, and the American eagle will rule over us."

Pepe returned with the news that fifty thousand men had volunteered in the United States and their army was already marching west. Don Manuel and the Assembly heard the news too and implored men to defend their country.

"The invader has already set foot on our sacred soil," Don Manuel shouted and waved a paper in his hand. "This is a declaration made by General Stephen Watts Kearny at Bent's Fort. He had the insolence to announce that he would enter New Mexico today. To arms, men! With God's help we will repulse this criminal invasion and save our beloved country."

Only two hundred men volunteered to join the five hundred in the militia. Other men took their panic-stricken families and fled to the remote mountains.

"There was some slip. Speyer got through with his guns and ammunition, and Manuel wants to use them," Pepe told Tules. "But the militia will be wiped out over night. The prisoners who were turned loose by the Americans say there are five thousand well-armed men in their army and sixteen cannon. They have crossed our border now and will be here in a few days."

At the end of the week the hot August sun glared on the plaza, and the church bells and bugles called every inhabitant to come to the Palace to hear an official announcement. Tules stood with her

305

household in the hot, dusty plaza and thought of that other day when Manuel was first appointed Governor and people cheered him as the great leader. Now they waited for him in terrified silence. Women loosened their rebosos to cool their shoulders, and men wiped the sweat that ran down under their high, peaked hats. They huddled in hopeless, muttering groups like frightened sheep. They gave Don Manuel a half-hearted "Viva!" as he ascended the rude platform in front of the Palace portál and began his speech.

"Fellow countrymen," his loud voice boomed out as his arm stretched toward them. "At last the moment has arrived when our country requires of her children a decision without limit, a sacrifice without reserve, under circumstances which demand everything for our salvation.

"Questions with the United States of America, which have been treated in a dignified and decorous manner by our Supreme Government, remain undecided. They concern the inalienable rights of Mexico over the usurped territory of Texas. On this account it has not been possible to maintain diplomatic relations with the Anglo-American Government, whose Minister has not been received in Mexico. The armed forces of that Government are advancing through this department. They have crossed our northern frontier and are now near the Colorado River. Hear then, fellow citizens, the signal of alarm which calls us to battle. . . ."

When Tules realized that Manuel was determined to drive his helpless army into battle she stopped listening to his bombastic words and watched the bright sun glint on his gold braid, buttons, epaulets, and tricolored plumes at the top of his helmet. The blue uniform was too tight for the rolls of soft fat on his huge body, and his dark face perspired and worked with emotion. He threw out his arms and pled with all his oratory, but his black eyes perceived that he aroused no enthusiasm. Tules watched his futile gestures and thought bitterly that Manuel's last vanity would cost many lives. Pepe nudged her, and she listened again.

"Be assured that your Governor is willing and ready to sacrifice his life and all his interests in the defense of his country. Comrades, if

306

we are honestly united, victory will be ours. To arms, men! With God's help we shall save our beloved country. Dios y libertad!"

Don Manuel's followers led the cheers with loud cries of "Viva Don Manuel! Dios y libertad!" but there was little response from the crowd. Women sobbed and pulled their black rebosos over their faces, and men hunched dejected shoulders.

"Manuel forgot that he said the American army could never cross the Trail," Tules murmured as they started home. "Now he will save his face by sending the pobres to be murdered."

"There is still time to persuade him," Pepe said mysteriously.

# 29

THE NEXT day Tules understood something of what Pepe meant when everyone repeated the joyful news that the Americans were sending an advance courier to arrange for peace. On Wednesday Captain Philip St. George Cooke and Don Santiago Magoffin rode into Santa Fe under a flag of truce. They had an escort of twelve men and had come for a parley with the Mexicans. Governor Armijo received them at the Palace and returned their call, but there was more business he wished to discuss that night.

"Don Manuel sent an order to keep our private room clear for the meeting with the Americans at ten o'clock," Tules told Pepe breathlessly. "He warned us to stay away. He said his soldiers would guard the doors."

"Bien." Pepe's white teeth flashed in a wide grin. "You watch the front door, and I will see who goes in the back. Victorio is small enough to hide in the chest beside the fireplace in the private room. I will bore holes so that he can breathe and hear. I will lock the lid after he gets in, and no one will suspect."

That evening Tules watched the gilt-framed clock that hung on the wall of the sala. Pepe had wound it, but she wondered anxiously if the hands had rusted and slowed down. She smoothed her black velvet skirt, adjusted the jade-green shawl over her shoulders, and fidgeted with the long gold chain that hung over her high bosom. She moistened her lips frequently as she watched the door. The sala was crowded, and smoke hung over the men who argued and drank at the bar. The monte tables were deserted, except for a few idlers who made small bets to fill in the time.

At nine o'clock Captain Cooke and Don Santiago Magoffin came through the front door, and Tules moved quickly to greet them.

"Doña Tules, you grow more beautiful each time I come here."

308

Don Santiago Magoffin bowed with courtly grace and garnished his fluent Spanish with Irish flattery. His light-brown hair receded from his high forehead and gave his face a severity that was contradicted by his twinkling blue eyes. The sharp, clean lines of his jaw rose above his flaring white collar and black stock. His long black broadcloth coat with the black velvet collar was conspicuously American. "Permit me, Doña Tules, to present Captain Cooke of the First Dragoons. I told you, Captain, that the high point of your visit to Santa Fe would be an introduction to this beautiful lady and this famous sala. Doña Tules, will you do us the honor of joining us in a bottle of your excellent champagne?"

Tules bowed and motioned to Santiago Flores to take Don Santiago's beaver hat and black satchel, but the American smilingly waved him aside.

"With your permission we will keep our fixin's," he laughed. "In these days a man might have to run before he could find his hat."

"Of course, Don Santiago," she said, but she was suspicious of the black satchel. She managed to bump her knee against it as she led the way to the bar. The satchel was heavy enough to be filled with gold. Under her lashes she watched Magoffin set the satchel down carefully and guard it with his foot as he leaned negligently against the bar.

She turned to the young Captain who held his stiff shako, with its insignia of crossed muskets surmounted by an eagle, under his arm. His erect military carriage and smart uniform with the light-blue trousers and dark-blue jacket gave her confidence. His keen eyes noted the faces around him, the position of the doors and windows, and the clock ticking on the wall. His face wore the set smile of a stranger who did not understand the rapid Spanish chatter around him.

Don Santiago Magoffin interpreted for him with easy ways and a suave Irish smile. He knew everyone in the sala, for he was the most popular of the American traders. For many years he had taken his wagons from St. Louis to Chihuahua and had a reputation for generosity, good humor, and love of good food and wine. Tonight he ordered champagne for the crowd and seemed more concerned with the age and bouquet of the wine than with the state of war. His friendliness overcame the fact that he and the Captain were alien enemies in a hostile camp.

While Don Santiago inquired solicitously as to the health of the families of the men around him, Tules and the young Captain talked but watched the clock. When the hands pointed to five minutes of ten, Don Santiago casually finished his wine, tipped the bartender lavishly, and bowed to Doña Tules. His eyelids drooped over his twinkling blue eyes as he picked up his heavy satchel and sauntered with Captain Cooke toward the door of the private room.

As soon as the door closed behind them, men chattered excitedly about this mission. Some declared that the Americans were caught between the shears of having their supplies cut off at the back and facing the Mexican army at the front and had sent Magoffin to make overtures for peace. Others insisted that the Americans wanted to compromise for the Texas claim of all the land east of the Río Grande. No one doubted that Don Manuel had entered the private room by the back door and was now deciding their fate.

Tules listened to the talk and fitted together hints of Manuel's plans. She moved from group to group, for she wanted everyone to remember that she had been in the sala all evening if there was any question of spies. She appeared calm, but her fingers played nervously with her long gold chain.

After midnight the door opened, and Don Santiago and Captain Cooke came out alone. She went to them quickly and tried to guess the outcome of the secret meeting from their blank faces.

"It is late, Don Santiago, and you must be tired. A little wine . . ." she offered, as she looked at him sharply.

"A thousand thanks, Doña Tules," he smiled. "We start back early tomorrow, and we must deny ourselves further pleasure tonight."

She walked with them to the door and again touched her knee against the black satchel. It was light, empty. Her shoulders relaxed with relief as she bowed them out.

She ran to her room but waited an hour for Pepe and Victorio. She walked the floor as she imagined that they had been caught or murdered. At last she heard Pepe's signal and flung open the door.

"I had to wait until it was safe to unlock the chest and get Victorio out," Pepe grinned. "He almost smothered. . . ."

"Tell me, Victorio," Tules jerked at his shoulder. "Don Santiago's satchel was empty when he left. Did he give Manuel the gold?"

"I could not see, but I heard the clink of gold." Victorio rubbed his thumb and forefinger in the sign for bribery. "They talked a long time. I could hardly breathe. I could not understand all of it. Don Manuel said he was satisfied, but the other, Don Diego Archuleta, he would not agree. . . ."

"What did he want?" Tules demanded.

"He didn't want to give up the country. At last the gringo with the voice like music said that Don Diego could keep the other side of the river. The Americans would only come as far as the Río Grande. Does that mean that Don Diego will be Governor?" Victorio's shriveled face frowned at this confusion.

"Manuel will be able to persuade him," Pepe said. "He weighed more by fifty thousand pesos in gold when he left the back door. As you have said so often, linda, money buys anything."

But the next day Tules was puzzled by Manuel's frantic preparations to defend his country. Evidently he had taken the bribe but intended to fool the Americans. His zeal sent officers scurrying to collect supplies and drill troops. He renewed confidence by telling that his ammunition wagons had come through safely and the army would have new guns and copper bullets. He sent soldiers to clean the four cannon in the Palace compound and boasted that the fine Texas cannon he had captured four years ago at San Miguel would now kill the Tejanos.

The Assembly met to plan the defense of Santa Fe. They would barricade the roads and fight from house to house. The Army of the West was coming closer every day, but no one believed that it could get through Apache Pass. The Americans would be annihilated in that narrow, strategic cañón, and Santa Fe and the Province would be saved. For the next two days men took heart and worked with new hope to defend their homes.

When Manuel strode into the sala and commanded Tules to come to the private room her knees shook, and she looked wildly for Pepe. She did not see him but signaled Santiago Flores to stand close to the door.

"As you know, the enemy has invaded our sacred soil," Manuel said abruptly, when she stood before him. "They will be upon us in a few days if we do not turn them back. Everyone must help, sacrifice themselves and everything they possess to save our country at this desperate time. I have come to get one thousand pesos from you. . . ."

Tules's red head jerked up at this demand, and she looked at him swiftly. One thousand pesos! Twice as much as he would demand from any rico! Did he fill his pockets from both sides?

He saw her defiance and sneered, "That is a small sum to prove your loyalty. It may quiet the suspicion that you and your pelado husband favor the gringos. I am in a hurry. Get the money."

Tules caught her breath at this threat but knew that she would have to comply.

"Come," she whispered to Santiago, as she hurried toward the money room. "He demands one thousand pesos. Help me count it."

"He is bleeding all the ricos," Santiago said. "He made the Vicario give him all the tithe money and the church plate and livestock. That would be all right if it could save the poor soldiers, but it will stick to his pocket."

"Válgame Dios, I did not know a man could be so crooked!" Tules's voice shook with anger.

She handed the sack of gold to Manuel, looked steadily into his black agate eyes, and said, "I question the valor of sending our poor men to be slaughtered."

"Would you let these ruffians seize our country without a blow?" he scowled. "Have you lost all courage, honor?"

"A boy does not lack courage when he cannot whip a man," she answered and looked at him with scorn. "As for honor—what do you

312

know of honor? If you are found out, men will curse your name for generations."

"At last you have confessed that you are a traitor." Manuel's lips tightened as his eyes measured her. "You will not have another chance. The time is short for you and your stinking buffalo hunter. When the time comes, I will fasten the rope around your neck and let you hang."

When he left she shook with fury. Her anger left no room for fear, and her thoughts raced with any plan that would destroy this tyrant before he destroyed her.

She no longer doubted his duplicity to the Americans. He boasted loudly of his plan to fortify Apache Pass, five leagues south of Santa Fe. Tules remembered that the high, red granite bluffs rose on either side of the one road. A hundred armed men and four cannon concealed above the bluffs could wipe out the American army as it marched down the road.

"The Americans must not march into that trap, Pepe," she cried. "You must get word to them. Men are already at the Pass cutting timber and making ready to set up the cannon. Manuel sent the cannon down there this morning."

"Take courage, my little bird," Pepe quieted her. "The Americans know all this. They have good spies, too. They will be warned in time and march around the mountain instead of through the Pass. It may delay them a day in reaching here."

She tried to find comfort in Pepe's words, but she was frightened. The Mexicans were used to guerrilla tactics from their long war with the Indians, but the Americans knew little of such fighting. If the Army of the West was wiped out by guerrillas, treachery, ambush, there was no hope. She wished that she could fight with the Americans.

The Army of the West was marching closer each day. On Wednesday morning General Kearny and his forces rode into Las Vegas and accepted a peaceful surrender. The General made a speech from the roof of the courthouse, offered the strength and friendship of the United States and promised civil and religious protection to all who swore allegiance. The Alcalde and the leaders of the town took the oath to the American flag. The army marched on and accepted the peaceful surrender of the settlements of Tecolote and San Miguel.

This news filled Santa Fe with wild terror. The enemy was only ten leagues away and would be here tomorrow unless it was stopped at Apache Pass. Families fled to the mountains, carrying bundles and driving burros loaded with household goods. A second detachment of soldiers departed for Apache Pass, but the terrified citizens were now afraid that nothing would stop the Americans. They fastened shutters over every window, barricaded doors, and planned to fight from house to house. The lookout on Atalaya Hill watched the road winding east over the wide plain to give the signal the moment he saw the Americans approaching in the distance.

Pepe said they must avoid suspicion and barricade their house like everyone else. Besides, that would give them protection against looters until the Americans learned which were friendly houses. The sala was strangely quiet and deserted. In the late afternoon Tules and Pepe stopped to rest on a bench under the shady portál. After dark Pepe would go over the short trail across the mountains with last messages for the Americans.

"There is trouble between the officers," Pepe frowned. "Mutiny would change our plans. Manuel and Diego Archuleta had words. Each wants to command. Manuel is a coward, but Diego has courage. He would die for his country. He may force Manuel. . . . Pues, we shall know by this time tomorrow."

Pepe wiped the sweat from his worried face. The sultry air was heavy with the sweetness of honeysuckle growing over the portál. The earth was parched from long drought. The leaves of the rosebush by the well had yellowed and fallen, and under the tamarisk trees dry seeds covered the ground like red pepper.

"Listen!" she exclaimed. "I hear cannon!"

"You are nervous, my little bird," Pepe laughed. "That is thunder. Thank God the rains have come."

The parrot and the mockingbirds in their amole cages chirped and ruffled their feathers with the first hint of rain.

314

"Mexicans know how to creep over a dark, wet road, but a storm will make it worse for the Americans," Tules said.

"You must have faith." Pepe patted her hand. "God will provide, but it's wise to gather a good pile of straw, too. I must start now."

"Ah, Pepe, may all the saints protect you." Tules kissed him. "Take care, mi alma. I would die if any harm came to you."

That night the storm raged with the violence of booming thunder and vivid lightning flashing through the shutters. Tules listened to it with the grim satisfaction that the driving rain would ruin Manuel's fine uniform. Ojalá that this would be his last stand and he would never come back!

Her thoughts followed Pepe over the dark, slippery trail where danger lurked. Spies might lie in wait for him, stab him, push his body over the edge of a cañon. "Madre de Dios, take care of Pepe," she prayed.

His honesty and courage had given her new values. At first she could not understand Pepe's indifference to money. Her experience as a pobre had driven her to the harsh belief that "With silver, nothing fails." Silver was protection, a barricade against injustice, a key that turned any lock. She had worked and schemed and gloated over the stacks of silver in her sala. It had brought her fame, luxury, power—but also fear and shame.

She sat up suddenly to stare into the dark room as if the blinding flash of lightning had also revealed to her the startling discovery that silver did not bring the real happiness of life—not her young joy with Ramón, nor María's unselfish love, nor Pepe's deep devotion. She reached over in the dark to touch Pepe's pillow and whispered, "Madre de Dios, bring him home safely. Then I will tell him that I have discovered a new proverb—'With love, nothing fails.' "

Another deep roll of thunder reminded her of cannon and tomorrow's battle. She shuddered over the defenseless men who would die for a lost cause. The long power of Spain was over, lost to the impelling force of a young, vigorous nation whose destiny was to push West with new ideals.

It was not surprising that a new race of men wanted this western country. For four centuries men had been drawn by the lure of this strange, beautiful land, tried to penetrate its secrets, its unknown riches, its mysterious, crystalline silence.

Tules always thought of the country as the breathtaking view after she climbed up the deep cañon of the Río Grande and looked out over Taos valley. She closed her eyes to see again the brilliant sunlight on the tawny sand overlaid with the gray green of sagebrush covering the wide valley, the purple shadow of the deep gorge that twisted through it, the massive blue mountains piling up to sharp white peaks. Beyond the valley the country reached on and on to farther flat-topped mesas, sheer red walls of cañons, and the faint blue outlines of distant peaks against the tremendous dome of the pulsing turquoise sky.

She remembered that childhood day when she had puzzled as to how the country had changed so quickly from Spain to Mexico. Tomorrow it would be called America; but the country would still be the same. Men had come and gone through it with their shouts of victory, but the shape of the mountains, the sunlight on the wide plains, the stillness that breathed of eternity did not change. The words of Tío Florentino came back to her as a far echo: "The puny cries of men in this land are like the wind that travels swiftly before the sun, but leaves no shadow."

She woke at dawn and opened the shutters to take a deep breath of the fresh, clean air. The sky was newly washed, and the bright sunshine dried the parched earth that had soaked up the heavy rain. She welcomed it as a good omen for this important day of August 18, 1846, but she turned back to the room with anxious thoughts of the battle that had begun at Apache Pass. She woke Victorio and Chico and sent them to the plaza to bring her the first reports. She was drinking her last cup of coffee when they rushed back.

"Don Manuel has fled!" Chico panted. "Early this morning he started for Apache Pass, but when he was three leagues out he ordered his men to surrender."

"Surrender!" Tules cried with unbelief.

316

"He took two hundred dragoons and started for Galisteo at a gallop. He has fled to the Río Abajo," Victorio added.

"But the others—the men at Apache Pass?" Tules cried.

"Don Manuel sent word to them to come home. They left the Pass before dawn," Chico said.

"María Santísima, this is beyond belief!" Tules gasped. "Don Diego Archuleta—did he run too?"

"Don Diego tried to hold the army. He pled with the soldiers not to give up. They said they could not win and it was useless to be killed. Don Diego could do nothing, and he rode to the Río Abajo too." Chico shrugged.

"Thanks be to God, but I can't believe it," Tules cried.

"It's God's truth," Victorio said, and his dwarfed body trembled with excitement. "The Americans are marching down a clear road. They will be here this afternoon. The plaza is wild, and people don't know what to do. I am going to climb to Atalaya for the first sight of the Americans."

Tules pulled her reboso over her head and ran to the plaza. She saw the Lieutenant Governor, Don Juan Bautista Vigil, and ran to him to verify this wild story.

"Yes, Don Manuel has gone," he nodded soberly. "At last he saw that it was useless. The surrender will spare many lives. I tried to tell him this two weeks ago. He says he will gather forces in the Río Abajo, but he is finished. He left me to receive the Americans."

"What will you do?" Tules asked.

"What can I do?" The old man turned up empty palms and shook his gray head. "I will receive them in the Palace as gentlemen and pray to God that this is best for my poor country."

The lookout on Atalaya Hill sighted the Army of the West in the distance as it came up on the mesa from the cañon at Apache Pass. When he flashed the signal hysterical people ran from house to house like frightened ants, repeating stories of the tortures the barbarians would inflict. No one knew what to expect.

Pepe came home after noon, a happy grin on his tired face. "God works miracles even when he uses cowards," he said as he kissed Tules.

317

"We have seen the last of Don Manuel. He ran with his pockets filled with gold from both sides. Now he has less to fear from the Americans than from his own people. They would gladly cut off his head."

"Did he plan this all along?" Tules asked.

"Quién sabe?" Pepe's heavy eyebrows shot up as he shrugged. "Diego Archuleta was wild. He called the men cowards to give up their country without firing one shot, but he could do nothing. It is not easy for a patriot like Diego to accept this. But the American army will be here by three o'clock. I need a river to wash off the dust. We must get ready. . . ."

That afternoon the August sun beat down on the crowds that swarmed into the plaza and over the flat roofs. Pepe, Tules, and their household pushed into the deep shade under the portál at the west end of the Palace. People whispered in stricken voices of what the Americans would do. They were unprepared for this swift, surprising turn of fate. Pepe's young daughters clung to his hands, their black eyes wide with fright. At three o'clock the smallest one, Carmel, cried, "Listen! Horses! Drums! God save us!" She began to cry, and Pepe lifted her in his arms.

A wave of muttered sound rose in the hot air as people fell back to make way for the Army of the West. The advance guard entered the plaza from the southeast side and rode around to the center door of the Palace. Tules breathed faster as she heard the bugles and the rapid beat of the drums. She raised herself on tiptoe to watch General Kearny ride in at the head of his troops. He sat stiffly erect and looked straight ahead, his face thin and stern under the short vizor of his high shako. Gold eagle buttons and insignia shone against his dark-blue uniform. He reined in his horse, dismounted, and walked with quick, decisive steps toward the delegation waiting under the portál. Don Juan Bautista Vigil stepped forward, and the representatives of the two warring Governments shook hands.

More and more American soldiers formed a long blue line around the plaza with their colored guidons fluttering above them. The bright sunshine glinted on the guns of the infantry and the sleek horses of the cavalry.

318

Soldiers climbed to the flat roof of the Palace to raise the new flag. Tules stepped into the street for a better view. The flag was pulled up slowly and reached the top of the mast. The Stars and Stripes caught in the breeze, unfurling its broad bands of red and white and the stars on the blue ground. The drums beat, and every soldier raised his hand in salute.

"But listen! Cannon! They're coming to kill us!" Rafaela screamed. The scream was caught up by everyone around them.

"Have no fear, amigos," Pepe's strong voice shouted. "The cannon are on the loma. They will fire thirteen salutes to our new flag. Thank God the cannon are not turned on us."

People crossed themselves as the cannon boomed and children counted the thirteen salutes. Glass splintered and fell out of the Palace windows.

"Viva los Americanos!" Pepe shouted.

Several men joined Pepe in exultant cheers, but most of the people were too stunned, too confused to do anything but stare at the new flag and the new army drawn up around the old plaza. Tules turned to watch Don Juan Bautista Vigil take General Kearny's arm and escort him into the Palace. The Mexican war was over before it began in Santa Fe, and now New Mexico was part of the United States.

"Viva los Americanos! Thank God for this glorious day!" Tules cried as she threw her arms around Pepe.

# 30

THE PALACE of the Governors basked in the hot August sunshine, unconcerned by the drama enacted before its doors. Its thick walls had heard the secrets of Spanish conquistadores, Indian chiefs and Mexican governors. Now it calmly accepted an American general and a fourth government.

Above the flat roofs of the town, the towers at either end of the Palace had been the pinnacles of men's ambition and the heights to which the humble people raised their eyes. Today a flagpole in the center of the plaza rose higher than the towers and the bright American flag rippled in the summer breeze.

Dust from the plaza rose in suffocating waves with the restless activity of the new conquerors. General Kearny rode out of the plaza with his troops to subdue any resistance Manuel Armijo and Diego Archuleta might have fomented in the Rio Abajo. Ten days later he rode in again to report a friendly welcome from the powerful Lower River families. He received delegations of Pueblos, Utes, Comanches and Apaches who came to the Palace to swear allegiance to the new government and sent a cavalry troop to bring the resisting Navajos to terms.

Santa Fe had been a goal the Americans expected to gain only after a hard, bitter campaign. After its bloodless surrender it became the stepping stone for the last thrust to the Pacific. General Kearny led part of his troops through the southern Gila desert to join the conquest of California.

Since this was no time to fight Britain as well as Mexico, the Oregon dispute had been settled by a compromise boundary above the mouth of the Columbia River. This gave the United States the forests of the Northwest, lands and ports of California and the wide plains and mountains of New Mexico and Texas. In this decisive year of

320

1846 the American nation added one-third to its continental area and held undisputed domain from ocean to ocean and from the Gulf of Mexico to Canada.

Santa Fe, at the crossroads of the trails, was strongly guarded to permit troops to move West. After General Kearny left, Colonel Sterling Price took command with the second section of the Army of the West and the Mormon Battalion. Three thousand American soldiers overran the plaza and four hundred white-topped wagons rolled in to trade without paying import duties or diligencia. The traders boasted of retaliating for the long injustices they had suffered.

Armijo's faithless surrender left the ricos too numb to assert themselves. When numbness passed they felt the pains of the vanquished and chafed under galling orders from the arrogant gringos. The ricos' old prerogatives were ignored and their power and herds of sheep had no importance. They muttered that it would have been better to die for their country than to live under the ignominy of these American upstarts.

The appointment of Charles Bent of Taos as governor and Don Carlos Beaubien as one of the three supreme judges added to their resentment. The Taos group had always been "outsiders" who had undermined the power of the ricos.

While the ricos chafed the pobres rejoiced in the new freedom and justice. They were astonished that the American soldiers were not permitted to loot when they had so little money. The soldiers complained that they had not been paid in four months and their summer uniforms were not warm enough for chilly autumn nights. They sold "eagle buttons" from their uniforms for a little cash.

Tules discovered that Rafaela treasured a dozen of these brass buttons and had fallen in love with an American soldier named Frankie. Rafaela's pock-marked face was radiant when Tules offered to take her, Raillitas and Carmel in her carriage to see the new Fort Marcy the soldiers were building on the foothill above the Garita.

The girls giggled and peered at the soldiers' camp on the high mesa while Tules studied the solid adobe walls rising above the slope of the hill. The cannon set in these heavy breastworks commanded all

321

approaches to Santa Fe and made Fort Marcy the pivotal stronghold in the Southwest.

Tules ordered Romulo to stop the carriage on the high bench of the mesa to look at the view spread below them. She turned to look behind her at the towering peaks of the Sangre de Cristo, where frost had turned the aspens to gold flames between the dark evergreens. Above timberline the mountains pyramided to round bare Baldy, already wigged with the first snow. As she looked, reflected sunset light bathed the great barrier in violet radiance. Blue sky and clouds were suffused with rose while a clear band of light outlined the horizon. It was a moment of unearthly beauty, glowing and fading while Tules marveled at it.

When the warm glow faded the mountains were bleak and Tules turned away from them to face the blazing sunset. Golden light washed the adobe houses of the town below, nestled close against the foothill. Gray smoke curled from chimneys and filled the clear air with the incense of burning piñón. Beyond the town the tawny plain spread on and on until it stopped against encircling mountains. To the west the high escarpment of the Jemez was broken by mesas and cañons. To the south three ranges piled against each other in graduated shades of blue; first the low dark cones of Los Cerrillos, then the medium blue of the Ortiz Mountains and beyond them the sloping sides of the Sandias almost melting into the blue of the sky. As the sun plunged over the western rim the mountains glowed with incandescent violet light, as though they were transparent shapes lighted from within by purple flames.

In that wide landscape the huddled town was the only sign of man's habitation. Three armies of conquerors had crossed that desert with no more effect than cloud shadows drifting across the prairie and over the timeless mountains. They had suffered thirst, hunger and exhaustion to follow the lure of the unknown, the mysterious beauty of a strange land. As darkness rose from the tawny earth the land seemed to be sucked back into the elemental forces that had shaped it with millions of years of sand, wind, and rain.

Tules' eyes sought the Ortiz peaks where she had known the terror

322

of wild lonely mountains. It was hard to remember her life with Ramón when they washed gold in the placers at El Real de Dolores. That was so long ago and so much had happened since then that it was like the life of another girl.

Life was a road where the past was forgotten in trying to see beyond the next turn. Pepe was sure the road ahead would be safe under the Americans and his good friend Charles Bent but Tules felt there would be pitfalls. She knew that people were still restless and the ricos muttered of revolution.

She acknowledged that her disappointment was colored by the surly manners of the Americans. At first they had linked her name with Armijo's and watched her as a traitor. The slight respect she received now was only because Governor Bent had passed word that Pepe and Tules were loyal. But Pepe had gone on the annual buffalo hunt and was not here to see that American officers recognized his wife's position and dignity. Por Dios, the Americans spoke to her in the same insulting tone they used to Cuca. They were too ignorant to perceive the distinction between the owner of the best monte sala in New Mexico and a procuress.

Tules shivered as darkness snuffed out the burning sunset and ordered Romulo to hurry home. Santiago Flores met them at the door and grumbled, "You are late. A young officer came to talk to you. He will come back later."

"What now?" Tules demanded. "These Americans are worse than a plague of locusts with their new regulations."

"Perhaps he wants to collect another tax or tell you that all gambling is prohibited," Santiago shrugged.

"I have paid the tax regularly," Tules' eyes flashed. "As for that thin-lipped General who says that gambling is a vice and should be wiped out . . . Válgame Dios, Americans are fools! What would men do if they did not gamble?"

"He would do better if he prohibited these American sharpers from St. Louis and New Orleans. They have loaded dice, marked cards for their poker and their three-card monte is a disgrace to the profession," Santiago said.

"We have a proud, honest profession but Americans think all gamblers are crooks," Tules tapped her foot with irritation. "The officers have not invited me to their ball next week. I've gone to every rico ball for years but now I'm ignored. After all I did to help them get here without a battle! I wish Pepe was here to see that these American burros treated us with proper respect."

"Here comes the young officer," Santiago said from the side of his mouth. "Be careful. Your temper cost us too much one time."

The young man stopped before Tules, flushed awkwardly and said, "Colonel Mitchell asked me to present his compliments, ma'am. I am his aide, Captain Moore. May I see you alone?"

Tules looked at his blond hair, blue eyes and embarrassed face, nodded curtly and led the way to the private room. She wished again that Pepe was here to handle these strange men. She poured wine and watched the young captain's face flush as he accepted his glass.

"Colonel Doniphan has been ordered to march south to join General Wool at Chihuahua and we have to outfit his regiment," Captain Moore explained. "Our men left Missouri in a hurry and have only their summer uniforms. They will need warm clothing this winter. . . ."

"Yes, I have heard them complain of the cold already." Tules' voice was sympathetic but she watched the captain warily. So this was the way the Americans demanded graft! She would tell Pepe that the Americans were no different from Perez or Armijo when it came to forced "donations."

"This campaign has proceeded so quickly and the orders to march to Chihuahua came before we expected them," Captain Moore pulled at his blond moustache and cleared his throat. "My commanding officer is embarrassed by being temporarily out of funds. . . ."

"But the great United States is rich," Tules countered.

"There is no time to send a messenger to Washington and back. Even to send to St. Louis for money would require weeks. We march soon and we must have money to buy food and supplies now. Colonel Mitchell thought you might let us have one thousand dollars. . . ."

324

"That is a large sum," Tules protested, though she knew she would have to pay it for the protection of her monte tables.

"Yes, ma'am, but we know that you lend money. If you could let us have it right away, Colonel Mitchell would sign the note and it would be repaid within ninety days by the United States treasurer. . . ."

"You mean that you want me to *loan* the United States one thousand dollars? A note to be repaid with interest?" Tules demanded. She kept astonished relief out of her voice while she pretended to hesitate over the size of the loan. If Pepe was here he would gladly loan the money without interest; but Pepe did not understand business. The old market training urged her to make a hard bargain. These gringos needed the money; now they could pay for the way they had snubbed her. She shook her head and said slowly, "These are hard times, señor. My country is poor. We welcome the Americans but we do not comprehend their ways. We would be glad to help but we are treated like ignorant peons. If I could talk to your Colonel Mitchell . . . No doubt he will go to the Officers' Ball?"

"Of course, ma'am. You can see him there and talk it over."

"But I have not been invited to the ball," Tules' red lips pouted while her eyes smiled invitingly at the young man.

"That was an oversight, ma'am, I'm sorry. You know how busy we are. Perhaps they thought that at your age and with your husband out of town . . ." Captain Moore floundered in embarrassment and swallowed hard. "If you care to go, the officers would be honored. . . ."

Tules cursed him inwardly for referring to her age but smiled as though she had a sudden, pleasant thought. "As you say, my husband is out of town, so perhaps Colonel Mitchell would escort me himself? It would give us a chance to talk of the loan. . . ."

Captain Moore's fair skin flushed redder but he said quickly, "Of course, ma'am. Colonel Mitchell will consider it a privilege."

Tules rose with smiling dignity and dismissed the young man. "Our country is restless. It requires a little time to accustom ourselves to new ways. I could tell Colonel Mitchell many things. . . . We will discuss the loan at the ball."

She received a formal written invitation the next day and started at once to plan a new gown. She sent for the seamstress and rummaged through the well-filled chest until she found a velvet in pansy purple richly brocaded in white and blonde lace for the ruffles on sleeves and fichu. She stood long hours before the mirror while the hem was pinned in the pleated purple satin underskirt and brocade draped over the fashionable bustle.

"But, Doña Tules, I do not comprehend this of the pillow," the seamstress diffidently touched the bustle.

"It is the style of the Americans," Tules insisted. "Pepe says bustles make ladies look like burros carrying panniers at the back; but what does a man know of style? I have bought a bonnet and cloak for the street."

She reached for a small hat of corded garnet velvet trimmed with a long, curling plume and set it over one eye. Then she pulled a broadcloth cloak over her shoulders and cocked her head toward the mirror to inspect the first hat she had ever owned.

"Ah, Doña Tules, it is of such beauty," the seamstress cried, caressing the plume. "The hat is almost the color of your hair. But your head will feel the cold without a shawl."

"The gringas do not cover their heads," Tules said loftily. "I will give you my old shawl."

She had not been as pleased and excited in years. She was almost glad Pepe was not here to laugh at her frenzied preparations. He never knew what she wore; she was his "little bird" and he never noticed her plumage. But the American officers and the strange gringas, like that young Doña Susan Magoffin, would see that Doña Tules was still the most stylish and handsome lady in Santa Fe.

Cuca, Rafaela and the little girls helped her dress for the ball. She remembered the young Captain's remark about her age and spent extra time applying rouge and powder to hide her wrinkles. At last she was ready—russet hair parted in the middle and wound in curls on either side, high-heeled gold slippers twinkling under her purple skirt, diamond earrings, and necklace shining at her throat. She dabbed perfume on her lace handkerchief and fan and nodded approval of her figure in the mirror. Her green eyes were alight with triumph when Colonel Mitchell handed her into his carriage. He did not understand that Rafaela was to accompany her as her maid and had to make room for the girl.

The carriage drew up at the door of the old Fonda, now patriotically called the "United States Hotel." The ballroom fluttered with American flags and bunting and many kerosene lamps flared against the white walls. Officers in their blue uniforms and ladies in their best silk gowns filled the room.

"We are just in time for the Grand March," Colonel Mitchell said with a quizzical smile as he offered his arm. They marched around and around the room to the jingling music of a guitar, mandolin, and Indian drum. Tules bowed and smiled to friends and preened with satisfaction as she saw the ladies look enviously at her stylish purple gown.

Between dances she sat regally in her chair with Rafaela curled up like a human footstool for her gold slippers. Her green eyes flashed as she exchanged compliments with the officers but her face sobered when Governor Bent whispered of trouble with the descontentos in Taos.

At last she sighed happily and turned to Colonel Mitchell. "Your captain spoke to me of a loan, señor. I shall be honored to loan the United States Government one thousand dollars at two per cent interest per month." She waved aside his thanks with the golden tongs holding her cigarrito and beamed with satisfaction as she whispered to herself, "Por Dios, it is true that silver buys everything."

The news of the badly needed loan brought Tules flattering respect from the officers. By the time Pepe returned from the buffalo hunt Tules was, once more, an ardent supporter of the Americans. Pepe brought back buffalo robes, wooden pails of lard and strings of dried meat to be sold by the vara.

"I have saved such delicacies as the tongue for the officers and my friend Governor Bent," he said, but a frown darkened his good-

327

natured face. "I must warn Bent of trouble Diego Archuleta is start-ing at Taos. He tells everyone that Armijo sold out the country and forced him to agree when Don Santiago Magoffin promised that the Americans would only come to the east bank of the Rio Grande. Archuleta and the Montoyas tell the Indians that the Americans have not kept their word and should be driven out of the country."

"Governor Bent told me something was wrong in Taos," Tules nodded. "What does Padre Martínez say?"

"You know that wily old fox. He is too smart to show his hand but his brain leads the others. It infuriates him that his old enemy, Charles Bent, is governor. He advises the boys in his school to become lawyers instead of priests. He says lawyers are better fitted to ride the burro of democracy than priests. This Taos revolt can be serious and even spread to Santa Fe."

"But the American army is here," Tules reminded him.

"Only part of the army is here," Pepe shook his head. "General Kearny has gone to California; Colonel Doniphan has gone to Chihuahua. The remaining troops are scattered, some in Albu-querque, some at Cebolleta, and half the men in the garrison here are sick. At best the Americans are outnumbered sixty-five to one. If the descontentos can unite the country for revenge and get sup-port from the Indians . . ."

"But you always said the Indians were for the Americans."

"Yes, but they expected the Americans to let them do away with the Mexicans forever," Pepe made the sign for cutting throats. "They do not understand peace after two centuries of war. They would rather count scalps and be sure. Archuleta is poisoning their minds with lies and whisky. They would wipe out the Americans and then the Mexicans and take this as their own country again."

"You must tell the Governor to banish Archuleta in Taos and Tomás Ortiz here or put them out of the way," Tules exclaimed.

"Bent does not believe that the people would dare revolt," Pepe frowned. "Even though he has lived in Taos, he believes with the other Americans that the surrender of New Mexico was final. A new flag doesn't change the customs of the country overnight. The

328

ricos know only one way to hold their power—revolution. They oust one man, put in another. They cannot understand that that way is over. They say now that they were wrong to give in without a fight and they may succeed in starting a rebellion."

Governor Bent laughed at Pepe's worries and told him bombastic talk was typical of the Mexicans. He said no one would dare defy the mighty United States. Pepe went back to the sala to sing his comic songs but he watched men whisper and nod over some secret plot.

"They plan a general massacre," he told Tules grimly the next day. "The leaders are here from Taos, Santa Cruz, San Miguel and the Rio Abajo. Bent will not believe that these men plan a revolt of the whole country at one time. They had the first meeting last night."

"Did you tell Bent of the meeting?" Tules asked.

"He won't believe it is serious," Pepe sighed. "Not even when I told him that his old enemy, Padre Martínez, was here pushing the plan. He thinks everything was settled when the army marched in. If all the Americans are killed, it will mean a long guerrilla war before the United States can conquer this country again."

"Bent should know that," Tules exclaimed.

"I told him the meeting was a family council of the ricos, all related by blood and willing to die for each other. They set the signal for the midnight bell next Saturday, December 19 —"

"But that is only five days from now," Tules cried.

"They postponed the date to give more time to rouse the whole country. They meet again tonight at the Pino's. Válgame Dios, if we could only listen and find out the new date."

The Pino's house was a block away on dusty Calle San Francisco. Tules knew that the sitting room, where the meeting would be held, looked out on the back patio but it would be closely guarded by family peons. The room had high barred windows and thick adobe walls muffled all sound. Tules said no one could hide under the dirt floor or behind the sparse furniture. Pepe went out to the corrals. He could think better outside.

After half an hour he came back beaming and unfolded his plan. "The sitting room has a small high window on the patio and one pane of mica is broken and stuffed with a rag. If we could climb up the cottonwood tree and take out the rag, we could see and hear."

"But, Pepe, you are too heavy to climb out on a limb," Tules reminded him.

"Victorio could make it," Pepe grinned. "He only comes to my belt but his arms are twice as strong as mine."

"Victorio! Of course!" Tules clapped her hands and then hesitated. "But it is dangerous. If they found him, they would cut his throat."

"He will take that chance," Pepe said. "He wants to be a soldier."

"He would do anything for you," Tules smiled.

Victorio grinned with pride and threw back his humped shoulders when they told him. After dark he would climb into the tree from the roof, lower himself to the window and work out the rag. Rafaela would run over the upper passageway of continuous flat roofs and listen beside the chimney where sound was funneled from the room below. If one was caught, there was still a chance for the other to hear the plans. Rafaela's dull eyes glowed with eagerness to save the life of her soldier, Frankie.

To throw off suspicion Tules and Pepe made themselves conspicuous in the sala that night. Pepe sang to his guitar and Tules hovered over the monte tables but her eyes watched the slow hands of the gilt clock. After midnight she nodded to Pepe and joined him in their room.

"We shouldn't have sent Victorio," she cried. "He would be back by now if they hadn't caught him. Pobrecito!"

"A man can die in no better way than by serving his country," Pepe quoted.

An hour later they heard Victorio's signal and dragged him in. His shirt was torn from the branches but his shriveled face was alight with success. Rafaela followed him, her face, hands, and reboso black with soot from the chimney. Both ran to the fireplace to warm their numbed hands.

"I almost froze," Victorio's teeth chattered. "The dogs barked and

330

I thought the mozo would see me but he had his eyes on the ground."

"Who was there?" Pepe asked quietly.

"Twenty men," Victorio counted them on his fingers. "The three Pinos, the Vicario and Tomás Ortiz—he will be governor; then Diego Archuleta, who will head the army; then his father-in-law, Don Antonio Maria Trujillo; next to him, Padre Martínez of Taos and two other padres I do not know; then Don Santiago C. de Baca, Don Augustín Durán, and Don José Maria Sanchez. The mother of the Pinos was the only woman. The men signed their names and she hid the paper up in the vigas. . . ."

"The traitors plan to kill all the Americans at once," Rafaela cried, her eyes wide with fright.

"When? What date?" Tules demanded.

"Midnight of Noche Buena," Victorio said. "That gives them nine days to get ready. They said that Noche Buena was the American fiesta of Christmas and the soldiers would be drunk and it would be easy to kill them in their beds. The signal will be the midnight bell for the Misa del Gallo. They will hide in the church, rush out and seize the guns in the Palace and kill everyone. In every settlement it will be the same signal of the bell for midnight mass. Diego Archuleta left tonight for Taos to prepare everything there."

"Go to Governor Bent and tell him now, Pepe," Tules urged.

"He won't believe me," Pepe frowned. "It is better for you to go to Colonel Price. He trusts you because of your loan. Make him believe this. There is no time to lose if Archuleta has already left for Taos."

Early the next morning Tules put on her new velvet hat and cloak and went to the office of Colonel Price in the Palace. When she told him of the plot he called in the Secretary of State, Don Donaciano Vigil, to discuss this serious news.

"I told Governor Bent of the conspiracy but he refused to believe it," Don Donaciano nodded and checked the list Tules handed him. "These men must be put in prison at once. We will follow Diego Archuleta to Taos and send the Alcalde to take Tomás Ortiz here before he can do more harm."

331

"I will see Governor Bent and act immediately," Colonel Price agreed and then turned to Tules. "I don't know how to thank you, Doña Tules. Every American here owes his life to you. Without your loyalty this would have been a bloody mess."

In spite of Governor Bent's mild protests most of the conspirators were locked in jail by noon. A few hours later Don Augustín Durán and Don José Maria Sanchez signed a written confession of the whole plot.

Tules raged when she heard that Tomás Ortiz had escaped, disguised as an Indian servant girl. "The trouble is not over," she cried. "Those two leaders, Diego Archuleta and Tomás Ortiz, will never stop plotting until they are buried."

Noche Buena passed in noisy Christmas revel instead of massacre. On the surface everything seemed happy and peaceful but Tules' long training made her suspect that the ricos had not forgotten their grievances. After the report of Colonel Doniphan's victory at Brazitos on Christmas Day the ricos conceded that the American army might conquer all Mexico but their thoughts were still vindictive. Manuel Armijo had not dared to return from Durango but word came that Archuleta and Ortiz were riding at night from village to village. If they could rouse the Indians and the ignorant country people they might still incite a general riot.

Early in January the trial of the conspirators began and Tules and Pepe went to the packed court room in the Palace every day. They were astonished to see that an American lawyer, Captain Agney, had been named to defend the prisoners. He argued that these men were not traitors since they had not become citizens of the United States; they had suffered from misguided loyalty but now they promised to become patriotic Americans. The judge reprimanded the prisoners and set them free.

"These gringos are too soft," Tules muttered. "They will learn that the only thing a Mexican understands is a kick in the pants, but it will be too late. They have planted the seeds of more trouble."

"The Americans think they are planting the seeds of justice and good will," Pepe said patiently. "Those seeds take a long time to bear fruit and we may not live long enough to see them. Charles Bent persuaded the judges to be lenient. He said it was better policy. He is a good man and he cannot believe that men are evil. He is going to Taos tomorrow to see his family. I will go with him."

"Oh, no, Pepe, you have done enough," Tules caught his arm. "There is always trouble in Taos. Diego Archuleta has come out of hiding now the trial is over. He will make trouble there. I beg you not to go."

"Charles Bent has been my friend for many years," Pepe said. "I tried to persuade him not to go but he says that Taos is his home and the people are his friends. He fed them and cared for them when they were sick. He says he can talk to them and settle this trouble. He needs me and I will go with him."

"Oh, Pepe, for the love of God, don't go," Tules begged and threw her arms around his neck. "We have been through so much. Stay here with me and enjoy this new life. I need you, too. I have a feeling you will have bad luck. Ah, lindo, I would die if any harm came to you."

"Hush, my little bird," Pepe kissed her. "You know that I can take care of myself. Bent may be right. He may talk to the descontentos and draw out the poison. He is the best friend our people have and he is my friend. I will come back within a week."

When Tules could not dissuade him, she packed tortillas, baked buffalo tongue and venison for a lunch to tie on his saddle. He left with Governor Bent before dawn for the long, cold ride to Taos.

# 31

TULES OCCUPIED herself in the sala to keep from worrying about Pepe. Her heart was filled with foreboding in spite of the carefree relief men showed now that the trial of the conspirators was over. The three Pinos took the oath of allegiance and loudly toasted their lawyer-defender, Captain Agney. The Captain stuck out his chest and answered with a Missouri saying, "If you can't beat 'em, jine 'em." In gratitude for Tules' help the American officers policed the sala, kicked out drunken soldiers and made themselves at home.

"Business is good," Santiago Flores whispered and rubbed his hands as they assessed the crowded monte tables.

Tules nodded as she looked at the stacks of silver in front of the dealer, Augustus de Marle. By habit she stroked her ring as she watched the bets. It felt heavy and cold and sent a shiver up her spine.

"Watch for trouble tonight," she cautioned Santiago. "I feel bad luck around us. I wish Pepe would come home."

"Don't worry about him. He can take care of himself," Santiago reminded her. "He said he would be away a week."

Six days passed without word from Taos but on the morning of the seventh day Rafaela burst into Tules' room and shrieked, "Madre de Dios, what fiends to kill that poor man in such a way!"

"What do you mean, Rafaela?" Tules asked. "Stop crying. I can't understand you. Who was killed?"

"Maria Santisima, don't you know that the Indians killed Governor Bent two days ago? The messenger brought the news this morning. They will march on Santa Fe. We will all be scalped, murdered. . . ."

"Governor Bent murdered!" Tules cried. "What of Pepe? Did you hear anything of Pepe?"

She could get no sense out of the blubbering girl, caught up a black shawl and ran to the plaza. She was short of breath when she pushed into the waiting room of Colonel Price's office. "Is this true?" she gasped as she waylaid a young officer.

"Yes, ma'am, we were fools to believe these lying hypocrites," he said sternly. "The messenger says all the north is in arms. The people of Don Fernandez de Taos and the Indians went wild; broke into the stores and drank wine and whisky all night. Archuleta and the Indian leaders, Pablo Montoya and Tomasito, harangued them to kill all Americans. We'll hang every traitor this time but that won't give Governor Bent his life."

"Pepe?" Tules cried. "What word . . . is he all right?"

"I don't know," the officer said. "The messenger said Governor Bent was warned to leave but he would not run. The drunken mob came to his house before dawn and yelled for him to come out. He tried to reason with them through the door but they broke it down, shot a dozen arrows into him and scalped him. . . ."

"Maria Santisima," Tules choked, "was Pepe with him?"

"We only had word about his wife and children," the officer said. "Mrs. Bent and her sister dug a hole through the adobe wall with a poker and shovel, pushed the children through and crawled through themselves. They begged the Governor to come but by that time the Indians had broken in and scalped Bent. Neighbors helped disguise the women and children and they escaped."

"The fiends!" Tules cried as tears ran down her cheeks. "I must find the messenger. God grant that Pepe escaped too!"

She waited restlessly in the outer office while the messenger finished his report to Colonel Price.

"It's a revolt of the whole province, the plan of December," a man said, who waited beside her. "Diego Archuleta and Tomás Ortiz planned it and kept the secret this time. They will march on Santa Fe, kill every gringo and everyone who sympathizes with them. The Indians are on the warpath and they show no mercy. . . ." Tules stiffened in dread, recalling the raid on the Salazar rancho.

"Do you calculate that the Army of the West can be licked by drunken savages with bows and arrows, mister?" a tall, lanky Missourian drawled.

"Your troops are scattered," the man shrugged. "Even your horses graze at Galisteo ten leagues away. How will you move your cannon?"

"Kearny and Doniphan should have stayed here," Tules cried. "They were fooled because they marched in without firing a shot. We tried to tell them the ricos would not give up so easily. Now they are ready, armed. . . ."

"You don't know our Uncle Sam nor them boys from Missouri, ma'am," the Missourian drawled. "We'll lick these dirty greasers if it takes the hull United States. Our men are comin' from Albuquerque on the double-quick and day after tomorrow our cannon will roll north. Our boys have been itchin' fer a fight and now they'll shore tear up the earth."

Tules saw Don Donaciano Vigil come out of the office and ran to ask him about Pepe.

"I have not heard his name mentioned on the list. Don't alarm yourself, Doña Tules," he patted her arm. "Pepe hunted buffalo so many years that he knows how to look out for himself. But this is a sad day for our country. Would to God that Kit Carson had been in Taos instead of California! He could have stopped the riot. He will grieve for Bent. If Bent had only listened to us!"

"I am sick with fear. . . ." Tules gasped and swayed dizzily.

Don Donaciano caught her arm, guided her into Colonel Price's office and made her sit down.

"Forgive me . . ." she gasped and pressed her hands over her heart to stop the pain. She recognized the messenger talking to Colonel Price, staggered toward him and cried, "Pepe? Is he all right?"

"I saw him that night," the man nodded. "He tried to get Governor Bent to leave. He had the horses saddled and ready in the corral. . . ."

"Then he got away!" Tules exclaimed.

"No," the man muttered, "the Indians caught him in the corral. . . ."

336

"Maria Santisima, if they murdered Pepe I'll kill them!" Tules shrieked. "Pepe! God have mercy! Ay de . . ." She swayed and caught wildly at her breast as the terrific pain squeezed her heart. She gasped, "If Pepe is dead, let me die. . . ."

Men laid her on the sofa, brought water and ran for the Frenchman, Dr. Mercure. She fought for breath but tried to hold her body rigid against the agonizing pain. The doctor mumbled "Heart attack" and forced her to swallow sharp-tasting medicine. She was hardly conscious that she was placed on an army litter and carried home.

By night returning consciousness brought bitter grief for Pepe. Only Pepe could save her from this suffocation of being sucked down, down in quicksand. She was lost in hopeless sorrow and let the tears stream from her swollen eyes. She tried to comfort Pepe's little daughters but found no words.

The next day Chico shook her shoulder and said, "I am going to Taos with the Volunteers in Captain St. Vrain's company. Let me have one of your mules."

"Yes, take it," Tules mumbled. "Find Pepe. Bring him back."

Later Victorio stroked her hand silently until she opened her eyes and found him kneeling beside her bed. "Oh, Victorio, you loved Pepe too! How can we live without him?"

"I go to Taos to avenge his murder," Victorio told her.

"No, no, Victorio," Tules protested as she looked at his dwarfed body. "Stay here. I can't let you go, too!"

"Captain St. Vrain has given me permission to ride with the baggage wagon. I will be a soldier," Victorio said proudly and tried to straighten his humped shoulders. "Pepe said I could shoot as well as any man. I will kill those fiends who scalped Pepe. Give me your blessing."

"Ay de mí, God is punishing me. He takes everything from me," Tules cried as she looked into Victorio's eager eyes. She made the sign of the cross and whispered, "Go with God."

Rafaela sobbed that her soldier, Frankie, would freeze in the heavy snow as he marched with the American army to Taos. Then she exulted over good reports of the battles at Santa Cruz and Embudo where American guns and cannon had routed the insurrectos.

Five days later Santiago Flores rushed in with news from Taos. "The Americans won but it was a fierce battle—four hundred gringos against fifteen hundred Indians and Mexicans. They barricaded themselves in the pueblo and shot from the high windows and roof of the church. The next morning soldiers ran through the rain of bullets and arrows and blasted a hole through the walls of the church. When the roof burned people ran out and begged for mercy. The Americans hanged the Indian leader, Tomasito. They should have killed all of them."

"Madre de Dios, what of my Frankie?" Rafaela screamed. "And Chico and Victorio?"

"Quíen sabe!" Santiago shrugged. "The army left to settle trouble in Mora and Las Vegas. The insurrectos attacked on the Mora, killed eight gringos and burned Turley's Mill. They will track the insurrectos but they can't search all the lonely cañons."

"Ay de mí, they'll hide and pick off the soldiers like rabbits. . . ." Rafaela sobbed.

"There will be a victory celebration here tonight," Santiago watched Tules' sad face. "You should come into the sala for a little . . ."

"No, I never want to see the sala again," Tules shook her head. "You take charge of it now. Pepe is gone and my life is over."

The next day Rafaela ran to her shrieking the death wail. "Madre de Dios, a messenger from Taos says Frankie and Victorio were killed. . . ."

"Victorio too!" Tules murmured as she lifted dull, heavy eyes. "Pobrecito! But he died as a soldier. God give him peace!"

She had cried so much that her eyes and heart were dry. Her long hands hung listlessly as she heard Rafaela sob. Every few minutes the girl lifted her swollen face and screamed, "Frankie! Victorio! Pepe! Come back. God have mercy on us and bring them back!" Cuca took the hysterical girl out of the room.

Tules' strength returned slowly but she refused to leave her room.

338

She huddled by the corner fireplace and hardly heard the chatter of Pepe's daughters or Cuca. She listened with mute lips when Chico returned with a glorified account of his battles. He said Victorio had been shot as he drove the baggage wagon close to the walls of the fortified pueblo church. He had been buried near Pepe in the campo santo.

"Pray for them," Tules murmured. "I will join them soon. This doctor gives me medicine to strengthen my heart but it does no good. My heart is broken."

When the long summer days came she sat under the portal in the patio and watched luminous clouds drift across the blue sky. For the first time in her life she sat in idleness, only moving to keep within the cool shade. She counted each bright hollyhock unfold and lazily followed the flight of velvet-winged butterflies and hummingbirds as they hovered over the sweet-scented honeysuckle. She listened to the mockingbirds in their amole cages imitate distant meadow larks and smiled as the parrot's raucous voice scolded them. Sunny days slipped by like a vacant dream while she waited for Pepe to waken her with his love.

She sighed when the great cottonwood tree near the corral turned to gold and the autumn chill drove her inside to sit by the fireplace again. Her body had lost its supple slenderness and she moved slowly. She wore an old pair of Pepe's moccasins on her swollen feet and hid them under her black cotton skirt. She did not care what she wore or how she looked. She refused to see anyone but her family and Santiago when he came to make his reports.

In spite of the doctor's warning, she craved rich food and found her only pleasure in eating. She showed Rafaela how to pat tortillas to a proper thinness and brown the puff-paste squares of buñuelos in hot, deep fat. She stood over the cook as she whirled the wooden pestle to make foaming, hot chocolate. The kitchen was aromatic with the herbs Tules used as she tried old recipes for cakes sprinkled with anise and cinnamon.

In the spring Santiago Flores came to her, his black brows drawn together in worried frown. "I have managed the sala for a year now,"

339

he said. "You are better and you must come back. Business does not go well."

"But why?" Tules asked. "The Americans have given us peace, thank God. You say we have a new governor, this John Calhoun. He was an Indian agent and he will even subdue the Navajos."

"Yes, the American ways are better," Santiago agreed. "The Americans have captured Chapultepec in Mexico City and the war is over. Santa Anna will not care about the loss of these northern provinces if he can get the foreign armies out of Mexico."

"Then why do you bother me about the sala?" Tules shrugged.

"Everything has changed," Santiago turned up empty palms. "The new law requires a license of two thousand dollars a year for a gambling sala."

"Two thousand dollars! Válgame Dios, that will ruin us!" Tules exclaimed with a return of her old spirit. "Get the account book, Santiago. I will have to collect my loans to pay this license. I loaned money to the United States when they needed it and now they will ruin me. I will talk to that Governor Calhoun. . . ."

They went over the account book and counted the cash in the money room. The sala had run at a loss and Tules blamed herself for indulging in idleness and not paying attention to Santiago's reports. Now she would have to take charge again to save the sala.

Submerged energy came back as she called Rafaela to help her dress. Even by lacing her corset she could not squeeze into her old dresses. "Bien, I will have new dresses," she said. "Tonight it is better that I should wear this cheap black cotton skirt. One should look poor to ask for a reduction of taxes."

Rafaela washed her hair with amole roots and Tules frowned at the white hairs glistening among the red. "Tell Cuca to bring the Spanish dye," she ordered. When Cuca finished Tules' hair had a bright copper glint.

"That is the color your hair used to be at Manzano when the salt air bleached it," Cuca beamed and rested her fists on her fat hips. "Thank God you have come to life again. You are younger than I am. It was foolish of you to act like a dead stump. . . ."

340

"I have lived three lives already," Tules smiled affectionately at the concern on Cuca's hard, painted face. "By now we should have grandchildren to take care of us and let us smoke by the fire in peace. Your hair is dyed black and mine is dyed red but we know what is underneath."

"You are still handsome and your eyes shine again," Cuca flattered her since her business depended upon the popularity of Tules' sala. "You will put the old life and spirit into the place again."

Tules shook her head as she studied her face in the mirror. There were deep lines around her mouth and eyes and across her forehead. She massaged the loose flesh under her chin and said, "At least my fingers are not too stiff to deal cards." She pushed diamond rings over her swollen joints and wound three gold chains around her wrinkled throat. Her green eyes flashed with the old challenge and she held her shoulders back as she walked toward the sala.

She caught her breath as she looked into the familiar room and remembered Pepe's laughing eyes when he played his guitar near the orchestra. Santiago Flores ran to welcome her and they spoke to the few men at the bar. Tules was shocked to find the monte tables almost deserted and the sala dingy and dilapidated.

"We will close the sala for a week," she announced. "It must be cleaned and refurnished. We will open again with a big fiesta."

Tules decided that the house must be white inside and out to advertise the renovation. Women coated the long low walls on the outside with white plaster and smoothed glistening yeso on the inside. A width of small-figured red calico pasted over the lower part of the wall prevented the yeso from rubbing off.

Tules jerked the faded red velvet curtains from the deep windows and ordered them burned. She remembered that Doña Trinidad Armijo had called the velvet curtains "rags" and wished she could burn all memories of the Armijos in the same fire. She hoped haughty Doña Trinidad had no comforts on the isolated ranch at Lemitar where she and Manuel hid.

When the windows were washed and tobacco stains scrubbed from the plank floor Tules took pride in the sala again.

"The foot of the master is the best fertilizer for the land," Cuca quoted and nodded at these signs of returning life.

The crowd at the opening fiesta was almost like the old days except that Pepe was not there to improvise a welcoming song. Tules wore a new black silk dress, jewels and brilliant-studded combs in her copper hair. Her figure was matronly but she moved with grace and distinction. An artist drew her portrait and young gringos questioned her for stories of old times. Once again she was a figure of legend, mystery and fame.

Governor Calhoun did not come to her fiesta so Tules went to his office the next day and used her wiles to persuade him to reduce the two-thousand-dollar license. The Governor said sternly that it was his duty to enforce American laws but suggested that she employ a young lawyer named Hugh Smith to study her case. Tules remembered that Pepe said "Americans don't give bribes. They hire a smart lawyer."

Hugh Smith advised her to pay the license before the taxes grew worse and to put her cash in the new bank, which had opened in the rooms to the north of her sala. Tules was distrustful when she handed over sacks of good, hard dollars and received nothing for them but a little book with black figures.

Every morning she took the winnings to the bank but each month there was less profit for the house. The first influx of Americans had passed. Gold had been discovered in California and adventurers rushed through New Mexico to reach the booming gold camps.

Tules found notes for old loans and set about collecting them. One was a loan to George Coulter for five hundred dollars. He ran the rival monte sala in the United States Hotel and had taken away most of the trade the year Tules sat idle. Now he complained that she had taken the trade away from him with her newly furnished sala. He offered to pay half the loan in cash and the other half in percentage if she would game at his tavern for two weeks.

Santiago Flores objected to the plan but Tules tossed her head with the old spirit, "Por Dios, we will win both ways. I will recover my loan and then bring the crowd back from that cheap tavern."

"You are not strong enough to deal monte all night," Santiago protested. He added slyly, "It is because you are flattered that even your rival acknowledged that you are the best monte dealer in the territory."

The first week's percentage was favorable but Tules said, "The gringos go to that tavern, but few ladies play. It is not gay and friendly like the old days."

"Gringos have no pleasure," Santiago shrugged. "They are all business, business. If our people lose, they wait until good luck favors them next time. If the gringos lose, they are angry. I wish you would not go to that tavern again. You look tired."

"It will only be another week," Tules said. She did not add that her heart fluttered and her breath was short after the long, exhausting nights at the monte table.

When she sat down to deal the next night she automatically rubbed her ring but it felt cold and heavy. She looked around to see who had the evil eye and saw many strange faces. She recognized Captain Moore who had asked her for the loan to the United States four years before. He was no longer the fresh-cheeked young officer. His civilian clothes were rumpled and dirty, his nose was the color of red wine and his tongue was thick. At Tules' warning glance Augustus de Marle touched his pistol on the table before him. Moore won two hundred dollars on his first bets and then began to lose.

Tules' fingers had regained their old suppleness the past week. She dealt the layout on the four squares on the green cloth, waited until the bets were placed, then drew the cards from the bottom of the pack and placed them face up. Augustus de Marle's long arm swept in the losing bets and paid the winners. He took Moore's last dollar.

"God damn you, you dirty crook," Moore cursed. "Thash my dollar on the sish spot and you pay me double. Give me my money or I'll . . ."

Tules saw him pull out his pistol and wave it wildly toward her. She bent swiftly to the left and the bullet whizzed past her. Moore aimed at de Marle but missed him. De Marle and the other men

343

grabbed the wild pistol and pulled Moore out of his chair. He cursed drunkenly and fought the men who dragged him away. In the noise and excitement Tules felt the old pain clutch her heart and slumped over the table.

Dr. Mercure scolded and shook his finger with his quick French gestures. "This you cannot do again, madame. The heart is bad and you are no longer young. You must make life slow, quiet. One more time like this, madame—pouff—c'est fini."

# 32

TULES DRAGGED herself out of bed to look at the fresh snow that had fallen before the New Year's dawn of 1852. It sparkled with a thousand diamonds in the cold clean air. A powdery bit fell softly as a blue jay flew out of the brittle vines. Beyond her window white frosting edged the brown walls of low adobe houses. The first dazzling rays of sunshine warmed the towers of the Palace and threw them into high relief against the snow-powdered mountains and the turquoise sky. Tules sighed as she looked at the familiar scene and thought of the years she had lived in this house. A new year was beginning but she would not live to see it through. She would not listen to the spring wind nor watch for the first green leaves.

It would not matter to her that this country was now a territory of the United States, governed by new men and new laws. She was too tired to adjust herself to new ways, as the ricos and padres had done. The revolutionists of five years ago were now leading citizens. Padre Martínez of Taos and the vicar, Padre Juan Felipe Ortiz, had been the first two presidents of the Council. Diego Archuleta and Tomás Ortiz held important offices. Tules shrugged and repeated to herself the Missouri saying, "If you can't beat 'em, jine 'em."

Manuel Armijo was the only politician who had not returned to Santa Fe. He stayed within the safety of his ranch at Lemitar and managed his trading wagons in the south. Men said he was a mountain of fat and his Dearborn carriage sagged under him as he drove over the sandy roads. Tules shook her head as she thought of imperious Manuel turned into a lump of suet.

But everything had changed, even in her own house. Last year Rafaela had died in the typhoid epidemic and she missed the girl's patient devotion. Raillitas and Carmel took care of her now, but they were young and inexperienced. Carmel's round face and laughing eyes reminded her of Pepe and she longed for Pepe's hearty warmth. All the joy of life had passed with Pepe. Without his love and courage, her days were empty.

Santiago Flores managed her sala and his wife, Refugio, managed her house. Their little daughter, Delfinea, and Pepe's girls made up her household. They sat with her through the dark nights when she fought for breath. It was only her fear of the smothering darkness that forced her to struggle to live in a lonely world.

Cuca was the only friend left from the old days. She sat beside Tules' fire and burnished the dull hours with her earthy wit. Today she gave Tules a cheerful New Year's greeting and bustled around the room like a hungry hen. She cocked her head to one side, looked at Tules' gloomy face and scolded, "Válgame Dios, at least you could wish me good luck for the New Year. Your face is as long as the Mother of Sorrows. With all your money, you have nothing to worry about."

"At last I have learned that silver buys nothing to feed the heart —not even one easy breath," Tules sighed. Maria used to say "Dry bread eaten with love is better than a banquet eaten with sorrow. Pues, when the years give us sense we are too old to use it. I am tired. . . . Ask the Vicario to come to see me tomorrow."

"You don't need the Vicario," Cuca's painted face grinned cheerfully. "You look better today. You'll deal monte again. . . ."

"No, some morning I will not be here and there are certain matters to settle first." Tules raised her chin with her old determination. "I will arrange with the Vicario for the best funeral money can buy and I want you and Santiago to see that it is carried out."

"Whatever you say," Cuca shrugged. "Shrouds have no pockets."

"When that time comes I want to wear my best black silk and this plain gold ring. It has brought me luck. I count on you, Cuca. Relatives forget as soon as the eyes are closed."

"We will do what we can," Cuca agreed but her eyes had a greedy gleam.

"These matters of the bank confuse me. I like to feel the weight of money in my hand. Then I know . . ." Tules lifted the blanket

346

that covered her in bed and pointed to the largest of two heavy money sacks lying beside her. "This is for the church. . . ."

"Dios de mi vida, that will make up to the Vicario for the hard ways of this new archbishop. Lately the Vicario has had to water his wine," Cuca sniffed. Everyone knew that the young Frenchman, Archbishop John B. Lamy, had started a thorough house cleaning of the churches and priests in his new diocese. Padre Martínez in Taos rebelled against the strict regulations brought from Rome but the deposed Vicario accepted the new superior with tolerant grace.

"I owe the church for many years . . ." Tules mused.

"Pues, you would be bored with nothing to do in Purgatory. If masses get you through there with dispatch . . ." Cuca nodded, rubbed her thumb on her first finger and sighed. "The path to Heaven is steep but the road through life is harder. You insure yourself for eternity while I worry about a crust of bread for today."

"You have found out every secret since I was young, Cuca. Can you shut your lips on one more?" Tules shifted her body in the narrow bed and watched Cuca's small eyes squint with wariness. She lifted up the smaller money sack with both hands and tested its weight. Then she held it toward Cuca and said, "Take it. I want to be sure you have a crust of bread when I am gone."

"Madre de Dios, do you give this money to me?" Cuca cried and took the heavy sack. "But it must be a thousand pesos! I have never had a hundred pesos of my own in my life. What will I do with it? Ah, niña, this is too much." But as she said it, she hugged the sack to her plump bosom.

"Tell no one you have it," Tules warned. "Bury it deep."

"But how can I thank you?" Cuca cried and tears ran through the paint on her old cheeks. "Now I can have a little place of my own, even one room. I can stop haggling with men, driving those girls. I can take off these cursed corsets and sleep all night. Ah, Tules, you are good. You must get well. Then we will laugh about all we did yesterday and drink wine to tomorrow."

Tules shook her head. "Go now and hide the sack. I am tired."

The next morning the Vicario made the sign of the cross as he

347

came near her bed and said, "I was afraid when you sent for me.
. . . But you look better."

"I told them to tell you not to come ringing the little bell, Padre.
I only wanted a visit with my old friend." She smiled at the concern
on his red face and motioned for him to sit by the fire. He had hurried to her without shaving the grey stubble from his jowls or changing his grease-spotted cassock.

"If you wish to confess . . ."

"If I recalled my sins I could not repent. I would enjoy them all
over again," Tules teased him. They smiled with the knowledge each
had of the other through long years. "My heart is battered, padre.
Soon it will refuse to march. Now, while my head is clear, I must
settle my affairs and arrange for my funeral."

"There is no need of such haste," the Vicario shook his head but
answered her questions about fees for the funeral. She groaned over
the cost and called Heaven to witness that everything was too dear
but she insisted on a high mass. Then there was fifty dollars for each
time the bearers would rest their shoulders and place the casket on
the ground; fifty dollars for tolling the bell when she died and again
before her funeral; thirty dollars for the grave and thirty more for
digging and filling it; charges for vestments, incense, holy water,
candles and the great cross, musicians and chanters. The Vicario put
down each item with the stub of a pencil, added them and handed
the paper to Tules. She took the paper cautiously and bent her jaded
eyes on the total.

"More than sixteen hundred dollars! For the love of God that is
too much!" she cried.

"You could give up the tolling of the bells. You won't hear them,"
the Vicario pursed his heavy lips.

"No, no," Tules protested. "All my life I have heard the bells
toll for others. I must have them."

"A low mass would cost less," the Vicario suggested shrewdly. "And
you could save on candles and music."

"But I want the high mass and many candles. And how could I
go to my grave without music? We forgot the wine for each of the

men who carry me. They must toast me in a last adios." She watched the Vicario add the item of wine and sighed, "It costs more to die than to live."

"But these costs you must charge to pomp and vanity, my daughter," the Vicario reproved her. "It is true that they are the blessed rites of the church, but they are not necessary. You know that only one thing is necessary—the love and forgiveness of God—and that is free to all who repent."

"Each is as God makes him, sometimes even worse. God knows my life and I cannot change it now," Tules shook her head. "Besides there is satisfaction in a good funeral. Make out the bill and I will pay it now. Relatives never dig graves as deep as their pockets."

She unfastened the money sack and began to count out the gold while the Vicario's knotted fingers signed the bill with his name and rubric. "Times have changed. I am too old to fit into new ways. I shall retire and let young men carry on the faith. But it would ease your heart to receive the blessed sacraments. If you want to confess . . ."

He watched her shake her head and saw the lines of suffering on her pale face and the tired droop of her eyelids. Soberly making the sign of the cross, he left her.

She dozed and woke with relieved satisfaction of the morning's business. A grand funeral would be her last triumph. She could almost smell the incense and see the candles and the great gold cross, hear the music and chanting. The price was high but she had made a good bargain. The Vicario had only listed the cost of a funeral but she was paying the debts of a lifetime.

By her intention it included prayers for lost Doña Carmen and old Caterina, for her mother, "Nana Luz," Rafaela and Maria. It paid for the marriage mass she and Ramón did not have and the burial of her only child. It asked forgiveness for the murder of Ramón and Pedro and mercy for those souls who died in anger and violence. It comforted her with prayers for Pepe and Victorio. She closed her eyes longing to feel Pepe's strong hand guiding her through the darkness.

The next day she sent for the young attorney, Hugh Smith, who had brought suits to collect her bad debts. He would know how to write her last will so there would be no mistake with these new American laws. Her mouth drooped as she thought that it was no bargain to give away everything she owned. Her hard-won money would run through the fingers of her only heirs, Lucita and Chico.

She left Lucita her house, furniture, silver plate, carriage, clothes and jewels. She hoped Lucita would save the jewels, at least, for her children. Chico had gone to the California gold fields, returned in rags and she had given him money to pay his debts. She left him half her stock of mules though she knew he would sell them in a week. She appointed Santiago Flores guardian of Pepe's daughters and left enough to care for them until they married. After she signed her shaky signature and rubric to the will, Santiago, Don Gaspar Ortiz and the Vicario witnessed it and promised to act as executors.

"You will be easier now," Santiago rubbed his hands with satisfaction over his part of the will. "When it is warm you will come to the sala again. The blood runs slowly in this winter wind."

"The wind leaves no shadow," Tules sighed.

When they left Tules pulled the covers around her and shivered. Her forehead and feet were clammy with cold sweat. Cuca brought hot stones and stirred the fire but it did not relieve the deathly chill. She turned her face to the wall as slow tears gathered in her eyes. There was nothing more to do. She felt as naked as though she had already been stripped of her grave clothes.

She woke with the pain squeezing her heart and looked around the dusk-filled room with terror. She was dying, alone and helpless. She held herself rigid against the pain, sucked in the air and shook in panic. Like a frightened child she longed for her mother's comforting hand. Her thought reached out for Maria who had been as dear as a mother.

"Maria, help me," she cried aloud. "It is dark, I am alone . . . afraid. Help me, Maria! Ay, Madre de Dios . . ."

Cuca heard the scream and called to the girls to bring more hot stones and vinegar water.

"Pobrecita," she murmured as she moistened Tules' dry lips. "Death knocks at every door, though the poor welcome it and the rich try to drive it away. I will send for Lucita."

When Lucita came Tules' dulled mind thought she was. Maria. She called constantly for Maria to help her, pray for her, give her peace. "Get the Vicario, Maria," she begged. "You told me of the love of God but I would not listen. Pray now that He will be merciful . . ."

When the Vicario came her sunken eyes stared at him. "I must confess," she mumbled. "I have many sins . . ."

"Do you repent in your heart?" the Vicario prompted gently. "Ask God to forgive you. He will hear you."

Her voice gained strength as she poured out the burden of her sins. The Vicario placed the wafer on her lips and anointed her with holy oil. She murmured, "Now I can go. I am clean and at rest."

"Go with God, daughter," he murmured as he blessed her.

After midnight she woke and gasped for breath. "Maria," she called in panic, "stay with me. It is so dark. I am afraid. Light more candles, Maria. Don't leave me."

Cuca and Lucita lighted the candles and brought them close to the head of the bed. Tules pulled herself up with a final spurt of strength and stared beyond the room. "Maria Santisima," the words fluttered out with her last breath, "such glorious light . . ."

# Glossary

Free translation and spelling conform to local usage in New Mexico, where the harsh Castillian z has become the softer Latin-American s. Indian words are also used for native herbs, place names, and so forth.

## A

**abayalde Mejicano**
Mexican face powder

**abigeo**
cattle thief

**acequia**
irrigation ditch

**adiós**
good-by

**aficionado**
enthusiast

**agua fria**
cold water

**aguardiente**
Mexican brandy

**A lanzas!**
To your lances!

**alcalde**
sheriff

**alegría**
homemade rouge

**alma de mi alma**
soul of my soul

**almueres**
15 pounds (dry measure )

**alza**
place your bets; ready

**amole**
soap root

**arroyo**
dry gulch

**Arroyo Hondo**
Deep Gulch

**a sus órdenes**
at your service

**Atalaya Hill**
Watchtower Hill

**atole**
corn meal gruel

**Ave María Purísima**
For heaven's sake

**Ay de mí**
Woe is me

**Ay, qué caray, hombres**
What the hell, fellows

**Ay, qué hombrecito**
What a fine little boy

## B

**baile**
dance

batea
flat bowl

Bibirón
great snake (mythological)

bien
well

bienvenida
welcome

biscochitos
short bread

bruja
witch

brujería
witchcraft

buñuelos
crullers

buscones
searchers

## C

caballada
horse herd

caballero
gentleman

cabrón
he-goat, fool

caciques
Indian chiefs

cállate, hombre
shut up, man

Callejón de los Burros
Burro Alley

campo santo
cemetery

Cañon del Infierno
Hell's Canyon

354

cantina
bar, saloon

cantón
canton, province

capitán
captain

Caramba!
Darn it!

caravana
caravan

carreta
oxcart

carreteros
cart drivers

carros
carts, wagons

Catalán
Catalonian

centavo
cent

chamaco
boy, kid

chicharrones
cracklings

chimajá
wild parsley

china
Chinese, curly-head

chiquita
little one

chulo
darling

chuza
gambling game with balls

ciboleros
  buffalo hunters

cigarrito
  cigarette

comadre
  godmother

comandante militar
  military commander

cómo no
  of course, why not

cómo te va
  how do you do

con permiso
  if you please

con su licencia
  with your permission

copla de amor
  love verses

corbels
  wooden brackets supporting beams

cordilleras
  mountain range

corrida
  sporting event, or,
  ballad

cuándo
  when, although

cuartillo
  quarter cent

curandera
  medicine woman

### D

dedalera
  digitalis

descontentos
  malcontents

diligencia
  graft (slang)

Dios de mi vida!
  Good gracious!

Dios mio!
  Good Lord!

Dios te salve!
  God save you!

Dios y Libertad!
  God and Liberty!

dueñas
  chaperones

### E

El Gallo
  cock, chicken pull

El Ojo del Gigante
  Giant's Spring

El Real de Dolores
  mining town of Dolores

El Viejo Amor
  My old love

empanaditas
  small mince pies

entrada
  entrance

### F

fanega
  1.60 bushels

fufarraw
  to spend lavishly

### G

galán
  gallant, dandy

gambucinos
  underground miners
garita
  prison
gente fina
  fine people, upper class
gobernador, -a
  governor, governor's wife
gringo
  American
grito
  cry; proclamation of revolution
grito de Dolores
  Proclamation from Dolores
guapo
  handsome, stylish

## H

hacienda
  country home
Hasta la vista
  Until I see you again
Hasta luego
  Until we meet again
Hola, compadres
  Hello, comrades
hombre
  man
hombrecito
  little man, male child

## I

inocente
  innocent, half-wit
insurrectos
  insurrectionists

356

## J

jaboncillos
  small soap cakes
jacál
  cruc̄e brush shelter
jerga
  handwoven carpet
jornada
  day's journey
jota
  Spanish dance
joven
  youth, young fellow
junta
  meeting
juzgado
  jail

## K

kiva
  Indian council chamber

## L

La Bajada
  The Descent
Laguna del Perro
  Dog Lake
La Paloma Blanca
  White Dove
linda mía
  my sweet one
loma
  hill top
Los Cerrillos
  Little Hills

Los Luceros
  village of Lucero family

Los Padillas
  village of Padilla family

## M

madre
  mother, camp cook (slang)

Madre de Dios!
  Good Heavens! (lit., "Mother of God")

maldita puta
  cursed bitch

maldita sea
  curses on you

malva
  wild mallow (medical herb)

mamá
  mother

mamacita
  dear little mother

manifiesto
  proclamation

mantilla
  lace scarf for head

mantón de Manila
  embroidered shawl from Manila

manzano
  apple tree

María Santísima
  Holy Mary

mayordomo
  head overseer

mescal
  liquor from maguey plant

mistela
  hot spiced brandy

monte
  mountain

mozo
  servant

muchacha
  girl

muchos años
  many years

mujeres
  women

mulas
  mules

muletas
  red flag used by bullfighters

muy borracho
  very drunk

muy hombrón
  very manly

## N

Nana Luz
  Grandmother Luz

niña
  little girl

no hay mas remedio
  no remedy

no importa
  it doesn't matter

nombre de Dios
  for God's sake

novio
  bridegroom, fiancé

## O

ojalá!
   would to God! . . .

Ojo de Dolores
   Dolores Spring

olla
   pot

órdenes
   orders

oshá
   wild celery (medical herb)

otro toro
   another bull

## P

padre
   father

Padre Jesús
   Lord Jesus

Padre Mina
   Spirit of the Mines

paisanos
   countrymen

parroquia
   parish

paso doble
   Spanish dance, two-step

patrón, -a
   master, mistress

pecadores
   sinners

pelados
   paupers, tramps

pendejo
   fool

Penitentes
   Penitent Brothers (a religious
      order)

peón
   day laborer

peso
   one dollar

peyote
   intoxicating plant

pobrecitos
   poor things

pobres
   poor people

poncho
   blanket coat

por Dios
   for God's sake

por el amor de Dios
   for the love of God

por favor
   please

por la vida de quién sabe quién
   goodness knows

por mi amor
   by my love

por qué
   why

por supuesto
   of course

portal
   porch, veranda

posole
   hog and hominy

pronunciamiento
   proclamation

pues
  so then

puestos
  market stalls

punche
  native tobacco

**Q**

qué hay
  hello

que hombrón
  what a man!

que mala suerte
  what bad luck

querido
  beloved

qué tal
  how goes it?

quién sabe
  who knows?

**R**

rancheros
  ranchers

real
  coin (12½ cents)

reboso
  shawl

ricos
  rich people

Rio Abajo
  Lower River

Rio Arriba
  Upper River

rubia
  redhead

**S**

sala
  drawing room

sal Andaluza
  Andalusian salt

sal drástica
  purgative salt

salud, amigos
  to your health, friends

salud y pesetas
  health and wealth

Santo Niño
  Christ Child

saqueo
  sack, pillage

señor, señora
  mister, mistress

serape
  blanket

siempre para ti
  always yours

sierras
  mountains

siesta
  afternoon nap

simpático
  congenial

sopaipillas
  puffed pastry

sub-comisario
  sub-commissioner

## T

tecolote
owl

Tejano
Texan

tequila
clear brandy

tía, tío
aunt, uncle

tierra amarilla
yellow earth

tierra azul
blue earth

tlaco
small Mexican coin

tonta
fool

torreón
tower

tortillas
thin corn cakes

tostón
half-peso

trasteros
cupboards

triste
sad

## U

un momentito
just a moment

## V

válgame Dios
bless me (figurative)

vámonos, hombres
let's go, fellows

vaqueros
cowboys

vara
short yard—32 inches

verdad, hombre
that's the truth, man

Vicario
vicar

vigas
ceiling rafters

viva
hurrah

viva Dios y la nación
hurrah for God and country

vivan los Americanos
hurrah for the Americans

## Y

yeso
gypsum

y tiempo para gastarlas
time to enjoy them

## Z

zaguán
open hallway

Page 17—Triste es la vida del hombre
Que viene decirte adios.

How sad is the life of this unhappy man
Who comes to bid you farewell . . .

Page   60—Tus ojos son estrellas
           Tu boquita un coral
           Tus rizitos en la frente
           Son dignos de amor. . . .

           Your eyes are like the stars above,
           Your little mouth like bits of coral,
           My heart is filled with deepest love
           For tender curls upon your forehead.

Page  232—Por todo mal, mescal;
           Por todo bien, tambien.

           Brandy helps everything bad,
           And the same for everything glad.